MICHAEL
MARSHALL

BLOOD OF ANGELS

HarperCollins*Publishers*

HarperCollins*Publishers*
77–85 Fulham Palace Road,
Hammersmith, London W6 8JB

www.harpercollins.co.uk

Published by HarperCollins*Publishers* 2005
1 3 5 7 9 8 6 4 2

A catalogue record for this book
is available from the British Library

ISBN 0 00 716396 7

Set in Minion and Din by
Palimpsest Book Production Limited, Polmont, Stirlingshire

Printed and bound in Great Britain by
Clays Limited, St Ives plc

For Ralph Vicinanza

Acknowledgements

My thanks first to William R. Corliss, volumes of whose *Sourcebook Project* provided background information and inspiration; and to Richard Pogue Harrison, whose *The Dominion of the Dead* helped focus some ideas. A huge thank you to my excellent agent, Jonny Geller; to Stephen Jones, David Smith and The Junction Tavern for their various forms of support during the writing of this book; and to everyone at HarperCollins for their inspired work on this and its predecessors – especially Jane, Amanda, Sarah, Joy, Kelly, Dominic, Fiona, Ingrid, Damon, Jane Harris and everyone in sales here and abroad.

Mad props to Paula, as always, and – welcome, N8.

Blood of Angels

How speedily shall time hide all things in darkness!
How many has it hidden already!
Marcus Aurelius
Meditations VI – 59

Key West

They came for him where he worked. They came on a good, hot afternoon when business was brisk and Jim was thinking he'd give it another hour at most and then call it quits and start the evening early. The dock was awash with tourists of all shapes and sizes, cruising like a school of brightly coloured fish with no particular destination in mind. Meanwhile they ate. They munched. They wolfed down everything the cafés and strolling vendors of Key West had to offer, from burgers and burritos to ice cream and sugar-dusted churros still hot from the fryer. Those with a spare hand drank, too, sucking frapps and iced teas and sodas large enough for small children to swim in. It was just after three in the afternoon. The food being consumed couldn't be a late lunch or an early dinner. Jim was confident all of these people would have taken a meal at midday: he was equally sure they'd be hunkered down again at seven, moving up to linguine and grilled swordfish and fancier burgers washed down with cold glasses of Chardonnay. Meanwhile they browsed, like huge, affable locusts; like

1

lucky cows in an endless, reasonably priced pasture. Their dedication was striking. If you let your mind wander you could believe these bodies were merely transportation devices for roving digestive systems capped by mowing teeth. You wondered what would happen if the food supply suddenly ran out; you wondered if, after a pause, the heads that housed these voracious mouths would slowly turn to take in the people around them, and decide they must be the next course.

Or Jim did, anyhow. He tried not to, but the thought still came. He was leaning against the rail on the north side of Mallory Square, an expanse of terrace and promenade which linked the hotels and restaurants of that side of the island with the sea. The cruise liners docked here overnight, multi-storey behemoths which dwarfed the hotels, disgorging further herds of credit card-holding grazing stock. A scant but welcome breeze came in off the shallow waters behind him. Jim held a camera loosely in his right hand. A bag over his shoulder carried packs of Polaroid film and a flat box of the folding cards he'd had printed up to hold his pictures.

Jim Westlake took photographs of tourists. He'd been doing it for years. There was a licence he was supposed to hold but he'd never got one and it didn't seem to be a problem. He didn't bother anyone at their tables or walk up and down hollering, jumping in front of strollers with a cheesy grin. He'd never been a salesman and didn't look like trouble. He was sixty-one years old, just starting to sag a little in the cheeks but still broad-shouldered and tall. He wore pale blue slacks and a white short-sleeved shirt, which he hated, but looked the part. His hair was mostly grey and swept back and he wore sunglasses against the glare off all the decking. He spent his days around Mallory, or walking up and down Duval Street, and when he saw the right kind of people he simply offered to take a photograph. Many would shake their heads firmly, bothered by the prospect of unplanned expenditure, and some would walk by without even acknowledging his presence. A few would pause, think a moment, and decide what the hey, we're on vacation. They would have toured the Hemingway house by then, stood on the southernmost point and taken a glass-bottomed boat out over the reefs. They'd be having a good time overall, and that's what photographs are for – to prove to others and ourselves that we've enjoyed ourselves, got some sun on our faces, forgotten about the daily grind for a time.

They'd most likely have their own camera around their neck, of course, maybe even a digital one, and Jim understood that the days of his profession were numbered. Pictures were no longer rare, immediacy no longer unusual. If you came to him you could get a shot of the two of you without having to ask some stranger, however, and Jim was good at getting kids to smile. The picture came slipped into a commemorative card with 'Having A Rest In Key West' printed on the front, and the stock was heavy and the typeface classy – a great gift for mothers back home, personal and yet effortless. The tourists could see that the photographer took pains, too: if he wasn't happy about the first shot, he'd take another – at no extra charge. He did this gracefully, slipping the first picture into his bag without even making you see it, so you didn't have to confront your bad side. Fifteen bucks wasn't cheap, but Jim had found he got more business at that price than for five. Five bucks was just some guy taking a picture. Fifteen was a genuine souvenir.

It was never going to make him rich, but Jim didn't want to be rich. Numbers were of no interest to him any more. He did okay, and okay is by definition good enough. He had believed that this might be the way he spent the rest of his days, quietly getting by. But when he saw the two men coming up the boardwalk, not eating, something told him they were headed his way.

One looked to be around forty, perhaps a year or two younger, the other in his early twenties. Both were fit and trim. The latter wore a black T and khaki army pants, and exuded a boisterous confidence that he was a force to be reckoned with. The older had on a charcoal suit and white shirt. He looked comfortable despite the heat, and also as if he didn't in the least care whether people took him seriously or not.

3

The younger man approached first. Jim smiled, held the Polaroid up. 'Want a picture?'

Living in Key West, you saw a lot of same-sex couples.

The young man said nothing, just stood looking him up and down. He was about five inches shorter than Jim. There was some kind of appraisal going on, but it wasn't clear to what purpose.

Eventually the kid spoke. '*You're* James Kyle?'

There was a note of something in his voice. Jim shook his head regretfully.

'Got the wrong guy, son. Name's Westlake. Sorry.'

The young man nodded, but didn't move.

Jim played for sheepish. 'You here about the licence? I figured it wasn't such a big deal these days.' He nodded towards a small group of portrait painters, sat in a huddle at the bottom of Duval, promising to make people look like Brad Pitt and Dolly Parton. 'Plenty people just set up and get working, take their chances. But if it's a real problem, then, you know, I'll be happy to . . .'

He stopped talking, leaving a gap to fill. It stretched but the guy didn't fill it. Just stood there with an unreadable expression on his face. There was an old scar about an inch and a half long under the boy's right cheekbone. Jim wondered how he'd got it, and sent the perpetrator a nugget of goodwill.

'Look, son . . . what do you want, exactly?'

The young man turned his head. 'I can't believe this is him.'

Jim realized he was talking to the other stranger, who'd suddenly appeared by his side. That worried Jim a little, someone being able to get that close without him noticing. It made him feel old.

'It's him,' the man said. 'You remember me, James?'

Jim turned in his own sweet time, and yes, of course he did. It had been a long time, and the man had aged but only on the outside. The eyes were the key, eyes that looked fine at first but soon revealed themselves to be devoid of genuine warmth, emotion or life. Jim had been cold in his time, no doubt, but this man looked like he'd never been anything but: as if he'd slid out of his mother's womb silent and calm and with bad thoughts already in his head. Jim didn't know his name, but he knew who he was. He was a man Jim had hoped – and come to believe – he would never see again.

He was the Forward-Thinking Boy.

'I remember. What do you want?'

'Got a job for you.'

'Don't need a job. I already got one.'

'We made an agreement, James.'

'Long time ago. I did what you wanted, then you stopped asking. I figured it was over.'

'No. You knew this was the way it could be.'

'Say I decide to forget about all that. Say I just walk away.'

'Then you'll be in jail before dark, unless you're already dead.'

Jim looked away across the dock. Seabirds whirled overhead. One of the glass-bottomed boats was chugging into harbour fifty yards away, shards of sun splashing off its windows. People waited to get on, and people waited to get off. Many were eating ice cream. It was all the same, but now it was different. There was sweat on the back of his neck, but the rest of his body felt cold.

When he turned back the younger man was still looking at him with his cool blue eyes, and there was something happening around the corners of his mouth. The muscles twitched, as if he was stifling a smile.

'What do you want from me?' Jim asked, dully now.

The older man reached into his pocket and pulled out a padded envelope. Jim took it.

'You would need to be in position in three days. And the instructions will be very specific.'

Jim put the envelope in his bag. 'Why me?'

'Because you owe us, and because I trust you to make it happen. Don't worry. You'll enjoy it.'

'I don't do that kind of thing any more.'

The man looked at Jim as though he were a fool. He had disengaged. This was over. He was ready to get on to the next thing, whatever that might be. The younger guy still stood there, staring at Jim. With that little grin waiting to get out.

Before anyone knew what was happening, Jim had his left hand firmly placed at the kid's lower back. With a short-arm punch too small to be noticed by most passers-by – even if they hadn't been blocked by the deliberate positioning of Jim's back – he drove his right fist into the boy's stomach, just to the side of the central pillar of abdominal muscles. Planted it like a piston triggered by an explosive charge. The effect was like slamming the kidney between two bricks, and the expression on the kid's face was very worthwhile.

'Suck it up,' Jim said, leaning forward to whisper in the kid's ear. 'You're as tough as you think you are, it shouldn't be so hard.'

He patted the lad's shoulder and stepped back, unhurried, out of range. He was pleased to see the boy's face was sheer white, his neck tendons tight as mooring ropes. It wasn't just the corners of his mouth that were twitching now. The boy made a sound, finally, and it was like a dead person trying to grab one more breath.

Jim turned to the other man, who looked calm and unworried and very slightly amused.

'I'll do this. Then it's over,' Jim told him.

Then he turned and walked away.

Jim's house was a forty-minute walk north, tucked into a scrubby neighbourhood on a small island nobody noticed when driving to or from Key West. The house was small and did not have a swimming pool. It did not even have an especially good view, though if you sat on the porch and positioned yourself carefully you could glimpse the ocean through the trees. At certain times of year.

Jim sat on a chair so positioned. He was sipping from a glass of iced tea spiked with fresh mint leaves, and not seeing anything at all. His neighbour Carol arrived hectically home with her two children, and waved across the forty feet between their front yards. She got no response, which surprised her. Mr Westlake was private but unfailingly polite, and always had a smile for her little angels. He

had taken the cutest picture of them, a photo which sat next to her side of the bed. Perhaps he'd received bad news, she thought – he was kind of old, after all, and holding an envelope in his hands. She decided she would call around later, on some pretext or other, but then Amy and Britney started arguing about nothing in particular and she concentrated on getting them inside to where there was an all-singing and all-dancing comedian (the television, the blessed tube, the tireless mother's helper) which would take them off her hands and let her cool down a little and concentrate on her main job for this time of day, in this kind of heat, which was delaying her first glass of wine.

The screen door clacked loudly behind the family as it went indoors, and Jim came back to himself. He looked at the envelope in his hands but did not bother to pull the contents out again. Inside was a cellular phone and a piece of paper listing the name of a town and two lines of instructions.

Part of his mind had already started the journey. He had hoped it would not. He hated the man who had come for him, for knowing that it would, that he would not simply throw away the envelope and take his chances. If someone else knew you better than you knew yourself, where did that leave you in the equation? He stared through the gap in the trees towards the ocean, but the view did nothing to help. Had he really begun to believe that it was over, that a decade had somehow undone the past and dissolved it back to nothing? If so, he was evidently a fool.

He drank the last of the tea and went inside, where he washed the glass and left it to drain by the sink. He owned precisely one glass, one set of silverware, one soup bowl, and one plate. This had never proved inadequate. The house had been furnished and decorated enough that a casual visitor would not think it overly sparse. When he'd first arrived in the Keys this had been in case he had to move on again at short notice. In the intervening eight years, as his mind had calmed and his life found a balance, he had realized he simply liked it that way.

Why have two, when one will do?

Why have one if you don't need any at all?

He walked up the staircase to his bedroom, where a small suitcase was already packed. His clothes and camera were *in situ*. A space about seven inches wide and ten inches long waited to be filled. He went to the empty cupboard and squatted in front of it. Though his knees let him know how they felt about this, they remained up to the task. As the asshole in combat pants had discovered, Jim's body was not easily giving up the struggle against time.

He lifted the mat from the bottom of the cupboard and raised the loose board. Not the world's most original hiding place, but if he'd had the slightest concern that anyone might come looking, then nothing would have been hidden there. Under the floor was a shoebox. He pulled it out, replaced the board and mat.

He put the box in the space in his suitcase. He closed the case, locked it, and then left the room without looking back. He wanted to, but did not. He did not want James Kyle to see this place. It belonged to Jim Westlake.

Downstairs he made sure all the windows were closed, and the back door locked, before leaving the house. He walked down the path to his clean white car and put the suitcase in the back.

He sat motionless in the driver's seat for a moment, looking at his little house. Perhaps he could leave Jim waiting there for him, standing quietly inside. Perhaps he could do this thing as James, and come back, and carry on as before. Perhaps this afternoon had only happened because there remained that thing, that possession of James's, that object he should have gotten rid of a long time before. A small and battered metal saucepan. Didn't look like much, but . . .

If you wanted to be nothing, you had to have nothing. He knew that. Had known it a long time. And yet still . . . he had kept it. Just hadn't been able to throw it away.

This was why Jim had made such a good photographer.

He understood about souvenirs.

8

Eventually he started the car. As he pulled away from the kerb he saw his neighbour standing in the window of her kitchen. He lifted his hand to give his standard wave.

Carol smiled and waved back, glad the old guy was back on form, not realizing that it wasn't Jim Westlake she was watching but an unknown person named James Kyle; a man riding into the past from the present, driving from this world towards hell.

Part 1: The None

There exists an allegiance between the dead and the unborn
of which we the living are merely the ligature.
Richard Pogue Harrison
The Dominion of the Dead

Chapter 1

My name is Ward Hopkins, and some of this happened to me. I was present, and the events moved the air in front of my face like a flock of birds taking chaotic flight. Had I done differently, things might have turned out otherwise. Better. Worse. I don't know. I choose to believe in free will – at least, I think this is a choice that I make – but also that the loci of our movements are constrained: that we have pre-ordained arcs within the chaos of life's endless flight, and that invisible forces are manifest in our paths. We all run, we all hide, we lie awake in the night, flustered and confused, made small by the shadows in our lives.

Time is a lake, getting deeper year by year, drop by drop. Surface tension, the electric presence of our staccato acts, keeps us scuttling like water bugs on its surface, unmindful of the depths we traverse. We're safe, afloat in the now, until we stop moving and begin to sink into the past. Only then do we realize how important all those yesterdays were, how they hold each present moment to the sun;

and how many people we leave behind, stricken in time like ambered insects. We think that it matters in the meantime, which route we take across the surface. We trace our complex patterns, and watch those of people who walk close by, seldom raising our eyes above the horizon or squatting to examine the path. But trees which overhang the edges of the lake will sometimes drop leaves into the water, causing ripples which we experience without understanding. Rain falls, too, from the future, sometimes heavily.

Time really does pass. Once in a great while, however, something will stir deep down beneath the surface of the lake, a thing that is long gone in time and yet still alive. This creates a deep, roiling wave, a cold current which affects everyone who lives on the surface, pushing some of us together, others further apart. Most ride the wave; some are engulfed; few realize that anything has happened at all. The creatures that live below us are rarely sensed, trapped deep in the occluded past.

Sometimes they do not merely stir, however, but rocket upwards to break the surface. They disturb us in the night like the shrieking whistle of a runaway train: a train bound across dark hills for somewhere you will never see, though the whole world may hear the crash of it reaching its destination.

Some of this happened to me, but not all of it.

I'll tell you what we know.

The first email had come a few days before summer ended. Nina and I had spent the afternoon in Sheffer, the nearest shopping opportunity to where we were living. A very small town in the Cascade Mountains of Washington State, Sheffer has a main drag of wood-fronted buildings divided by five cross streets which fade into fir trees without much ceremony or regret. The town has a market and a café that serves good food, as well as selling second-hand books and CDs and curios of no value whatsoever. There is a pharmacy, a sundries-and-liquor store and a place for ladies to get their hair cut the way they did when Jimmy Carter was president. The town is home to a couple of upmarket bed and breakfasts and three bars, with a motel conveniently just up the road in case you lose track of the time or drink a little too much to drive home. In our case, both had been known. There is a small railroad museum, a police station run by a good man, and that's pretty much it. It's a decent place, and some nice people live there, but it's little more than a wide spot in the road.

Our temporary residence was smaller still, a log cabin that had once been part of an old-fashioned resort down on the Oregon coast. At the end of the 1990s a retired couple from Portland bought three of these cabins, moved them up on the backs of trucks, and installed them on a forty-acre lot at the end of a failed subdivision in the forest thirty minutes north-east of Sheffer. The husband had died soon after but Patrice was still going strong. She reminded me a little of my mother, and if Beth Hopkins had still been alive it would have been tough to choose who to bet on in a fight. Patrice offered us the use of one of the cabins after we extricated her from a situation out in the woods. We thought about it, made some arrangements, accepted the offer.

Patrice's acreage backed onto national land and had its own big pond. If you looked out across it on an autumn afternoon it was easy to believe mankind had never existed, and it was easy not to mourn the lack. Our cabin was on the far side, half a mile from the road. It had a sitting room with a fireplace and a kitchen area, plus a bathroom and a bedroom. It was plenty big enough. My life had condensed to the extent that I could store my possessions in the trunk of a not-very-large car. We had one of those too. It belonged to the woman I had first been introduced to as Special Agent Baynam.

Nina. She was presently out on the porch in front of the cabin. The air was cold but not bitter and had a relenting quality about it that said winter knew its time was not quite come. Nina was supposed to be watching the sun go down, but I knew she wouldn't be. Just having your head pointed in the right direction does not count. The sun was probably grateful for the break. Being glared at by Nina when you're trying to slip gracefully below the horizon is more pressure than any celestial body needs.

I was in the kitchen area of the cabin putting together a salad, and making a meal of it in more ways than one. Nina had been quiet for most of the day, quiet in the manner of a large rock resting halfway up a hillside. I had asked if she was okay and received affirmatives which were unconvincing but non-negotiable. I have no idea why women do this, but there's nothing that can be done about it until they're good and ready to talk. I knew that we were going to be having a conversation soon – it had been brewing for a week – and I was in no hurry for it to start. Consequently the salad was taking on baroque proportions. Any culinary aesthetic had long departed and it looked more as though someone had decided to conserve on counter space by tossing the whole salad bar into one bowl. I had gone as far as steaming some French beans on the stove and was waiting for them to cool in a bowl of ice water in the sink.

To kill the time I wandered into the living area and flipped open Nina's laptop. I had one of my own but it wasn't really mine and was hidden in the roof space of the cabin. The material on it was backed up, encrypted and stored on a server far away. The files on the laptop were the earliest versions I had, however, and retained a kind of precedence in my mind. Strange how the human mind confers status and antecedence even on digital data, on electrons which can be everywhere at once and hence nowhere at all. We have to believe that things begin somewhere, I guess. Otherwise, how can they stop?

I checked my email accounts once every couple of weeks at most. I wasn't really in contact with the outside world. The one guy who used to email me regularly was dead. It was his laptop which was stowed in the roof. The only mails I received now were sporadic opportunities to harden or lengthen my penis, be showered with college grants, or view footage of whichever bubblehead was currently juicing her celebrity through suspiciously well-lit home movie footage. The non-specificity of these invitations, their generic inapplicability, made them even less meaningful than total silence.

Maybe that's what I was hoping for. Further quietness, additional white noise, and through these a promise that this thing we were calling life was going to continue for a while longer.

So when I saw I had a single email, and that it appeared to be to me in particular, I suddenly felt very still.

The subject line said just: WARD HOPKINS?

I didn't recognize the sending address. It was a Hotmail account, favoured lair of spammers but not exclusively so. It had been sent to an address of mine which I'd had for many years but not used in two or three. It didn't seem likely a message to that account could have any current bearing on my life.

I opened it. It said only this:

I need to talk to you.

No you don't, I thought. *Goodbye.*

I pulled the message towards the trash but something made me hesitate. Should I at least make a record of the sending address? Deletion is not the same as negation, as I had reason to know.

I heard a creaking sound from outside and turned to see Nina heading towards the door. She was wearing black jeans and a thick brown jacket I had bought her down in Yakima a couple of months before. She looked good, but grouchy.

I quickly shut the computer and went over to the kitchen.

'Ward, I done stared at that sunset as long as I'm able,' she said. 'Where the hell is the food?'

'Coming right up.' I took the beans out of the water, shook them a little, and spread them artfully on top of the other stuff in the bowl. Nina watched this in silence, staring at the result with what appeared to be genuine bafflement.

'*Voilà*,' I said. 'The salad to end all salads.'

'You're not kidding. How about a few pine cones on top? A pair of squirrels, in a tableau. I can fetch a couple if you want. Or, like, a whole tree or something. Say the word, maestro.'

'Stop, stop.' I held up my hands. 'Really, I don't do it for the thanks. Just the pleasure on your face is enough.'

She smiled, a little. 'You're an idiot.'

'Perhaps. But I'm your idiot. Come on, give it a try. Actually, you have to. There isn't anything else. I used it all up.'

She shook her head, then smiled more genuinely. Spooned some salad out onto a plate, and then added an extra scoopful, to show good intent. Pecked me on the cheek and carried her plate and the wine bottle back out onto the porch.

I followed. Talk minus a half hour and counting, I reckoned.

We ate for a while.

The air was still soft, but had edges within it now, carried down off the higher reaches of the mountains. It wasn't a salad kind of evening. After about ten minutes Nina set her fork at a 'that's enough of that' angle. Her plate was still over half full.

'I'm sorry,' she said, when she saw me noticing. 'You've gone to a lot of trouble.'

'Way too much. It sucks. It's the Salad of Shame. I told you we should just have bought a big box of Izzy's fried chicken.'

'Maybe.'

'Definitely. You should trust me on these things. I have junk-food wisdom. It's a gift. On any given day I'll be able to predict the best type of junk food to have – not just for me, but for the tribe as a whole. In epochs gone by I would have been a snack shaman. I'd have consulted bones and read portents in the sky, and finally pronounced: "Lo, guys, you'll be in the mood for tacos later, so try to snag a mammoth when you're out." And I would have been right.'

Nina was looking at me. 'Are you still talking?'

'Not me. It must be the wind.'

The lake was assuming its twilight form, black and glasslike.

Nina stared out over it for a while, and finally she spoke. 'What are we going to do, Ward?'

18

There it was. I realized what I'd been trying to put off was not a conversation after all. It was just that. A question. *The* question.

I lit a cigarette. 'What do you *want* to do?'

'It's not like that and you know it. It's just . . . it can't last. This is no way to live.'

'No?'

'I don't mean it like that. You know. I mean these circumstances. I mean not having a choice.'

I took her hand. The summer had been good to us, despite everything. We had mainly stayed around Sheffer. Got to know some of the locals while keeping our heads firmly down. Got to know each other, too: when we'd accepted the use of Patrice's cabin we'd only been together a week, though our lives had been linked for six months before that. Since soon after my parents had died. Or been murdered, as it turned out. Nina knew most of what there was to know about my past. I knew stuff about her, too. More than anyone, I suspected, including a man called John Zandt who had once been our friend but appeared lost to the world now.

The three of us held secrets it would have been better not to know. That was why our life was this way.

We went for long, long walks in the woods, cooked healthy food on a barbecue I'd made out of flat rocks. Nina laughed when she saw it, pointed out I'd somehow made it in a half-assed Prairie style. It worked, though. With all the walking and helping Patrice and others with manual work, I was in the best shape I'd been in for years. The injury I'd received to my shoulder five months before didn't trouble me any more. While I'd lost some pounds Nina had gained a couple of ounces, and – though she was never going to be called anything more than slim – it suited her. We'd been on a couple of road trips too, driving east and south more or less at random. They made us feel less like we were in hiding. We had to go down to LA on two tense occasions and on the second of these fetched a few things from Nina's house, a precarious structure perched in the less fashionable side of the Malibu Hills. We couldn't stick around long enough for her to put the place on the market – in the unlikely event anyone would want to buy it – and in the end we secured it and left it as it was.

Which, in a way, was what Nina was talking about. Fundamentally everything was still the way it was, however much I might want to pretend otherwise. We had boarded up our windows but the world was still out there. Nina had a job, for a start. A serious job. Her negotiated leave of absence had been stretched to the point where it squeaked: she was going to have to either resign or go back. My own position was more fluid. I had worked for the CIA, some years before. I specialized in media surveillance. In the end, they let me go. Actually, as my friend Bobby had been fond of pointing out, I walked – just ahead of a mandatory polygraph test.

We talked around the subject for a while but we could sense this hiatus breaking, and neither of us wanted it to. It had been like being held in a giant's warm hand for a spell. We could feel that hand lowering, preparing to put us back down.

'We'll decide something,' I said. 'But for tonight life could be worse. I sit here with you and I don't feel I'm lacking much.'

'Well who would? I am, quite literally, a peach. Attractive, smart, even-tempered. The perfect companion in all ways.'

I raised an eyebrow. 'I'm not sure I'd go that far.'

'No? Name a failing.'

'Well, you shot your last boyfriend.'

'It was an *accident*.'

'Yeah. So you claim.'

'I do. It was.' She winked. 'But it won't be next time.'

I laughed, and the question went back to hide under its rock for a while longer. We sat out there on the porch, talking and watching the lake darken to a void, until it was too cold and we went inside. Later we lay in bed together and I listened to the trees and Nina's breathing as she slept, until I could no longer tell the sounds apart and I was asleep too.

Five months may not sound like much, but it made this one of the longest relationships I'd ever had. It still felt mildly miraculous to me. It felt like somewhere I could live. I didn't say anything about the email I'd received, nor about the second – with exactly the same subject and message – which arrived two days later. I deleted this one and buried the other deep in a folder. Simplicity has not been a feature of my life, nor the sense of having a home. I fought their departure in the only way I could. By hiding.

For a few more days, it worked. It was only on the morning when a car pulled up the track towards Patrice's cabin that I accepted nothing – no smile or white lie or overblown salad – would be enough to stop the world coming to find us again.

Chapter 2

The call came at just after eleven in the morning. I was down near the lake, screwing around with some big pieces of old, grey timber I had salvaged from an afternoon helping patch a barn. I had thought maybe I could make a rustic table out of them so we could eat close to the lake without having to drag the small one off the porch. In my heart of hearts I knew we could not be eating outside for much longer, and I further suspected that anything I made would not long stand the rigours of supporting anything heavy, like a full glass of wine. I heard the three short beeps of Nina's cell phone ringing in the distance but didn't give it much thought. The cabin didn't have a phone. If one of our acquaintances in the area wanted to get hold of us, it was her cell they called. I kept clattering around, holding bits of wood together in a speculative fashion, until I looked across to see Nina standing on the porch, white-faced.

'It's Patrice!' she shouted. 'Someone's coming.'

I dropped the tools and walked quickly back up to the cabin. My head felt clear, my chest cold. 'How many?'

'One vehicle. So far.'

While Nina ran back inside I reached under the porch and pulled out something long and heavy wrapped in a thick plastic sheet. I loaded the rifle quickly, my ears burning, listening for any sound from the other side of the water.

When I was done I went inside. Nina had our two handguns out on the table. 'Anything yet?'

'No,' I said, taking my gun and pocketing it. I kissed her and then hurried back outside. I stood for a second and looked across the lake again. I could now see a car outside Patrice's cabin. You couldn't get a vehicle any closer. Any person or group of persons heading our way would have to make the last two hundred yards on foot. There were only two possible routes: following the rough path around the lake shore, or cutting up around through the trees to approach the cabin from the back. Both were mine to hold.

I picked up the rifle and looped around the cabin, climbing a narrow ridge which was well hidden in trees. I kept low and went about a quarter of the distance around the lake. There was a vantage I had found which gave a good view towards the path thirty yards below, but which would be hard to spot from the lower ground. I hunkered low at the trunk of the largest tree, wedging myself for stability. I pulled the rifle up into position, got it locked into my shoulder. I had spent hours out in the furthest reaches of Patrice's land, practising. I had little doubt that from this range I would be able to hit whatever I aimed at, and no doubt whatsoever that I would be willing to try.

One car. Four men, most likely. Assuming there was not another vehicle waiting out on the road. And that other men had not been sent to come at us through the forest. If so, I would hear Nina shooting before she heard me.

After six minutes I began to hear faint sounds of approach down and to the left. Feet crunching amongst the leaves on the path, carried on the clear air. I waited, willing my heart steady and quiet,

23

trying not to think about what would happen if I had to shoot. About where we would go, what we would do. About whether it would even be an issue, or if the best of us both would seep into the indifferent ground right here, red for an hour, brown for a few days, then indistinguishable from the other mud and dust. That last thought was easiest to push away. I have no intention of dying. Not now, not ever. I simply don't think it's necessary. Sooner or later the world will just have to see this my way.

After another two minutes I saw a flash of movement down at the bottom of the rise. Enough to tell it looked like two men, three at the most. That was either good or meant they had backup elsewhere. I leaned backward and glanced left along the ridge. I couldn't see anyone else. I turned back and waited the twenty seconds it should take for them to come level with the next sight line below. It took nearer to forty, which gave me pause. They weren't coming quickly. I didn't know what a measured approach might indicate, and you're going to want to respond very differently to caution or covert expertise. I still didn't know how many there were, either: as they crossed the second clear space a flat blade of sunlight flashed off the lake beyond, filling my eyes with yellow-white.

Then they were behind trees again. I had one more, final, window. Two or three guys – it ultimately didn't make a lot of difference. We'd still have to drag them out into the woods, lose them somewhere deep.

I stood and edged forward between the trees to a second position where the line would be clearer, and my safety about the same. A confusing shot coming from behind them might give me an extra two seconds, my position disguised by shatter-echoes from the surrounding trunks.

I dropped to one knee and sighted. I saw the first glimmer of dark clothing through the trees, five yards short of the clear space I was waiting for them to reach. Thirty seconds ticked by.

Then I heard something.

Didn't know what it was at first. Then I realized it was the sound of Nina's phone ringing again.

I froze, aghast. This was a bad error for Patrice to be making. Very bad. She shouldn't be checking what was happening. This had been agreed. If she saw someone, she called Nina. If she subsequently heard a shot she was supposed to call a friend in Sheffer. That was all. Otherwise she was just supposed to sit tight in her cabin and pretend to be out, or dead, or both.

The men below had stopped too. They must have heard the phone. They weren't in clear enough sight for me to be sure of taking one out with the first shot. Without that . . .

I heard a faint murmur of voices. The men deciding to go on, perhaps, realizing the distraction of the phone could only have made things worse for the people waiting for them.

They moved again, and finally they were in clear sight. Two men, tall. Both dressed in dark clothes.

Forty yards from me. Not a head shot. Go for body mass. Be sure. I took a shallow breath and held it, sighted along the barrel. Gently applied pressure to the trigger.

I saw a flash of movement, someone walking quickly from the direction of our cabin towards the two men below. The flash was a rich brown, the colour of . . .

I jerked my head up off the rifle, just in time to hear a woman shouting below. Nina's jacket – so Nina's voice?

I found myself on my feet again, without thinking, heading down the hill carefully but fast, rifle still in position and finger still ready to pull – but no longer understanding what was going on.

I ran down to station myself twenty yards behind the intruders. I hit the path just in time to see Nina a hundred feet ahead, storming around the corner towards the men now caught between us. They had stopped walking. One was still holding a phone. The other turned to look at me, and slowly raised his hands.

'Hey, Ward,' he said. 'Be cool.'

'For God's *sake*, Charles!' Nina shouted at the man with the phone. 'What the *hell* do you think you're doing?'

*   *   *

25

They sat on the porch. We stood a few yards away. Neither Nina nor I trusted ourselves to be nearer them yet, though coffee had been poured, Patrice had been stood down, and the sweat on my scalp was now cold.

'We could have killed you,' Nina said, not for the first time. She was still full-blown furious, hands on hips.

'I still might,' I muttered.

The two men sat in the chairs where we normally ate. The second man, the one who'd greeted me, had said nothing so far except to decline sugar. He was rangy and tall with his hair cut short. His name was Doug Olbrich and he was a lieutenant in Special Section 1, the LAPD Robbery Homicide division dedicated to high-profile murder cases.

The first man, whose limp I had noticed even from a distance, was Charles Monroe. He was a Special Agent in Charge at one of the FBI's field offices in Los Angeles, and he was Nina's boss. I had met him only briefly, immediately prior to his receiving a number of gunshot wounds from an assailant who had attacked us in a diner in Fresno five months before. He was lucky to be alive, though he had probably spent many weeks feeling otherwise. Judging by the care with which he sat down, that time was not over yet. The man who shot him – and me too, in the shoulder – was dead. Nina had killed him in the forest a couple of miles from where we now stood, on the day we met Patrice. Nina had seen her boss only twice since, on our two brief visits to LA, when she had been required for debriefing and evidential hearings towards the trial of the killer we had caught that day.

'Why didn't you call ahead?' she said. 'By which I mean yesterday, not when you're halfway around our lake? Killing you is trouble we really don't need – however *unbelievably* appealing the idea seems right this second.'

Monroe put his mug on the table. 'Would you have been here when I arrived?'

'Of course we would.'

He didn't believe her. Olbrich meanwhile was gazing out at the trees, happy not to be involved in this part of the conversation. But I could read a good deal of tension in his face.

'And you would have taken the call in the first place?'

'Charles . . . oh for God's sake.' She rubbed her face with her hands, and picked her own coffee up off the rail.

'Monroe,' I said. 'What do you actually want?'

'From you, nothing. You are not an employee of the FBI, which is the organization I work for. Nina too, as I hope she recalls. You're not a cop either, and never were. I gather you once worked for another agency in what may loosely be termed "intelligence", but from what I hear that was a long time ago and you are not exactly missed. So far as I am concerned you can walk off into the forest and never come back.'

'Ward saved your life,' Nina said.

'Really? The last thing I saw was him pulling you out of the back of a restaurant and leaving me pinned in a booth. The shooter followed you. I survived by default.'

'A selective account,' I said, though privately I agreed with him. I'd been more concerned with prolonging Nina's life, and my own, than I had been with his – especially after he'd taken what I'd assumed were mortal wounds. I had found I could live with this decision.

'People,' Olbrich said, 'this isn't getting us anywhere.'

'Nina and I weren't *intending* to go anywhere,' I snapped. 'She had an agreement with this asshole which precluded him revealing our location – including to you. He's broken that already and I'm guessing that's just the beginning. You haven't come here to bring Nina's mail, Monroe, so what the hell do you want?'

'Nina,' Monroe said. 'It's time for you to come back.'

Bang. Just like that, I knew Nina's question of the other night had been answered. It was always bound to be this way. I shook my head, and walked a few paces.

'I don't know if I'm coming back,' Nina said. 'I like it here.'

'Is that a resignation? Really? If so, get a pen and paper. I'll need it in writing.'

Nina looked at me. I shrugged, meaning this was her gig, her call and decision and life.

'Come on, Nina,' Monroe said, voice caught between irritation and an attempt to sound reasonable. 'You know the score. I got you leave because the circumstances were exceptional.'

'Plus about two million years' worth of owed time.'

'You ran out weeks ago. As you know.'

'Okay,' she said, dully. 'So maybe I will retire. Maybe I'm done with this stuff. It's not like we're making a discernible difference.'

'That's not true. There are ten years' worth of killers in jail because of you.'

'Putting someone away after they've killed two, four, six people – what kind of win is that? It's wiping up a dropped glass of milk. Fine, the floor's clean for a while. But you still don't have any milk. The victims' families still get up every day feeling like death. It all still happened and we're after the fact.'

'Unless you find some way of going back in time,' Olbrich said, 'That is the nature of law enforcement.'

Nina coloured. She had meant the observation personally, as a reflection of what she felt. By not taking it that way the cop had made her feel dumb.

Monroe evidently realized this too. 'Also,' he added, quickly, 'There's something else. I need you.'

'Nah, you don't,' she said, shaking her head firmly. 'You got plenty of other bitches. Some of them bright sparks even understand causality, I'll bet.'

'Nina, I came a long way to see you and I don't have a lot of hours to spend on this.'

'So fly back to LA. Have a safe trip. Call ahead next time and bring flowers or muffins or something. You were evidently very badly brought up.'

'I'm not going back to California. The FBI have been asked to assist a homicide investigation in Virginia. It's messy and it could be a serial killer, or that's what the local cops think. I want you to come with me.'

Nina shook her head again. 'I'm not . . .'

'Nina – they think a woman did it.'

Nina was down by the lake shore. She had been there ten minutes. I knew every second that passed meant it was more likely she was going. Her stance said that everything near her, the trees, the lake, the mountains and probably even me, was insubstantial to her now. I stayed up at the cabin with the others. Neither of the men made any attempt to start a conversation with me. Olbrich checked his watch several times.

'So explain this to me,' I said. 'You've got a body out east and maybe it's Fed business, maybe it's not. What I don't understand is why your pal Olbrich is here. I don't care how you define LAPD's jurisdiction, but Virginia is a long plane ride away.'

The men looked at each other. 'Tell him,' Monroe said. He got up gingerly, stepped down off the porch. 'This is his business, even if nothing else is. And we have now run out of time.'

He walked straight down past me and towards Nina.

'The Henrikson person,' Olbrich said, when the other man was out of earshot. 'He's your brother, right?'

He was referring to the killer we had caught in the forest, a man who would soon go on trial for the murder of a woman called Jessica Jones in Los Angeles, and another from Seattle, Katelyn Wallace, whose body had been found forty miles from where we now sat. The case was ironclad. Following that a further trial would take place concerning the deaths of a number of teenage girls in LA five years previously, a series the LA media had called the Delivery Boy Murders. Matters there were more complicated.

'We're twins,' I said. 'But I never knew him. His real name is Paul. He calls himself the Upright Man – the Delivery Boy crap was

Monroe's idea, remember. Paul doesn't work alone, either. You know all this. It's in Nina's report.'

'Actually, it's not,' Olbrich said, looking away. 'It was determined that your more general allegations confused the case.'

'What I said was true,' I said. 'Nina knows it. Paul worked for a conspiracy of killers, procuring victims to order. He did other things too.'

'Monroe's in charge of the investigation, not Nina.'

'Monroe is in charge of his career. Anyway – what about it?'

'After your brother was discharged from hospital he was transferred to Pelican Bay. The supermax near the border with Oregon.'

'I thought that was for gang psychos, the Aryan Brotherhood and Low Riders and Black Guerrillas.'

'Usually it is. But Monroe was convinced your man needed to be in a Secure Housing Unit until trial – 24/7 solitary lockdown in a place with no windows and guards who regard fatalities as paperwork. After seeing what he did to those women, it was hard not to agree. So Monroe swung it. The Corcoran and Tehachapi facilities wouldn't take him, so he was sent north to the Bay. In three months he survived three murder attempts, one from a member of staff – who's still in hospital. But then . . .'

Olbrich breathed out heavily, and that was enough to steal his thunder. Especially when I saw Monroe talking down by the water-line, and Nina suddenly raising her head to look up at me. She started walking back fast.

'Don't tell me this,' I said. I could hear the blood rushing in my ears, feel it hesitate in my veins.

'Two days ago he was released for transport back to Los Angeles. We don't know what happened en route, but a hundred miles south something sure as hell did. We have the armoured truck, most of it, and the bodies of two of the guards were found within a half mile. The other two are missing. The assumption is they're dead too.'

'No,' I said. 'Assume instead they helped Paul escape.'

'Monroe knew you'd say something like that. Said you were a conspiracy kind of guy. A killer under every bed.'

'You know what I'm talking about. You helped John Zandt. You got information for him. He was tracking Paul.'

'I helped John because I knew him when he was in Homicide, and he'd been a stellar cop. He's not any more. There're two outstanding murder warrants against him, for a start.'

'Yeah. He killed a man who organized the transport of young girls to their deaths, and someone who helped abduct them in the first place.'

'Careful, Ward. If Zandt ever reappears you may find yourself having to repeat that in court some day.'

'I don't condone what John has done. But when I have the time and feel safe, I'll go dance on those two guys' graves.'

'Safe from who?'

'Who do you think? The people behind this. This is not a delusion. Why do you think Nina and I have been up here all this time, living under false names? You think we're on some back-to-nature thing? Or that we're just really fucking shy?'

'I thought it was because of your brother. I know you were involved in his capture.'

'No,' I said, coldly. 'It wasn't about him. We assumed the California penal system had that situation under control.'

'Ward,' Nina said. Monroe approached a few paces behind her, his hands clasped behind his back. He had the air of a man whose task was completed, who'd seen it go as planned, and was now ready to get on with his day. 'He told you?'

'Yes. Congratulations, Charles. You just lost one of the most dangerous men on planet Earth.'

'We'll find him,' Monroe said.

'No you won't,' I said. 'Not a chance. Anyone finds anyone, it'll be him finding you. Good luck when that happens.'

'I don't think it will be me he's looking for.'

31

'Right,' I said. 'So shouldn't you have told us about this a little earlier? Like one and a half days ago? Or have you had agents sitting in Sheffer since then, watching to see if he would head up this way, using us as bait?'

'Of course not,' he said.

I didn't believe him, and that meant Sheffer was no longer safe. I wasn't convinced Paul would necessarily come looking for me. But there were other people who might.

'So Olbrich's here to ask if I know where Paul is?'

'Do you?'

'No,' I said. 'And right now I wouldn't tell you if I did.'

I smoked on the porch while Nina packed. Monroe and the cop stood some distance away, impatiently. I spent a while staring at the back of Monroe's head. A clean shot no longer seemed enough. I wanted to grab him by the neck and drown him in the lake. I wanted to do it and sell tickets. Cheap tickets, with free snacks.

'I'm done,' Nina said.

I looked round to see her standing in the doorway, carrying a bag. She had changed into the kind of clothes she used to wear. A Fed suit. She looked different. She looked businesslike, professional. She looked . . . actually, she looked kind of cool.

I stood up. 'Agent Baynam, present and correct.'

'I hate this too,' she said, coming closer. 'You believe me, don't you?'

'I do,' I said, keeping my voice low. 'Because I think someone's been ignoring Monroe's calls for a while now. True?'

'Could be.'

'You should have told me he was ringing your bell.'

'You're right,' she said. 'And I'm sorry. My bad. But tell me, who's been ringing yours?'

'What do you mean?'

'The night you made that ridiculous salad. You closed the laptop without quitting out of email. It was sitting there next time I used the computer.'

There wasn't much to say. 'You got me.'

'So who's trying to get in touch with you?'

'It's an old address of mine. It could be anyone.'

'I don't think so. You're a nice man, underneath it all, but you're really not that popular. It's not going to be an invitation to go bowling. There's a world out there that means us harm, Ward. You need to find out who this person is.'

'You're the boss.'

'Correct. Remember that at all costs.' She leaned forward and kissed me. 'Later,' she said.

She walked down to the lake and walked away with the two men. It seemed to me that she was gone, disappeared, long before she passed out of sight.

I spent the afternoon closing down the cabin. I cleaned up, shut down the boiler, put the shutters over the windows. I spent much of this time trying to think of somewhere specific to go, and failing. Pointing the car east and driving was the best I could come up with. I went up into the roof space and retrieved Bobby's computer. I left it charging up while I carried a few things around the lake to Nina's car, parked behind Patrice's cabin. I explained to her that Nina was gone, and that I would be soon. I told her to be careful, to watch out for strangers, and to be in contact with the sheriff if she suspected anything at all. She made me a cup of coffee which just made me feel more alone.

When I got back I checked my email. There was nothing, which kind of screwed things up. It was all very well Nina telling me to find out who'd been trying to be in contact, but the email with the return address was on her machine. I still wasn't convinced it was an interaction I needed to have. Maybe she thought it was Paul, trying to track me down. If so, she wasn't thinking straight. The email had been sent while he was still in jail.

I was about to shut the machine when I noticed it was down-loading something after all. I flicked to a progress window in back and realized email was coming into one of Bobby's accounts. I'd left his addresses active in the software, out of respect or superstition, not wanting to close down this last vestige of his life.

There were three emails in his in-tray. All were titled 'CALL ME', and the most recent had been sent three weeks before. I'd have called them spam without thinking except the Hotmail address they'd come from looked familiar.

I opened the most recent:

> Bobby – are you there? There's strange chatter all
> over and I need your brains. Now.

Like the ones to me, it was not signed. Why? I could only assume the sender thought Bobby and I would recognize the sending address. I thought a moment, and then copied the address into an email from my own account. I typed:

> It's Ward Hopkins here. Bobby's dead. Who are you
> and what do you want?

Then I hit SEND before I could think too much about it.

I knew the best thing was just to leave quickly, but I was finding it hard. I took a last look around, as my father had taught me to do on family vacations, checking rooms one by one and shutting each door behind me. I couldn't find my coat for a while but then realized it must be hanging behind the front door, which was open. Didn't remember putting it there, but hey – it had been a stressful day.

I pulled the door to grab it and realized it wasn't the only coat there. Nina's brown jacket hung next to it.

She'd left it behind.

For a moment I felt like a teenager, then made myself mentally shrug. Too bulky to go in her bag. Not in keeping with the sharp Fed look. You're thirty-nine years old, Ward. Get a grip.

Then I noticed there was a folded piece of paper sticking out of one of the pockets. It was a note, in Nina's writing.

Silly me. I'll freeze to death. x

I had a destination after all.

I locked up the cabin and set off south towards Yakima, where there was an airport. I figured I'd stay the night there, and fly on to Virginia in the morning.

Chapter 3

Lee John Hudek would later say he knew something was going down right from the start. He couldn't recall when he'd first sensed it, but he had a feeling for sure. This was something he'd remember, because he didn't believe in that spooky shit. At all. That was for the hucksters down on Venice Beach, and drunk girls with cheap tarot decks, or Pete Voss at a pinch – Sleepy Pete seemed to think he had some otherworldly voodoo vibe going on because his mom was an eighth Blackfoot or Buddhist or whatever the fuck. He primarily seemed to believe this when he was stoned, however, and though that was most of the time Hudek was convinced it was utter bullshit – both in Pete's case and worldwide. Hudek had understood from an early age that the world worked in hard, straight lines, and that the curvy crap was for losers. The world likes get-up-and-go. The world likes people who get in its face. Sleepy was kind of an airhead all around, no doubt, but he was big and loyal and did a slow but steady job of selling product, and he was long-term crew, so whatever.

What Hudek did remember was this:

Sitting in the car with Pete on the side and Brad Metzger in back, parked at the end of the turn-off on Tujunga Canyon Drive. They had the roof down, catching rays while they waited. And waited. The car belonged to Hudek, paid for in cash. Most in his position would have some souped-up retro boat – he did too, for a while – but recently he'd decided a businesslike Merc sent better signals. The cops gave you less grief, too. Not quite yet twenty years old, Hudek also owned his house outright. Nothing pimp, merely an unobtrusive three-bed in Summer Hills, but it had a pool and a big double garage and the size of his television was something to behold. Pete and Brad lived over in Simi Valley, south of Santa Barbara, with their respective parents. Everybody they knew did, having done little in the year since school except learn that jobs no longer dropped out of the trees in California and that having played mildly impressive ball in high school meant jack shit to the outside world.

They were parked with the car pointed back up the track, the dusty, shrubby wall of the sub-canyon rising steeply on the right-hand side. It was hot. Sleepy was playing a hand-held video game that went ping, ping, beep. Brad was droning on about the chick he was boning and whether he should pay to have her nose done. Having boned the chick in question himself, Hudek was of the opinion that Brad's ability to bear her company would not outlast the post-op period, especially as the short-term potential for blowjobs would be critically diminished. He would let Brad figure that out for himself. If the guy was thinking about throwing that kind of money at a chick, he was being paid too much.

Paid too much by Hudek, that meant.

'I fucked her, man,' he said suddenly, on a whim. 'Year ago.'

Brad was silent for a moment. Then he started talking about some other girl.

When Hudek looked at his watch again it was seventeen minutes after one. They were over a half hour late now. That was unique. It was a pain in the ass to drive right across the Valley to do this, but that's the way it had always been. Hernandez had always been reliable, too, so Lee didn't mind doing it his way. This was not being reliable, which meant the pain in the ass became much more acute. Especially now. Now that he had the Plan, reliability was going to be key.

He glanced at his watch again, unnecessarily. Still seventeen minutes past. For just a moment it looked to him as if the sweep of the second hand was slowing, as if this minute was swelling and might burst.

Maybe that was it. Maybe that was when he got the twitch, had his odd feeling; the intimation that the day was heading down a road towards a future that was not yet signposted.

Then it was eighteen past.

He heard a lighter spark behind him. 'Brad, don't smoke in the car.'

'Fucking roof's off, man.'

Hudek turned in his seat and stared at the boy in the back.

Brad shook his head, opened his door, got out. He walked a little way from the vehicle, over to the canyon wall. Sat on a rock and smoked the cigarette down. What he wanted (fuck, *needed*) was a joint, but while Lee blew hot and cold on cigarettes he was uniformly down on people doing weed at work. Brad was going to be glad when this bit of work was done. It always freaked him, a little. Nothing had ever gone wrong yet but drug buys were drug buys – a fizzy thing to endure even if you didn't have an All-Star hangover, which Brad most certainly did. He had spent the previous evening hanging around the pool with the Reynolds kids and a bunch of others over in Santa Barbara, the Reynolds Seniors out at an attorney-rife party down in Hollywood, cocktails and canapés and jokes about the new DA. Meanwhile their kids juiced their own party mix: wine, weed and Xbox. Brad wound up passed out in a bedroom with some girl. Not the one who wanted her nose fixed, Karen, who had some big-deal family dinner she couldn't get out of. Just some fifteen-year-old from the High, whose name he never found out but who evidently liked cocaine a whole lot and who he really, really hoped would have forgotten about the whole episode. At 7 a.m. Mr Reynolds came into the room, went to the closet and chose a tie.

As he left he said, 'Good morning, Bradley.'

'Morning, Mr Reynolds,' Brad mumbled.

That was that. Mr Reynolds looked like he had stuff on his mind. Maybe some big law case or something. Hopefully not the fact that his teenage son and daughter were zoned on Valium half the time, supplied by Hudek, via Brad.

As he sat on the rock Brad was more interested in the question of whether Hudek really had slept with Karen Luchs. It was possible. You never knew with Lee. Though Brad had known him most of his life, walked the same halls and kicked, caught and dribbled the same balls, he never felt he'd gotten to the bottom of his friend. There were questions unanswered. Like where Lee got his drive. Like how he knew how to do things. Like how he was one of those guys you wound up working for, instead of the other way around. Maybe he had screwed Karen, maybe not. Most of them had screwed most of the others at some point in time. It didn't really matter in the end, probably.

Brad looked up when he heard a polyphonic snatch of the theme from *The Simpsons*, saw Lee put his Moto to his ear. The conversation lasted about a minute. Hudek didn't raise his voice, but he seldom did, so that didn't prove much. Finally he flipped the phone shut and crooked a finger at Brad.

'Delay,' Hudek said, when Brad got to the car. His eyes were hard to read.

'Delayed how?'

Hudek shrugged.

'That's kind of fucked up, Lee,' Brad muttered. The sun had made his head hurt worse. 'Lot of people waiting.'

'I know that.' Hudek shrugged again. 'Can't do it now, is all. Have to be this evening. No biggie.'

Far as Brad could see, it actually was kind of a big deal. It had never happened before, point one, and point two it was Saturday and a ton of people were waiting for weed and coke. The later they took delivery, the later it would be before they could stop driving around doing drops and start partying themselves. But Hudek was staring out through the windshield in a way that said he was unhappy enough already, so instead of saying anything Brad reached in and got the gun from where it had been lying ready in the rear seat footwell. He took it around back and put it safely in the trunk for the journey home, wrapped in a beach towel. As always, he felt a lot happier when it was put away.

He dozed off on the way back across the Valley, as Hudek drove a steady fifty along 118, not saying a word. Sleepy played his game all the way home. Beep, beep, ping.

The sun poured down, making everything flat and bland.

After dropping the others off at the Belle Isle mall Hudek drove around the Valley, not heading anywhere in particular. Wound up at a table outside Frisbee's with a cheeseburger and chilli fries, watching cars go by. Anyone glancing his way would have seen a blond kid, sport-toned build and medium tan, clean baggy jeans and a T-shirt that wasn't cheap. A single barbed wire tattoo around the left bicep (no faux gang crap for him) and looks that weren't head-snapping but would pass for decent anywhere in the continental USA. Standard-issue local fauna, in other words, the young male of the species that roamed this particular valley plain.

His phone rang a few times and he answered it, methodically fielding enquiries as to why people hadn't received their goodies yet. He knew these people socially, and no one got uptight. It was all cool. Lee would provide. He always did. Always had, anyway. The one person who didn't call was the guy he most needed to hear from, with a new time/place to meet. It was getting, as his dad would say, 'most unusual'.

Like a lot of his friends, Hudek got on okay with his folks. The difference was that while most tolerated their parents because they gave them so little grief, floating in the background of their lives, giving rides where needed, making cash available for clothes or counselling or rehab, and only intermittently taking time out of their busy careers to wonder aloud if their son or daughter might seek some kind of employment, ever, Hudek genuinely semi-dug his father. When he was around. Hudek Senior was in real estate development, and travelled a lot. He seemed to have plenty contacts and made outstanding amounts of money, and yet he wasn't ostentatious with it. Both he and his wife owned a lot of very expensive stuff which never even left the house, and was tidied away when guests came. He had a sense of humour, too. Lee's choice of ringtone was an in-joke with himself, in recollection of – many years before, when he was just a little`kid – seeing his father watching *The Simpsons* and laughing hard when Homer turned to his children and said: 'Remember – so far as everybody else knows, we're just a normal family.' Ryan Hudek's motto was similar, and unusual for his place and era: if you understand what you're worth, not everybody else has to know.

Lee had taken that on board, along with a lesson enshrined in countless movies and reinforced every week in real-life cop TV. Showy gets attention, and attention isn't good. So far as most people would ever know, Lee was just another boy with not much to do on a hot Saturday afternoon. That much was cool with him.

After a while he remembered it was his mother's birthday. He picked up a card and a bottle of the stuff she wore and drove around to their house. His dad was out somewhere, golf probably, so Lee went straight out back.

Lisa Hudek was semi-reclined on a lounger by the pool, wearing dark glasses and not doing much. She accepted the unwrapped gift and a kiss and smiled in her son's direction, or at least nearby.

Lee sat out with her for an hour, watching the flickering of the water in the pool, while his mother drank steadily from a tall, frosted flask. Finally the cell rang and it was Hernandez.

Revised meet was seven thirty. Yes, very late, but that's the way it was. Deal with it. They'd beep him a venue later.

Oh, and this time could he come alone?

Hudek muttered 'Yeah, right,' and went inside to make some calls.

At seven fifteen he pulled to a slow halt halfway up the block where Roscoe Boulevard crossed Sennoa Avenue. At the junction fifty yards down was a gas station, as he'd been told. Opposite was a low building Hudek had driven past many, many times in the last few years, without giving it much of a glance. When he was a kid it had been a buffet restaurant, and he was pretty sure the family had eaten there a couple of times. Then it went out of business, became a carpet store and a car spares place and a variety of other things before becoming fundamentally invisible. One of those places, sometimes boarded-up, sometimes in generic business, that drifts slowly off people's mental radar.

'Okay,' he said, turning off the engine.

'Very, very far from okay,' Brad said, shaking his head. This time he was in the passenger seat. Sleepy Pete was in the other car, with Steve Verkilen, the fourth member of the inner crew. They were just around the other corner from the gas station. Brad could just see the front of their vehicle. It wasn't reassuring him much. The pistol was under Brad's seat, but that wasn't helping either. Something was making him suspect that tonight it was finally going to get used. That wasn't good. It wasn't there to be used. It was there to be owned, for other people to know you had it. Once, just once, they had sent a burst across the front of some guy's house in the night, as a warning, when they knew for certain he wasn't home. Using it for real was a whole different bag of shit. It stopped it being an even remotely reassuring object. Brad thought he could sense the thing radiating coldness up through his seat: feel it limbering up, waking and stretching, sipping a coffee and saying, 'Well, kid, what did you *think* I was for?'

The fact there was a second gun under Hudek's seat only made things worse. It was there next to the bag of money.

Brad lit a cigarette in the hope this might make a difference. 'Front's locked and boarded. How are you supposed to get in?'

'Door around the back.'

'Are you really going to do this?'

'No,' Hudek said. '*We* are.'

'Lee, look, man. Look. It's . . . if they specifically say just you, what are they going to do if we both turn up?'

'That's what we're here to find out.'

Brad started to reply, and found Hudek was looking at him. He realized immediately that there was nothing he could say. Not in the face of the fact he owed money, and that Hudek was the only place it could be found. If Brad said anything more it could only be by opening the car door and walking away, and if that happened the future was a poor and unknowable place without drugs or money or a position in life.

'I could have just brought you along as usual,' Hudek said. 'Not told you what they said. But I kept you in the loop.'

'Okay,' Brad said. 'Okay.'

Hudek sent a beep to Pete and got one back. They watched as Sleepy and Steve got out of their car and walked across the junction, disappearing up the other street. Waited until there was no one likely to pass by, then they got out of the car, pulled the pistols out and wedged them quickly down the backs of their jeans. Jackets on over the top, bag of money in Hudek's left hand. Hudek looked at Brad and nodded curtly. Ready to go. Just two guys out for a stroll. You could almost hear the soundtrack start to play.

Oh yeah, Brad thought, feeling faintly nauseous. *We're fly as all hell. This fucking cool, what could possibly go wrong?*

He followed Hudek across the road, his head up and his stride regular and strong. They walked straight into the small lot in front of the building, and headed around the right-hand side. A narrow passageway here gave access to another, bigger lot around the back. This was empty apart from a battered square of tarpaulin lying in a crumpled heap over to one side. At the far end was a low concrete wall, as Hudek knew from a drive-by two hours before. The other side of this wall, hidden around the side of a rusted dumpster, would be Pete and Steve.

When they were halfway across the lot, Hudek stopped. He had to admit the place was a good choice. Broad daylight, yet completely hidden from the road. A doorway was visible in the long, flat expanse of the back of the building, but he didn't head straight for it. He glanced around the lot instead. Listened. Took his time, looking for all the world like a predator on his own territory.

Brad admired his cool. Admired it a lot. And really, really hoped it would be enough.

'We told you to come alone.'

Brad's heart nearly leapt out of his chest. The voice had come from behind them. Of course.

'Turn around,' it said. 'Slowly.'

Hudek and Brad turned together to see three men standing ten feet away. All were lean, dark-haired, dark-eyed. Must have waited until they saw them come around the back, then followed up the passage. Oh Christ.

The only one Brad recognized was Hernandez, their regular contact. He was around thirty and had a face like a second-hand axe. He shook his head at Hudek.

'We told you to come alone,' he said, again. The inflection was exactly the same the second time.

'And I heard you,' Hudek said. 'You told me to suck your dick, I wouldn't be doing that either.'

Hernandez pursed his lips and nodded soberly, as if in appreciation of the response, its genre appropriateness, as if the older man was a digitized bad guy in Grand Theft Auto VII and this was Available Riposte number 3.

He turned to the guy on his right, and nodded some more. This guy nodded back. They both looked at Hudek and nodded.

The moment went on a beat too long and the whole thing was beginning to seriously freak Brad the fuck out.

'You said to meet you inside,' Hudek said. 'What's this crap out here in the lot? What's the creeping up on us about?'

'To check you'd followed instructions,' Hernandez said.

'You seriously think I was going to?'

'We hoped.'

'Life is full of disappointments, dude. Deal with it. Can we get this done? I've got half the West Valley waiting on a high.'

'Maybe we find some other rich kid to run our shit. Someone who does what he's told like a good boy.'

'See, you're getting mixed up about something,' Hudek said, theatrically shaking his head. 'Really just, completely turned around. You seem to think we're going to stand here and take this kind of crap from you guys. That's sort of not going to happen.'

'Is that right?' Hernandez was smiling again now. Brad didn't like it when he smiled. It was not convincing. He needed lessons. Brad realized one of the other guys was holding a gun, casually, down by his side. Probably always had been, but he'd been too wired to notice. *Take their crap, Lee*, he thought, urgently. *Please, Lee, let's just take their crap and get out of here.*

'Pete,' Hudek said, suddenly, his voice loud. 'Why don't you come join us?'

There was silence for a long moment. Sleepy Pete did not appear from around the side of the big metal block.

Brad glanced dismally at Hudek, and saw that for the first time the other boy's eyes looked a little confused.

Nonetheless Hudek spoke again. 'Steve?'

More silence, broken only by the sound of a car honking over on the intersection, a world away.

Hernandez cocked his head. 'Pete? Steve? Who would these people be? More uninvited boys? More Valley rats?'

Hudek said nothing. Kept looking at the dumpster.

Hernandez looked at the guy on his right again. 'You guys know any Pete or Steve? You come across anybody like that?'

'Yeah,' the guy said. 'Think we did.'

He walked over to where the big square of tarp was lying bunched against the side wall. Lifted one corner.

Brad stared. Lying under the tarp were Pete and Steve. Their mouths had been secured with silver duct tape. Probably their arms and legs too, because they weren't moving. At least, that might be why they weren't moving.

The guy let the tarp fall again.

'Shouldn't have done that,' Hudek said. His voice was low and flat. He slipped his right hand into his jacket and around the back. 'You should not have done that.'

'You should have come alone.'

'Untie them.'

'Fuck you.'

Hudek pulled his hand out. He was holding the automatic pistol. 'Fucking untie them, man.'

They went to and fro on it for a while, but Brad barely heard. There was a constant voice in his head now, blotting out almost everything else. *I'm twenty years old*, it was jabbering. *This is too soon. This has not been enough. I thought I was grown, but I was wrong. I do not want to have sex or take drugs or drink beer any more. I do not want to be here. I want to be home, watching* X-Files *reruns and eating ice cream. I want to be ten years old.*

'You piece of shit,' Hudek said, evidently resting his case.

Brad tuned back in. The other guys' guns were no longer by their sides. They were pointing at him and Lee. It was all going very wrong but Brad knew what was expected of him, and he pulled his own gun out. Nothing good could happen now. Five guys with guns. You do the math.

Hudek raised his pistol, pointing it squarely at Hernandez's chest. The guy appeared utterly unmoved, and for the first time Hudek was sure, completely sure, that this man had killed people, and more than once. Hudek's mind possessed a low clarity which Brad's could never hope for, but just at that moment their thoughts were pretty much the same. This was it. This was the point where it all unravelled.

'Okay,' he said, 'If that's the way it's got to be . . .'

There was a loud clicking sound, from behind. Then a soft bang, like wood hitting cinder block.

Hudek saw Hernandez's eyes swivel. He and Brad turned.

The door to the back of the building was now hanging open. A man in a business suit was standing there.

'Just get in here,' he said. 'For Christ's sake. We're waiting.'

Brad was at least as surprised as Hudek, but he couldn't have spoken. Couldn't have said a single word. It was left to Hudek to find voice, therefore, and he barely made it either. He didn't even notice Hernandez taking the opportunity to thunk Brad on the back of the head, or hear his friend dropping bonelessly to the lot.

He just stared open-mouthed at the man in the doorway for a full five seconds, and then finally said:

'Mr *Reynolds?*'

Chapter 4

The interior of the building was hot and dark, lit only by a few bulbs hanging bare from the ceiling at apparently random intervals. Every now and then one of these illuminated some debris from one of the structure's previous commercial incarnations: a pile of mouldering carpet rolls, unidentifiable pieces of motor vehicle, bits of oblong machinery Lee Hudek dimly recognized as belonging in the kitchens of restaurants. It smelled of dust and heat. He followed Mr Reynolds through a large room, along a corridor, and then through a door into an even bigger, darker space, which stretched the remaining length of the building. Mr Reynolds stepped aside there, leaving Lee suddenly in front. It was clear he was supposed to keep walking. There was a light down the far end. Presumably that was where he was supposed to go. He considered, just for a moment, the idea of not doing so, of turning and trying to force his way back out. The notion didn't seem to make much sense. Brad was out in the lot still, Pete and Steve too, having Christ knows what done to them by Hernandez and his pals. It wasn't clear what the future held for Hudek, either.

He guessed he might as well just find out.

He walked forward into the gloom. He felt his footsteps ought to echo in a space this size, but they did not. Maybe there were more heaps of trash out of sight, deadening the sound. Maybe it was because it was so fucking hot. The air felt as if it had been trapped here a long, long time, as if it was palpable, and swallowed sounds. People too, perhaps.

The light was coming from a single lamp, positioned in the middle of an empty patch of floor. It looked like something out of a cheap motel, or a movie, a straight wooden upright capped by a large shade, once white, now aged and dusted a sickly cream. Next to it was an armchair: big, threadbare, a colour that would be nameless even in good light. Sitting in this was a man.

'Hey, Lee,' the man said. 'Remember me?'

Hudek stopped about twenty feet short. This wasn't because he thought it was the protocol. It was more because, for reasons he'd have found hard to explain, he didn't want to get too close.

The guy wore a dark suit over a dark shirt. He looked to be in his late thirties and was well-built but underweight. His hair was short and his skin was pale. His face was so harshly down-lit that it was hard to make the features out properly, but as far as Hudek knew, he'd never seen this dude before in his life. He looked like a large dog of uncertain temperament, sitting upright in a chair, very awake. Ready for a walk. Or dinner.

'No,' he said.

'Good.' The man regarded him in silence for a while. His gaze was impersonal, as if Hudek were a landscape painting of indifferent quality for which he might be able to find some hanging space. In a back room, most likely, or the corridor where old coats and broken tennis rackets were stowed. 'So how have you been, Lee?'

Hudek shrugged. 'You know, okay.'

'Good. That's good. Take a seat.'

Hudek was confused. Then he realized the man was indicating something, pointing with a raised left hand. Lee turned to see that a wooden chair had appeared just behind him. All he had to do was bend his knees to sit down. So he did.

He still had the bag of money for the deal which was evidently so *not* going to happen, clenched in his hand. He put it down. His heart felt as if someone was tapping his chest with a hammer, not yet quite as hard as they could, but enough to bend the ribs a little.

'You were asked to come alone,' the man said, as if he'd just remembered something of minor importance. 'You didn't. Why?'

Hudek struggled again to work out the best thing to say. 'It just didn't sound like a good idea.'

'I get you. The guys you've been buying from ask you to bring the money, without any backup, and they dick you around over the time, that's got to make you nervous, right? So you think, hell, I'll bring some pals, I'm not going to just do what I'm told. I'm the man. I'm Lee John Hudek.'

'Exactly.' Hudek nodded enthusiastically, glad to finally be on solid ground. Whoever this guy was, he clearly understood.

'If you do that again,' the man said, 'if you disobey an instruction, however complex or simple, then the police will never find your head. I will kill you, and everyone you've ever cared about, and then your troubles will have only just begun. Understand?'

Hudek just blinked at him.

'Do you understand?'

'Shit, yes. Of course. I get you, man, I really do. I'm sorry.'

'Excellent.' The man nodded, suddenly affable again. 'See, that's really important, Lee, because I need to feel that I can trust you. *We* need to feel that, okay?'

'Sure, sure,' Hudek said, head bobbing in rampant agreement. He was now convinced he was going to die. 'But . . . when you say "we", who is that, exactly? I mean, I thought Hernandez was . . .'

The man said nothing, but instead lifted both hands off the arms of his chair, and raised them, palms up.

From out of the darkness, four men appeared. Two were in middle age, the other two a good deal younger. One of each group was expensively attired. The others had dressed to go without notice in a crowd.

'We're the people you buy your drugs from,' the man said. 'We distribute them through Hernandez, amongst others. Welcome to the next level, Lee.'

It took about a minute for Hudek's heartbeat to return to something like its normal rate, by which time the other men had faded back out of sight. He was effectively alone with the seated man once more.

'Tell me something,' the man said. 'Do you have any ideas?'

Hudek paused. What did *this* mean? 'Like . . .'

'Well, you're good at what you do. We're happy. Solid turnover, and you've kept it low key. Is that all you want? Are those the limits of your skies?'

Hudek hesitated again. He thought now he understood what was being asked, but he didn't want to get it wrong. 'Well, yeah, I mean, I have thought about something.'

'Why don't you tell me what that is?'

'Spring Break,' Hudek said.

'What about it?'

'I got a plan.' Hudek took a deep breath. 'Every year, you got millions of kids on Spring Break, right? Florida in particular, I'm thinking about. It gets bigger every year, more like a theme park, with your sponsored this and MTV that and your big business muscling in and all that shit. This year I was down in Panama City, checking it. And I'm thinking. Bottom line. There's four hundred, five hundred thousand kids coming to that one town over the season, March to April. They want beer, they want wet T-shirts, they want to get laid. They want *drugs*. Even if they don't know it yet, they do. It's around, of course, you can get drugs no problem, but it's not organized. It could be better. A *lot* better.'

'I see,' the man said. 'And you're figuring . . . why should it just be the IBMs and AT&Ts of the world who are getting their hooks into these young tigers? If corporate America is invading the Break, why shouldn't Lee John Hudek get in there too, tap into that customer base?'

'Exactly. You had a tight crew there, worked hard, you could shift a truly awesome amount of drugs. I want be that guy.'

There, it was done.

The Plan was out in the open. Hudek had never actually said it out loud before. Doing so had made him feel even more confident.

'It's an idea,' the man said. 'But it's not original, and there are three problems with it. I'm going to explain them to you, okay?'

Hudek nodded, his heart falling immediately.

'First and biggest is the cops. There are plenty of dealers working the Break already, of course. They're small-time or kicking back to the local law. Spring Break is huge business for these places, Lee. Towns can make a quarter billion dollars a season, can stand or fall on how many of these beer-swilling fuckheads they can pull into their nightclubs and bars, burning up their licence to go wild before they go get their dull jobs and disappear into the long grass. The towns know there's drugs around. It's part of the deal. It's contained, it's understood. But if the place gets awash and it splashes all over the front pages, it's all over for that town. The law's job is to ensure that doesn't happen, that a balance is struck – and the cops skim a little for their boat upgrades and retirement funds too, of course. You know a lot of Florida cops, Lee? You got those connections? You got experience in dealing with Panhandle law at ranking officer level?'

Hudek shook his head.

'I assumed not. Second issue is supply. Even if you get the cops sweet and put your people in there – and you'll need quite a few, and you'll need good communication, transport and storage facilities, which the cops might even be able to help you with – then you'll have the problem of product. How are you going to finance this? I don't know how much of your allowance you got in that bag there, but it isn't going to cover it.'

Hudek had known this was the tricky part. 'I thought,' he said, 'I thought maybe it could be a pay afterwards kind of deal.'

'Someone lends you the drugs, sees if you can shift them on, if not you give them back with your receipt and their ten per cent? And they turn a blind eye to all the stuff that's missing, the pills and coke your dealers have sucked into their own heads or bartered for fucks on the beach? That really what you thought?'

Hudek shrugged, his face hot. It was, of course.

The man in the chair didn't laugh, but someone in the shadows did.

'Finally,' the man said, 'where were you actually going to find these altruistic benefactors? You go nosing around trying to make contacts down South, Miami gangbangers will have you in pieces before you've opened your mouth. Some of those Cuban homeboys make the Crips look like Martha fucking Stewart.'

'So it was a dumb idea,' Hudek said, deflated. He looked down at his hands.

'No, Lee. It's a *good* idea. It semi-happens already. But it hasn't been done properly, you're right. You'd need a reliable and large-scale supply of drugs, and a way of laundering the money taken. You'd need to take advantage of pre-existing law enforcement relationships and have the wherewithal to refresh those ahead of time. You would need someone to help you avoid stupid mistakes and/or winding up face down in a swamp. You would require serious backers, in other words.'

Hudek looked up. The man was staring at him, hard.

'Backers who trusted you, who knew that you could be relied upon. Who knew you always did what you were told.'

Hudek nodded. He didn't quite trust himself to speak.

'You would need backers, in fact, who might want you and your crew to prove themselves: who might ask you to do them a favour or two first, to show good faith. Do you understand?'

'I think so,' Hudek said. 'What do you want?'

The man smiled. 'We don't need to get into that right now. Soon, but not just at this minute.'

He looked at Hudek a while longer, and nodded. 'Great to see you again, my friend. On the way out you'll be given what you came for. You can take your own bag back with you this time, as a gesture of our good will. Spread the cash around your crew. Make people happy. We'll be in touch soon regarding the other thing.'

Hudek stood up. 'Will I be working with you on it? I mean, direct?'

The man shook his head, and Hudek found himself feeling relieved. 'I'm just a day tripper. Other things I have to do. You'll work with Hernandez. Play nice. Watch and learn. He's good. You can pick up some things. For future positions you might hold.'

He winked. Hudek risked a smile.

The man indicated with his head. Hudek got the message, turned and walked away.

Mr Reynolds was waiting for Lee in the corridor. He led him back out through the building, across the middle of the large room with its dangling lights. Hudek felt light-headed and shaky and euphoric all at once, and altogether unable to deal with the fact that he was being led out of the building by Stacy and Josh Reynolds' father. He'd blanked this particular piece of weirdness while confronted with the man in the chair. That guy had a way of focusing your attention.

Just before they got to the exit, Mr Reynolds stopped. 'Don't mention my being here,' he said. 'I offer people advice on occasion, that's all. Legal counsel is available to everyone.'

'That's fine, Mr Reynolds.'

'Make sure Bradley understands that too.'

'I will. He does what I tell him.'

Mr Reynolds nodded. 'I'm sure. I'm sure they all do. You don't get the guns back, I'm afraid.' He reached into the shadows and pulled out a small bag. It was bright red and had a white Nike logo on it. 'But this is for you.'

Hudek pulled the bag's zipper back a few inches, and saw it contained the usual mixture but in greater quantity, a real bumper crop. Just at the moment he wasn't equal to working out what precise level of income it all represented. 'Thanks,' he said.

'You're welcome, Lee. But if I *ever* hear you've been selling that shit to my kids, any of it, at all, you'll rue the day you were born.'

Then he turned and walked away.

Hudek walked the last couple of yards and opened the door. Stepped out into the parking lot.

It was still light, which kind of amazed him. He glanced at his watch and saw only thirty-five minutes had passed since they'd pulled up in the car. Unbelievable.

Standing in the middle of the lot were three guys. His guys.

He walked over. Brad looked kind of woozy. Pete and Steve were red around the mouth from where the duct tape had been. All appeared shell-shocked, and quiet, and all were smoking. Just for once, Hudek wished he could join in.

'They told us to wait here,' Pete said. 'Hernandez and the other two fuckheads. They . . . I don't know. They waited with us for a while and then . . . just fucking went. The whole thing was seriously fucking odd, dude.'

Brad blinked, seemed to come back into himself. He looked down, realized what was in each of Hudek's hands. He frowned at the red bag. 'You've got the drugs?'

'Yes.'

'And you've still . . . got the money.'

'Right. It's like, a bonus. It's all cool.'

Brad shook his head. He looked like his brain was in need of a reboot. 'So – then, what the *fuck* was all that about?'

'It's cool,' Hudek repeated. 'That's all I know.'

He led the others out around the side and back onto the road. Lee wasn't actually sure what had just happened. He just knew that he had come through it stronger, and that he was now dealing with a different order of professional. One thing he was absolutely *not* going to do was underestimate the people he had just met. Especially the guy in the chair. The threat he'd made could be interpreted as just being the kind of thing that people said to underline a point. Florid. Movie-speak. But Hudek didn't believe that was the case. He believed the man had meant what he said, would follow through, and had perhaps even understated his intentions.

And he still didn't remember meeting him before.

'I knew something bizarro was going to happen today,' Sleepy said, rubbing his wrists.

'Pete,' Brad said, 'shut up.'

'No, seriously. I had this weird fucking dream just before I woke up. I was in the mall and I went to McD's for lunch. Except it was night, you could tell because the big windows behind where the tables are were dark, but it felt like lunch. And instead of buying like a burger or something, I asked for a salad, which you'll agree is pretty fucked up.'

'Beyond amazing,' Brad said. 'Hold the front page. Alert CNN. That's some crazy shit, bro.'

'No, that's not it. I *asked* for a salad, okay, but they didn't give me a salad. They gave me this huge bag of Fritos. And I enjoy potato chips *more* than the next guy, but I didn't want any right then. I wanted a fuckin' salad. And so I said, jeez, hand over the green shit, dude – what's your fucking problem? And this guy who was serving just kind of smiled at me, and he didn't look like your normal server droid, he was much older with grey hair and he was big and he looked kind of weird and scary. He took the chips back though, and handed me a McD bag, folded over. I walked away and then suddenly I was in the parking lot and I opened the bag and saw it *still* wasn't a fucking salad.'

'What was it?' Brad asked, despite himself.

Hudek tuned them all out, gazing up the street into the Valley, savouring the moment, knowing it was here and now where his life kicked into a higher gear. It was already hard to believe what had happened back inside the building, in fact it too felt a little like a dream or something he'd watched on TV – but the bags he held in each hand said it was not.

'Apple pie,' Pete said. 'I wasn't going to go all the way back in the mall to sort it out, so I just opened it and took a bite. But the filling was all red. And it was absolutely freezing cold.'

Brad stared at him. 'That's it? That's *it*?'

Suddenly all their cell phones started ringing at once.

'Okay,' Hudek said. 'The customers are getting restless. Let's get it on.'

Back inside the building, the other men had stepped once again out of the shadows. Someone flicked a switch and the room was bathed in light.

'He'll be fine,' the man in the chair said. He stood up, slowly, stretching his shoulders and back. 'But tweak him anyway. Then we're good to go.'

Chapter 5

Jim sat at a table in the window of a place called Marsha's, in South Carolina. He had followed 95 up as far as Savannah and fifteen miles north from there made the turn-off onto 321. He had made slow progress all the way from the Keys, and already taken a day longer than the journey merited. Had stayed in the slow lane of the freeway all the way north, just another grey-haired guy in an old car, the kind you whip past on your way to somewhere or other. At first this had been partly because it was a long time since he'd made such a drive: he'd barely used the car in the last eight years, except on local grocery runs. He soon got used to the sensation of road passing under the tyres again, however, and could not blame caution for his speed. Nor sheer perversity, though that was also a factor.

Heavy clouds were gathering overhead. It was only just after five o'clock, and yet outside all was muted and dark. The word at the counter, which Jim could hear without effort, was that they were going to see some serious rain this evening, and it was about time.

The waitress came by and refilled his coffee without asking. He smiled, and she smiled back, and then waddled off to perform some other kind deed. Jim watched her reflection recede in the table's napkin dispenser. Her hair was dyed a funny shade or two of lurid blonde and had she been a refrigerator you could have stored a lot of food inside. And yet there was something very appealing about her, something true about her ordinariness. Strange how it could be that way. Good, capable hands and a nice attitude made more difference than people thought. Jim realized, with mild wonder, that it had been over a decade since he'd had sex. The thought brought him little but relief.

He stirred a spoonful of sugar into the brew and looked out the window a while longer. It was coming down to it, now. He had dragged his feet, made as if coming north meant fighting some natural slope in the landscape which his car was not equal to. Now he was only an hour or so from his first destination, and·it was time to stop pretending. He was going where he was going, unless he stopped now. There were miles still to drive, but they were getting fewer. This was the time, this lacuna. If he was going to not do something, now was the time to start not doing it.

The feeling in his guts was one he recognized. A hollow tension, so muted it could perhaps be hunger. He glanced at the menu propped up against the sill and rejected its contents once more. He knew he should have something to eat. Someone two tables over had taken a corned beef sandwich a little while back and it had smelled fine, the bread lightly toasted, sauerkraut warm and rich, the sauce good and thick the way Jim liked it. He had always had very specific tastes in food. Maybe if he ate, the feeling would go away.

Did he want that?

He did not know. He truly did not know.

So he sipped his coffee until it was finished and then left, leaving a dollar tip on a dollar fifty purchase, hoping it went to the right waitress.

When he got back in the car he noticed the bag on the passenger seat, and was confused for just a moment. Of course. He barely remembered buying the contents, at an outlet mall a little south of Jacksonville. But he had bought it, he knew, just as he had acquired a much heavier item before even leaving the Keys, and so he supposed that meant he had made his decision.

And it didn't matter anyway. It had already been made for him. The sphere turns, and the heart pumps and blood flows, regardless of what you feel on the subject.

Eighty miles up the way he took the turn to Benboro. He took a wrong fork soon after that and had to retrace a little. It was not an area he knew well, nor one which made great effort to make things easier for outsiders. People would only ever be passing through. There were patches of anonymous woodland now and then but usually the land was flat either side of the road.

After Benboro it was simpler – there was only one road out of the town, such as it was. A mile along it was a big tilted sign on the right. It had been pale green last time Jim saw it, but in the intervening years it had been repainted red: some while ago, judging by the state of it. It looked as though the job had been done by someone who was dimly familiar with letters as shapes, rather than as things that conveyed meaning.

BENBORO PARK, they said.

He pulled over and headed up the access road. He had known it would still be here: impulse calls once every couple of years had proved someone still answered the phone at the number for the trailer park. He had not stayed on the line long enough to find out if it was the old woman he had met, or to ensure the park itself was still in business. People lived there, had done so for years. There was no reason for it to go under, turning families and old couples and wild-haired single individuals out into the unknown. Benboro town itself had the dynamism of an old sock. Nobody was going to be developing subdivisions or building a business park outside it anytime soon.

And what was it to him, anyway?

Yet still he had called, every couple of years.

60

The drive took a curving path that had probably looked artful on the original plan, scrawled on an envelope in some long-ago developer's office shack, but in the real world was just plain long-winded. By halfway along you could see the unlovely sprawl of the sixty or so trailers in sixty or so different designs and states of repair. Unlike many such facilities, the roads they were situated on did not follow a simple grid. The guy with the envelope evidently had a taste for the ornate. Jim imagined this made finding a particular resident far from easy, which probably had both bad and good sides. Luckily he knew exactly where he was going. On the far side of the park, over where a stand of trees marked the beginning of a forty-yard strip of waste ground which led down to the bank of a feature-less river, was a line of four low wooden buildings. They were very large, ramshackle. Two were used to store old junk and materials relevant to the maintenance of the park. The others were parti-tioned into storage areas which were for hire.

At the entrance to the park, Jim pulled over. A gateway affair – two grey metal poles with a board held between them over trailer height – confirmed this was indeed Benboro Park and not Bel Air or heaven or the best of all possible worlds. On the other side, the road split. In the centre of the division was a trailer painted the same red as the sign on the main road. This was Site No. 1, and in it lived the woman who ran the park. Hannah, her name was. Assuming she was still alive.

He got out of the car. The clouds were heavier now, charcoal and frosted and pregnant, but the rain had still not begun to fall. Jim hoped it would sooner or later, if only for the sake of the old boys perched at the counter in Marsha's, to whom it had sounded like a big deal. Though it would spoil the fun of a little girl he now saw, playing by herself in the road outside a trailer down the right-hand fork. She was singing to herself, quietly. It was a nice sound.

As he walked over to No. 1 he reminded himself of the story he'd told long ago. He had just gone through a long and arduous divorce, that's right, and this was everything he'd been able to save for himself. Wasn't much, but it had sentimental value. He wanted it somewhere safe, away from lawyers and their familiars. He was on his way down to Miami. Friend of his said he might be able to get him a job in a hotel there. Failing that, he might head for Arizona, or Nevada, try his luck further west.

He knocked on the door, listening to the sounds of television from inside. Before very long the door was opened.

'Yessir?'

It was the woman he remembered. Additional years of pickling in a trailer full of cigarette smoke had turned her skin the non-colour of a once-white dishcloth. Dry, grey-brown hair was pulled into a ragged ponytail that said she knew she looked like shit, and honestly didn't care.

'Hi,' Jim said, smiling broadly. 'Hannah, right? Don't know if you remember me?'

'Can't say that I do, no. You're not from the park.'

'That's right. I rented storage space from you a little while ago. I need to get to it.'

'Okay,' she said. 'What's the number?'

'Seventeen,' Jim said, keeping his voice steady.

She wandered off towards a cataclysmically untidy office area in back. This was the point, Jim knew, where things could get sticky. He waited just outside the trailer, eyes on the road. The little girl had disappeared.

A couple of minutes later Hannah came back. 'Little while ago is right,' she said. 'It's been twelve years. You only left enough for five.'

'I got held up,' he said.

She nodded. 'You the fellow who was heading off to Australia?'

'Miami. That's right.'

'No good?'

'It's okay. Kind of hot.'

'Hot? Don't talk to me about hot. This summer was a bitch, and it still ain't rained. You owe me money.'

He gave her the bundle of bills he had prepared. She counted it.

'I haven't allowed for inflation.'

She laughed. 'Ain't no inflation round here. We can't afford it.'

Jim smiled. 'I want it for another year, if that's okay.'

'All right by me, and I see the money's here.' She handed him a small, rusty key. 'Goodnight. Leave the key on the step.'

Then the door was shut, and Jim was finished.

As he drove through the park, heading for the far side, he was bemused at how easy it had been. He had arrived late, that night twelve years ago, and in an intense frame of mind. His cover story sucked, and yet Hannah had actually given him a ride back to Benboro so he could catch a bus for Miami. He had booked five years and then disappeared for over twice as long. You'd have thought she would be . . . well, whatever. He'd evidently just made a good choice, that was all, divining correctly that storage turnover out here would not be high. Or perhaps she'd just sold his belongings long ago and was sitting in her trailer now, door bolted, laughing over his money.

He parked outside the third of the big sheds, and walked along to the fifth big door. He used the key to unlock it, and went inside.

Space 17 was a simple rectangle partitioned off within the big interior, ten feet wide by twenty deep. It was immediately evident that it still held what Jim had left behind.

He pulled the cover off and let it fall to the ground. Then just stood and looked at it for a moment. He had meant to be businesslike about this, but he could not help but pause.

For something that looked so luminous, the object in Space 17 was remarkably prosaic. It was an old VW camper van, in white: a vehicle in neither good nor bad enough condition to draw the eye. There was the big window in front, for optimum visibility. None in the sides. The quarter-height one in back was obscured by a thick white blind. You couldn't see the interior but it held a minuscule kitchenette and a tiny divided-off sleeping area at the back which ran the width of the van, and was just about feasible if you weren't too tall and didn't mind lying on your side and drawing your legs up a little. It was everything a travelling man needed. This partic-ular travelling man, anyhow.

Jim walked back to his car and got the two bags out. He opened his small suitcase, put his hand into the shoebox, and pulled out the old set of car keys. Felt funny with them in his hands, with the worn plastic fob, a free gift advertising a school craft fair eighteen years ago. He was becalmed by it for a moment, remembering that afternoon, recalling buying it. Another life.

Back in Space 17 he unlocked the camper's driver-side door and threw the lighter bag across to the passenger seat. Then he carried the heavy bag to the back of the vehicle. He drained the small amount of gas still in the tank and replaced it with new. He removed the van's battery and swapped it with the one in the second bag, then carried the dead one back outside and stowed it in the trunk of the car. Walked back to the van.

It was time to see. Could be the electrics had gotten damp. The oil would have settled. It had been a very long time.

He climbed in the front, feeling the seat settle under him like an old friend. Stuck the key in and turned it without ceremony.

A click, and nothing.

Turned it again. The van coughed, farted, and then chugged gamely into life. Jim shook his head fondly, not the first person to admire the efficiency of Volkswagen's engineers.

'Welcome back, old horse,' he said.

Ten minutes later he placed the key on the step of Site No. 1 and walked back to the quietly chugging van. He sat in the front and waited while a middle-aged couple wandered across the road. Neither gave him a second glance. A more-or-less white van. Whatever. And of course Jim was over sixty now, and men of that age are seldom assumed to be up to much. The car he had arrived in was in Space 17, covered with the tarp. Inside it were the clothes Jim had been wearing. He was now dressed in black jeans and a faded denim shirt, purchased at the outlet mall. Not the kind of thing Jim Westlake wore. More the style of someone called James Kyle, a teacher and householder and all-round regular guy.

The little girl was back out in the street again, still playing by herself. Jim frowned. Someone should be keeping an eye on her. Some adult should be sitting on the step, drinking a beer if necessary, but keeping her within view. The people who lived in Benboro Park probably knew each other pretty well but that wouldn't always be enough. It was easy for bad things to befall the young. Too easy. The ease of it was depressing. The world should be organized so that the innocent and unblemished remained so, should be configured and maintained so that every person lived their span and got to its end thinking, 'Well actually, that wasn't so bad.' How often did it work that way? Everyone spent their time staring in the wrong directions. Instead of caring about corner offices and tidy lawns, about this season's hot shoe style or diet or celebrity; instead of obsessing over what other people think of them or over what they thought about themselves, people should be paying attention to other people, to each other's kids and parents and wives and pets. They should be dedicating themselves to protecting these magical things, the living loved ones, because only when something is gone or broken do you realize how wondrous and unique its completeness was. But people didn't consider this ahead of time, because they were stupid. They didn't, because life holds many distractions. They didn't, just because.

It was one of the reasons he had done what he did, in the old days. To show them what they should be caring about. To commune with the essential, the one. Or so he had told himself, occasionally: but he told himself a lot of stuff back then and most of it wasn't true. In that regard he had been just like everybody else. Inside, he thought, we are all two people, lying to each other. The only difference is the size and deadliness of the falsehoods we tell.

Within a few miles the van had warmed up well, and seemed to be enjoying being back on the road. Jim retraced his route until he could rejoin 321, and then continued north into the twilight, storm clouds still following after.

Chapter 6

Nina stood in Raynor's Wood wishing the men would be quiet so she could concentrate. She had spent the morning in the Thornton police department being briefed and looking at endless black-and-white photographs of a dead man who had been found six feet from her current position. Much of this had been superfluous. After Olbrich had left them to head back to Los Angeles, she and Monroe had done little on the journey east but talk about the case. She was prepped. There were not too many facts to go around. The more you repeated them the more they bloated, like bread left out in the rain, swollen and fundamentally substanceless. Monroe was now standing twenty feet away down by the stream with a gaggle of cops, rehearsing the same stuff. She tried to tune him out but immediately began to hear another voice, this one much closer.

'See the bushes? That's how come nobody saw it earlier.'

The speaker was Joe Reidel, a stocky young homicide detective. He was one of a number of cops out of the Cathridge County

Sheriff's office who'd been in Thornton working the case since the previous morning. The local police did not seem to resent the CID presence at all. They seemed cool about the FBI too, though it had been Reidel who'd initiated the contact. It was easy to gain the impression that this town didn't much like having dead bodies turning up, and would be happy for someone else to make the problem go away. Reidel was the only man who had not yet told Nina the facts his own way, given them his own special spin. Maybe if she let him do so then they'd all *shut up* and let her get on with thinking her own thoughts.

'I see,' she said. Raynor's Wood curled around the north side of the town. A flat stream ran through the middle of it and much of the ground on either side was prone to bogginess, settling out into still pools above which clouds of midges hung. The body had been found half-in and half-out of one of these, a few yards to the side of an odd hump in the ground. A stand of bushes had obscured it from the path down by the stream, and Nina dutifully stood and observed this conjunction for a moment. 'Still – not a major attempt to hide the body.'

'No. And this is a popular walk.' Reidel pointed up the rise to where the wood thinned. There was a small parking lot at the top. 'They don't actually call it "Lovers' Lane", but that's what it's for.'

'Though it's actually not as nice as all that.'

'It's a small town. I guess you work with what you've got.'

'Still no sign of the guy's clothes? No blood?'

'Nope.' The detective indicated around. 'It's a tough scene because of the leaves and twigs and general forest crapola, but I'm pretty sure it was undisturbed before our scene-of-crime techs got on it. The couple who found the body kept well clear.'

'Forensics on the stab wounds in the chest and stomach indicate the victim was dressed at the time of death?'

'Very likely. Fibre traces in several of them. Though there are two in the groin area which are notably clean. So maybe . . .'

'. . . a sex act was under way when the attack started. Right.'

Nina reached into the envelope under her arm and pulled out two of the pictures of the victim *in situ*. The first was a general view, largely replicating, she supposed, the sight the discovering couple had come upon. A body, in a wood at twilight. It was large and pale and just lying there. It was so incongruous that at first you barely registered its sex, though the body was completely naked. It was lying on its back, legs out sturdily straight. There were cut marks over its belly and chest. It was a male chest.

The second picture was from closer in. It showed that the victim's head was partly under water, only the chin and nose breaking the surface. The eyes were open under the surface, and the mouth too. The photo was sharply focused and you could see how the hairless parts of the body had a clammy-looking texture, like a piece of raw meat which had been lying on the counter too long. The body's left arm was out to the side, as if in sleep. The right was cocked upwards slightly, breaking the water like a fallen branch. There was nothing at the end of it.

'No sign of the hand yet?'

Reidel shook his head ponderously. He did not have the air of a man who was going to wander off anytime soon.

'Clean, too,' Nina said. 'Seventeen stab wounds, plus the amputation. Yet the body is not smeared with blood. And no rain the night before, or during the day until it was found.'

'Which suggests the victim was murdered elsewhere, stripped and mutilated, and then brought here. Maybe.'

'Time of death sometime the night before last?'

'Correct. Body dumped then too, the pathologist thinks, determined by the relative density of bugs and micro-organisms on it. And the amputation was post-mortem. Which helps with the lack of blood. Leave it until the guy's dead to cut off his hand, it's a lot less messy.'

'Though still hard work,' Nina said. She flicked through the notes once more. Hand removed with two or three chops from something heavy and sharp, rather than a sawing action. Still waiting for a full blood work-up to come back. 'And the nearest place you can park is that lot up the slope, correct? Long way to carry a two-hundred-pound body. Especially for a woman.'

'The body has some cuts and general contusions on the back. The theory is it was dragged down.'

'Still. I wouldn't want to pull it that far, and I work out. Used to, anyhow.'

'This has sex all over it and the victim wasn't homosexual. He's a forty-six-year-old married man with two kids.'

'Married men are sometimes homosexual. Or don't you see much of that down south?'

The man smiled. 'Ma'am, I was born up in DC. You can see pretty much anything you want there, if you know where to look. But the victim is a man to whom local gossip ascribes pawing hands – on female behinds. Who was also an occasional customer at local bars – never left with a woman that anyone can testify to yet, but spent time talking to them. Including the ones behind the bar, one of whom went so far as to describe him as a "pussy-hound". We'll be talking to the night shifts later. None of which proves he wasn't gay, of course, but in terms of direct evidence the ball's in your court. And while you're at it, you'll be wanting to explain the trace of lipstick found on the victim's neck.'

'I'll try to find some evidence this is a serial killer, too, rather than just a one-off homicide. Which right now is all it is.'

'You're the expert.' Reidel pinched out the end of his cigarette, and replaced the butt carefully in the pack. 'Guess I'll leave you to your thoughts, Agent Baynam. Let me know if ya'll need anything.'

He wandered off down the slope to where the other guys were. After a few moments Nina heard a laugh float up.

She turned away. Spent a few moments considering the slope.

Nina and Monroe went alone to talk to Julia Gulicks and Mark Kroeger. Both lived in Thornton but worked together in Owensville, the nearest sizable town. Their walk in Raynor's Wood had come in the evening of their fifth date. They had not yet slept together. They were taking it real slow, evidently wondering if this might be the one. They were two kids, really, and yet they were not actually kids at all. Twenty-nine and twenty-five.

They were interviewed in the meeting room of the company they worked for. Neither seemed comfortable, but Nina supposed that wasn't surprising. After three weeks of covertly meeting after work at a bar a hundred yards down the street, their nascent affair was now presumably the talk of the water cooler. Nina believed she detected in Gulicks a species of considered privacy that was not unlike her own. Over the age of twenty, this stuff is not a game, and it's most definitely not a spectator sport.

Monroe was leading the questions. 'You stayed in the bar until what time?'

'Around nine,' Kroeger said. He had a soft voice and a few early grey hairs around his temples. 'A little later than we usually do, because, well, recently we'd gotten in the habit of going on to the Italian Kitchen. It's a couple of blocks further.'

'How come you didn't go there last Thursday?'

Kroeger seemed to colour, glanced across at Gulicks and then down at the floor.

'Well,' Gulicks said. Her hair was a striking red, her skin pale but tawny with freckles. 'We've kind of been through this?'

'I know,' Monroe said. 'But please.'

Nina tried not to smile, and tuned out. It was in the notes, teased out of them by Reidel in the previous day's interviews. Most of it had come from Kroeger. Thursday night had been the Night. He had known it. He thought Gulicks had known it too. This unspoken factor had conferred a formality to the evening, conversation stilted by the dark matter of the thing not being said. They met after work, going to the bar on Union as usual. Their first two semi-dates had taken place here, and for the next two they had gone on to the Italian. The staff were cheerful and good at treating people like couples. Dates two to four inclusive had featured kissing of an increasingly fervent nature. Date five stepped up to the plate knowing it was time for a big swing of the bat. Neither person was sure if this evening would involve food. Neither wanted to ask. Nina was willing to bet there had been two apartments back in Thornton in states of unusual tidiness that night. Hers probably even had clean sheets on the bed. He wouldn't have gone quite that far (not even realizing, perhaps, that it was an option) but it would have been recently made, at least. Both fridges would have held a single cold bottle of very decent wine – no more, as both were declared light drinkers. Sofas had been straightened, bookshelves arranged with the brainiest books centre stage. And yet neither had felt equal to saying 'Hey, why don't we go to my place?' Neither suggested moving on to the Italian, either, because it tended to leave you feeling kind of full and heavy, which is not conducive to, well, you know.

So they sat closer. They kissed, a little, but not too much because it wasn't the right kind of place and also there was a twenty-five minute car journey to get back to Thornton, and you didn't want to peak too early. Gradually the conversation began to turn from general matters of the day and to the season, how the weather was actually kind of nice, and now perhaps – well that's an idea: why didn't they go for a walk? Might not be too many more evenings they could still do that. And so he settled their tab, and they walked down the street a while, but there wasn't a great deal to look at in Owensville if the truth be told and they got to his car pretty soon. Then the drive back to Thornton, both of them thinking it might still be a little early yet. And so as they passed the turn-off, just a half mile out of the town, Julia had a brainwave and suggested . . .

'Why don't we park up and go for a walk?'

Monroe nodded. 'Is this a walk with which you're acquainted?'

'No,' Gulicks said. 'Well, yes. I know the wood, everyone does round here. There's a lot of families go there during the day. But I've never . . . gone there at night before.'

'Me neither,' Kroeger said.

Aw, sweet, Nina thought.

'But it is used that way by local residents on a regular basis.'

Gulicks and Kroeger nodded together.

'And you walked a little way, and stopped, and that's when Mr Kroeger spotted something behind the bushes.'

Kroeger dutifully described how they had walked about a hundred yards down from the lot, and then along the stream for a while. He had looked up, his arms around Ms Gulicks, to see something pale lying with an arm outstretched. The two had gotten closer, seen what it was they'd found, and then used a cellular phone to call the police.

Four hours later they got back to their own apartments, alone. Thursday had not been the Night after all. Nina reckoned it might now be postponed a little while. The image of a corpse is not easy to erase from the inner eye. Kroeger still looked queasy at the thought.

'The victim has been identified,' Nina said. 'A local man called Larry Widmar. Either of you know him?'

Both shook their heads, and that was the end of that.

Monroe drove back to Thornton. Nina had been in a car with him many times before, and noted that his preferred speed had decreased by a good ten per cent. Being shot seemed to have affected his willingness to take risks, as if his body was feeding him signals of caution. He looked older, too. Nina understood how that could be. She had been shot herself, almost a year before, soon after meeting Ward. It had happened at a place called the Halls, up in the mountains near Yellowstone. One of the men involved in the murder of Ward's parents had tagged her in the chest, just under the collar bone. For a while afterwards she'd felt old too, as if cold winds had a way to blow straight through her. Now she felt . . . she wasn't sure what she felt. It was strange to be back in the world again, to be doing her job. Insubstantial, unreal. She had a headache, too.

Locals cops would be working bars this evening, trying to find someone who'd seen Widmar on Wednesday night or any prior occasion. More would be on hand in Raynor's Wood to scare the hell out of any couple who decided that tonight was *their* night. Monroe and Nina were on their way to the final task of the day, interviewing the other person who could be said to be involved.

'What did Reidel say about me?'

'When?'

'You know when. When he came back down to the stream after bugging me while I was trying to think.'

'That you seemed invested in this not being a female killer. Which he felt was odd, given you seemed capable of cutting a man's balls off without thinking twice.'

'And you laughed at that?'

'Not me, Nina.'

'You know how dumb it is, assuming this has to be a woman.'

'Women kill people, Nina.'

'Not like that.'

'I can think of several who have been convicted for it.'

'Convicted isn't always guilty.'

'Actually, it is. That's how it works.'

Conversation petered out soon afterwards, which gave Nina a chance to look at the town as they drove back in. This was not something she particularly relished. She couldn't put her finger on why, but she didn't like Thornton. Objectively it seemed nice enough. It was in the south-west corner of the state, thirty minutes from Smith Lake and an hour from Blue Ridge National Park. The main road from Owensville brought you painlessly into a small commercial district. You could get a burger from a Renee's, get lubed, store things or ship them, buy a lawnmower or stay in a chain hotel. You could keep going straight out the other side, too, and miss the older part of town altogether. But if you took a left by the Ponderosa, the road wound you over a hill, past a big old church and a high school. This was a collection of big buildings of mildly Gothic flavour, poised confidently behind an open space of lawn and trees. Across the street was a smaller building housing the Sleepyheadz kindergarten. After this the road took you down into a pleasantly tree-lined old town district, a couple of streets with a Starbucks and restaurants and places you could get things nicely framed. Nothing was more than two storeys high, all wood-fronted, and the leaf-strewn pavements were of herringboned red brick. People strolled hither and yon, carrying the local newspaper under their arm. Nice young moms with trim figures and a toddler stopped to spend the time of day with each other. A UPS van purred up and down, delivering goodies. This area slipped down-market for a few blocks and then the streets thinned out into larger plots holding wooden houses clinging to pretensions of grandeur. Soon afterwards, open countryside again, a third of the town surrounded by Raynor's Wood, which spread for quite some miles to the north.

It was the kind of place that every year fails by a narrow margin to make it into somebody's compendium of America's Most Charming Little Towns. And yet she'd been here less than twenty-four hours and just didn't like it.

She tried to allow for the fact that she'd first heard of the place as a murder scene, which lent a flavour to an environment, the knowledge that however nice it might appear, this town had placed two individuals in murderous opposition. How did these people come to interact in this way? Was the town not in some way impli-cated in what happened within its boundaries? You expect people to kill each other in cities: in our hearts we know they're too big and place strangers too close together and without explicable contracts of moral exchange. But small towns . . . surely they were supposed to provide support, to embody an epitome of commu-nity that stopped this kind of thing from happening?

Nina had been doing the job for too long to entertain naïve ideas about local community or rural idylls, however, and she knew that while urban centres turned in the big numbers of fatality, the smaller towns often contributed the baroque.

No, there was just something about Thornton. Something not quite right.

The Widmar house was a mid-sized Queen Anne with a covered brick porch in front. Gayle Widmar was in her late forties, spruce, and had expensive-looking hair even after thirty-six hours of grief. Her children were with her sister forty minutes away and Gayle would be joining them just as soon as this interview was over. An overnight bag was ready in the hallway. The house had the baffled silence of a domicile in which everything had changed.

Mrs Widmar sat in a high-backed chair in the middle of a large sitting room, while Nina confirmed background. Gayle's husband Lawrence – she never once called him 'Larry' – had owned 'a chain' of dry-cleaning establishments (the chain numbered two, as Nina already knew) and a part-interest in a thriving pizza place in the historic district. He was on the school board. They lived in this neighbourhood, though they could have afforded something more expensive, because it was where they had both grown up. They had been married twenty years.

Mrs Widmar's manner was clipped and strained, as is often the case with spouses of the violently deceased. They need support but are distrustful of the world. They feel obscurely accused. They believe people are thinking that if they had been better in some way, then this awful thing would not have happened to their partner. Five per cent of the blame for every murder rubs off on those closest to the victim, and they are unconsciously furious at the dead for putting them in this position: especially for having to deal with it without them, as a terribly out-of-practice single individual. They are also attempting to come up to speed with the realization that murder is not some fictional conceit, imagined for the purposes of entertainment, but actually happens: and afterwards no credits roll, and life has to continue to be lived even if you have absolutely no idea where the deeds to the house are kept, or who services the lawnmower. It is never comfortable to discover that reality and fiction are closer than you realized. You wonder what could happen next. Might aliens exist also, or ghosts?

As Monroe led Mrs Widmar through confirmation of her husband's last known movements – on Wednesday night he had gone for dinner with his pizza partner, not returned, and she had reported him missing at 7 a.m. the following morning – Nina looked at the pictures on the mantelpiece. In them Lawrence Widmar looked so average as to be almost remarkable. Off-the-rack smile, bouffant greying hair, a pillar-of-the-community-sized gut. You could picture him standing in a bank. You could picture him making a solid contribution to a PTA meeting and rigorously supporting the school team. You could picture him in a bar, too, pulling his stool a little closer and asking what the lady will have. Unfair, perhaps, but death leaves such a big question behind it that almost any answer can seem like it might fit.

'You husband's partner says they went their ways around ten thirty,' Nina said. 'Do you have any idea of where Lawrence might have gone after that?'

'No,' Gayle said. 'He goes for long walks sometimes, in the evening. He has done . . . he did for the last three or four years. It was his idea of a fitness regime. He didn't like gyms.'

'Did he used to go any place in particular that you're aware of?'

'No. Just around the town.'

'Not Raynor's Wood, for example?'

The woman looked at her coldly. 'The last time he would have been there at night was over two decades ago. With me.'

'The local cops seem convinced your husband was murdered by a woman, Mrs Widmar. What's your reaction to that?'

'The same as yours.'

'Which is?'

'It's bullshit.'

'He never had any affairs that you're aware of? I'm sorry to ask you that, but . . .'

'I know. You have to. And my answer – as it has been to everyone who has asked it either directly or indirectly over the last two days – is no.'

'And you can't think of anyone who might have a desire to harm him?'

Mrs Widmar shook her head fervently, and briefly looked close to breaking down. She blew her nose aggressively and then blinked at her knees for a moment.

'I loved my husband,' she said. 'I still do. He was a decent man, and a good father. It sounds trite, but it's true. The kids are going to miss him. A lot. But . . . he was just a guy. Just a normal guy.' Finally she looked up. 'I just don't understand it. Why would anyone want to kill a man like that?'

'"Why" isn't always there to be found.'

'And how come the FBI are involved in this?'

Monroe stepped in. 'There are aspects of the murder which attracted our attention.'

Mrs Widmar smiled tightly. 'Well, focus that attention. Find who did this to us.'

'That's our job,' he said.

But she hadn't been talking to him.

Nina and Monroe walked back down the road. The sun was getting low in the sky and the light was slanted and golden.

'What do you think?'

'We know she can't have done it,' Nina said. 'And I don't see her being involved in any other way. There's no incentive for the business partner to have dropped him?'

Monroe shook his head. 'They were old friends, guy had nothing to gain and a lot to lose. He seems more upset than the wife.'

'She's plenty upset,' Nina said. 'Trust me.'

They reached the car. Nina waited for Monroe to unlock it, but he seemed distracted by a house across the street. It was smaller than the Widmars', and in significantly worse repair. It appeared to be for sale, though it didn't look like the vendor was exactly putting his heart into the task. Eventually he turned back.

'Widmar had a reputation. In a quiet way. One of the girls who worked in his store, plus a waitress in the restaurant. Occasional inappropriateness.'

'I know. Reidel told me. And evidently at least some of Widmar's walks ended up in bars. But the fact his wife didn't know this does not prove he had some double life or was a total scumbag. Men of a certain age talk to barmaids. Harassment remains harassment, but hands can wander without their owner being one of Hitler's henchmen. Not everyone has your moral fibre, Charles, or your level of self-control.'

'I'm not saying Widmar was a bad man. And I don't appreciate the sarcasm.'

'Sarcasm? Your fibre is legendary.'

'Nina – why are you busting my balls?'

'Just for recreation, I think.'

'I don't believe so. You have a reason for everything you do. And now is the time to tell me about it, because I won't ask again.'

'Okay.' She cocked her head. 'Ward told me that everything we gave you has been pulled from the Jones/Wallace case. That Paul's back to just being a lone psycho again.'

'Christ, Olbrich. He's a good cop but Jesus does he talk.'

'Maybe he felt he owed Ward something, what with having mislaid his psychotic brother. Of whom I assume there is still no sign? Despite your confidence yesterday?'

Monroe shook his head.

'So – true or false, Charles?'

'There's no evidence anyone else was involved in the Jones and Wallace murders, which is what the trial pertains to. Hopkins' rants about an alleged conspiracy of serial killers could do nothing but muddy the waters.'

'You know what they're called, Charles. They're called the Straw Men.'

'I know what you told me. I don't know it's true. And it's not something I'm ever going to try to prosecute.'

'And that's nothing to do with the fact that if they were mentioned in court, it might slip that you got a tip-off concerning the location of Jessica Jones' body? Doesn't *that* somewhat suggest some other person or persons were involved? But we wouldn't want *those* waters muddied, right?'

Nina finally noticed a man was standing in the garden of the house opposite, and was watching with interest as he hosed water over his lawn. She realized she had been a bare few decibels short of shouting, and dropped her voice. It shook a little.

'Let's hit it back to the hotel, Charles. I want to be somewhere generic. I've had enough of this town for one day.'

Chapter 7

The car pulled in to the front of the Holiday Inn a little before seven o'clock. I was standing in the parking lot. Partly because I could smoke there without being glared at, also because I had no strong desire to run into Monroe. The two of them got out of the car and were joined by someone who'd been waiting outside.

I watched the three of them walk to the lobby and disappear inside. That was slightly weird. The third man was not far off my height, with only a slightly heavier build. It was almost like I was outside my body, or my life, and looking in. That's not a good feeling. This sensation intensified during the time I spent waiting, watching the three shapes in room 107 on the ground floor. When I was younger I might have thought that being a man loitering in a parking lot with a gun in his jacket would be cool in some way. In fact it just makes you wonder if you'll ever be let back inside.

After forty minutes the second man came back out of the hotel and drove away. Eventually it seemed like there was only one shape in Nina's room. It stood motionless behind the curtain for a while.

I went into the hotel, swung around the far side of reception and walked along the corridor. I knocked on her door and it was a full minute before it was opened.

Nina had taken her shoes off, and thus looked about two feet shorter than usual while being about the same size. She looked tired, and wary.

'How did you know what hotel I was in?'

'Called the cops, said I was a Fed underling and had an important package for you.'

'Christ. And the room?'

'I asked at reception,' I said. 'Security in this town is not iron-clad. I should warn you that if al-Qaeda decide to take out the Thornton Savings and Loan, they may well pull it off.'

She didn't smile. 'Did I make a mistake coming here?' I asked. 'It's just, I thought someone left me a note.'

'Sorry,' she said, and stood aside.

I walked past her into the room. Other people's hotel rooms are strange. Unless you've entered it with them, been present at the initial dispersal of case, jacket and small change, peered hopefully in the bathroom together and pulled the curtain aside to establish the view isn't all that great, they always feel like someone else's nest. The dampness of another person's towel is private. Maybe that's all I was feeling.

'Nina, are you okay?'

'I'm fine,' she said, in an un-fine way. 'This is the first day I've been out in the world for a long time. I hadn't realized how used I'd got to being the way we were.'

There was a pot of coffee sitting on the desk. I helped myself to a cup and sat in an object which some designer, somewhere, had evidently believed would function as a chair.

'Is that all it is?'

She sat cross-legged on the end of the bed. 'Maybe.'

The coffee wasn't great, but I soldiered on with it. Nina stared at the mirror above the desk.

'Tell me,' I said. 'Tell me why you're here.'

'It's my job.'

'No,' I said. 'It is, but that's not why. Monroe knew you'd come out for this one. Why?'

She smiled at her hands. 'I keep forgetting you're not stupid.'

'Me too. It's an easy mistake to make.'

She looked at me, rolled her eyes, and seemed okay for a moment. Then her face clouded again. She slowly let herself fall back until she was lying rigidly on the bed, eyes on the ceiling.

I sipped quietly for a few minutes longer, until she finally started talking.

'When I was young,' she said, 'there was this woman.'

Nina grew up in Janesville, Wisconsin. She was an only child. Her parents got on well with each other, and with her. She was smart and good at sport. For some reason this had not translated into having large numbers of friends. She did not take the bus home from school with the other kids, but walked to where her father worked and waited on a bench outside. He drove them home, talking about his day, or, on infrequent but memorable occasions, sitting in churning silence. When she turned thirteen she got with a crowd at last, and became a little more sociable, but for a number of years that was how each afternoon ended. The walk from school, and then a sit, getting an early start on her homework or just watching the world go by. She liked to do that, and only accepted the offer of a seat in reception when the weather really was too cold or wet (and Janesville got plenty wet, and plenty cold). It was not a great part of town but her father could see the bench from his office window, and the security guy on the door kept an eye out for her too. Perhaps things would be different now, but back then, the arrangement was fine.

Opposite the office was a bar, on the ground floor of the only Victorian building left in a street of concrete oblongs. One of the things Nina watched was the people who came and went from the bar in the late afternoon. She was always intrigued. You saw all types. Businessmen in suits who walked in as if they had a meeting there, but who sat in the window alone, and not for long. There were the old guys, too. You only ever saw them go in, or come out. The length of time between the two was too long to wait. It might be years. They wore thick coats and moved with slow deliberation and had grey stubble on their chins. There were also guys who were not so old but not businessmen either, who came and went from the bar like busy birds. It was hard to imagine what they did when they were not inside. Slept, maybe, or did whatever it was that meant they had just enough money for another beer.

And there were the women. Not too many, but some. After a while Nina came to recognize one of these.

She first saw her when she was about eleven, and then on and off for the next two years. Nina first noticed her because she looked a little younger and prettier than the other women who went to the bar, the majority of whom were, frankly, dogs. She had a lot of brown hair and wore tight jeans and a sweater without any sleeves. The second or third time Nina saw her, the woman noticed her back – and winked from across the road. Occasionally men spied the young girl sitting on the bench opposite, and looked at her, and when they did it made Nina flush. She didn't like it. But when this woman winked, it was okay. It made her feel a little grown up.

They never spoke. The woman never crossed the road, or waved. But maybe twenty or thirty times over the next few years, her and Nina's gazes interlocked. Over that period Nina watched the woman change. Nina never saw her too close up, so perhaps she had never been as young as her clothing suggested. But she got a lot older, and fast. It was like each time you saw her something irrevocable had happened in between. She put on thirty pounds. Her hair went blonde and then red and then blonder and then back to something like brown, but not in a good way. Parts of her face went rosy, the others pale. The only thing that stayed the same was her walk, the way she approached the bar as if this was the first time she'd been there but she'd heard good things about it and was confident of a fine time within. She looked that way even when it became so that she was generally staggering a little even when she arrived. By this point Nina didn't really like to see her any more. It was like watching someone whose life was running on faster film, as if every step this woman took counted for a thousand of ours. But still now and then the woman would notice her, and wink. A slow wink, that just said, 'Hi, I see you, and you see me, and that's okay.' On the last few occasions Nina actually wondered whether the woman could still see her at all, or was just doing it out of habit. Still, it happened.

Meanwhile, bodies were being found.

Three in two years. Then a fourth, and a fifth. Men's bodies found in parked cars, dead of gunshot wounds. Men who started the night looking for something cheap and easy, and who saw in the next day minus their wallets and their lives.

Three weeks before Nina's thirteenth birthday, a woman was arrested. When Nina saw the news report, sitting with her parents on a Thursday night, her mouth dropped open.

It was the woman.

The woman who winked.

It was a big story, Wisconsin's prequel to Aileen Wuornos, Florida's more notorious man-slayer of a few years later. They called Janesville's killer the Black Widow, though she was neither black, a widow nor a spider. They found out how she had been abused as a child, by at least two family members. They heard how in recent years she had been passed around by men at parties until she lost consciousness, and then passed around some more. They hinted at what she would do for little more than a drink, or even just the promise of one. None of this was presented in mitigation, but as titillating proof of her guilt.

The woman claimed she was innocent, and Nina believed her. Nina had watched her walking down the street on summer afternoons, had seen the spring in her step. No one who walked like that could do these things. Someone, somewhere, was lying.

Then it seemed like she might be guilty after all – at least, that's what her attorney was willing to plead. Yes, his client had wielded the gun. But in self defence, always. She had wound up in bad situations with men, and it had been her only escape.

Nina didn't believe that either. By now she was following the case avidly. She scoured the papers and magazines for more information, kept her eyes peeled for reports on the television. Whenever she heard someone talking about it, at school or on the street, she slowed, tried to hear what they were saying. She became a sponge, absorbing everything, until it became a part of her.

A month later came the next episode in what was rapidly becoming a soap opera. The woman had reversed her claim. She was completely innocent again, and had never been anywhere near any of these men. Her attorney had also tried to rape her, she said. And the judge. Everybody was trying to fuck her over both figuratively and literally. Every man, and every woman too.

Not me, Nina thought, as she watched. Not me.

'But then . . .' Nina tailed off, and said nothing for a moment.

I kept silent, as I had done throughout. When Nina spoke again her voice was thick. 'Then there was this five-second piece of film, showing her coming out of court and being helped into a car. It was raining, and her hair was plastered down all over her head. She'd lost pounds again, but from the wrong places. It was like she'd lost weight from her mind. She looked across the top of the patrol car before she ducked her head, glared straight across into the television camera. And you could see it in her eyes.'

'See what?'

'She did it. I knew right then that she had killed them after all. You looked in her eyes and knew she was guilty, that she had been there and fired the gun. But I knew she was not guilty, too. I knew she had done these things, but also not done them. And I wondered how that could be. And how there could come a time when there was no winking left in her head.'

I thought about that for a moment. 'What happened to her?'

85

'She went down for all five. Killed herself eight months later. Got hold of a spoon, broke off the end, and pushed the shaft into her throat after lights out. They said it probably took about three hours for her to die.'

Nina was quiet for a full five minutes. Then I realized the rhythm of her breathing had changed, and that she was asleep.

I watched her a while, then opened up my laptop and plugged it into the phone. I hadn't had a chance to check email during the day, to see if my mystery correspondent still had something to say.

The hotel's connection was slow. While I waited, I found myself thinking about my own father. These messages from the ether reminded me of the last communication I had from him, a single-sentence note left inside a chair in their house in Montana. When you die, the loose ends are what prove you have been alive. The cans of food no one else likes. The greetings card not sent, its Cellophane now dusty and yellowed, the price sticker faded and historically cheap. My parents had left plenty such loose ends. Through them I had discovered my brother Paul and I had been unofficially adopted as babies after a confrontation with my natural father, a man who had harmed my mother. My parents abandoned Paul on the streets of San Francisco a couple of years later, believing the two of us were better kept apart, and not knowing how else to achieve it. The organization my natural father had belonged to was still in operation thirty years later, and my dad – and bear in mind Don Hopkins was just a realtor – tracked them down to a luxury development in the mountains above Yellowstone. They killed him and my mother. The group was small and very well hidden, but it had money and it had power. I knew this group now as the Straw Men. The detective called John Zandt had told me he believed the Straw Men had been in America for three thousand years or more, growing rich on the profits of prehistoric copper mining in the Great Lakes area. He claimed that a loose confederation of men and women had settled there, arriving from different parts of the globe and many different eras, united in a hatred of the world's increasing civilization: and further claimed they had subsequently been responsible for everything from the disappearance of early settlers at Roanoke to old Indian legends of violent tribes of bearded men, as they tried to resist later settlement of a land they believed to be theirs. I wasn't sure how sane Zandt still was, however. He had doubts about my character too. I had failed to take two opportunities to kill the man who had murdered his daughter. My brother, Paul.

But I suppose one's own life always seems more complicated than other people's.

Finally the machine pinged. I had a message. I opened it. It said:

> Ward –
> It's Carl Unger. Bobby's dead? What the FUCK?
> I've come across something strange and it's ringing a
> bell with a matter Bobby called me about a year
> back. He mentioned your name in connection with it.
> It's important.
> Call me **now**. 202 555 9733.
> C

I read the message twice, sat back to think. I didn't remember the name, but that didn't prove anything. It had been a few years since I worked for the CIA and it's not like they send newsletters saying who got married and how the softball team's holding up. I'm also not great with names. To me they always seem tangential to the person, like a favourite jacket they just happen to wear a lot. The email implied I had known this guy. But it could be I'd known him at one remove: the text suggested he'd known Bobby better, and the third sentence was particularly convincing in this regard. Bobby Nygard had been a tough bastard. I too found it hard to believe he was dead, and I'd been there the night it happened.

I checked Bobby's email address book. He had no listing for anyone called Unger. Proved nothing – I wasn't in there either.

Bobby was a surveillance professional, specializing in computers and the internet. Who knew what weird ways he had of obfuscating his life? I could find no emails from Unger prior to the recent attempts – either from this address, or from someone of the same name from a different one. A more official-sounding .gov domain, for example. That didn't prove much either. Bobby evidently archived and purged his mail on a regular basis. The earliest here was dated less than a month before the point where our lives had re-entangled: less than a week later, he'd been dead.

I knew Bobby had called some people in those last few days, trying to chase down leads he and I had uncovered. It was certainly possible that Unger was one of these contacts. Was I ready to take that risk? And for what? If you kept re-reading the email, and had an optimistic heart, you could maybe believe this Unger guy might have information that would be of use to me. You could believe otherwise, too. 'Optimist' is not something I have printed on my business card.

'Tell me, Bobby,' I said. 'Is this guy for real?'

There was no reply. I'd tried asking him questions before, and he'd never once come back to me. Contrary fucker. He'd been full of advice while he was alive.

I opened the email again and transcribed the phone number into my cell phone. I wasn't going to call Unger. Not yet. First I would ask Nina what she thought. If our lives were connected, which I hoped they were, then she had a say.

I woke to the sound of thumping. Someone was banging on the room door, hard. For a bad, fuzzy moment, something made me think it was Paul, that he'd somehow tracked us down in Virginia. Then I realized he wouldn't knock, however vigorously.

I sat up, back tweaking from the chair. The room was dark but for a parking lot glow through the curtains. I looked across at the bed but Nina wasn't there. Clock said it was just after 11 p.m. Felt a lot later. Like the day after next.

I groggily got to my feet and saw that the door to the bathroom was shut. Slash of light underneath it. I went and stood outside.

'Nina?'

'I'll just be a minute. Who's at the door?'

'Room service with attitude.'

'You ordered this late?'

'No,' I said. 'Joke. Never mind.'

Bang bang bang on the door again. I lurched over, squinted through the security thing. Remembered too late all the movies I'd seen where somebody gets shot in the eye that way. Luckily I recognized the face on the other side, fish-eyed though it was.

'Monroe,' I said, trying to sharpen up. 'And he doesn't look like he's going to go away.'

'Christ. Let him in.'

I yanked the door open, caught the agent about to hammer once more.

'We heard,' I said.

He pushed straight past. 'What are you doing here?' he muttered, though he didn't look very surprised.

'I come free with the deluxe suites,' I said. 'Look under your bed, there's one of me in your room too.'

'Fuck with this investigation and I'll have you arrested.'

'Duly noted.'

Nina came out of the bathroom. I'd assumed she was showering or something, but she was still dressed. She looked a lot more together than I felt. She always does.

'What's up?' she said. 'We get a hit in one of the bars?'

Monroe grabbed Nina's coat off the bed and handed it to her.

'It's a little bigger than that. Somebody else just turned up dead.'

Chapter 8

It was only a little after eight and the party was *happening*. It was *going on*. It was tight and happy and just swinging into the end of the beginning, kind of the best part. There were oldsters due home but on past form the Luchses were mellow hosts. They'd stroll out back, stand around being hearty for fifteen minutes and then retreat to the master suite with the curtains drawn. So long as nothing caught fire, they were cool. Meanwhile the pool was full of hooting boys and laughing girls, and people were dancing to some guy who was mixing songs off his iPod and out through a speaker system over by the keg. That could be a real pain in the ass, some tune-junky levering his taste in people's ears, but this guy had a cool Nu Indie/Alt. Country vibe going on and Brad wished him nothing but the best.

Brad was in a lounger under the big old tree in the centre of the main lawn, and he was feeling fine all round. There had been a sticky moment when the chick from a few nights before had seen

Brad and Karen together and looked like she might want to make something of it, but she'd evidently got hold of some powder in the meantime and was already way too cheerful to care. Karen was currently standing by the pool chatting to some friends Brad didn't know. She had talked to her mom and it had been determined that if she really wanted her nose done they would pay for it, not least so they could influence which surgeon she went to: most of Mrs Luchs' pals were bionic one way or another and she had sound intelligence on the subject – though curiously she'd never gone under the knife herself. When Karen first mentioned their offer Brad felt a brief flicker of regret, as if something had been taken from him. Within two seconds he realized it was responsibility and a significant expense, both of which he could live without. Though, Lee having kicked a big chunk of the drug windfall back to the crew, Brad's finances were actually significantly rosier than usual. He was more or less back to zero again now, naturally, but he was wearing new Zpatuula shorts, Penguin shirt and CK briefs, and there was an extra foot of CDs and console games on the shelf at home. He'd bought himself an iMac for . . . some purpose or other, it would probably come in handy and the store had been, like, right there. And when Karen turned to give him a little wave, the necklace he'd given her glinted in the early evening sun. He was looking forward to watching it sway later on. A little K, swinging back and forth.

He sat and drank his beer, listening to the music, content for the moment to be alone. He sometimes thought that was the truly cool thing about having a lot of friends.

It meant sometimes you felt okay about being alone.

Cut to an hour or two later and he was sitting around the other side of the pool with a bunch of people and Karen was on his lap. She'd had her hair cut for the party and it was mid-length and glossy. They were just talking in general and listening to some dude who was saying how his uncle was going to set him up with

91

cash to start a dotcom telling uncool kids how to be cool and Brad was thinking that sounded like a pretty cool idea and that he should maybe think of something like that for himself. He tried for a few minutes, stroking Karen's neck, but nothing came. Maybe later. He'd scaled back on the beer now because he'd taken one of the new pills – didn't have a name but they were red and had an 'A' on them, so maybe they were called A. Very laid back but you stayed sharp, or at least when you looked at things they had sharp edges, unless you moved your head too fast in which case they kind of sparkled. It made the fairy lights strung from the trees look fabulous. Lot of people on A tonight. It was proving very popular. Good news for Lee, and good news for Brad. Good news all round.

After another couple of minutes the dotcom dude had talked just a little too long and Brad found his attention wandering. The music guy had either passed out or found a friend and there was something mid-tempo but okay playing. Brad semi-recognized it but couldn't be sure. The Luchses had come and gone already and the party was in that full-on mid-evening mode when it seemed like it would last forever. The best part, for sure, maybe even better than the beginning of the middle. Brad was thinking maybe he'd get up in a while and go find some food or something when he saw someone unexpected the other side of the pool.

It was Lee. Brad hadn't even known he was there. Lee didn't party much. He was actually kind of a serious guy. Case in point, he was on the phone right now. All around him were people laughing and exercising their right to chill the fuck out, and there was Lee looking heavy and frowning like he was dealing in stocks and shares. Buy low! Sell high! Funny guy, really.

As Brad watched, Lee ended the call. He seemed to look off into the distance for a moment. Then he turned his head slowly around, as if looking for someone. Brad wondered who it might be. Lee's head stopped moving, and the A made the halt look robotic. He saw Brad, and nodded.

Brad nodded back, smiled. Lee, his friend.

Lee shook his head to indicate the previous movement had not been a mere greeting, and crooked his finger to make his point.

The person he'd been looking for was Brad.

Brad kissed Karen on the neck. 'Back in a second, babe,' he said. 'Got to go talk to Lee.'

She hopped off and he got up and headed over through the crowd of people. His leg had gone to sleep from having Karen on it and he limped slightly as he made his way around the pool.

'Hey,' he said, when he got there. 'Good party, huh?'

'How fucked up are you?'

Brad blinked. So much for the small talk. 'I'm cool,' he said. 'Couple beers.'

Lee nodded. 'Good. Need you to come with me.'

'You got it. You going for burgers?'

'No. Are Pete and Steve here?'

'Steve, no. He's . . . I don't know where he is. But Sleepy's around somewhere. I saw him earlier. I think.'

'I'll go around the side, you head through the house. See if you can find them. Meet me at the car. And splash some water over your face.'

'What's up?'

'We have to go do something.'

'Yeah, I'm getting that, but – what?'

'Brad, just get moving.'

Lee peeled away and moved off through the dancing people. Brad shook his head to clear it a little and found he felt largely okay. He headed up around the top of the pool, keeping half an eye out for Pete and a quarter of an eye out for Steve, who he was pretty sure wasn't actually at the party at all. He glanced towards where Karen had been, too, hoping to indicate he was going off for a while, but she wasn't there any more.

The house was pretty much empty for now, quieter than it would be in a few hours when it had cooled down and people were in the mood for being more horizontal. No sign of Pete or Steve. He found his way out the front with only one wrong turn. Forgot about the splashing thing but he felt fine.

The driveway was full of cars, including Karen's new sharp blue BMW, and there were a couple of small groups of people hanging out. Brad located Lee's car and stood by it. He waited a few minutes and then took out a cigarette. Found he'd left his lighter out by the pool. Shit. How annoying was that?

'Looking for this?'

He turned to see that Karen was suddenly there. She was holding out a flame.

He grinned, took it. 'My angel of mercy. Or of fire. Definitely an angel, anyway.'

'You say the nicest things. So, what's up? Doing research for a career in valet parking?'

'Just waiting for Lee.'

On cue, there was the sound of feet on gravel and he turned to see Hudek approaching.

'On his way,' he said, to Brad. 'Hey, Karen. Great party.'

'Why, thank you.' Karen stretched. 'We do our best. So where are you young blades headed?'

'Just out for a ride,' Lee said. 'Pick up some eats.'

'There's stuff out. Enough guacamole to hide a baby in.'

'I know. I had some already. But I got a specific hunger. By the way, there's people over there waving to you?'

Karen turned and saw a red Porsche idling at the front door. Two figures stood by it with the air of people who didn't want to leave without saying goodbye but who really had to go, kind of *now*. Karen squinted to make them out.

'Right, Sara and Randy. They got to split early. Okay, so, duty calls. Drive carefully,' she said.

'Always do,' Lee said. 'You know that.'

Karen smiled quickly, looking a little uncomfortable. She leaned forward and pecked Brad on the cheek.

'Later,' she said, then ran back towards the house, arms already wide to hug people goodbye.

They waited for a couple of minutes and then Sleepy Pete appeared. He looked quite stoned, but less than you might expect, though he was munching diligently from a sizable bag of Doritos.

'So, what's up, guys?'

'Bit of work. You coming along?'

'Absolutely, dude. I'm all about the work ethic. You know that.'

'My man.' Hudek pressed the blipper and the car let out a quiet squawk. The doors unlocked. 'Brad, come in front with me.'

Lee hit the radio and turned it up loud. Drove out through the gates and then along the winding road through the ranch, past all the other big private gates, to the bigger main gate of the Faircroft Ranch community. Security guys there flipped them a wave without even looking. Point of gated communities is to stop people coming in, not going out, and not a single person in Lee's car was even slightly black.

Hudek stuck to the main drag through Santa Barbara, driving responsibly and well. After ten minutes he switched to 192 bearing north. Brad watched the lights as they passed, headlights and streetlights and signage. Some song came on the radio that he recognized but he didn't know what it was. His head was mainly full of wondering what the 'drive carefully/you know that' exchange between Karen and Lee had meant. If anything. And also, why were they going north?

'Hey – turn it up,' Pete said. 'This *rocks*.'

Hudek jacked the volume in the back speakers but pulled it down in front.

'Lee, what's up?' Brad said, finally. 'Where are we going?'

'Hernandez called,' Lee said, quietly. 'He has a last-minute thing. His people are unavailable. He needs a couple of guys to stand behind him.'

'And that would be us? You're fucking kidding? Lee – last time I saw that fucker he cold-cocked me with a gun.'

Lee nodded, his eyes on the rear-view mirror. 'I hear what you're saying. But this is a good sign, Brad. This is important.'

'Since when are we the hired hands? Jump, do this, whatever?'

'We can't bail first time we're asked a favour. So we're going to do this thing, then we're going to get some serious-sized burgers, go back to the party and do some heavy chilling. You on that?'

Pete was singing along in back, oblivious. Brad shook his head, but not in denial. He took out a cigarette and lit it.

'Dude . . .'

'Lee, fuck you. The lid's off and we're driving. I want a fucking cigarette, I'm going to have one.'

Hudek smiled. 'That's fine, man. Go nuts. What I wanted was a yes or no.'

'Well, fuck, yes. I guess. Though, you know, I don't know.'

Hudek winked at him and then suddenly swerved over to the kerb. This freaked Brad out until he realized Hernandez was standing on the street corner, a bag over his shoulder.

'Whoa,' Pete said, through a mouth full of potato chips. 'What's *he* doing here?'

Hernandez walked up to the car, looked down into the back seat. 'Where's the other guy?'

Hudek took his time about answering. It felt good to be in control. If he decided to, he could just pull away. Leave the asshole standing there.

He killed the music. 'This is short notice, don't you think?'

'Notice for what?' Pete asked. 'And seriously, why are we mixing with this shithead?'

'We're going to help him out,' Lee said. 'Give him a ride some-where he needs to be. Okay?'

'Yeah, whatever,' Pete said, dubiously. 'I guess.'

'Great.' Hudek looked back up at Hernandez, and smiled. 'You getting in the car, or what?'

*　　*　　*

Under Hernandez's direction Lee drove up into the hills. Golf courses, more ranch communities. It wasn't an area he knew well. You could make a case for it not being an area at all, except in real estate terms. They drove a little further into the Santa Ynez and then on some more.

'Are we going all the way to Nevada?' Pete asked at one point. Otherwise he and Brad were quiet in the back.

Eventually Hernandez indicated a turning on the left. It didn't seem to be signed for anywhere. Lee drove up it for a couple of miles, into scrubby semi-forest. After a time they crested one of the hills and started a slow descent. By now the road was pretty basic, and after another eight hundred yards it ran out altogether. As it did so it widened into a big gravel-and-dust parking lot surrounded with trees that blended into the inky twilight. It appeared empty.

'This it?'

Hernandez nodded.

'What time are they due? And who are these people?'

'They're just like you,' the man said. 'Nothing to worry about.'

'So how come you need us here holding your hand?'

But then a set of headlights came on at the other end of the lot. Brad felt his heart give a heavy double-thud. Lee just felt good to be in the car with the drugs. People bringing bags of money to *you*: that was a step in the right direction, for sure.

'That them?'

'Yes.' Hernandez opened his door. 'You, Pete, whatever your name is, you wait in the car.'

'No way.'

Lee looked at Hernandez. 'What's the problem?' It felt weird talking to this guy as something like an equal. Weird, but good.

'You and the other kid I saw stand firm in the parking lot. This loser I just remember with duct tape around his mouth.'

'There were three of you and two of us,' Pete said. He sounded angry, which was rare. 'You want to go one on one, right now?'

Jesus but you're dumb, Pete, Brad was thinking. Three figures were now silhouetted in the lights of the distant car. *Staying in the car sounds plenty good to me.*

'No, thank you so much,' Hernandez said. He turned to Pete and smiled one of his bad smiles. 'Big guy like you, what chance would I have?'

Pete shut up.

'Get behind the wheel,' Lee said. 'Just in case.' He was pleased to see Hernandez nod. The older guy unzipped his bag and pulled out a gun. He handed it to Hudek.

Brad shook his head. 'How come we need that, if this is going to be so . . .'

'Brad, shut up.'

Lee slipped the gun in the back of his pants. He saw Hernandez reach behind and touch his own lower back, as if to check the position of a weapon there. Okay, so they were good to go.

The three of them got out of the car. Pete climbed over and into the driver's seat. 'Be careful,' he said.

Hernandez led the way. Lee walked a little behind and to the right, Brad to the left.

One of the guys at the other car called out. 'Hey, Emilio. Who's with you?'

'Friends,' Hernandez said. 'It's cool.'

Brad looked back and forth between the shadowed faces. One of the guys was probably Brad's age, and probably from a similar background. The other two looked older. One had a shaved head. There was something hinky about them. What was with the standing back, for example? There was a way of doing these things. You walked over, they walked over, you met halfway and swapped bags, maybe had a quick cigarette or shared a line in some ridiculous pretence of conviviality, then split.

Why weren't they coming forward?

Lee was thinking the same thing, but maybe these people thought they were proving something making them do the extra work. Some kind of petty power play, to make themselves look big. Lee didn't think that was going to happen, and he was right. Hernandez stopped walking forward. He and Brad stopped too.

'Okay guys,' Hernandez said. 'You stuck there, or what?'

None of them said anything, and something suddenly dropped into Lee's head like a hammer.

None of the three men was holding a bag.

'Hernandez . . .' he said.

Then they started shooting.

No warning, nothing said. Just arms suddenly out front, caps going off. Clack clack clack.

Lee stumbled backward, reaching for the gun in the back of his pants. Hernandez was much faster. He had his gun out and was firing shots towards the other car, scooting quickly out towards the right, heading for the trees.

Lee saw Brad frozen for a moment, and remembered the guy had no gun. He saw him try to work out what the fuck to do and then break into a run towards the left-hand side of the lot.

Lee yanked at his gun. It was stuck. Yanked it again – got it out and started firing.

Two of the guys had leapt into the back of the car. The other was hurrying around the back. He fired in Hernandez's direction, but missed.

Lee shot at him, once, twice. Missed both times.

Then the guy swivelled and let one off at Brad, who was going nowhere dangerous to them and didn't even have a gun and was only here because Lee had told him to be.

Lee saw Brad shudder and trip and fall. Saw him clatter into a tree and wallop over to hit the ground full length.

Then the car was rocketing past him, spraying him with flint. A final shot and Lee swore he felt it move the air above his head.

Forty-five seconds, at most. And it was over.

Lee stood a moment, feeling like the whole world had flipped, as if the universe had punched to negative. 'Oh, shit, Brad . . .'

He ran to the edge of the lot where Brad was face down, and was amazed to see his friend was still moving and that he was not covered in blood. He rolled over and his eyes were on Lee's. There was a lot to read in his face but it was not a story about pain.

Lee stared, grabbed him. 'Fuck, man – I thought they got you. I thought you were fucking nailed.'

Brad sat up, shook his head. 'Me too. Just tripped, though. Big rock. Just tripped.'

'It probably saved your life, man. Jesus.'

'Yeah. I got a lucky rock.'

They looked at each other, eyes wide, and laughed. It was a shaky laugh. It wasn't really a laugh.

Hernandez shouted from thirty yards. 'Is he shot?'

'No!' Lee shouted back. Adrenalin was still pumping through him like a jolt of uncut cocaine. 'But what the *fuck* just happened here?'

'I don't know,' Hernandez muttered. 'But we're leaving. Now.' He walked quickly towards Lee's car. 'We got to make some calls.'

Lee stuck a hand out and Brad grabbed it. Allowed himself to be pulled upright. Brad's brain really hadn't caught up with recent events. Most of it still lived in the world of sixty seconds ago. Evidently bad stuff had happened in between, but he felt like he'd missed most of it. He was somewhat amazed still to be around.

'Come on,' Lee said. 'Let's get out of here.'

Lee knew what they'd just experienced was something very significant. Hernandez was going to want to fuck those guys up bad. And Lee Hudek was going to be there with him. As of tonight he was not just one of the kids who turned up with the money.

He grabbed Brad's shoulder and helped him move faster.

Brad was limping heavily, but equally keen to be somewhere else. He did his best and hurried over towards the car. He was thinking that he wished the A would cut out for a moment, just so he could get his head together, when he noticed Hernandez had stopped a few yards short of Lee's car.

'What?' Brad said. He turned his head towards the vehicle.

There was something sitting in the driver's seat.

It was something awful. Something had come out of the forest and the night and sat in their car. It was terrible and it was ugly but it was very still.

It was Sleepy Pete.

'Oh Jesus,' Brad whispered. He looked at Lee, but Lee was staring at Pete. Brad forced himself to look again. 'Oh, no.'

Below the shoulders everything was okay. It was still Pete. He was sitting upright and the bag of Doritos was still in his hands. But one of the bullets meant for Hernandez or Lee or Brad had passed them by like a migrating bird ignores a hundred miles of sea, and found the place it had left the barrel to land. It had taken away about a quarter of Pete's head. It had entered the right side of his face halfway up and ploughed through the cheekbone and into the brain, tumbling out the other side at the top via a ragged hole. Pete's remaining eye was still open. The dregs of his nose were pulled out of true.

As Brad stared, he thought at first that the left eye was just glistening, still wet, and then he realized it was trying to move.

Then Pete's jaw dropped open. And a dark stain bloomed on his crotch. And Pete really was gone.

Chapter 9

'There's no choice,' Hernandez said. 'Listen to me.'

Brad was sitting on the ground, arms wrapped around his knees. He was on his third chain-smoked cigarette, which meant the conversation had been going at least ten minutes. Brad knew he had to listen but wanted no active part in it. When he tried to think it was like walking across hot coals, coals that stretched to infinity in every direction. Except the coals felt bitterly cold.

Lee shook his head. 'I went to school with this guy. There's got to be some other way.'

Hernandez's position was simple. The body had to disappear. They couldn't leave it here. It had to be got rid of. Soon as it was found, the cops would be all over it. Rich kid with his head blown off was not a situation that just went away. The event had to be erased. Lee had managed to muster a detachment that Brad found almost incredible. Okay, his voice didn't sound completely steady all the time, and he was rubbing his lip with one finger and not looking at the front seat of his car any more often than anyone else. But he'd come up with the idea of somehow posing Pete's body somewhere it could be interpreted as a drive-by, or a mugging gone horrendous, or *something*. He was sticking with the notion but Hernandez was having none of it.

'Listen to me, Lee,' Hernandez said again. He spoke quietly and Hudek realized this was the first time the man had referred to him by name, rather than as 'kid' or 'hey you'. 'We don't have any more time. We're out of town but someone would have heard the shooting anyway. We've got to make this go away now.'

Lee nodded. Thought about it. 'Okay,' he said. 'Let's do it.'

They opened the driver's-side door and got Pete's body out, supporting it at first so that it came out gently but then the remains of the head lolled and something viscous started to slip out onto Brad's hand and he let go in a spasm at about the same time Lee did and the whole thing wound up falling out onto the gravel. Lee took his T-shirt off and used it to wipe the worst of the mess off the car seat while Brad and Hernandez took a foot each and pulled the body around to the back of the car. Slowly, so the head didn't bounce up and down. They opened the trunk and Hernandez got the beach towel out and wrapped it around Pete's neck and head and then they lifted the body up and bent it around so it would fit, which was not easy. Then they shut the trunk.

When the body was no longer visible it was better. Brad stood watching while Hernandez went around the car scuffing up the gravel, gathering bits with blood on them and scooping them up into the Doritos bag. He was very thorough.

Then they all got in the car. They drove out the way they'd come and then took a left to head up further into the hills. The park was shut and would have been a bad place anyway but they found an access road and drove along it for quite a while. Then they parked and got Pete out of the trunk and carried him or it along a walking trail for about half a mile. Pete had been big in life and he was very heavy in death. Heavy and hard to manage and still warm, with hands that seemed too big and made of fingers. By the time they cut off the trail and headed out into nowhere Brad's back ached like someone had driven a nail into the base of his spine.

Eventually Lee said this had to be far enough and they stopped and left the body by a tree. There had been no shovel in the car, of course, so they used their hands and the car jack. It took a time and was very tough work, even though the ground was not too hard and they went at it together. They dragged Pete across to the hole but he did not fit, so they rolled him out the other side and made it larger. In the end they got him in. There was some discussion about whether they should leave the towel in place. Lee thought it was as safe there as anywhere else. Hernandez said Lee should take it somewhere and get it burnt. Brad wanted it to stay in place so he would not have to look at Pete a final time, though he felt bad about feeling that way and would not have wanted to explain it to Pete. In the end, Lee won. It was a cheap towel. You could get one like it anywhere. Brad was glad.

Nobody was sure whether you could leave fingerprints on a body. They thought not but Lee used his bloody T-shirt to wipe it just in case and then threw it in. Then as an afterthought he rolled Pete over and used the T to tie his hands, to confuse matters in case it was ever found. They pushed most of the dirt back over the body and then each went in a different direction and found the biggest logs they could carry. They positioned them over the grave in a way that looked kind of random and Lee walked ten yards off and looked back and though it was hard to tell because it was dark he thought it would do. He threw the remainder of the hole dirt around. He stood for a moment, looking at what they'd done, and then just shook his head.

They walked back to the car without saying anything.

Lee kept the lights off until they were near civilization. He drove back down to town at a steady rate and pulled over to drop Hernandez off where he indicated.

The man stepped out onto the kerb and then turned back.

'I'm going to call some people right away,' he said. 'The man you met. I'll let you know how we're going to handle this. Tonight.'

Lee just nodded, looking straight ahead. Hernandez shut the door and walked quickly off down the street.

Lee put his foot down and hammered down to 101 and through Ventura and Oxnard. Then abruptly slowed and took a right and headed out to the beach.

They parked up and got out, still without speaking. It was impossible to know what to say except blunt monosyllabic words that didn't help. Lee brought the Doritos bag with him and as they climbed up over the dunes he dispersed the contents slowly and thinly, letting the wind carry as much as possible away. By the time they got to the shore the bag was empty but he walked straight into the sea with it and washed out the interior before shredding it into as many pieces as the shiny material would allow. He let these fall into the sea, the wind catching them like pieces of moonlight.

He walked back up to where Brad was standing swaying in the sand and the two of them stared at each other for a while.

'Sleepy Pete,' Lee said.

Brad just shook his head. 'Fuck, Lee. Fuck.'

They walked back up over the dunes. Lee found an old sweatshirt in the trunk and put it on and drove into town. They pulled over at the first Starbucks they saw and bought vanilla lattes and drank them in the car as they drove on to the big Frisbees on Jolacha Ave. They bought three big bags of burgers there, confused and scared by the bright lights and the strange noises made by the till, and the way other people just stood around talking and laughing and asking for barbecue sauce as if absolutely nothing had happened. They walked stiff-legged back to the car.

Drove through town and up to the Faircroft gate. 'Be cool,' Lee said, quietly. Brad smiled vaguely into space.

A security guy came over to the car. It was the one Lee had talked to when he first arrived at the party. The exchange was short and friendly. Lee offered him a burger and the guy nearly said yes but then evidently remembered he was supposed to be on Atkins or not accept stuff or maybe just hadn't finished a pizza in the booth, and contented himself with waving them on.

Lee drove away and into the estate, past all the big gates.

'Pull over,' Brad said, after they'd gone a few hundred yards. Lee pulled over. Brad got out and vomited on the side of the road. The vomit smelt of beer and sour blood, of stagnant water and forest dust.

He got back in the car and Lee drove the rest of the way.

When they turned into the Luchs driveway there were still plenty of cars. Lee parked up and killed the engine. Took his hands off the wheel and clenched and unclenched them a few times.

'Okay,' he said. 'Now we have to go to this party. Have some fun.'

'You're kidding.'

'I'm not. We have to *be* here, understand what I'm saying?'

Brad understood. They got out with the burgers and went around the side. There were still about thirty people hanging out and the party was still going and the mixing guy had reappeared and was doing his thing but it was different now. The music sounded flat and out of time. A few people homed in when they saw the Frisbees bags.

'Anybody seen Pete?' Lee asked, casually. 'His name's on one of these. Two, probably.'

And people laughed and said no, they hadn't seen him in a while, and someone said they thought he'd gone off to some other party.

Brad thought, *Yeah, that pretty much covers it. Some whole other party altogether.* He was glad he'd already thrown up.

Suddenly there was a hand in his, and Karen was by his side.

'Thought we'd lost you,' she said.

He smiled and said 'Nah' and handed her some fries.

An hour and a half later Hudek pulled up in the street outside his parents' house. He checked the place for lights and thought about what he was going to do.

He had already gone to a 24-hour car wash. In fact, he had been to two. He'd done the first at a place where they knew him and then driven twenty blocks to another, where they didn't. Only an exterior job each time, of course, and he'd only used the first location because none of the guys he recognized were on duty and so he was just another young guy in a nice car.

The bodywork was in good shape. Less so other parts. The driver's seat and upper part of the driver's side door, for example, which were okay to the naked eye but Lee knew this wasn't clean enough. He could sell the car in a little while. But not immediately, and he was surprised by how much difference it made, knowing one of your best friends had died right where you were sitting.

He could get it fixed in the morning, but he found it was something he wanted finished now. He wanted to be able to get up tomorrow and know this event was yesterday's thing. Of course it would not be. Pete would be missed, and soon. But if the car was sorted out then he could get on with just not knowing anything about anything.

To achieve this he had to tick some tasks off:

Check there were no stones or dust left in the treads of the tyres which could be traced back to that fucking parking lot, or the access road they'd driven to get to where they buried him.

Give the trunk a thorough clean for specks of gravel and blood. The towel around the head had been a good touch but it was soaked almost through by the time they pulled him back out. Destroy and replace the lining if necessary.

And clean the front seat and the rest of the interior. Clean it well.

The lessons of half-watched episodes of *Forensic Detectives* had not been lost on Lee, though he'd never realized these were things he had needed to learn. The garage at his house would be perfect for all of this. The lighting was good, clinical. But first he had in mind to stop by his parents' house, assuming there was life there. There were two reasons for this. His dad had stuff in the garage which would help in what he had to do. Cleaning materials, solvents, tools, Hudek Sr's car always looked just so, and he had the stuff in bulk so he wouldn't miss anything Lee took. The second reason was that Lee felt that being seen around was a good idea. *Yeah, I saw him that night. No, he was fine, very relaxed, why do you ask? Oh no, that's impossible. Sorry, quite impossible.*

He could see that though his parents' bedroom light was turned off, his dad's study looked inhabited. He parked and locked the door and let himself in quietly. Poked his head in the study but though the computer was on, his father was not *in situ*. Walked through into the kitchen and saw the big doors there were open.

There was a shape sitting in a chair out by the pool.

He stepped out. 'Dad?'

The figure's head turned, and Lee saw that it was him. He was smoking a cigar. Sitting quietly out there by the pool by himself.

'Hey, kid,' he said, he said softly. 'What are you doing here?'

'Driving by, thought I'd say hi if you were still awake.'

'That's nice. You want a drink?'

'Sure. A beer'd be cool. Though better make it Lite.'

'That's right. You were at a party this evening.'

'Uh-huh. The Luchses.'

'Nice house.'

Lee shrugged. 'Yeah. Kind of showy, maybe.'

Ryan Hudek smiled, and went in the kitchen to get his son a beer. He clapped Lee on the shoulder as he walked past.

That was the moment where Lee came closest to losing it, but it passed. After that, there was never any going back. He sat out with his father for a half hour, and then excused himself. His dad nodded, stayed where he was. On the way through the house Lee ducked into the garage and picked up what he needed, arranging the remainder so no one could tell anything had gone.

Then he drove home, put the car in the garage and made himself a strong pot of coffee. He had shoved Hernandez's gun under a pile of stuff in one of the drawers in the storage unit in the garage. He felt bone-tired now, and he needed to make sure he was sharp and observant and tonight of all nights drugs were not the answer.

Caffeine was as much as he ever needed. While he waited for the pot to perk he tried to think about Pete, and found it better not to. Pete was dead. That's what it came down to in the end. Nobody had made him do anything he didn't want to do.

While Lee cleaned the car he found himself looking at his phone every few minutes. It had been three hours now and Hernandez still hadn't called.

Chapter 10

I don't know how you'd describe it. It wasn't forest, it wasn't open land. It was at the north-west extremity of Raynor's Wood. It was basically nothing, acres and acres of it, spread thinly with trees and bushes and criss-crossed with watery channels like the lines on a very old face. Apparently there was a small town half a mile away, but you wouldn't know it. It wasn't an area that was of use to anyone except bugs and birds and the small, furry wildlife who fed on them. I'd seen something like it in New Jersey once and they called it the barrens. I don't know how local parlance had it, but that seemed as good a name as any, especially under a cold grey moon.

I had followed Monroe and Nina out into the parking lot and got in the back of their car. There was some heated discussion over this but Monroe wanted to get moving and evidently decided not to get into a fight over it. He drove through town and out the other side and for a further ten minutes until he saw a local police car by the side of the road with its flasher going. Monroe pulled in behind this and followed as he was led down a series of roads to nowhere and finally onto one that cruised in a long straight line. The leading car eventually pulled over onto gravel. There were two other vehicles parked a little way up the road, and what looked like a scene-of-crime truck.

Two cops got out of the car, one in uniform and one in a suit. The second looked like the guy I'd seen with Nina and Monroe at the hotel earlier.

'Who's he?' this one said, when we walked up to them.

'A colleague,' Nina said. 'Problem?'

'No, ma'am. Call your mom. Get her to bring us a picnic.'

'Leave it, Reidel,' Monroe said. 'Just take us there.'

The guy called Reidel looked at me. I looked at him back. Then he turned and started walking off along a track by the side of the road. We followed.

A couple of hundred yards down it we began to see flashes and glints of torchlight in the distance. The ground was getting wetter. It was a sodden obstacle course of bracken and sudden ankle-deep squelches.

'So who found this one?' Nina asked. 'I don't believe anyone's desperate enough to come here to make out.'

'Local old guy out walking, collecting wood. He carves fallen branches into snakes, apparently, sells them at the craft fair. He actually found it early evening, but he's had some mental health issues and got freaked out and wasn't sure he'd actually seen what he thought he'd seen. Took him a few hours to build up to calling. He's kind of relieved right now.'

'Who would want a wooden snake?' I asked.

'You got me, sir.'

The line of incident tape was a little further on. On the other side was a shallow channel of water, maybe three feet wide, though rushes either side made the difference between water and boggy ground hard to call. The water stretched out left and right, curving around, creating an indistinct island about forty yards across. There was something on the far side of it, but the main focus of attention was nearer the front. A small knot of men stood around something on the ground. A heavy-duty lamp had been set up on a stand, throwing white light on their heads and shoulders.

Riedel went under the tape and led us towards a place where two wide boards had been laid across the water.

'One at a time,' he said.

We walked out across a makeshift bridge, which bent markedly in the middle and seemed unlikely to last the night. A couple of wet steps and then the ground was more solid.

The scene-of-crime people stood back as we approached. Already you could tell that something bad was in prospect. In the still air, the odour had a keening, unavoidable quality to it.

'Good timing,' one of the techs said. 'We're just about to move it. Him, I mean.' He stood by and shone a flashlight steadily on what we'd come to see, adding a second set of shadows.

Monroe caught sight of it first. 'Jesus,' he said, calmly.

On the ground was a man, lying on his right side with one arm trapped underneath. He looked like he'd been dropped from a height. He was wearing blue jeans and a dark green checked shirt, both extensively stained. His head was twisted around awkwardly, as if he'd been trying to glimpse the moon through the trees. His eyes were open and he was probably about thirty-five, though it's not always easy to tell with corpses. Sometimes death seems to smooth away a few years of care, along with a portion of character. Some small animal had also made it away with part of one of the man's cheeks.

The harshness of the lighting made the whole thing seem like a photograph, emotionally flat, until you remembered what your nose was trying to tell you and realized this thing was real, right there in front of you. Monroe's reaction was not to any of this, however, but to what the positioning of the left sleeve of the shirt revealed. It had been rolled up to just above the elbow, and it was clear that the arm was missing most of its flesh. Not through decomposition, though that had definitely played a part – the smell was really not good, at once both acrid and wet – but through someone removing large portions of it, taking much of the arm back to the bone. Once you'd seen this, you realized that the rest of the body under the clothes also looked reduced. The face was that of a man of medium build, maybe a little heavier. The way the clothes hung over the body, and the dark, dry stains, suggested that what you could see on the arm would be mirrored over the rest of the corpse. Could be the work of animals, but why burrow under the clothes and yet leave most of the face?

I turned away, and was glad to see I had not been the first. Nina was looking over at the far side of the island.

'What's that?'

'Come see.'

Riedel led us across the uneven surface. At first it was hard to make out what the object was, just that it seemed to be picked out by the moonlight. When you got closer it suddenly folded into comprehension.

What I'd noticed when we first got there turned out to be a white shirt. It was clean and not too large and it had been arranged over three thin upright branches of a bush, to look a little as if it was hanging on a line. The bush was close to one of the island's five trees.

Nina, Monroe and Riedel stood and looked at this for a few moments, and then grunted more or less in unison.

Perhaps even more than the body, it had that effect on you. I wondered whether the snake-carving guy had noticed this first, and if it was this which had actually freaked him out the most.

There was a muffled sound from over at the body, and one of the techs swore. He lifted his head and called over.

'Guys – you'll want to see this.'

We dutifully traipsed back over to the body, which had been carefully turned onto its back. This had revealed the right arm, which was in exactly the same condition as the left. Sleeve rolled up, flesh mainly removed. There was one notable difference, however.

The hand was missing.

'Okay,' Reidel said quietly, after a moment. '*Now* can we call this a serial killer investigation?'

*   *   *

'At least four, five days,' the coroner said, watching the body being loaded onto a stretcher. Some gunk he'd smeared under his nostrils to combat the smell made him look like he had the world's worst cold. 'Could be a week, though the removal of the flesh and organs makes it harder to tell. I'll be more precise when he's back at the lab, but I still won't be able to nail it to the clock. This is not a good environment to be dead in.'

He was right. Even with the midnight blue of the sky beginning to soften, this was no place you wanted to be. Four long hours had passed since we'd left the hotel, and I was wide-eyed and running out of cigarettes. I had kept quiet and out of the way in case one of the grown-ups remembered I was there and sent me up to bed.

I watched as the remains were carried precariously off across the narrow bridge. The island seemed different immediately, as if someone had turned off an inaudible soundtrack. There is a glamour about a dead body. It confers something extraordinary on a place, claims it for our kind. You can observe many aspects of reality – streams, animals, trees, the sun – but the thing that makes the biggest difference (that between a loved one and a dead body) is not tangible. A corpse must have been the first thing that made us realize how powerful and important things could exist which were yet not visible. This opens the way to an abstract universe: without corpses there would be no viruses, radio waves or quarks. It introduces powerlessness into the human world, too. Ritual and its condensates – gods – are merely a wrapper around this emptiness, this thing we cannot grasp. I wondered who the dead man was, and in whose life he was going to leave the biggest hole. I was glad it wasn't mine, and I felt for a moment abject and alone. However far I walked on this planet, I would never find my parents waiting. Bobby would never buy me another beer. A year after the fact, I didn't seem to have made much progress internalizing any of this. I forgot it all, for hours and sometimes days at a time: but when I remembered it didn't seem to have become any more explicable. I was never able to think 'Oh, right, they're *dead*. Of course. Okay. Got it.' Maybe I never would. Perhaps the death of the loved one simply cannot be apprehended. Maybe you just have to think about something else, forever.

I lit one of my remaining cigarettes and listened to other people saying things.

Monroe was still making notes. 'You're sure the defleshing didn't take place after the body was dumped here?'

'Yes. There's been a little, the face for example – definite teeth marks, rodent of some kind – but the majority was hacked off,' he said. 'A big knife, cleaver, something of that nature. There were cut marks across the humerus. And a scrape along the tibia. Probably see a lot more when the clothes come off. Heavy and sharp. The same instrument used to remove the hand, I'd guess.'

Nina nodded. 'I'm surprised there wasn't more animal damage after that long.'

'After how long?'

'Five to seven days. What you just said.'

'Ah,' he smiled, holding up a finger. 'Not what I said. He's been dead for that long. But not on this sorry piece of real estate. I'd say he's been out here twenty-four hours at most.'

Nina looked at him silently. I knew the look. It meant, 'Give me the information without making me ask for it, or you'll be sorry.'

The coroner was wearing a wedding band. He knew the look too. 'The flesh on his back is relatively intact,' he said. 'And there's evidence of pooling on the dorsal surfaces – blood settling to the lowest point of the body after death. It's consistent across the back and remains of the buttocks and calves, whereas the body . . .'

'Was found here lying on its side.'

'Exactly. So it was somewhere else for a period immediately post-mortem, laid out flat on its back.'

'The question is, where?' Reidel said. 'Guess you don't have any clues for us on that?'

The coroner shook his head. 'See what forensics scrape up. But I wouldn't hold your breath. The hope would be there'd be something distinctive about where he was lying, dust, debris, earth. But if he was naked there then much of any evidence would have been cut off or brushed away when the clothes were put back on.'

Monroe nodded. 'So the removal of the flesh could be an attempt to hide where the body was stored.'

'Could be.'

'Or not,' I said. I was looking out across the island again, struck by a sudden thought.

'What, Hopkins?'

'What do you think that shirt's about?'

'I have no idea at the present time. It may not be relevant.'

'Of course it is,' I said. 'Dead body and an article of clothing out here, with nothing else for miles around? I'd say there's a pretty clear line of relevance.'

'Perhaps whoever brought the body here just discarded it as they left,' Reidel said. 'Which could give us a direction of departure.'

'I don't buy that either,' I said. 'Discarded why? It's clean. No blood, nothing. Looks like it just came out of the packet.'

Nina was looking at me. 'So what do you think?'

'Come and look,' I said.

I started walking. After a beat, they followed.

When I got to the shirt a tech had just finished taking photographs of it and was about to remove it from the bush.

'Wait a second,' I said. I motioned for Nina to go stand behind the shirt. 'Notice anything?'

She looked down at the shirt, shook her head.

'Not the shirt itself. Stand with your shoulders parallel to it. Look straight ahead. Tell me what you see.'

She moved slightly. Looked ahead. 'The lamp.'

'Right. Where the body was, in other words. The shirt's been posed,' I said. 'It's standing in for someone. It's a witness.'

The three of them stood and looked back and forth for a few moments. 'Okay, maybe,' Nina said, nodding.

Monroe looked only semi-convinced. 'But how does that speak

to whether the removal of the flesh was about removing evidence of where it had been stored?'

I shrugged. 'It may not,' I said. 'But if someone's gone to the trouble to put that shirt there, they're making a point. Creating a tableau, or a scene. Maybe even recreating one. You've got to have a reason for bringing the body all the way out here. They previously had it somewhere they could hack the flesh off without being discovered. Somewhere safe, in other words. But then they chose to bring it all the way out here, where someone's going to find it. So the positioning has to be important. Maybe the removal of the flesh was to make the body lighter.'

Three people were frowning at me. They looked like a row of question marks.

'You guys must be tired,' I said. 'The *lighter* the body is, the easier it will be to carry. Someone wanted to do this, and do it here specifically. But they knew they weren't strong enough to carry the whole thing. So they hacked off as much weight as they could without compromising the overall integrity of the body.'

'So it's someone who knew they wouldn't be able to carry it all this way, and took steps to make it feasible,' Reidel said. He paused. 'Like a woman, perhaps.'

'Well, yeah,' I agreed. 'Though . . .'

Monroe was looking at me curiously. Nina was staring at the ground. Reidel had an odd kind of smile on his face.

'What?' I said.

The car dropped us in the lot of the hotel. Monroe and Reidel were going straight to the morgue to follow progress on the initial forensic examination of the body. The dawn was beginning to come up.

'I'm sorry,' I said. 'I didn't realize I was stepping into an ongoing debate.'

Nina shook her head. 'It was good thinking,' she said. 'I think Charles was actually impressed.'

'Doesn't prove it's a woman,' I said. 'If I had to carry that thing all the way out there then I'd want it as light as possible, too. That wasn't a small man. And even a dead midget is far from light.'

'Is this the voice of experience?'

'No,' I said. 'I think it was Confucius or one of those guys. Look, let's go see if they'll serve us some coffee.'

'Ward, it's not even five a.m. yet.'

'You got a gun with you?'

'Of course.'

'Me too. They'll serve us. They have no choice.'

We went into the hotel and I found someone and was charming at them until they agreed to find coffee just to make me go away.

The lounge was L-shaped and we walked the cups out to the furthest extremity of the long arm. It probably would have made more sense to go back to the room but there's something about the dead that makes you want to stick to open spaces for a while. We sat and sipped to the sound of distant people vacuuming.

After a time Nina's pager beeped. She looked at it. 'The bloods on the first guy are back,' she said. 'Traces of a Rohypnol-style substance. Which means pre-meditation.'

'Of something,' I said. 'Though not necessarily murder. Is that something a woman would do? Use a date rape drug?'

'Not if she was hoping to get laid.'

I told Nina about the email purporting to be from someone called Carl Unger, claiming he'd known Bobby and that he needed to talk to me soon. We knocked it back and forth and then she thought for a moment. 'Call him,' she said.

I nodded, and we sat quietly for a while.

'I looked it up,' Nina said, eventually. 'In the last decade there's not been a single murder in this entire county. Not a one. Now two bodies in a week, outside the same small town.'

'They got themselves someone serious.'

'Yep.'

We stayed there, drinking cooling coffee, as the world outside slowly got lighter.

Chapter 11

Meanwhile a man was still out on the road, a man who no longer had any hesitation about going where he was going.

At the end of the previous afternoon Jim Westlake had reached Petersburg, the place specified in the instructions he had been given in Key West. He had parked in the lot of a Publix supermarket on the outskirts. He got out and stretched his legs and waited until five o'clock exactly. Then he pressed and held the 1 button on the phone, which had been programmed to call a number. The identity of the number had been obscured. He supposed that had he been young and technically minded, or if he found and paid someone who was, he might be able to establish what the number was. It was not obvious how this might help, and so he had not bothered.

The phone rang three times and then was picked up.

'It's me,' Jim said. 'I'm here.'

'Good, good,' said a voice. It sounded like the older of the two men from Key West. The Forward-Thinking Boy. Of course. Always him.

'So what now? You going to give me an address?'

'You're going to have to get that for yourself.'

Jim laughed sourly. 'You been to Petersburg? It's not New York but it's no bump in the road. You want this done smartly, you're going to have to do better than that.'

'Well,' said the voice, 'here's where I misled you a little. You've got a little driving to do yet.'

'Where am I supposed to be?'

Without hesitation, the voice on the line mentioned another town. Jim was quiet. Utterly quiet.

'You still there, James?'

'Yes,' Jim said. 'And *fuck you.*'

'About what I thought you'd say. Which is why you're sitting where you are, rather than where you're supposed to be.'

Jim looked at his left hand, down by his side. It was trembling a little. He clenched it. 'I'm not going there,' he said.

'You are,' said the voice. 'You have to, and not just because I say so. I knew that if I told you this down in your nest in the Keys then you wouldn't do it. That would have been a mistake, because if you don't do this you're screwed. You left a loose end a long time ago. It's just come badly undone. You have to fix it, and while you're there you're going to do work for us too. It's important work and it's personal to me and you're not going to mess it up.'

Jim looked away across the lot. The supermarket flashed in the sunlight. Families went to and fro, pushing baskets empty or full. Bringing food, fetching food. Hunters of the aisles, gatherers of the low carb and shrink-wrapped.

'Okay,' he said. 'Just tell me. The truth this time.'

'Wait where you are,' the voice said. 'Further information will arrive. Then get on it. This matters to me, to us, but it's your life at stake, not mine.'

The line went dead.

Jim stood there by the van for a few minutes, and then the phone made a series of weird noises. After a brief pause it did the same thing again. The screen told him to press a particular button, so he did.

A picture came on the screen. A woman's face. He pressed another button at the prompt, and was shown another tiny photograph, of another woman. Underneath each photograph was a message. It was the same each time.

It just said KILL THEM.

Lost in time. Lost in numbers. Lost in things gone by. Jim was roused again by the sound of bawling. He realized he had been standing leaning against the van for God knows how long. Just standing there, zoned out in the parking lot, staring down at a cellular phone.

'He kicked me. Mommy, he kicked me.'

Jim turned his head. Across the way were two young boys, standing at the back of an SUV. The boys were maybe seven years old, and already stocky. The back of the vehicle was open wide like jaws, stuffed full of bags of brightly packaged food-like materials. Enough for a small African country for a month, you'd have thought. The kids had been left there while their mother trekked the basket back to the collection point, about fifty yards away.

Stupid. Really stupid.

The one who'd been kicked was howling and red-faced. The other kid was watching this with a concentrated expression, as if evaluating the experience. You kick, he cries. How interesting.

As he climbed up into the van and started the engine, Jim thought how, to the person overhearing it, the kicking child is nowhere near as annoying as the kicked one, the child who stands bawling, 'He kicked me, he kicked me,' over and over again. Yes of course the child who did the kicking is an asshole, and yes, he started it, and yes kicking is wrong. But it's the whining child you want to go and kick for yourself. You want to punish it for the puling self-righteousness of the wronged, for the attempt to parlay weakness into backdoor power. What the kicked kid wants is for an adult to come along and thump the kicker. He wants to do a violent deed *without having done it* – to receive advantage without the responsibility of action. This is the kind of kid who will grow up to sue a neighbour's ass off because he tripped on the neighbour's path, after an afternoon spent eating the neighbour's hotdogs and drinking the neighbour's beer.

Jim pulled out of the space and wound down the window. The mother was still forty yards away, on the return journey.

'Hey, kid,' Jim said.

Both children turned to look up at him. Jim spoke to the bawler. 'Either kick him back or shut the fuck up.'

The kid blinked at him, still mechanically sniffling.

'You got it? Stop fucking whining.'

The sniffle stopped dead. The kid nodded, quickly. His face was white.

'Good. Keep it that way. Or I'll come back and get you.'

Jim wound the window back up and headed out of the lot, back out of town, and onto the highway.

He drove straight through the night. Drove due west, staying in Virginia but sticking to minor roads once he was clear of Petersburg. He was on his way. Now he really had no choice.

He was going home.

Part 2: The Many

Places have an effect, for good or bad.

David M. Smith

The Morality of Place

Chapter 12

Oz Turner took a deep breath and let it slowly out again, lips flapping like a dispirited horse. It was ten forty-five on a Monday
morning in September, it was cold, and it was raining. September
sucked. Mondays were The Week's Only Just Started And Already
Feels Old, and the present hour was a quarter of Are We Having
Fun Yet? You factored in the precipitation, which was light but
determined, and you truly had a morning to forget.

From his desk against the window he looked down at Lincoln's
main street with a jaundiced eye. A couple of locals walked along
it, heads bent. They went into Jayne's Stores, and the street was
empty again.

Hello boredom, my old friend.

He got up and shambled to the kitchenette, past two empty desks.
The paper rarely saw two employees at once; a full house of three
would take the outbreak of war, the arrival of space aliens, or the
county fair. While Oz waited for the water he heaped four teaspoons

of coffee into a cup and added a further three of sugar. His most recently ex-wife had dedicated a deal of time to ragging him over his caffeine consumption, and he still took pleasure in not having to give a crap any more. Pain in the ass that woman could be, really. Fun under the covers, of course, though as she was currently manifesting that with some other guy (and had been for three years, for the first of which she had still been married to Oz), this had turned out to be a mixed blessing. Oz had long ago decided that the world of women could be divided into shy, inhibited ones who stayed faithful and from whom you strayed; and gutsy, come-hither ones who strayed first and strayed fast and far. He'd tried both – married both, matter of fact – and neither had worked out. He hoped there might be a middle ground someplace, but allowed it might be getting late for him to find out.

He had been staring at his reflection in the kettle for five minutes – at least, he assumed it was him, though hair and beard looked far too uniformly grey, and excessively bushy for general tastes – before he realized it had boiled. Back at his desk he stared disappointedly at the screen for a while, cradling his coffee on his gut. The morning had added five hundred words to his current article, but they were no good. So the Newport Tower down on Rhode Island looked surprisingly Norse in construction. What of it? The subject was old ground. Oz's angle was The Pig-headed Blinkeredness Of The Establishment, Not To Mention The Powers That Be. It was his whole approach to life. But he was a professional, too. You can't just say the thing time and again. Even if no one ever read his section (which seemed all too possible), or skimmed it and thought it was a joke (and he knew for sure that some did), you had to do it right.

Otherwise – what was there?

He selected, erased. Started again. The next half hour of the morning passed without too much of a fight.

When he heard a *thunk* from outside he looked up.

A car had appeared in the street outside Jayne's. It was noticeable because it was parked nose out, a feat of bravura which would have taxed most locals well beyond their limits: also because it was a rental, big and black, with Colorado plates. Someone was standing at the front. Above average height, broad shoulders, dark hair cut very short. His face was lightly stubbled and kind of gaunt. He was looking right up at the windows of the *Lincoln Ledger*.

He glanced away, up the street, then down. The action had a professional look about it.

Oz leaned forward and watched, intrigued by a fanciful notion. The guy reminded him of the Terminator. Not that he was anywhere *near* as wide or pumped as Arnie had been in those days, nor was he dressed head to toe in black leather. Anyone like that rode into Webster County, Massachusetts, it would have been on the news by now. News that was broadcast out of a small studio a couple towns away, from a chair that Oz himself occupied for an hour a week in the dead zone from midnight until one. 'The Oz-Man's O-zone', its audience a handful of bilious insomniacs, syndication rights still very much available.

No, actually the guy was lean and compact and the resemblance came only from the way he stood; from an apparent indifference to the rain, a sense that it, and probably many other things, didn't matter to him at all.

Call me Woodward, Oz thought, or colour me Bernstein if you will: but that guy hasn't stopped for a comfort break.

He turned to grab his digital camera. It took him thirty seconds to locate the device under piles of reference material, and when he turned back, there was no one standing in the street any more.

'Oh, crap,' he muttered, peering quickly left and right up the street. Must've gone into the market after all, some passer-by needing cigarettes or a soda. Lincoln could rest easy. Any potential excitement had been averted.

Then somebody knocked on the door.

Knocked hard.

Oz turned in his chair, neck tingling. That couldn't be so. Shouldn't be, anyhow.

It happened again. Three heavy raps.

Oz stood slowly. Took a couple of steps back, to where he had a clear view of the *Ledger*'s door. Top half was frosted glass.

A blurred shape was visible through it.

Oz waited to see if the person would knock again. Then he realized it was brighter in the office than the stairwell, and if Oz could see whoever was out there, they could sure as hell see him. No point knocking again if you know someone's already heard.

Oz squared his shoulders – which had minimal effect, but made him feel a little more bullish – and went to open the door.

The man from the street was standing on the other side.

There were beads of moisture on his long coat. He stood with his feet a little apart; solidly planted, very still, yet giving the impression of someone ready to move quickly in any direction he chose. He looked at Oz. His eyes were green and sharp.

'Are you Oswald K. Turner?'

'How did you get up here?'

'Came in the door, walked up the stairs.'

'Just opened the street door, right?'

'That's correct.'

'No. It was locked, dude.'

'I didn't notice.'

'Didn't . . . right. Whatever you say.' This wasn't something Oz was prepared to make an issue of. The longer he stood with this guy, the more he wondered if he was a cop. Or a soldier. Or a full-on Man in Black. Something heavy, that's for damned sure.

'Can I come in?'

Oz thought that was curiously polite of him, given he looked like a guy who was used to going pretty much where he wanted.

'Depends,' he said, warily. 'What do you actually want?'

The man reached into his jacket and pulled out a piece of paper. Held it up so Oz could see. It was an interior page from the *Ledger*, printed three weeks before. The article carried the Oswald K. Turner byline and was entitled 'WHEN WILL THEY TAKE THIS SERIOUSLY?'

'I want to talk about this,' the man said. 'I want you to show it to me.'

'Go *out* there? It's raining.'

'I'm aware of that.'

'My car's in the shop,' Oz said.

'Mine isn't.'

'There's a serious walk even when you get there. Uphill. And it's on private land. And the owner doesn't like me much.'

The man didn't say anything, merely inclined his head about five degrees and kept looking at him. Oz got the picture. They were going to go see this thing, they were going now, and they were going if it started hailing, or snowing, or raining cows.

'Are you with . . . somebody, or what?'

'Me?' the man smiled, kind of. He looked out of practice. 'No. I'm just an avid reader.'

'And do you have a name?'

The man looked at him coolly for a moment, as if making a judgement.

'My name is John Zandt.'

The man drove in silence, speaking only to get directions. Oz kept quiet too, exercising his observation skills. Maps and books were spread across the back seat. The car had six and a half thousand miles on the clock, the journey indicator said six thousand two hundred. It was possible the hire place hadn't remembered to reset it before giving the car to this guy or some previous fellow, but Oz didn't think so. The car smelt a little of cigarette smoke, but otherwise was factory fresh. Oz thought Mr Zandt had been on the road for a while, or drove fast, and possibly both.

Oz took him up 112 and then a right onto 51C – or Old Pond Lane, as it was called. It wasn't obvious why: the road did pass a pond on the left side, but the area was full of water features and there was nothing to suggest why this one was considered worth mentioning. Oz saw the guy glance at it as they passed, and guessed he was wondering the same thing. He had no way of knowing that the man was observing a resemblance between the small lake and one in Vermont he had stood by, a little over a year before; that he was trying to remember what his life had been like then, and could not recall.

Fifteen miles up the way Oz pointed to the right again, and they started up the rough one-lane road that skirted the edge of the Robertson state forest, a near-thousand acres of trees and foothills that people went hiking in once in a while.

At the end of it was a gate. 'Going to have to park here,' Oz said. 'Do the rest on foot, like I said. It's a couple miles.'

The man nodded, killed the engine. Got out. Waited for Oz to do the same. Then locked up. Waited for Oz to lead the way.

The first few hundred yards made Oz nervous, because it involved going up what was effectively Frank Pritchard's driveway. The Pritchard farm backed into the park and was surrounded by it on three sides. Getting where they were going was a lot easier if you took this short-cut through Frank's property, ducked back onto national land, and then came back onto private property at the end. Problem was Frank, who was not big on local heritage. Last time he'd seen Oz slinking around he had threatened to destroy the damned thing, with conviction, and while waving a shotgun.

They left the road without incident and dipped into the forest, where Oz soon stopped feeling he was leading the way. He had to point out the direction every now and then, but the other guy walked fifty per cent faster than Oz's usual pace, taking rises and stream beds as if it was all level ground, and before long Oz was red-faced and hot.

'Been here a while,' he panted, at the other guy's back. 'Another twenty minutes aren't going to make much difference.'

The man stopped, turned to look at him. But he did seem to walk a little more slowly after that.

Oz kept them on a rough north-east bearing up into the hills.

130

'Aw, crap,' he said, a little later. He stopped walking, and pointed. 'Bastard's repaired the fence.'

He rested a moment, hands on his knees. Part of him felt relieved. Where they were headed was now the other side of a new eight-foot wire fence. This meant they couldn't go on. Game over, weird guy. Been nice not knowing you.

The man walked up to the barrier, looked at it. Reached into his coat, and pulled out a small tool. In about forty-five seconds he had clipped a five-foot vertical slash in the wire.

'Oh, great,' Oz said, but the man was already climbing through.

Oz followed. What else was he going to do?

Once they were back on Pritchard's land, it wasn't far. About three hundred yards in the lee of a ridge, then a sharp left and over a small hill. The other side was a little steep, and they came down carefully. When they reached flat ground again they were faced with another very similar hillock, about six yards in front. Trees grew all around, and the undergrowth was tangled. Oz led the guy around to the right, then stopped.

'So there you are,' he said, with a touch of pride. 'There's your root cellar.'

He was about to say more, go into his spiel, but the guy held up his hand and so Oz shut up instead. The man walked closer to what they'd come to see. It wasn't anything outstanding to the naked eye, and in fact would have been easy to walk past without noticing, as people had for many, many years.

Hidden amongst tree roots and random bits of rock, there was a small rectangular recess in the side of the hill. The bottom of the recess was the ground; the sides were slightly bowed and consisted of stones, not unlike those which lay around, but set together in a dry wall construction to create supports about a foot wide and three feet high, a little over two feet apart. Across these lay a flat lintel stone. On top of that, earth.

The man squatted a moment and looked at the opening, tracing a finger over the joints between some of the stones. Then he stood and looked over it, sweeping his gaze across the hill behind. Pulled a camera out of his pocket and took a couple of pictures. Walked around the base of the hillock a little way, observing the relationship between the door and the hill.

Then, his eyes still on the feature, he came back to where Oz was waiting.

'Okay,' he said. 'Now you can talk.'

In 1869 a resident of a homestead near Lincoln – then a hamlet of little size or repute – was foraging for firewood in the forest when he came across something odd. A stone construction, something that looked like a very small doorway. The next day he and his son cleared the undergrowth, and moved a collection of large stones which appeared to have been inserted into the mouth of a tunnel beyond: it was hard to see how they could have got there otherwise, and what function they could have had except to impede access. The son was sent inside, with a candle. He discovered the tunnel continued into the hillside for approximately eight feet, before broadening into a round, arched chamber with a diameter and height of around three metres. That night the son, who was talented with a pencil, drew what he had seen. The next day his father went in himself, navigating the narrow tunnel with some difficulty. He was inside for forty minutes, and when he emerged he instructed the son that they were going to block up the entrance again. To prevent children or livestock becoming trapped inside, he said, though neither were common to the area. He was also firm that they speak of this to no one outside the family. The son recorded the events in a private diary, which was discovered in an archive in Lincoln's small museum – along with the drawing – over a hundred years later.

A local curiosity, nothing more. An abandoned root cellar, very likely, built to preserve vegetables in the lean early years, its stone construction enabling it to outlast any sign of the cabin it once served.

Except that on February 1, 1876, the *Boston Journal* had reported the discovery of another underground chamber near Dedham, south of that city. Over the course of the next five decades hundreds of similar chambers were discovered across New England – in Massachusetts, Vermont, New Hampshire and Connecticut. Usually, but not always, associated with hillsides, they were of two types: simple covered passageways, often formed by taking advantage of natural crevices in rock; or more complicated beehive structures, like the Lincoln chamber, dry-walled and corbelled to arching ceilings. Both forms were usually covered and in-filled with earth, moulding them into the hillside or ridge where they were found.

It didn't take long for some people to notice the similarity of these structures to stone chambers built in Europe a long, long time before America was supposed to have been discovered. Mainstream archaeology was firm on the subject, however; these were root cellars, built by early colonial settlers – since moved on or died – and forgotten until rediscovery. Some of them (like the Dedham chamber itself) seemed to become mislaid again, and the phenomenon faded into obscurity.

There the matter rested until the 1960s, by which time enthusiastic amateurs had grown so clamorous in their desire to read something else into the chambers that the archaeologists had to take charge of the subject once again. The pros weighed in with a wealth of tedious data concerning the lack of pre-Columbian artefacts in the area, the fact that the distribution of the discovered structures largely mirrored known colonial settlement patterns in New England, and that oral and historical traditions confirmed the existence of stone root cellars. QED, in effect – now go away and leave this to the professionals. But the amateurs pointed out that some chambers seemed to have an astronomical orientation: one at the Gungywamp site in Connecticut, for example, which featured a channel markedly similar to one in the prehistoric New Grange monument in Ireland. An accident, said the archaeologists. But a sample of charcoal taken from a chamber in Windham County, Vermont, was radiocarbon dated to around 1405, said the amateurs. Carbon dating is notoriously tricky, the archaeologists scoffed (except when it backs up what *you* say, countered the amateurs). And even if most of them *are* root cellars, others are ludicrously large for that purpose, the amateurs further insisted, by now quite bad-temperedly.

'Whatever,' said the archaeologists, sticking their fingers in their ears. 'Go away.'

'But something tells me you know all this,' Oz muttered, tailing off. 'Half of it is in that piece in the *Ledger*, for a start.'

He had grown uncomfortable under the man's steady gaze, and for once in his life wanted to stop talking. Everybody's heard of the thousand-yard stare of the Vietnam vet. This guy's seemed to reach for maybe ten times that distance – which was unsettling, especially if it was boring straight through your head.

'What's inside?'

Oz laughed. 'Yeah, right. You think I've been *in* there?'

'You've written about this place three times that I know about, and you've never gone inside?'

'Look at the entrance,' Oz said. 'One of the questions over these things is why the openings are usually too small for easy access. Now look at me, dude. How's your spatial awareness? You see me fitting up there? Even if there weren't a shitload of rocks in the way?'

There was silence for a few moments, and then Oz glumly watched the man taking off his coat.

It took over a half hour. The rain had thinned to little more than mist by the time the guy was having to stick his torso into the hole to reach far enough to pull out more rocks. Oz did what he'd been told, which was to take the ones he was passed and put them in a neat pile to the side. Then there was a slight but distinct change in the echoed sound of the man's breath, and he emerged slowly, pulling with him a rock far larger – and flatter – than any of the others.

'It's open,' he said. He looked at Oz.

'Not that I don't want to, man,' Oz said, and now that the way was clear, he really sort of did. 'But I'm a little too old, too chunky, and *way* too claustrophobic. Went in one of these up in Vermont eighteen months ago, had a much bigger entrance, and I still felt like I was being buried alive.'

The guy smiled very slightly at this, but Oz didn't think it was anything to do with mockery. More as if Oz had said something unexpectedly close to the mark.

Then he was down there, only his feet still visible in the mouth of the entrance, and soon nothing left at all.

Oz sat down on the pile of rocks and waited.

After ten minutes he leaned over and peered up the tunnel. A couple of yards away he could see a brief sweep of a powerful flashlight. The guy came prepared, that was for sure.

Oz sat back on the rocks. It was raining again and he wished he had a coffee, but otherwise he was feeling kind of psyched. Only a few hours before he'd been rueing a very average Monday morning, wishing something would happen. Well, it had. This, without question, was something happening. He had been to this place maybe fifteen, twenty times over the years. Sat close to where he was now, wondering what the purpose of the structure was. And now someone was inside, maybe finding out.

After another fifteen minutes he heard the sound of the man coming back. He emerged hands first, holding a couple of small, clear plastic bags. Each had something in it, though Oz couldn't see what. The man got to his feet, brushed off the worst of the mud, and picked up his coat. The bags went into the pockets.

'What you got there? What did you see? Is it like the drawing?'

'The drawing was pretty good.'

'So what did you . . .'

Then there was a cracking noise, very loud. Plus the sound of someone shouting. Oz turned to see Frank Pritchard striding fast up the rise towards them, a shotgun in his hands.

'Oh, shit. This is bad,' Oz said. 'This is precisely who we most don't want to see at this point.'

135

The other man watched the farmer's progress, wiping dirt off his hands. Soon the content of Pritchard's hollering was discernible. He was a little drunk, as usual, and he was determined that no goddamned bastard was going to just come on his land whenever he felt like it. He had his goddamned gun and he was going to use it this time, and he was confident that no goddamned jury in the land would convict.

He came to a halt and levelled the gun at them.

'Oh crap,' Oz said, now very scared. 'Look, Frank . . .'

Pritchard was waving the gun pretty wildly. If he pulled the trigger it was going to take off someone's head.

'We're busy,' the man called Zandt said, mildly.

The old guy shut up, like a clam closing in a snap. After a moment Oz realized the guy in the long coat was holding a weapon too. A gun had appeared from nowhere in his right hand, and was pointing directly at Pritchard's head. It was not wavering at all.

'I accept that this constitutes trespass,' the man said, in a calm, low tone. 'And as such, grieves you. But you're going to go now, and leave us alone. And if you see Mr Turner here again, you're going to look the other way and walk on by. Can we agree to that?'

'This is my land,' Pritchard said, with surprising clarity.

'We know that. We'll do it no harm.'

The old man seemed to subside, and then abruptly turned and walked. After a couple of yards he looked back.

'That thing's bad news,' he said. 'I'm telling you.'

'Yes,' the other man said. 'It is.'

Pritchard swore at no one in particular, and then stalked away.

As Oz watched him go, the other man bent to the pile of rocks and started moving them back into the mouth of the tunnel.

Within ten minutes no one was getting back in there in a hurry. This time the bigger, flatter rock was the last to go in. When you saw it blocking the entrance, you realized it had been designed that way.

The man stood. 'You never get more specific on where this thing is located, understood? Neither in print or on your website or in that appalling radio show.'

'Why? Now you've been in there . . .' Oz tailed off quickly when he saw the man looking at him. 'Okay,' he said.

The man took the camera out of his pocket and handed it to him. 'There's fifteen shots of the inside. The rest of the disk is full of similar material. Including the interior of the Dedham chamber.'

'What? No way. That was lost . . .'

'I found it again. Put it all up on your site, so I can get them if I need to.'

'But . . . why are you doing this?'

'People need to know. But you came here alone, went inside alone. Right?'

'Man, I'm forgetting your existence in real time. It will be a pleasure. Trust me.'

The man smiled, and this time it looked almost real. Then he turned and walked away.

By the time Oz got back to the gate the black car had gone, and fresh rain had begun to fill its tracks. Happily, a car came along only five minutes after Oz made it to Old Pond Lane.

Unhappily, it contained his ex-wife.

Chapter 13

In the morning things had happened fast. We were woken just after eight by a call from Reidel: a local cop had gotten a hit on Larry Widmar. He had been seen talking to a woman in a bar on the Owensville Road on the night he disappeared. Nina took details and arranged to meet him at the bar in forty minutes.

While she showered I called the number Unger had supplied in his email, after using a dark corner of the internet to confirm it belonged to a phone that was registered to a Mr C Unger, street address withheld. This looked good, down to Unger using his alleged intelligence status to keep information out of a database that wasn't supposed to exist in the first place. I still didn't want to use my own phone to call him, but other options were limited. Calling from the room or lobby or a public call box would place me even more securely than a cell trace. The only other approach was social engineering: borrowing a phone from a member of the public with or without their consent. All I'd be doing was transferring the danger to an innocent bystander – which even my training-wheeled moral system would find hard it to classify as 'good'.

So in the end I just called him, and after all that he didn't pick up. I was redirected to voicemail and told I'd reached Carl Unger's phone and I should leave a message. The voice didn't sound familiar, but they seldom do. I said who I was and that he was welcome to call me back.

Then we went out and got in my rental and headed for the bar.

Reidel was already there, standing with a woman in the middle of a parking lot that was cold and empty and bordered with mist. The bar sat by the side of the road about a half mile out of town, and was a long, flat oblong tricked up to look slightly like a boat. Why, when the nearest ocean was a long day's drive away, was hard to imagine. It was called 'The Mayflower'.

Reidel introduced the woman as Hazel and explained they were in the lot because the manager was late arriving to open up.

'So,' Nina said, showing her badge. 'Hazel – you want to tell me what you've told the detective here?'

Hazel was in her thirties and smoker-thin, decent looks heading calcified. Her voice sounded like you could use her throat to take the edges off things, and also as if she was more of an evening person. She stood with the body language of a woman who had about two minutes' good temper left in her at any one time.

'The guy in the picture I was showed. He's in once in a while, not often. Wednesday night he was here, though, mid to late, and I know it was Wednesday because I was pissed because it was supposed to be my night off but Gretchen went no-warning AWOL *again* but hell, that's okay – because bubble-butt is screwing Lloyd right now and so she's fucking golden.'

'Lloyd being the manager,' Reidel said. 'He hasn't been talked to yet. He wasn't here last night or on Wednesday.'

'Yeah, right,' Hazel said. 'Too busy getting it wet. He's married, you know. Three kids. Cute fucking kids, too.'

'Last Wednesday,' Nina prompted.

139

Hazel shrugged. 'I didn't talk to the guy and I don't really know him and all I told the cop was he was there, and I saw him talking to some chick with short hair who's in here sometimes, drinks vodka straight up. Personally I always thought she was, like, a woman's woman, but what the hell do I know?'

'Can you give us more of a description of the woman?'

'Your height, forty pounds heavier, pasty face. Wouldn't want to kiss her.'

'You think any of the other staff might know who she is?'

'Maybe Donna. But she's away till Thursday.'

We turned at the sound of a vehicle pulling into the lot. It was a red truck, and it parked right up against the front of the building.

'Or him,' Hazel added, folding her arms even more tightly. 'Assuming he brought his brain today.'

The guy who got out of the truck was in his late forties, slim and losing colour on top. He was trying hard for silver fox but came across more like a greying weasel with a tan.

'What's going on?'

'Police,' Reidel said. 'We're here about a customer of yours. Man called Lawrence Widmar.'

Lloyd looked immediately wary. 'Right. Guy who got killed.'

Hazel stared. 'He's dead?'

'Yes,' Nina said. 'He's the man who was found in Raynor's Wood. Didn't the policeman tell you?'

'No. He just asked if I recognized . . . I didn't know.' She pulled out a pack of cigarettes, fumbled for a light. I held one out for her. 'Thanks. Jesus.'

'I wouldn't call him a regular,' the manager said, moving smoothly into distancing mode. 'Came in here maybe once, twice a month. Didn't drink a whole lot. Sat in a booth, read a book mostly. Sometimes he'd talk to someone.'

'Women?'

'Yeah.'

'Hazel says he was in conversation last Wednesday.'

Lloyd looked at Hazel. 'You know the one,' she said. 'Big-faced. Short hair. I figured maybe she was a dyke.'

'She *is* a dyke, Hazel. I told you that. That's Diane Lawton. He was talking to her?'

'Sure was.'

'Wasting his time then,' the manager said, evidently baffled. 'I guess some guys are just plain dumb.'

Hazel gave him a look that would have scorched paint.

'You got a phone book in the bar, sir?' Nina asked.

The manager led her and Reidel over to the door. While they were inside I waited in the lot with the waitress.

She accepted my offer of another cigarette, in no evident hurry to get inside. 'You figure it's someone from Thornton?'

'Or nearby. This Lawton woman seem good for it to you?'

She frowned, surprised to be asked. 'Well, no, not at all. But I mean, I don't know about people who kill people. There's got to be something about them, right? You'd be able to see it?'

'Not really,' I said.

'For real? You known some killers?'

'A few.'

'What are they like?'

'Same as you or me. But they kill people.'

'But then . . . how come?'

'Got me,' I said. 'That's just the way it is.'

'I had a boyfriend once,' she said, after a moment. 'Seemed like he might hurt somebody some day. Just something about him, like, sometimes he looked at his hands funny. But he never did, far as I know. We broke up and one night he came around and sat in my yard. Didn't shout or nothing. Just sat out there. I thought that would be the night, but then he went away.'

'What happened after that?'

'Nothing,' she said. 'I'd see him around. Couple years later he got killed in a car wreck.' She shrugged. 'Don't know why I told you that.'

Nina and Reidel came back out. Nina stopped with Hazel a moment and thanked her for her time. 'I'd appreciate it if you didn't speak to anybody about this,' she said. 'At this stage all we want to do is eliminate Ms Lawton from the investigation.'

'You got it,' Hazel said, standing on her cigarette butt. 'Thanks for the smoke,' she added to me, and headed off towards the bar.

'Been making friends?' Nina asked.

'You know me,' I said. 'I'm hard to resist.'

Diane Lawton lived in a small house about a mile from the Mayflower, back into Thornton proper. It was twenty after nine by the time we got there but a compact car in the driveway suggested she was still at home. That, and some music wafting out of an open kitchen window. Light, baroque, with an oboe wandering happily around over the top. Bach, most likely, and probably enough to make her neighbours look at her sideways all by itself. Kids' toys littered the front yards of the houses either side.

Nina knocked on the side door and it was opened almost immediately by a woman who matched the description we had been given.

'Ms Lawton?'

The woman looked at us and nodded. She was about thirty with a round face and one of those mouths that seem forever on the verge of movement. You had to look hard to realize there were shadows under her eyes and that the movement the corners of her mouth were most prone to make wouldn't necessarily be upward.

'Yes,' she said. 'And you are?'

Nina held up her ID. 'Do you mind if we come in?'

'I'm on my way to work.'

'It should only take five minutes.'

'Should?'

Nina looked at her steadily. 'Ma'am, like it says on the badge, I'm with the FBI. We tolerate backchat on television for dramatic purposes. Not so much in real life.'

Lawton stood back and let us in. Her kitchen was homely and

full of macramé plant hangers and pottery storage jars that had been made either by enthusiastic amateurs or those undergoing occupational therapy in facilities with high walls.

She picked up a remote and muted the music. 'What's this about?'

Nina held up a picture. 'Do you recognize this man?'

Lawton smiled tightly. 'His name's Larry. I shouldn't be at all surprised if he's married.'

'He was. But he's dead now.'

Ms Lawton stared. 'Really? Wow.'

'You haven't heard about the body found in Raynor's Wood?'

'No. I was out of town all weekend. What happened?'

'That's what we're about finding out,' Reidel said. 'Some folks at the Mayflower say you were talking to him Wednesday night.'

'People round here do take a lively interest in other people's business, don't they? Yes, sure, we spoke for a while. He came and sat next to me.'

'Did you leave with him?'

'No, I did not.'

'Is that because of, uh, an incompatibility?'

Ms Lawton sighed. 'I work for a women's refuge in Dryford, Detective, because there are times when women need refuge. I'm not from around here and I wear my hair short because I hate it when it gets in my eyes – and also because I happen to think it looks nice that way. Probably I'm wrong about that, but I'm not actually a lesbian. Okay?'

'It's none of our business,' Nina said, glaring at Reidel, 'and personally I wouldn't blame you. Given the alternative.'

'I didn't leave the bar with him because I'm not in the habit of one-night stands. If I was then I'd've rolled out of there on the arm of enough good ol' boys that people would know where my interests lie. It also didn't happen because he was an asshole.'

'In what way?'

'*He* came over, bought *me* a drink, and then spent the entire time staring over my shoulder at someone else. Finally he said it'd been

143

nice, still not even *looking* at me, and then just left to go talk to her. Okay? That a sad enough story for you? Woman gets hit on and then the guy realizes what a dull lot she is and takes the hit back so he can trade it up?'

'It would be a sad story,' I said, 'if that's what it meant. Married guys who trawl bars are not looking for a mental workout. He spotted an easier mark, that's all. Either way he's been dismembered now, so I guess you win.'

She blinked at me.

'What did this other woman look like?' Nina asked.

'She had long hair,' Lawton muttered, as if this explained everything dire about the world. 'She was slim and *pretty* and she had long hair and it was red as all hell. A real fireball, I'm sure.'

Reidel looked up from his pad. 'Excuse me?'

'She was drunk, though,' the woman added, not trying to keep the spite out of her voice. 'So maybe you're right. I suspect she would have been an easier job than me. Like falling off a log.'

'Ma'am,' Reidel interrupted firmly. 'You said red hair, is that correct?'

'I did say that, yes.'

'You don't know her name?'

'No. But I've seen her in there before. A few times. Sits way in the back and slugs it down all night long.'

'Age?'

Lawton shrugged. 'Don't know. Mid-twenties?'

'Did you see her leave on Wednesday night?'

'Well of course,' Lawton said, as if we were all being unbelievably dim-witted. 'She left with lover-boy. I thought that was your whole point?'

There was a moment of silence, and then Reidel walked right out of the house.

Nina wrapped quickly and hurried outside after him. I followed. Reidel was already on the phone down by his car.

'What's up?' I said.

Nina's face was pinched. 'Do me a favour,' she said. 'Go back to the bar. See if that waitress recalls someone of this description being there that night or any other. Call me as soon as you know.'

'Has Reidel got something?'

'No,' she said. 'Or I hope not. But if I don't contain it fast then word is going to spread and someone's life is screwed anyway.'

Reidel closed his phone. 'I called Monroe,' he said. 'He'll meet us there.'

Then they were in Reidel's car and gone.

I drove back to the bar and went inside. It was cold and dark and had been garnished with nets, presumably in the belief that the *Mayflower* had played a key early role in America's fishing industry. The interior was long and thin and I could see why you'd come here if you wanted to drink somewhere other than home without it being general knowledge.

Hazel was desultorily cleaning the bar, or at least redistributing its grime. 'Hello again,' she said. 'If you're looking for Lloyd he's on the phone in back. Matter of national security, I believe.'

'Actually it was you I wanted to ask something.'

'Ask away.'

'If I say "slim, decent-looking, red hair", does it ring any bells?'

She nodded. 'Sure. We got one of those.'

'Friendly type?'

'No. Very much one of the "I'm not here" crowd.'

'She in here last Wednesday?'

She thought a moment. 'Maybe. Yeah, could have been, actually. She'd have been down the end, though. I was stuck up here. I can't be a hundred per cent.'

'Don't suppose you've got a name for her?'

''Fraid not. Sometimes you overhear and sometimes people will do the bluff handshake and hi-I'm-Bill thing, like that changes the fact they're drinking alone, but if you want to be convivial you'll go to one of the bars in town.'

'Would shithead know?'

She smiled. 'He might. He has this *mine host* act, when he can be bothered. Especially if they're cute. She'd count. Go ask him.'

I went down the corridor and found a door ajar. Beyond was a small office. The manager was stuffed into a chair with his feet on the desk. He was talking close into the phone and grinning in an unappealing way. He frowned and cupped his hand over the mouthpiece when he saw me.

'What do you want now?'

'Customer of yours. Red hair, attractive. Name?'

He gave me a couple of possibilities, cast doubt on her sexual preferences in either event, and then pointed out he was busy and the bar wasn't open yet and it would be nice if I could leave.

'A pleasure,' I said. 'By the way, women don't have to be gay to say no to you. And if they are, they deserve your respect.'

He stared at me as if I'd started speaking Swahili with a bad accent. 'Whatever,' I said. 'Have a nice life.'

I walked out into the lot and got Nina on the phone.

'And?' she said.

'Regular customer who keeps her head way down. Hazel can't say for sure about Wednesday night.'

'Did you get a name?' Her voice sounded tight.

'Only the first, and the manager's not certain,' I said. 'He evidently tried it on with her once or twice and failed.'

'What is it, Ward?'

'He thought it was either Julie or Julia.' There was a silence. 'Nina? Bear in mind the guy's an idiot.'

'I'll call you later,' she said, and the line went dead.

There was radio silence for the next four hours. I parked up in the historic district and killed time with breakfast and a chain of coffees. The local paper had a non-piece about Lawrence Widmar, glossing the facts of his discovered condition and majoring on his triumphs as a local businessman. It was too early for anything on the body found the previous night. Too early and . . . maybe something else.

146

Two of the people we'd spoken to that morning had no idea of the identity of a man who'd been found naked in the local woods a couple days ago. Okay, Diane Lawton wasn't exactly plugged into the town – but women who work in bars generally know what's going down. As Nina had pointed out in the small hours of the morning, this place now had two corpses lying in its morgue: but as I watched the people walk up and down, I didn't get a sense of a place that had been shaken to its core.

I tried calling Nina and got no response. I didn't have numbers for Monroe or Reidel and doubted they'd talk to me anyway. As I scrolled futilely up and down through my tiny list of stored numbers, I went past John Zandt's, and paused. Nina and I had both tried calling him over the last five months, never received a response. It rang, but no answer. You could leave a message, but he never called back. I still had an odd feeling about the idea of communicating with Mr Unger. Was it worth mentioning his name to Zandt to check it wasn't a name he'd come across? The last time I'd seen him it had been evident that – however crackpot a lot of it had sounded – Zandt had done heavy research into the Straw Men. If nothing else it would ensure someone else knew Unger's name if anything happened to me.

I sent John a quick SMS text message. Two minutes later the phone pinged to let me know it had been delivered, but there was no further response.

'Yeah, and fuck you too,' I muttered, startling a waitress. I went and bought my next coffee somewhere else.

I was sitting drinking it on a bench opposite a small park and considering heading back to the hotel when my phone rang. It wasn't Nina and it wasn't Zandt.

'Hello,' I said, sitting up straight.

'Is that Ward Hopkins?'

'Yeah, it is.'

'Carl Unger. Look, first, I'm real sorry to hear about Bobby. He was a good man. How did it happen?'

147

'He was murdered,' I said.

'Okay,' he said, evenly. 'Well, we'll get into that when we meet. Where are you?'

'You tell me,' I said.

'I don't have a trace on your cell, Ward. I'm asking because I want to talk to you and I don't want to do it over the phone.'

'Why?'

'That's a funny question from someone who used to monitor personal communications on a professional basis. Look, work with me here. I'm just trying to figure out a place to meet.'

'How about Greensboro?' I said. 'North Carolina.'

'Okay,' he said, immediately. 'Can you do tonight? I can be there probably around seven.'

'Call me when you land. By the way, what colour's your hair these days? You were going pretty grey last time, I think.'

'Mr Hopkins,' he said, patiently. 'We've never met. I joined the company a year after you left. Only reason I know your name is through Bobby, okay? If I can find one I'll wear a pink carnation. Otherwise I'll just stand up and wave.'

I cut the connection feeling foolish. If the guy was coming to kill me he was likely to succeed, on the basis of my cunning so far. I'd picked Greensboro partly because it's easy to get to by plane, mainly because it was in a different state to where we really were. I had been hoping to hear something in his voice suggesting he knew I wasn't near there, which would have shown he was running a cell-locate after all. I'd heard nothing of the kind. Greensboro was at least two hours' drive from Thornton, moreover, which would be a royal pain in the ass. I thought back over the conversation and realized he knew when I'd been with the company and what my job had been. Also that he could shoot me in Greensboro just as easily as anywhere else.

I hit the button to call his number back.

'Hey,' he said. 'What's up?'

'Change of plan,' I said. 'It would be a lot easier for me to get to a place called Owensville. Couple hours north-east of Greensboro, in Virginia. Can you do that?'

'No problem. Call it eight thirty or nine, though.'

I sat for a while, staring across the street and hoping I hadn't made a huge mistake.

The phone rang again. It was Nina. She sounded mad.

Chapter 14

'She'll be here in less than an hour,' Nina said, as she led me into a corridor of the Thornton sheriff's small office, where she paused for a second outside a closed door. 'There are cops out scraping together a line-up, but finding enough people with the right colour hair is proving tough.'

'I think I passed a candidate on the way in,' I said. Through a reinforced glass panel I could see the down-turned face of a woman in her twenties. 'The woman in the lobby is a few decades older and runs two hundred fifty pounds,' I said. 'No one's going to confuse her for the person you've got in there. Or believe she was someone Larry Widmar might work his charm on.'

'I know.'

'Diane Lawton in particular isn't going to think that.'

'No shit. Which is why Julia Gulicks is going to be under arrest very soon.'

A little further down the corridor was an unmarked door. Nina opened it and we entered a twilit room with a big one-way mirror on the right-hand wall. Reidel was standing leaning against the back. He and Nina went into quiet conference.

I took a better look at the woman who was about to become the chief suspect in a double homicide case. She was sitting behind a characterless metal and plywood table. Her face was still lowered, and I wondered whether she was looking at the table's scarred surface and absorbing its message. It was the table of bad news. It was a table whose presence said you were somewhere you really didn't want to be. Even the meanest restaurant would cover it with a chequered cloth.

After a few moments she looked up. You had to notice her hair first. It was long and wavy and an unusual colour: a natural red, but with a dark warmth, less like fire than a flow of deoxygenated blood. Her face had the peachy paleness that goes with such colouring, and her bone structure was good. Her build was medium-slim. She was wearing a sharp, dark business suit. She looked contained and composed. You could just about make her for involvement in some minor but complex corporate fraud of a type you'd never quite understand. Not for what I'd seen out in the barrens the night before.

On the other hand, as I'd told Hazel, you never knew.

'No lawyer?' I asked.

Reidel shrugged. 'Says she doesn't need one.'

'She doesn't look much like someone who hangs out in bars.'

'No,' Nina said. 'And Mark Kroeger says he's barely seen her drink. Two small glasses max per evening, leaves half of the second one.'

'Old alcoholic trick,' Reidel said. 'Hold back in public and when you get home yank the bottles out the laundry hamper.'

'Who's Kroeger?'

'Guy she was with when they found the body in Raynor's Wood.'

'Is he here?'

Reidel shook his head.

'So you're pretty convinced the woman in there did it,' I said.

151

'And that she didn't have an accomplice? Someone to help her carry two heavy male bodies quite a distance?'

'These are crimes of a type committed by a single individual,' he said. 'But thanks for the input.'

'That woman's got the reddest hair I've ever seen,' I said. 'It's like she's got a major head wound. Don't you think she might have made some effort to mitigate a feature that distinctive?'

'Not if Widmar's murder was an impulsive act, no.'

'But it wasn't. The bloods came back with traces of a date-rape drug. That doesn't say spur-of-the-moment. And if the body in the forest with all the flesh hacked off it is supposed to be hers too, then I'd say you can throw crime-of-convenience out of the window. And that time-lines before Widmar, right?'

'Remind me,' Reidel said, distantly. 'On whose authority are you here?'

'Mine,' Nina said.

'We'll see how Monroe feels about that.'

Nina turned away. Even in the low light she looked tired and unhappy. There was something wrong.

Monroe arrived twenty minutes later, flushed and ready to be televisual. Nina convinced him to wait until Diane Lawton had been given a look at the suspect, and to reinforce the press embargo in ad hoc operation.

They kept Lawton waiting forty minutes while they went through a debate over the women in the assembled line-up. Only one had genuinely red hair, the large lady I'd already seen. Two were variably auburn, the others plain brown – and none were packing locks in the same quantity as Julia Gulicks. Nina held her ground. A compromise was reached involving getting the women to tie their hair back.

'Agent Baynam's doing a bang-up job of defending her client,' Reidel said, by now genuinely angry. 'I thought we were in the business of establishing guilt. Or am I missing something here?'

Monroe went into the interview room and advised Gulicks to

152

request an attorney. She declined once again. He explained that representation was her right, that such a request would not be taken as evidence of guilt, and that her position could become serious much more easily without adequate counsel. She shook her head. I heard her voice for the first time over the intercom.

'I didn't do anything wrong,' she said. 'And I'm not even under arrest, am I?'

Monroe came back into the viewing room. 'We're doing it now,' he said. 'She's had her chance.'

The other five women were brought into the room and arranged. Gulicks wound up in a position second from the left. A screen was pulled down over the glass.

Then Diane Lawton was brought into the observation room. Monroe explained her role and reminded her that she was not to feel that she had to pick someone out: also that if she did make a selection, she had to be frank about her degree of confidence in that choice. She nodded. She got it.

Reidel leaned forward and raised the screen.

They'd done the best they could. Lighting in the room had been adjusted to prevent the women's hair colour from being too apparent. Tying it back made a difference too, pulling attention on to the facial features. I knew exactly where Gulicks was standing in the line, and it still took me a beat to pick her out again.

Lawton slowly turned her head to scan along the row from left to right, pausing for a couple of seconds on every face. Then she went back the other way.

Monroe was watching her face carefully. 'Are you able to pick someone out?'

'Yes,' she said.

'How confident are you?'

'One hundred per cent. It's not like Wednesday was the first time I ever saw her.'

'This is not just about whether you've seen someone in the

Mayflower,' Nina said, firmly. 'On that night or any other. It's specifically concerning who you saw with Lawrence Widmar last Wednesday, and who you believe he left the bar with.'

'I know that,' Lawton said. 'It's her. It's number two.'

Monroe nodded. Reidel smiled from ear to ear. Nina looked down at the floor.

Lawton was taken to another room to provide a formal statement. Police in Owensville had been asked to collect Mark Kroeger and bring him over for further questioning concerning the night of his last date with Gulicks. Monroe had gone to obtain a warrant for Gulicks' apartment and car, and to initiate the search of those areas. Two local cops had been dispatched to the Mayflower to elicit further witnesses for the previous Wednesday evening.

Everyone had been told to keep it as quiet as possible. So far it was holding. It wouldn't last, and as soon as the media got hold of it any trail of evidence would be irrelevant. News editors and couch potatoes are our keenest legal minds these days, it appears. I watched through the glass as Julia Gulicks was arrested on suspicion of the murder of Lawrence Widmar. She was offered and declined yet again the opportunity to contact a legal representative. She requested and was provided with a glass of water.

Reidel sat at one end of the table. Nina at the other. Gulicks looked pale but composed. Paleness could be the result of the strip light in the room. Composed appeared to be her natural state. Cold, even.

Reidel did the talking. 'You understand why you've been arrested?'

'You have a witness who claims I was in a bar with a man on Wednesday night.'

'We believe you met Mr Widmar in the Mayflower bar mid to late evening. That you drank and conversed with him for some time. Our witness says you left the bar together around eleven.'

'And then what?'

'Excuse me?'

'What happened then?'

'You tell me.'

'I have *no idea*. I have never been to this bar. I never met this man while he was alive. Your witness is just plain wrong.'

'You've never been to the Mayflower?'

'I'm not in the habit of drinking alone in bars.'

'Yes or no, Ms Gulicks.'

'No.'

'You sure you want to be that black and white about it?'

'I have no conception of what you mean.'

'What he means,' Nina said, 'is that we obtained your name from the manager. Who is not the person who just picked you out, but an additional witness we'll get a statement from later this evening. If you claim you've never been in the Mayflower, and two in-dependent witnesses say you have, you're not in a good position. Confirming that you frequent the bar is not an admission of anything else. Your case would be best served by avoiding simple untruths at this or any other stage.'

'Okay,' Gulicks said, nodding slowly. 'Thanks for the translation, scary lady. But I've still never been there.'

'You should listen to what the agent is telling you,' Reidel said. 'She's your unofficial counsel here. Having seen the body, I'm less inclined to cut you any slack.'

'I saw it too,' Gulicks said. 'And what hasn't been explained to me yet, even *a little bit*, is why I would have led someone straight to it. And then called the police, and waited until they came. I want to know why you think I would have done that.'

'In an attempt to establish innocence. You met Lawrence Widmar in the bar. At some stage you introduced a substance into his drink to impair his judgement. You left together and got into your car. You drove someplace, very likely the lot above Raynor's Wood. You murdered the victim and dragged his body down the slope to the position where it was discovered. At some point during the night or next day you realized you could lead your friend from your office to the scene under the guise of a romantic encounter, and thus

155

appear to be a bystander discovering the body. Kind of clever, but also kind of dumb.'

'Dumb is right,' Gulicks said, staring at him. 'You've got to be on drugs. That's the most ridiculous thing I've ever heard. On the basis of my hair colour you're going to file charges on that?'

'Not yet. We don't have to,' Reidel said, standing. 'We have three days. If we need an extension after that, we'll get one.'

Gulicks turned to Nina. 'But . . . you've got no evidence.'

'We'll get it,' Reidel said. He paused, looking down at her. 'And then we'll start on body number two.'

She stammered, just a little. 'What?'

'The other dead man. Guess you didn't realize we'd found him too.'

'I don't know what you're talking about.'

'That line's getting old, Julia. Don't worry – I'll keep explaining myself. Sooner or later you'll get what I'm talking about, and how serious we are.'

Julia Gulicks suddenly looked very young, and confused, and as if she had at that moment understood this afternoon was not just going to fade away of its own accord: that at least one of the people in the room with her really did think she was a murderer, and wasn't going to stop until he'd proved it.

She sat back in her chair and folded her arms. 'I would like to talk to a lawyer now,' she said.

She was left in the room with the door locked and a cop outside. Reidel went to expedite an attorney and to give Gulicks some time to stew in a small room with a very depressing table in it.

I took Nina out into the street for some fresh air, and so I could have a cigarette. When you can't even smoke in police stations you know the *Zeitgeist* has won. Nina's phone rang as we hit the pavement. She picked up and listened for a while.

'They got the warrant,' she said, when she was done. 'Gulicks' place is about to be turned upside down.'

'So hopefully they find nothing,' I said.

Nina just shook her head, but I couldn't tell what this meant. It was coming up for six o'clock.

'I got to go soon,' I said. 'I want to get there in plenty of time, size up a safe location before this Unger guy hits town.'

'I can't come with you,' she said.

'I know. I wasn't expecting it.'

'I wanted to cover your back.'

'You will,' I said. 'I'll hear your voice.'

'Tell me how careful you're going to be.'

'Careful. They'll be calling me Ward "Careful" Hopkins. I'll be a new byword for caution. There will be timid nocturnal forest creatures with big eyes, pointing and sniggering and calling me disrespectful names, all on account of my excessive prudence.'

'Seriously, Ward.'

'Yeah,' I said. 'I know.'

'Beep me before you go in.'

'I will.' I took her hand. 'Don't worry about me. Just go back in there and sort this thing.'

'Do you think she did it?'

'Nina, I don't know. It's not my job to even make a judgement. I'm just a civilian.'

'You know that woman I told you about?'

'What about her?'

'I think I fell asleep before I finished. Year and a half after she killed herself with the spoon, they pulled some guy over on a DUI in a place fifty miles from Janesville. Turned out he had a bunch of drugs and a couple of guns in the back of the car, wrapped in a bloodstained coat. So they brought him in. In the end they nailed him for a murder up in North Dakota.'

'So?'

'They also eventually made him for the killing of one of the dead guys in Janesville. Just a plain vanilla robbery-homicide, it turned out.' She smiled tightly. 'She didn't do it after all.'

'She didn't do that one,' I said. 'You don't know about the rest.'

'She was innocent on a charge of which she was convicted. That's enough. The case should have been . . .'

'Yes, Nina, but it was too late by then and that was her fault. Tell me something, honey – why are you here?'

'You know why.'

'No, I really don't. You wound up in law enforcement because of this one case, it seems to me, and it still screws with your head. Monroe knows this, and yet *this* is the job he wants to pull you back into the fold for? Why?'

'To stop the same thing happening to some other woman.'

'Maybe,' I said. 'Or perhaps because he wants a babe on board to make sure he's covered if it all gets politicized.'

I glanced across the street. A little way up it a car was parked. Two guys who were obviously reporters were standing by it. Thirty yards further along was a windowless white van that could easily hold covert TV cameras, or a whole nest of journalists ready to pounce. 'Look. Someone leaked already. It won't be long before this is coast to coast.'

'All the more reason.'

'Okay. All I'm saying is don't get pulled in too deep.'

'Right. Take it easy. Look after number one. Don't worry too much if the wrong person goes down.'

'That's not what I mean and you know it. I'm just saying the world will do what the world always does.'

'Thanks, Yoda,' she snapped. 'That's real heart-warming. So maybe you should just shrug and forget what happened to your parents, too. Nothing you can do about it now, after all.'

'That's not the same. They were my family.'

'Everybody is someone's family, Ward. Everybody, everywhere, at all times. It isn't about blood ties. It can't be. Otherwise we're all just Straw Men. Either people look after strangers and treat them like they matter, or the whole world goes down.'

'You're right.' I held up my hands. 'You'll do what you want to do. My advice is notoriously worthless anyhow. I'll let you know how I'm doing, okay? I'll call when it's done and I'll be back at the hotel soon as I can.'

She nodded, but didn't say anything. I walked away, feeling like I was going in the wrong direction.

Just before I turned the corner I looked back. She was still standing on the pavement outside the station. After a moment she raised her hand a little and waved, and something around her wrist glinted softly. I waved back.

She mouthed two words. I mouthed back that I would be.

Then I went off to meet a guy.

Chapter 15

Brad's heart turned over in a slow, laboured beat as soon as Mrs Luchs came out of the house. Karen's mother usually moved in a measured fashion. It was one of the distinctive things about her, like the fact that – uniquely amongst his friends' parents – she was a little overweight. Not fat, of course, and she carried those few extra pounds in a way which gave her more presence than the stick-insect treadmill martyrs. It was like a declaration she was sufficiently centred she didn't feel it necessary to slog herself off to the gym every day. Or, in her case, to pad downstairs to the one in the basement of her own house.

When she came out now she was walking with purpose, however, and a little too fast. Maybe he read it in her face, too, a subliminal signal that something unpredicted had come into her polished life.

Or perhaps he'd just been waiting for it.

It was a little after four and Brad was sitting out by their pool. Karen was swimming methodically from end to end. She'd just thrashed forty lengths and was winding down. She'd been a fixture on the swim team in school and still seemed to take it seriously. Brad wasn't sure why.

'Karen,' her mother said. 'Some policemen are here.'

Brad's stomach immediately went to battery acid. Karen came to the side and lifted herself out in one fluid motion. Sun sparkled off the water as it fell, and off the swinging K of the necklace.

She grabbed a towel. 'Cops? Why?'

'I don't know, dear. But they would like to talk to you.'

Two guys in casual suits had walked across the grass a few yards behind her. 'Okay,' Karen said. 'I guess.'

The detectives were largely indistinguishable from each other except one had a moustache and the other had paler skin, like he made an effort to keep out of the sun. The first held out a badge.

'Detective Cascoli,' he said. 'Karen Luchs?'

'Yes,' she said.

The cop looked at Brad. 'And you are?'

'Brad Metzger,' he said. His voice sounded fine.

'How about that?' the detective said. He got out a pad and flipped through it, tapped a page with his finger. 'There you go. Bradley M. You're on our list too.'

Mrs Luchs folded her arms a little tighter. 'What's this about?'

The cop ignored her, but politely, as befitted the size of her house. 'You're both friends of a guy called Peter Voss?'

'Well, yeah,' Karen said. 'Pete, yes of course. Why? Is he okay?'

'We don't know that, Ms Luchs, because we don't know where Peter is. He didn't return home on Saturday evening. Apparently he sometimes stays over with friends, so, whatever. But he didn't come back yesterday, or call home. So last night his parents got in touch with us.'

'Oh God,' Mrs Luchs said, her hand hovering around her throat. 'Really?'

'When was the last time you saw him?'

161

'Saturday night,' Karen said. Her voice was cramped and she sounded shocked. 'There was the party here, as I guess you know. Pete was around early, but then he went somewhere else.'

'Do you know where?'

Karen shook her head, looked at Brad.

'No idea,' he said. 'I saw him at the beginning, and then later he just wasn't around. We got some burgers and were looking for him, in case he wanted one, but I guess he'd already split.'

'Peter's mother said he got a lift to your party with someone called Andy.'

'Yes,' said Karen. 'They all got here together, that's right. But Andy was around to the bitter end. He always is.'

'And then he drove home?'

'He doesn't drink much,' Karen said, quickly. 'And actually, I think Monica drove. Yeah, I remember that. Definitely.'

The cop looked at her. 'Right.'

While he made a note on his pad, the other detective spoke for the first time.

'Mr Metzger,' he said. 'Some people we spoke to said you and Pete are good buddies. That correct?'

'Well, yeah,' Brad said. 'I mean, Pete's everybody's friend. But yeah, I guess you could say that. We hang out.'

'You don't know where he went after the party?'

'No.'

'And you didn't hear anything from him since?'

'No. I mean, I figured he slung out to some other party, got wasted, spent yesterday sleeping it through. I'd've called him this evening or something, maybe.'

'Would you characterize him as a person who gets intoxicated on a regular basis?'

'Peter Voss is a nice young man,' Mrs Luchs said. 'He's always extremely civil.'

'What we're trying to establish,' Cascoli said, 'Is whether he might have got himself into some trouble. Got a ride from someone he

162

didn't know too well, ended up in the wrong place, wound up in a bad situation.'

'It's possible,' Brad said. Everyone turned to look at him. 'I mean, I'm just saying, Pete's a friendly guy. He'll talk to anyone. It's what's cool about him. But . . . you know, he could have spoken to the wrong person, somewhere. I could see that happening.'

'Has this occurred before, that you're aware of?'

'No,' Brad said. His hands felt sweaty against his thighs. He crossed his arms. 'No. I'm just saying, you know, it's possible. But he's probably just hanging someplace, right?'

'Let's hope so,' the cop said. 'Because otherwise I think his mother is likely to go clean out of her mind.'

He closed his pad and put it back in his pocket. Got out his wallet and handed them both a card. 'You hear anything from him, call me,' he said. 'Tell him it doesn't matter if he's in trouble. We just need to let his mom know he's okay.'

Brad and Karen nodded in unison. Mrs Luchs led the policemen back up towards the house. The men looked like they should be carrying something for her.

'Well that's not good,' Karen said. 'God, I hope Pete's all right.'

'He'll be fine,' Brad said. 'You know Sleepy.'

'Maybe I should call around. Check if anyone's seen him. You know?' She grabbed her phone off the table, finger ready to speed dial. 'What do you think?'

'The cops are doing that already.'

'But we could get people out looking for him. Checking places, people's houses, key stores. Places the cops might not think of.'

Brad nodded. 'Yeah, why not, good idea.'

Karen sat cross-legged on the grass and started dialling, safe in the assumption that Pete just needed rooting out – and that she was the girl with the can-do to do it.

Brad waited for an excruciating twenty minutes. When she hung up her sixth call he said he'd remembered he had to run an errand for his dad. He'd call her later, see if she'd found anything out.

She was talking to somebody else before he even reached the house.

'We're fucked.'

'We're not fucked.'

'We are so fucked, Lee. We're *fucked.*'

'Why are we fucked, Brad? Answer me that. Tell me precisely how and why we are fucked.'

They were standing in the kitchen of Lee's house. As always it was eerily tidy, like a kitchen in a show home. Brad had never understood how Lee managed to keep it that way, even given the fact he never cooked. Everyday life messed things up after a while. Chaos encroached. Brad just shook his head. 'We're fucked,' he said, quietly.

Outside, Lee's car sat in the driveway. It too looked like an advertisement for the whole concept of 'clean'.

'The guy's gone missing,' Lee said patiently. 'The cops were always going to talk to his friends. Point two, Karen held the party which was his last known location. So they're going to talk to her too. All of this is predictable. The cops will soon come to figure he's just blown off somewhere and he'll be back, but in the meantime they've got to go through the motions.'

'But he won't be coming back,' Brad said. 'Remember? *He's not going to be coming back.*'

'I know that. But so long as he's gone, he's just gone. Nothing more. Pete's a world-class stoner. They'll already know that about him. I tell you now that their assumption will be that he just lit off. Figured he'd go snowboard pro and headed for Colorado. Or he's asleep under some skanky chick nobody knows about and will be back when he has to borrow some cash. They have to look busy but they'll lose interest soon enough. Cops are poor and live in crappy little houses and they hate people like us.'

'*She* won't, though,' Brad said. 'Pete's mom won't lose interest. Ever.'

At that moment he got a mental image of her, strong enough to make the real world fade away. Maria Voss was small and slight – Pete's dad had contributed all of his son's height and bulk – and she had long black hair and big brown eyes. The vision held for a second and then suddenly her eyes were full of tears, full in the way the ocean was full. Brad had never seen this happen in real life, but he knew exactly how it would look. Her face started to crumple and he could almost hear the scream that was fighting its way out of her mouth.

'Lee, this is real bad.'

'Nothing has changed. Brad, listen to me. Nothing has altered since the moment the bullet went into his head.'

Brad flinched. 'Christ, man, that's . . . cold.'

'*Listen to me.* You've got to get your mind around what's happened here. All this was going to happen right from that moment. We can't go back before the bullet, so we have to live in the world that comes afterwards. This is not our fault.'

'Of course it's our fault.'

'We didn't kill him.'

'We took him out there. We should have, we should have . . .'

'What? We should have *what*? What could we have done?'

'We shouldn't just have dumped him.'

Hudek shook his head firmly, a man who either believed he was right or who was simply no longer countenancing alternative views.

'Hernandez nailed it. Once it happened, there was nothing else to do. Pete was already dead. There was no point us going down with him, and that's all that would have happened.'

'Hernandez, right, yeah. Our good buddy. Has he called yet? Have we heard anything out of these so-called friends of ours?'

'No. But we will.'

'You're dreaming, Lee. We're nothing but a problem to them now. We're baggage. We're fucked.'

Hudek reached up and took him by the shoulders. Just looked into his eyes. Brad looked back, and all he saw there was calmness and strength of purpose. Slowly he started breathing more easily.

'Go home,' Lee said. 'Take a nap. Jerk off. Play some Xbox. Do whatever the fuck you have to do, but chill out.'

Brad went home. He tried some Xbox, and only then realized that almost every single game he owned involved shooting people. He didn't want to do that. He tried a driving game instead but it just meant going round and round in circles, and his head felt like it was already dizzy. In the end he lay on his bed. From there he could see his photo boards. They were covered in pictures from the last five years, at first laid out neatly and then just all over, on top of each other and four deep in some places. Parties, big school events, snaps of everybody hanging out. Good nights, happy days. Pete was there, of course. There was one of him and Brad in the back of Lee's old car. One of him in Brad's back yard. One of a bunch of them after a big game back at school, arms around each other, mouths wide in victorious bellows.

Eighteen months ago. Was it really only that long?

His phone rang. It was Steve Verkilen, the guy who'd lain in a parking lot next to Pete with duct tape around his mouth. He was breathless.

'Shit, dude. You heard? I just had Pete's mom on the phone. She sounded way strung out.'

'I heard,' Brad said, evenly. 'The cops came by Karen's. You any idea where he is?'

'Not a clue, man. Not a *clue*. Haven't seen him in days. Was supposed to meet up with him at Karen's party but I was wiped and didn't make it.'

'Yeah, well, he was there,' Brad said, thinking: spread the consensus. 'Then he split. Nobody knows anything after that.'

'Weird shit.'

'Yep.'

'Was going to call Lee, see if he heard.'

'I just came from there. You know Pete. He's out there some-where. Probably just lost his fucking phone.'

'Yeah.' There was a pause. 'We going to be doing a pickup this week, though? If Pete doesn't show up?'

'I don't know.'

'Well, keep me in the loop, okay? I need the money.'

Steve went away, leaving Brad to wonder what in fact they *would* do about the week's pickup. Hernandez seemed to have gone to ground. Steve wasn't the only one who needed the money. But could they just do it? Business as usual despite everything?

He lay on his back a little longer, trying to work things out, and then decided he didn't want to be able to see the pictures on his wall. He rolled onto his front, eyes closed, breathing the familiar smell of his sheets. Like Lee said, until they found something, there was no crime. Brad nodded to himself reassuringly, his forehead rustling on the sheets, and gradually started to feel okay. He turned over onto his back again and stared up at the ceiling for a while and eventually sat up and swung his legs off the bed. He felt tired and yet rested when he stood up, and even a little hungry. He decided to head downstairs, see if there were some Fritos in the cupboards. There generally were. Things just appeared. He walked along the upper gallery and down the stairs and realized he seemed to be alone in the house. His mother had been there when he got home, and his sister too, playing Smash Mouth way too loud. He walked into the kitchen and was surprised by how tidy it was. Usually a contained chaos was the Metzger family MO. This afternoon it looked like Lee's place, tidy all over, the Sub Zero gleaming like new, nothing even on the kitchen table, which had long been the eventual resting place of everything in the household that wasn't nailed down somewhere else. He opened the cupboard that usually harboured potato chips and found it empty. Completely, without even any dust. So that's where they'd gone – to the supermarket. Done a spring clean, now time to restock. Figures. He opened the next cupboard. It was empty too. He quickly moved around them all, and found it the same everywhere. A very serious spring clean, evidently. Though it was September, of course. A fall clean, then.

He heard a noise and turned to see where it was coming from. It was hard to describe, sort of like a quiet chewing sound. It sounded like it was coming from the back yard. Brad went to the window to look and realized it was night. He must have fallen asleep on the bed upstairs. Though . . . hadn't it been daylight five minutes before, when he looked out front to check for his mother's car?

Brad walked quickly back to the front of the house. It was clean in here too, he realized. Very, very clean. No magazines, no newspapers, no television remotes, and out the front it was still day. There was something wrong about this arrangement, but he couldn't put his finger on what it was. So he turned to deal with the other thing, the chewing/rustling he could still hear from out back. It didn't seem any louder but it didn't seem like it was going to stop either. He headed back into the kitchen and out through the big doors into the yard. It was very dark and cold outside but there was no wind. There were trees, however, ranks of tall trees which came right up to the back of the house. A few even seemed to spike up through the roof from the inside. He thought he could hear a stream too, somewhere not far away. There was an unusual smell. It was cinnamon, and sugar, and something else he couldn't get. He walked between the trees but nothing seemed to get any closer. There was a mole problem, though. Wherever you looked there were pathways running under the surface of the forest floor, like a network of swollen veins. They were moving. This was what was making the chewing sound, and as they shifted it was as if the ground itself seemed to become transparent. There were people under there, too. They were lying flat and their eyes were closed and most were missing something. The smell seemed to get stronger and Brad realized first that there was the scent of apples, and finally that what he could smell was a pie. A slim McDonald's apple pie, specifically, the kind that came with the warning that the contents were very fucking hot. None of the bodies had anything in their hands or in their mouths. There must be a pie somewhere, though. You could smell it. *Anyone* could smell it, Brad realized, his heart going cold.

If someone came out here they couldn't help but work out what had gone on.

There was a glassy rapping sound then, and he turned to see his mother and sister had returned from the store and were in the kitchen. His mother was unloading groceries and his sister was tapping on the window, trying to tell him they were back with Fritos and he didn't need to go looking for pies, that it would be better if he did not. He wanted to tell her it was okay and that so long as the pie remained hidden he was safe and everyone was safe. But the more he tried to walk back towards the kitchen, the smaller it seemed to get, and she began tapping on the window harder and harder and the sound was not so much like a tapping as the ringing of some bell, in a rhythm that was familiar and trying to tell him something. The smell of apples became overpowering suddenly, too sickly, nauseously strong and then—

'Fuck,' he slurred, jerking upright. He'd fallen asleep on his side and so banged his head on the wall. He flapped out with his hand, knowing now that the ringing sound was his phone. Finally found it where it had slid off the bed and fallen to the floor.

The screen said 'K CELL.'

'Hey,' he said. He opened his mouth and eyes as wide as he could, trying to wake up, half of his mind still somewhere else.

Karen didn't say anything. It sounded like she was crying.

'Babe, what is it? What's the problem?'

She sniffed, hard. He could hear her swallowing.

'Oh my God,' she said. 'They found Pete.'

Chapter 16

Lee sat on one of the couches in his parents' living room. The detectives sat opposite, the big windows behind making them appear as silhouettes. This was fine by Lee. It rendered them anonymous. He'd already figured the one with the moustache was the boss. That was all he needed to know.

'Do you want me to stay?'

Ryan Hudek stood in the doorway. He was dressed in chinos and a pale blue Lacoste and had reacted imperturbably to the arrival of policemen at his house. On being told they were looking for his son he had asked why, and stepped aside when it had been explained – after he had checked ID. Lee was glad his father was in the house. He felt curiously young this afternoon.

'No, that's okay,' he said.

His dad gave him a small upwards nod of the head. 'I'll be around,' he said. 'If you change your mind.'

The moustached detective looked down at his hands and waited until the sound of Ryan Hudek's footsteps had receded down the hall. There was the sound of the door to the back yard opening and then sliding shut again with a quiet thud. Then he looked up and straight at Lee.

'Okay,' he said. 'Sorry to come hunt you down at your folks' place, but you weren't at home when we called around there.'

'No,' Lee said, evenly. 'I was here.'

'Right. Very understandable. Friend of mine turned up dead, a good friend, I'd want the support of friends and family.'

Lee said nothing. Instinct told him not to volunteer answers to non-questions.

The detective paused, started again. 'I'm sorry to bring you the news about Peter Voss.'

'You didn't,' Lee said. 'I heard an hour and a half ago.'

'Someone called you? Who was that?'

'Couple people. Word went around fast. I still can't believe it.'

'You can't remember who the first person was?'

Lee pretended to think. 'Sorry. I was pretty shaken up.'

'Of course. When was the last time you saw Peter?'

'Pete,' Lee said. 'Nobody called him Peter. I saw him, guess it would have been late Friday morning.'

The detective frowned. 'You didn't see him at the Luchs party?'

'I don't think so. I got there a little late. Time I arrived, he'd gone, I guess.'

'So you'd be surprised if we said we had someone who'd seen you talking to Peter at the party.'

'Not majorly, but I don't remember it. Pete and I talked the whole time. I don't, like, make a note of the occasions. Why – did somebody say that?'

'No.'

Lee shrugged. 'Okay. Kind of a weird question, then.'

'So you saw him Friday. Under what circumstances?'

'At the mall, just before noon? We split some fries, then he went.

171

Had to go meet some guy, or something. Seemed to be a thing he didn't want to be late for, anyway.'

The first part of this was true. Lee had seen Pete at the Belle Isle mall that Friday morning, but from a distance and they hadn't spoken. Voss had been on his own, however, so nobody was going to know the difference.

'Did he seem to have anything else on his mind when you spoke? Did he seem unusual in any way? Worried? Distracted?'

'Not really. I mean, Pete was always kind of out there. We talked about how we'd hang out at Karen's on Saturday, early. He had some other party for later on that night, but he wasn't specific about it.'

The other detective spoke. 'You think it's possible it might have involved whoever he was going to meet after you on the Friday?'

Lee considered. 'Could be, I guess. But he didn't say anything about it to me.'

'And you heard nothing after that?'

'Nothing.'

'Peter's mom said her son seemed to have an unusual amount of cash last week. Bought himself new clothes, expensive gifts for her and his father. You know anything about that?'

Lee shook his head.

'Nice place you got over in Summer Hills.'

'Thank you.'

'Looks expensive.'

Lee shrugged. *You want to ask me a question, ask it direct.*

'How much information did your caller have? The first who told you about Peter. Whoever that was.'

'Nobody knew details. Just said that Pete was dead.'

Moustache made a show of referring to his notes. 'The body was found up in the Santa Ynez mountains, just shy of the Los Padres National Forest. It was hidden a few hundred yards off a hiking trail. Somebody blew most of his head off and tried to bury him but made a crappy job of it. Didn't dig the hole deep enough.'

'It's always the way,' the other detective said, meditatively. 'Just fucking lazy, most of these people.'

'Anyway, so, coyotes sniffed it out. By the time they'd dragged it up and been at it, it was in even more of a mess. Luckily some kids on bikes found it pretty quickly. But still. It was pretty bad.'

'Yeah, really,' the other guy said. 'Tore up. Heat, death and vermin. It's a bad combination.'

'Do you mind?' Lee said, loudly. 'This guy was my friend.'

Moustache looked up. 'Oh, I'm sorry . . .'

'No you're not. Just show some respect. For me, and for him.'

The cop stared at him and Lee stared right back.

'I apologize for our insensitivity,' the other one said, after a long, long beat. 'Occupational hazard.'

'Just don't talk to his parents the way you have me,' Lee said. 'Or you'll be living in a world of hurt.'

For just a moment, he felt a little rocked. Was Moustache actually the lead guy after all? For a second there, you wondered whether it was his pale friend who was the boss.

'We've already been there,' the cop said. 'But point taken.'

'Okay,' Moustache said, quietly, 'if we need anything else, we'll be in touch. You want to just check your cell phone for me, see who that first call was from?'

'Sure.' Lee got his phone out, hit buttons, completely someone who wasn't even a little bothered what the answer was. He found it and nodded. 'That's right. It was Brad. Of course.'

'Bradley Metzger?'

'Yes. Karen called him, he called me straight after.'

'Because you three guys were friends. Good friends.'

'That's right.'

The cops stood up together and Lee saw them to the door. As they stepped out of the house, Moustache turned. 'Oh yeah, one thing you could confirm. Did Peter usually carry his cell phone?'

'All the time,' Lee said. 'Why?'

'Can't find it,' the cop said. 'Not on or near the body, not at his house. His mom tried calling it, and it rings, so I guess the battery's not run dry yet. You didn't find it at your place or anything? He didn't drop it there sometime?'

'No,' Lee said. 'He had it when I last saw him Friday. In the mall.'

'Well, they're slippery things. Can fall out anywhere. We'll keep an eye out for it.'

Lee watched as they walked down to their car. He waited until they'd backed out of the driveway and then stood a little longer, staring out into the world, thinking:

You lied to the cops. The world's different now.

'Not so tough, were they?' said a voice.

Lee turned, startled, to see his mother standing just behind him in a silver robe. He hadn't even realized she was in the house.

She wasn't wearing sunglasses and her eyes looked floaty but she did appear to be seeing him.

'You did very well,' she said. 'The respect part was a nice touch.'

She ran her finger down his cheek, very briefly, and then wafted out of the room, to go who knew where.

'It's me.'

'Hey babe. You okay?'

Karen sighed. 'Well, kinda. You know.'

'Yeah. Where are you?'

'Out by the pool. Just sitting around. If I stay in the house Mom keeps coming by to ask how I am, which is nice of her, but, you know.'

'Yeah.'

'She's going to go see Pete's mom later.'

'I didn't realize they knew each other so well.'

'Well, I don't think they do, but, you know, Pete's dead.'

Brad nodded even though Karen wouldn't hear it. Pete was indeed dead. In a way the fact this had become public knowledge made it a little easier. It had changed from being a murky thing which had to be hidden at all costs, obfuscated in the hope the fact would simply fade away, to something irrevocably sharper and clearer. The known now accurately represented reality: the facts were in place. The job became making sure those facts didn't fall down and squash you flat.

Lee had called after the cops interviewed him and told Brad what he'd said. Brad had passed on Steve's enquiry about the week's pickup and Lee said he didn't know. Hernandez was still not returning calls. It didn't seem like a good notion on the whole but they'd see. Brad was relieved to hear this, as privately he thought it would be a fucking *terrible* idea to deal drugs right now.

'You still there?'

'Yes,' he said. 'Just, you know, thinking.'

'Yeah.' She was quiet for a while, and Brad thought she was maybe gearing up to sign off. But then she spoke again.

'Can I ask you something?'

'Sure.'

'You don't know anything about this, do you?'

Brad opened his mouth but nothing came out. He coughed and then tried again. 'What do you mean?'

'I mean, it's just, you and Pete and Lee were so tight, you know? I just wondered if Pete had some secret or something, something you guys knew about but weren't supposed to tell?'

'No,' Brad said, relieved. 'Yeah, we were tight. We were like blood. Pete didn't have nothing weird going on that I knew about.'

'Okay,' she said. For some reason the way she said it made him feel cautious again. Okay . . . what? Okay, thanks for the information? Okay, I believe you? Okay, I don't, actually – but I'm not going to call you on it right now?

'It's just . . .' she said.

'It's just what, babe?'

'You know at the party, when you and Lee went to get burgers? I saw you out in front of the house before you left?'

'My angel of fire. What about it?'

'Well, I was thinking about that earlier and I thought when Lee came around the side to meet you there, didn't he say something like 'He's on his way', or 'On his way', or something?'

Brad spoke very carefully. 'I don't remember it.'

'I'm sure he did. Something like that. Because, also, I went to see Sara and Randy off, but you guys just kept standing there. Like you were waiting for someone.'

'Nope,' Brad said. After a split second his brain provided. 'It was just, I was having a cigarette, remember? And Lee doesn't always like it in his car. I wanted to finish up before we left.'

'Oh, okay,' she said.

They talked of this and that for a little while, then just before the call ended, she said: 'Brad?'

'Yeah?'

'You think they'll get who did it?'

'I don't know,' he said.

'I do,' she said, quietly. 'I think they will.'

After he'd called Brad, Lee had left his parents' house and drove around a while before finally heading back to his own place. He went inside and fixed coffee and sat drinking it at the spotless table in the kitchen. He resisted the urge to pull the car into the garage and search it for Pete's phone. He knew it wasn't there. He'd have seen it when he cleaned the car on the night of the shooting.

But – assuming the cop hadn't been lying in an attempt to knock him off balance – it was kind of strange. Pete's phone was a fixture. He would have had it surgically implanted if he could. He must have had it with him that night. So where the hell was it?

It didn't matter. Most likely it had fallen out of his pocket, somewhere between the parking lot where the shooting had taken place and the spot where they'd buried him. Humping him along in the dark, nobody would have noticed. Whatever. Even if somebody found the phone it made no difference. It didn't tie them to what had happened.

But still.

176

For a moment he sat with his head slumped forward. It could have not happened. It could all so easily have not happened, not be true.

He took the call from Hernandez. He could have not done.

He said 'yes'. He could have said 'no'.

Small difference. Big difference.

It could all have not happened.

He remained sitting that way for ten minutes. Then he went out front, pulled the car into the garage, and searched it.

There was no phone.

He was washing up his hands in the kitchen when the doorbell rang. He assumed it was probably Brad come to freak out at him, but opened it to find a much older man standing outside.

'Mr Reynolds,' he said, confused by the fact there was no car out in the road. 'What are you doing here?'

The lawyer walked straight past him and into the house. 'I need you to tell me what you told them.'

'Told who?'

'The police, Lee. Who do you think?'

'Why do you want to know?'

'Because it's now my job to provide you with legal advice. Should it become necessary, which I hope it will not.'

'Did my dad hire you?'

'No he didn't.'

'So who . . .'

'Tell me, Lee. Every question, every answer. Every single thing.'

Lee ran through the interview with the two detectives. Reynolds listened closely. By the time Lee finished he was looking serious.

'You realize you're now an accessory to murder? You and Metzger would get serious jail time for that alone. You're not juveniles any more, hard though that can be to believe. If they tie this to the drugs and the DEA gets involved then you may as well throw away the key.'

'But how would they do that?'

'Why else were you in a deserted parking lot miles from anywhere in the dark? Why else would you hide the body?'

'It was an accident, or something. We got scared.'

'Uh-huh. And then you lied to a police officer. Bradley too. And are you confident there's not a single person who will testify that the two of you – with Peter Voss, of course – have been dealing all over the valley for the last six months?'

Lee thought about all the people he slipped packages to. All the houses he'd visited, the parties he'd been welcome at, all the hand-shakes and free beers and 'Hey, dude, great to see you' – none of which would mean shit when the time came and people were confronted with a cop in their parents' living room and they real-ized dropping Lee's name would avoid them serious trouble.

'This is all screwed up,' he said, quietly.

'That about nails it,' Reynolds said. 'You need this thing to go away, and fast. You understand that, don't you? You get just how fucking serious this is?'

Lee nodded. He felt tired. He felt nauseous. He'd get it together real soon, he knew, but just for the moment he felt like lying face-down down on the floor and never getting up. 'I get it.'

'Come with me,' Reynolds said. He opened the front door.

Hudek saw a car was now sitting in the road outside. It was black and had black windows too. The motor was running, but it was very, very quiet.

He locked the house behind him and followed the lawyer up the pathway. At the car the older man opened the door. Lee bent down to see two sets of seats facing each other inside. The whole interior was black, and smelled like it was made of shadows.

There was a man sitting in the middle of the seat which faced forward. It was the guy from the abandoned building. The guy he'd told the Plan to. The guy who, if he was honest, Lee could have lived without meeting again.

'Hey, Lee John,' he said. 'Come take a seat. We need to talk.'

Lee hesitated but knew there was nowhere else to go. He got in the car, sitting opposite. Mr Reynolds came and sat beside Lee. The door shut with a soft, expensive *clunk* and the car floated gently away from the kerb as if being picked up by a soft breeze.

'How you feeling, Lee?' the man said.

'Okay,' Lee said.

'That's good. Not spun out a little?'

'Well, a fucking tad, yeah. I've been calling Hernandez for three fucking days. Why isn't he returning my calls?'

'Because he's dead, Lee.'

Lee blinked, his anger flicked out like a light.

'He died the same night as your friend. Went looking for the guys who did the job on you. Didn't make it out the other side. Luckily we did a better job of hiding his body than you did with Mr Voss – though what we haven't been able to do is tie down the where-abouts of Mr Voss's cell phone, which I gather the police are getting exercised about.'

'Jesus,' Lee said. He didn't bother to ask how the man got his information. He evidently just had it. 'This is fucked up.'

'It's serious, yes, but it can be accommodated. We have to look to the future, always. The loss of Hernandez leaves us with a position to fill – and it'll put you in great shape for your Spring Break master plan. The *Plan*, right? Long live the Plan. Assuming we sort out this little local difficulty. Which I believe we can, with your continued cooperation.'

'That would be good,' Lee said. 'That would be . . . very good.'

'All part of the service.' The man sat back in his seat and looked at Lee for long enough for it to become quite uncomfortable.

'What?' Lee said. The man was wearing an open-necked shirt and Lee couldn't help noticing that he had something that could only be a scar from a bullet wound, high on his chest. And was that another scar, nickel-sized, a couple inches below the first?

'You still don't remember meeting me before?'

'No. I really don't.'

'Well, we're going to be doing real business together now. So let's do the introductions properly this time.'

He stuck out his hand for Hudek to shake. A copper bracelet hung from his wrist.

'Good to know you, Lee. My name is Paul.'

Chapter 17

Jim had thought he could drive past without incident. It was so long ago, and it was something he had trained himself rigorously to believe had happened to someone else. But not long after he had been past the old place he realized he was driving more and more slowly, as if his battery was running down. He stopped a couple of times, parked up by the side of the road for a while. Then drove off again. Puttering around. Through the forest. Back into town. Tightening circles.

Eventually he found himself trundling into the lot of the Renee's. He was hungry now, there was no doubt. He still hadn't eaten since leaving Key West. He got out of the van. As soon as he did so his stomach didn't feel empty any more. You could smell cooking oil wafting from the back of the building. Jim's guts wanted something, but not what they were going to sell in there.

He stood with his hands in the pockets of his jacket for a moment, enjoying the cold air, hoping it might cut through the clouds settling in his head, growing thicker and more stormy by the hour. Ever since he'd picked up the van things seemed to have become complicated, and it had gotten a whole lot worse since Petersburg. He had begun to feel as if things were coming to a point. It had been a long time since it felt like that.

What was that in his pocket?

He pulled it out, frowned at it. It was a pack of cigarettes.

For a moment this was so weird to him that he was afraid he'd somehow picked up someone else's coat. But he couldn't think where he might have done that, and a quick check in the other pockets reassured him it was his. So where had these come from?

Jim had not smoked in a long time. Jim had never smoked, in fact. James had, all through his teens, yes, and during the time he had spent in other countries. In the army, everybody smoked. When he got back, too. Teachers' common rooms could fume it up with the best. And then – during that other period. But not since. He had stopped dead when he reached Key West, quitting the habit like losing a finger. You adapted, lived your life to a slightly different rhythm: the calm, measured way of a Jim Westlake. But at some point in the last forty-eight hours he'd acquired a pack of Marlboro Reds.

He put the pack back in his pocket. He didn't want one. He didn't smoke. But he knew they were there.

For a moment, suddenly, he felt tired and angry at himself. These stupid divisions, as if they dissipated blame. It wasn't me, it was the drink. Judge, my hormones made me do it. Ain't nobody in this head but us chickens, and chickens don't carry knives.

He pushed himself away from the van and wandered around the block. He wasn't ready to get back in just yet.

The cigarettes hadn't been the first difference. That morning he'd noticed there was a small saucepan in the bag down in the footwell of the passenger seat. He didn't recall buying that either. He knew it hadn't been in the van, because everything had been disposed of. Also it looked new, not like the battered one which was in the shoebox. Wasn't anything strange or magical about it: he'd obviously just bought it, in the same way people found themselves finishing off a bag of chips that they'd resealed and put back in the drawer, without even realising they'd walked back in the kitchen to find them. He guessed sometimes your hands just reached out and did things. Maybe if there was a *real* division, then this was it. Your soul and body, united by a common enemy. Your maleficent mind.

He got rid of the new saucepan. He didn't need two.

There was nothing to see around the block, and by the third quarter Jim was ready to get back to the van and go. He was strolling past the back of Renee's when he heard something. He stopped, turned.

There was nothing to see except the scarred and shadowed back of a fast-food outlet, a concrete light-industrial oblong with padlocked doors and big metal containers for refuse, lacquered with the odour of things gone long-ago bad and hosed away. There was an eight-foot high chain fence which marked the boundary between the back of this business and the next, a place selling tyres. Alongside was a narrow alleyway, probably providing access to the rear of some key storage unit or other. Maybe where they grew the burger patties.

That's where the noise had seemed to come from.

Jim heard it again. Sounded like it could be a small animal or something, maybe, knocking itself against the lower part of the fence. Could be hurt.

Jim cared for animals. He guessed he should go see.

He crossed the sidewalk and a few feet of battered concrete and stepped into the alley. It was thirty feet long and ended in a shadowed wall that he couldn't see.

Yes, there it was – something small, right down at the end. Banging against the side of the fence.

He took a couple of paces towards it. Its movements were frenetic, as if it thought itself trapped – and yet surely all it had to do was turn this way and run out.

Strange shape, too. Must be standing on its hind legs. It was maybe three and a half feet tall.

Jim took a final step, bent down a little to get a better look.

A blurred pale face turned towards him.

It was a child. A child in a tiny dark overcoat, head bare, hair whipped around as it snapped back and forth and up and down. It/she was clinging onto the bottom of the chain fence with both hands, shaking it with all her might. Her face was blurred and pale and streaked with earth.

The fence rattled in the wind, but she made no sound.

Jim stumbled back out of the alley, across the concrete and back to the sidewalk. He stood there staring as he sucked in big lungfuls of air. The fence continued to twitter gently in the wind. Nothing else. Nothing else was there.

He walked quickly around the last leg of the block until he was back within sight of the van. He pulled out the cigarettes and a disposable lighter he found in the other pocket and started smoking again, just like that.

After the first few pulls it was like falling off a log, and it helped mask the smell of fat coming out of vents in the building, the oil in which the dead had been warmed to feed the dying. It was making him feel sick. Everything was making him feel sick. He felt old and wrong and yet full of strength, his hands cramping with power he did not know how to use.

Chapter 18

I wound up picking a place called Lucy's on Union Street in Owensville. It had as much character as an airport lounge but they let you smoke and it was either that or a Denny's. It was only as I settled into a booth on the side looking out over the crossroads that I realized this was the place Gulicks and Kroeger had used on their dates, where they had been the night they went on to find Lawrence Widmar's body in the woods outside Thornton. I considered asking the barman if he remembered them, using Gulicks' famously red hair as a trigger, but it could only make him assume I was a cop – not a good move if you want to sit unobtrusively in a bar. Patrons don't like it. It's like having your mom in the corner. Your mom, with a gun. Nobody needs that.

Unger called when he landed and I gave him directions. Then I waited a couple of hours, twiddling my thumbs and trying not to drink too much. After the night out in the barrens I felt tired and spacy and had the dry, relentless headache that comes from getting up too early and knowing it's a long time until you can sleep. I ate some aspirin which I bought from a late drugstore across the street, and periodically trooped to the restroom to splash water over my face, but the improvement was minimal and shortlived. In the end I zoned out, hoping my life wasn't now always going be like this: sitting in some bar, feeling tired and wondering if someone was on their way to kill me. I thought about the case Nina was trying to solve, but didn't reach any conclusions. I hoped Gulicks had done it. That way we could get ourselves out of all this sooner rather than later. It seemed a little convenient, red hair and two hops and a suspect in jail – but that's the way it goes sometimes. Eighty-five per cent of solved crimes are broken in the first forty-eight hours. Any longer than that and memories fade, people get things wrong, the world spins on to other dark deeds.

About a quarter after nine a cab pulled over on the opposite corner. I watched as a man paid the driver and looked across at the bar. He was short and not built for speed, but it had to be him. Sure enough, he got out and started walking towards me.

When he entered he casually looked around. I was the only person sitting by myself and taking no interest in either the game on the television or someone of the opposite sex. It wasn't a hard call. He did not pull out a weapon. Instead he came over and stood by the table, hands empty and by his sides.

'Ward Hopkins?'

We shook. His hand was hot and damp. He sat opposite, scooting along the banquette in an ungainly lunge. Thinning black hair was sticking to his pate. His suit was crumpled. He looked about my age, maybe a year or two older. His features were surprisingly sharp for a man carrying a spare fifty pounds. I waited while he efficiently attracted the attention of a waitress and ordered drinks. Then he looked back at me and smiled.

'I know,' he said. 'Name like mine, you were expecting Dolph Lundgren. Don't worry. I have grown accustomed to the faint sense of disappointment.'

'You're a good-looking man,' I said. 'Don't let anyone tell you otherwise.'

He laughed. 'Granddad dropped a "stein" when they arrived in the 1930s,' he said. 'My father kept talking about reinstating it, but it never quite seemed the time. Me, I've been an Unger since I was born, so whatever. I know the other part's there.'

The drinks arrived. Unger swallowed half his beer in one. 'Better,' he said. 'Lord, but I hate planes. Okay, first – what the hell happened to Bobby? I thought he was immortal.'

I hardly knew where to start, or whether I was really prepared to. 'This is a weird kind of situation, Carl.'

'I know that. You have no idea who I am and I walk in here bandying your best friend's name like we were lovers. I assume you did a check on my phone and found my identity is real, but got no further than that. That's the way it's supposed to be, of course. I will tell you that yes, I am carrying a gun, because I have no clue about you either. I assume you're doing the same. But one of us has to start talking, right? You want it to be me, that's fine.'

'Sounds good.'

'All right. This is what I know. We got a whole wing of people at Langley whose job it is to comb the ether, keeping an eye out for evidence of the terrorist mind. As you know. A few months ago one of these people is fiddling around in downtime and starts looking into email spam. Now. You remember when it started that some of that crap would turn up with bizarre words in the title or body?'

'To fox spam-filtering software.'

'Right – that was everyone's assumption. You load your spam with random words so that junk filters working on statistical assumptions are misled into thinking it's a genuine communication: because spam typically contains words like "sex" and "Viagra" and "loan", and not words like "bison", "strawberry" or "hobblede-hoy". But here's the thing. This assistant, she's called Ramona, she started collating all the examples she can find, literally tens of millions, and running stat. analyses on them. She's not expecting anything, just killing time.'

'I can imagine,' I said. 'I had a job like hers once.'

'The initial pass doesn't show much – pretty random distribution of words. So then she starts breaking them into sub-words too, just in case – units of meaning. So out of "house-sitter" you get "house" and "sitter", and "sidewalk" you get "walk" and "side". And suddenly things start to spike a little.'

He watched me carefully as he said: 'Two of the biggest peaks come on the words "Straw" and "Men".

You could have read my reaction from across the street on a dark night. I actually dropped my cigarette.

He nodded. 'This is my point. They're not the only ones – there's a hundred fifty or so that seem to have some kind of significance – but they're right near the top.'

'So what . . .' I stopped talking. I couldn't really work out what the implications of this might be. 'Christ.'

'Right. Actually nobody would have cared about those words except I remembered Bobby coming to me with an enquiry about the phrase "the Straw Men" months before, and I thought, well, that's weird. We downloaded copies of all the popular bulk emailers and random word generators, pulled their code apart, and couldn't determine any reason why these words should come up more often than any others. It began to look as if someone was putting them there on purpose. So I got thinking a little harder about spam. Some of it's no-brainer. You've got Nigerians with their "I have a bazillion dollars and I've chosen *you* to help me", a straightforward scam preying on the clinically stupid. There's your online Viagra merchants and loan sharks – pumping out cold calls and not caring if you even live in the right country, because it costs them nothing. But then there are other kinds, and the one that got me thinking was one you don't actually see any more: "Britney Spears Nude". It had always struck me, did anyone in the world *believe* that? Did they actually think, despite her being – at the time – a world-renowned virgin, that there'd *really* be nude pictures of her available on the net, for just five bucks ninety-nine? And if not, then what was this communication actually about? Anyway, so Ramona and I did a cull of spam – normal-looking ones, not random-word stuff – and started looking at them properly. Actually we chucked them all in a computer, to see what it could find.'

'Which was?'

'Nothing at first. An index of what the unscrupulous try to sell to the desperate. Things to make your dick hard. Pictures of women with unfeasibly large breasts. Degrees for people who can't spell. Sex, sex, sex. But then Ramona had a brainwave, booked time on the cryptography mainframe and threw it all in there. Still nothing significant for days and days, and I'm beginning to think the "straw men" thing is just a coincidence. Finally three weeks ago we got a hit.' He slugged back most of the rest of his beer. 'It looked like a straightforward spam for prescription drugs. But . . . you know about book codes, right?'

I nodded. 'Each word or letter stands for a word or letter in the same position in a known book. First word in first line might be first word of first chapter, third word in fifth line would be the third word of the fifth chapter, and so on.'

'Right, with a thousand variations. Completely blown once someone knows what the book in question is, but simple to use and hard to break without a tip. So once all the spam had been through the standard crypto attacks with nothing shaking, it was thrown across into software where the computer looks for grammatical constructions based on a few hundred thousand books it has stored. I was looking through the results one night, and I found a single sentence that leapt out.'

'What was it?'

'It said: Tomorrow is not the straw men, but rejoice.'

I shrugged. 'Okay, you got the Straw Men in there. But it doesn't sound like it means anything.'

'It wouldn't. Unless you knew this piece of spam only went out once, on a single day, when it was simultaneously delivered to millions of addresses all over the world. That was in the late afternoon of September 10, 2001.'

I stared at him.

'Right,' he said. 'These people knew what was going to happen. They knew the Twin Towers were going down, and they didn't try to stop it. They spread the word that it wasn't them, but they approved.'

'Holy Christ.'

'Everyone assumes spam is just spam, but one in a million isn't. If you know your communications are going to be of interest to the security forces, then what you most want to *avoid* is any sense of secrecy. So instead of sending a message to a particular person, you send what appears to be a non-message to a vast number of people. All the intended recipient or recipients need is (a) to be on the spamming list, and (b) to know the code. Everyone else throws it away. He or she gets the message. And even if we get lucky and break the code and realize there's a message there, it's hard to demonstrate it's a communication because it was sent out to so many people at once. Worst thing is, even if we find one saying "the assassination of the agreed head of state goes ahead on Wednesday at four o'clock", *we're no better off.* It doesn't lead us to anyone. How are we going to check the millions of addresses who got the mail, half of which will be one-shot accounts on Hotmail? It's impossible to find out who it was really sent to, who the genuine target was.'

'So they can send messages in plain sight, to whoever they like, and the recipients are protected and completely anonymous.'

'You got it. It's a fucking *nightmare.* All of the emails have been bounced around the net, of course – best we can do is suspect some of the more recent originated in Southern California, perhaps LA or in the Valley somewhere. So this is the point where I begin to get twitchy and start trying to get ahold of Bobby. There's evidently a communication system in place that's too fast-moving to get on top of – especially when we're entering the situation late and desperately trying to play catch-up.'

'What situation? Catch-up on what?'

Unger flagged a couple more beers. 'That's what we still don't know. It's why I'll fly down to see someone like you at the drop of a hat. The codes keep changing. We had some lucky hits for a while, but there's no way you can cross-check against every book in the world, and vowel/phenome analysis won't get you far. For the last two weeks we've been able to make no sense of anything at all, which suggests they know we're looking. Which might also mean they have a person or persons within the Agency, which I don't even want to think about.'

'Think about it,' I said. 'A friend of mine in the FBI got suspended after she started pushing too hard in the right direction. And a week ago someone who should be in jail was sprung right out of an armoured vehicle in California. These people are very seriously connected.'

'So who *are* they? What do you know about them?'

'My parents died a year ago,' I said. 'Up in Montana. It looked like a road accident. I was there for the funeral and I found something that got me looking at the situation a little harder. I found a videotape my father had made which mentioned a group called the Straw Men. Bobby only got involved because I called him for a lead on somewhere local I could get the tape ripped onto DVD. That should have been the end of his participation.'

'He never did know when to stop.'

'He did some digging and found there was no record of my birth in my home town. Cut a long story short, we wound up discovering I'd been unofficially adopted after my father killed a man who attacked my mother. He didn't mean to kill him, I don't think, but he was one of a bunch of strange people holed up in the woods and that's the way it panned out. We were that guy's kids.'

'We?'

'I had a brother too.'

'That you didn't know about? Have you met up?'

'Kind of. He's one of the Straw Men, and he's the guy who escaped from prison. He's a serial killer. He also abducts people for others to murder for kicks. He has a theory that mankind was infected by a virus tens of thousands of years ago. It made us more sociable, enabled modern society to coalesce by obscuring some of our natural enmity towards our fellow man. We started living closer together, began farming, developed the modern world. They don't like it. They want the planet back the way it was.'

Unger was staring at me.

'There's worse. We found evidence the Straw Men were behind the shootings at the school in Evanston, Maine last year – and probably other events as well, going back some years. If the Oklahoma bombing hadn't been nailed elsewhere, I'd say that was their kind of operation too. They have no limits. None at all.'

Unger sat still for a moment, and then reached across the table and took one of my cigarettes. I'm not even sure he was aware what he was doing, at first. He lit it, and then looked at me.

'Okay,' he said, quietly. 'Well, here's the other thing. Before the codes flatlined we were starting to get one phrase appearing consistently. We discovered it in a couple of major spam messages, and one night we found the phrase recorded on the phone systems of companies in thirty cities across the United States.'

He reached in his pocket and pulled out a piece of paper on which one sentence had been printed.

THE DAY OF ANGELS.

'Mean anything to you?'

'No,' I said, feeling very cold across the back of my neck. 'But it does not sound good.'

We traded what little information we had back and forth for a little while longer, but when Unger pointed at my glass again I shook my head.

'Got to get back,' I said. 'Going to be driving slowly as it is.'

'I was hoping to debrief you properly.'

'Not tonight. There's a friend I have to talk to.'

'Does she know about this too?'

'How did you know it was a she?'

Unger held his hands up innocently. 'Your tone of voice.'

'Yes she does.'

'Could I talk to her too?'

'I don't know,' I said. 'I'd have to ask her.'

'Okay.' He got a pen out and scribbled an address on the piece of paper on the table between us. 'Here's where I am tonight. The Days Inn, it's about five blocks, uh, east of here. Room 211. Assume I'll be there until around nine thirty tomorrow morning. You got my number, let me know. If you can come talk to me, I'll stay as late as you need. Is there anyone else I should know about?'

'No,' I said.

'It would be really good to talk to you both,' he said, and for once there was no trace of what seemed to be a habitual half-smile on his face. 'I have a bad feeling about homeland security. I think something dark is on the way, and this would be a terrible time for the Agency to drop the ball. We got murdered for it last time.'

'Iraq was hardly the Company's finest hour.'

He shook his head irritably. 'We did okay. The fuck-ups were PR spins, trailer trash out of control. Sure, it looked gross but that kind of thing has always happened – only difference is now we got digital cameras so we can share with the folks at home. The army was doing good in other places. The Company too. But the press don't know about that stuff. They're not supposed to. It's a *secret*. But the bottom line is 9/11 happened and it shouldn't have and the intelligence for Iraq II was group-thought a little too imaginatively and so someone had to take the fall – when the dust had settled and we'd done what we wanted anyway. Never mind that army's counter-intelligence was cut to nothing back in the early nineties. There weren't a hundred Arabic speakers left in the whole place. They weren't ready for the new world disorder. Nobody was. It's not nukes and battalions we've got to worry about now. It's armies you can fit in a car. Terrorism isn't James Bond or Tom Clancy. Even al-Qaeda is looking old school these days – now it's just some guy with a bomb. He walks the same roads as us. He thinks the same thoughts. But he's got a bomb. Only hope you have is through operatives who can work one to one, get inside an individual's head. Find out if he's a farmer or a fanatic. Find out where they're going to strike next. And that's *exactly* what they cut back – people like Bobby, though admittedly he couldn't speak foreign tongues to save his fucking life. Sorry, bad choice of words. But the point is they cut off our cocks and then wonder why we can't piss any more and it's a *lot* easier shafting the CIA than some raghead they can't even fucking find.'

'That *you* can't find,' I said. I wanted to leave. 'And if you're trying to convince me the Company deserve a Peace Prize then you're talking to the wrong guy. I worked for you people, remember. There's plenty of morally subnormal men working there and we in general have done a lot of dumb things over a long period of time. Why do you think everyone hates us so much?'

'Beats me,' he said. 'I swear to God, we mean well.'

'Can do better,' I said. 'And here's one thing you should know. The real bad guys are already inside the gates. They may even have been here before we were.'

'What do you mean?'

'I'll talk to my friend,' I said, standing up. 'Maybe I'll see you tomorrow.'

'I hope so. Don't worry – I'll stay right here until you're good and gone. But if what you say is true, one of these days you're going to have to trust someone – otherwise your life is one long arc out into darkness.'

'Trust,' I said. 'Yes, I think I remember the word.'

I shook his hand and left. As I crossed the road I glanced back at the bar to see him still sitting there in the booth. I'd deliberately parked the car some distance away and round a series of blocks that you'd have to have been tied to me with a rope to follow, and I left town via a road that could be taken as leading in just about any direction except the one I was actually going. As I drove back to Thornton I tried hard to work out what I felt about Unger. Part of me did want to trust him, to feel there was someone inside a recognizable agency who might be able to help us. Another part wasn't sure. Had he really guessed that the person I spoke of was a woman, just from the way I spoke? Was his question as to whether there were any more of us a general enquiry, or was it loaded? If he was allied to the Straw Men then it would make sense for him to try to gather us together. Wouldn't it?

The problem with paranoia is it's hard to know where to stop. As soon as you question something as fundamental as the human contract, all bets are off. The reason the Iraq torture pictures were shocking was not the events they portrayed. Excesses in Vietnam are well-documented. We know about POW camps in WWII. We've heard of heads on spikes in medieval times, knights burned alive at Agincourt, the inventive horror with which the Romans and Carthaginians terrorized each other in the Punic Wars. There has been no war without atrocity. War *is* atrocity, pure and simple: only greed, nationalism and faith help us pretend otherwise. The only shocking thing about the pictures was the act of photography itself, the realization that people wanted to record these events, that they believed there were other people who would want to see them too. Is that really such a long way from the killer who keeps a picture of his victims? Or a lock of their hair? The serial killer is sufficiently unhooked from his culture that he is able to commit this kind of deed on home soil – whereas most of us need the anonymity and distance of a foreign land, of being vaguely mandated through a declaration of war.

But other than that – how much difference is there?

US intelligence didn't fail to prevent 9/11 purely because of incompetence. The assumption is always that we're so much more capable than the rest of the world. They don't win matches, we sometimes drop the ball. Wrong. Sometimes the bad guys win because they're as good as we are. Strength of will and purity of hate will make up a *huge* technology gap. To believe otherwise is to be a country still stuck on Spring Break, goggle-eyed with the contents of our culture's wet T-shirts, the first heart-stopping whupping of our life just visible on the horizon.

After a while it started to rain.

It was a depressing drive.

I pulled back into Thornton a little after midnight. The town lay quiet under faint moonlight, flat and inexplicable as someone else's dream. I drove slowly past the sheriff's building, considered calling Nina. Realized that she'd either be too busy or no longer there. The car that had what looked like reporters in it was still present, but empty. Presumably they were inside, and the Julia Gulicks story would break tomorrow. The white van I'd seen was gone.

When I got to the hotel I saw Reidel's car parked out front and Monroe's a couple of slots away. I went inside, hoping that whatever late-night conference they were involved in was happening somewhere other than Nina's room. The bar and the restaurant were empty, however, closed in that hotel-specific way which seems to declare they're shut now, they were never fucking open in the first place, and they sure as hell never will be again. There was no one around in the lobby, nor at reception.

I shambled down the corridor, wondering whether I could reasonably tell the other cops to fuck off to bed. Or if I might do it anyway, reasonably or otherwise. That afternoon Nina had looked more tired than I'd ever seen before. She needed sleep. So did I.

I knocked on the door to give them due warning, and then opened it with my swipe key. Silence inside. I shut it behind me.

'Nina?'

No reply. The conference was evidently being held elsewhere. Did I even know what room Monroe was in? I walked down the little passageway past the bathroom, thinking maybe I'd just lie on the bed and let Nina join me in her own time.

When I got to the main room I stopped as if walking into sheet glass.

At first all I could see was blood.

Chapter 19

I knew I was making sounds. I knew because they were hurting my throat. I just didn't know how loud they must have been.

It looked like someone or something had been destroyed with a chainsaw. There were splatters of blood over the walls, the television set, the chairs, the bedspread, the big mirror on the wall. The room reeked of copper and death and there was so much dull red everywhere it was like a noise. For a second I was stunned into immobility. I couldn't get the scene to resolve itself into anything that made sense.

There was so much mess, in fact, that it was a long minute before I realized I could so far only see one body.

It was Reidel.

He lay underneath the window onto the parking lot, twisted as if he'd been thrown there hard enough to dent the wall. He'd lost half his scalp and his face was red-brown and wet. His eyes were open but there was nothing left to see out through them. It looked like someone had tried to cut his clothes off with a hatchet and then just lost it and started swinging wildly instead. There was a blood-lined slash across the wallpaper beside his head. There were far deeper cuts across his throat, arms and into the left side of his chest, and a pool of darkness on the carpet spreading two feet to either side.

One body.

Only one body.

I spun into the passageway and kicked open the door to the bathroom, gun held out and my finger a breath away from emptying it. It was surreally clean in there compared to the rest of the suite, and empty of people either living or dead.

I turned back into the main room and yanked the bed aside. Maybe I thought Nina might be hiding under there and hadn't realized it was me bellowing her name, or that something that had once been her had been shoved under there, part by part. I had it halfway across the floor when there was a sound from behind me and I whirled to see a woman in a hotel uniform standing in the passageway.

She started to scream like a big plane taking off.

'Go find Agent Monroe!' I shouted. 'Find him now.'

She stumbled backward, trying to get away. She was shrieking in earnest now and the noise and all the blood was making my brain white out and it took me a second to work out it was me she was trying to escape from. I had a gun and I was smeared with blood and there was something horrible slumped on the other side of the room. I'd have run from me too.

I stuffed the gun in my pocket and managed to grab her arm. Got the other hand on her opposite shoulder and held her still.

'It wasn't me,' I said, trying to keep my voice level, trying not to break her bones. Her eyes flickered around in their sockets, seeing everything but me. I put my face up close and said it again, louder. 'It wasn't me. Now go call the cops and *find Special Agent Monroe.*'

I pushed her away towards the door. She ran.

I tried to be methodical. I knew I shouldn't mess up the scene but I'd done enough damage already and I had to see. If Nina had to be found then it had to be me who found her.

I dropped to the floor and looked under the bed just to lay that idea to rest. I got back up and threw open the small wardrobe. Nothing but Nina's few clothes. I left the doors open so her body couldn't suddenly materialize in there, falling apart and leaking blood. I looked behind the big television, swept aside the curtains either side of the window. I had to step over Reidel several times in the process and I knew there was something particularly wrong about him but didn't immediately understand what it was and it wasn't my main problem right then.

I went pointlessly back out into the bathroom and looked in there once more, moving the door and shower curtain with my elbows, trying not to contaminate the room with blood from the other nightmare.

She wasn't there. She was nowhere in the suite. I couldn't make a value judgement on that fact. I just had to find where she was.

I ran out into the hallway and towards the lobby. I passed Monroe after ten yards, turning into the corridor in his shirt sleeves, looking old and confused.

'What's happened?'

'Reidel's dead.'

His mouth dropped but then I was past him and out through the front doors and into the cold parking lot.

I sprinted into the middle of it and back and forth searching in car windows but there was no one in any of them and no one was driving away and finally I slowed and stopped. Everything was still except for clouds scudding overhead.

There was no one to chase and nothing I could do. Whatever had happened had already happened and I was too late. In the distance I heard the sound of approaching sirens.

They were too late too.

*   *   *

An hour later I was perched on a kerb and smoking a cigarette. The hand which held it was smeared with blood. My jeans were too. I was staring down at the pocked asphalt to give my mind something to hold on to. I'd spent much of the intervening time in Nina's room and couldn't be in there any more. The barely-contained fury and panic amongst the local cops had melded with my own and turned my head into an icy ache of helplessness.

The hour seemed to have passed in jump-cuts. Nothing useful had happened. The time had merely fled, taking the initiative with it. I could see a couple of cops walking the lot, bent over, looking for signs of blood. I'd already tried.

I heard the hotel's automatic doors open and looked up to see Monroe coming out alone. The lobby behind him was full of milling staff and guests, with cops trying to get them to go back to their rooms or offices or anywhere so long it was out of the way. Half the guests looked scared. The rest looked like they'd lucked into a walk-on in some particularly juicy reality show. I wanted to go in and hurt them. Hurt them badly.

'Anything?'

Monroe shook his head. 'The hotel is being pulled apart. Basement, roof, every storage area we can find. But she's not here.'

I went back to staring at the ground.

'Every cop in town is in here or out there on the streets,' he added. 'All off-duty officers have been called in. Owensville, Andley and Smithfield sheriffs are on alert. I've notified the two nearest bureaus. People are on their way.'

'It's too late.'

'No it isn't. A federal agent has been kidnapped. We have a history of responding decisively to that kind of event. We look after our own. Whatever it takes, we'll get her back.'

'Where are you going to start looking, exactly?'

'There are road blocks already up at the three main routes out of Thornton. When other agents get here we'll get the whole town

200

locked down. We'll do a house-to-house if necessary. We'll find her if we have to pull this place apart brick by brick.'

I assumed Monroe couldn't hear the note of heroic desperation in his own voice.

'What time did you people return to the hotel this evening? How long before I found what's in there?'

'About an hour,' he admitted. 'Maybe a little longer.'

'Makes it over two by now. He could be in a different state.'

'He? Who do you think this is?'

'Who do you think? Someone's just attacked two of the key people investigating the murders. Reidel's been hacked apart with the same kind of weapon used on the victims, a heavy cleaver – didn't you see the slash in the wall?' I had since realized one of the things that had been wrong with Reidel's body. 'His hand was lying three feet away. This is down to your killer. Who else?'

'Julia Gulicks is still in a cell. There is a guard outside it.'

'Of course she is, Monroe – because *she didn't do it.* Nina was right. Your case is hot air built on Gulicks finding Widmar's body, muddied by an alleged sighting from a jealous woman in a bar. Even if Gulicks was guilty and astral-projected herself out of the station I don't believe she's capable of what happened in that hotel room. Reidel was built to fight and Nina could look after herself. You really see Gulicks taking them both down? Really? I mean, can you *see* it?'

'No,' he admitted.

'So it's a man, and it's someone who's done serious killing before. Gulicks is innocent and the real murderer has brought the fight to us and we have no idea who he is or what he's capable of.'

Monroe ran a hand through his cropped hair. I knew he cared about Nina a great deal but also that some loud and buzzy part of his head would be thinking how it looked to have an agent kidnapped on your watch, not to mention a butchered cop. He was forced to make a reluctant suggestion.

'It doesn't have to be the killer. Couldn't it be him?'

'Who?'

'Your brother.'

I stared at him. 'Why would he be killing locals here? And he was still in Pelican Bay when the John Doe got killed.'

'I know. But there's a version where Gulicks is still Thornton's killer, but your brother tracked you two here tonight. Nina shot him in the woods earlier in the year. Maybe he's come and got her back.'

This hadn't even occurred to me. 'And the hand-cutting is just a coincidence? I don't think so. And you'd better pray it's not. If it's Paul all bets are off.'

'I'm sure you're right,' he said. 'I just don't know where else to go on this.'

'Nobody in the hotel saw *anything*? No one on reception, no one on room service, no late guest getting back? Somebody got in that room and turned it into an abattoir and pulled Nina out of the hotel – and yet nobody saw or heard a thing?'

'We're still interviewing the guests but it's dead air. Room service stopped at ten thirty. The receptionist for the last three hours was the girl you scared to death. She spent the evening in the back office – standard practice: do prep for next day's business and only come out when someone rings the bell. Getting past her on the way in wouldn't be hard. Coming back out . . .'

'Nina was unconscious. Must have been.'

Monroe looked away. 'Or . . .'

'No,' I said. 'Not that. Unconscious.' I stood up. Jittery, needing to be on the move. 'I'm out of here.'

'Where are you going?'

'To do what I should have done an hour ago,' I said. 'Go looking. She's not here. So she's got to be somewhere else.'

I got a piece of paper out of my pocket and scribbled my cell number on it. 'Call me. The second. Anything at all.'

'I will.' He looked at me hard. 'You too. Don't think about dealing with this by yourself.'

'You think I'll promise you that?'

'No. But if you find him, I want to be there.'

'You won't stop me killing him.'

'I didn't say anything about stopping you.'

I drove around the town randomly and fast, windows open wide, listening for the sound of sirens. It occurred to me to go check the sites where the two bodies had been found, but the lot at the walk-down to Raynor's Wood was empty and I hadn't paid enough atten-tion to find the second murder scene again. I called Monroe with the idea and he said he'd send someone.

So I kept moving faster and faster, searching the town on a grid. I saw cop vehicles flashing in different directions but nobody paid any attention to me or stopped my car despite the fact I was driving like a maniac and – had they looked – liberally smeared with blood.

A second sweep brought me past the cop station and I pulled to an impulse halt. I was out of the car and walking up to the front doors before I knew what I had in mind. The interior was deserted, just one cop behind the desk looking tense. Luckily he was someone who'd seen me go in and out that afternoon.

'Sir, are you okay? Are you hurt?'

'No,' I said. 'I've just come from where Reidel got killed. Where's Gulicks?'

'In the cells. You can't go in there.'

'Yeah, I can,' I said. 'Call Special Agent Monroe. Tell him it's Ward Hopkins.'

I walked past him through into the back half of the building and headed down the corridor past the interview room from that after-noon. At the end was a sign indicating the overnight holding area, three grim-looking doors in a row. Another twitchy-looking cop with a gun was standing outside the middle one.

'Open the door,' I said.

'I'm not doing that, sir.'

I stood where I could see through the slot window in the cell door. The area beyond was small, nine feet by nine, dark except for light leaking in from the corridor. A narrow bed took up one side, a sink and a functional metal latrine on the other. A chair was positioned against the back wall in between.

Julia Gulicks was sitting bolt upright on it, head lowered. As I stared in through the slot, she raised her head. Her face was pale and her eyes were wide.

She looked straight at me. And something happened in her face.

I don't think it was a smile. But she did something with her mouth that wasn't right.

'Sir –' The cop from the front desk came walking fast down the corridor behind me. 'You've got to go. Right now.'

'I want to talk to her,' I said. She was still looking at me.

'That's not going to happen, Mr Hopkins. I just talked to Agent Monroe and he said not to arrest you but to escort you the hell back out of here, right away.' He put his hand on my arm. 'I don't want to have to . . .'

I shrugged him off. The guard cop was watching me closely. 'I'm going,' I said.

The cop shepherded me hurriedly back out of the station onto the pavement. He was extremely pissed and I knew I wouldn't be able to pull something like that again. Not that it had done me any good.

Except –

The look that woman had given me had meaning. No one smiles that way without something strange on their mind. Gulicks must know something serious had happened in town – the station would have been chaotic when news of Reidel's murder broke. She could have heard specifics through the door. Was she just reacting to that? To the news that the cop who'd harried her that afternoon had been killed?

I stood on the sidewalk, knowing the cop was still watching me from behind the desk. I had been exhausted even before I got back to the hotel after meeting Unger. Now I could barely think.

I sat down heavily on the steps.

Assumption, or hope: Nina wasn't dead. If the idea had been to kill them both, the attacker could have done it a lot more easily in the hotel room.

So: why would someone kill Reidel but take Nina alive?

Either the killer originally went there to murder them both and for some reason changed his mind, electing to kill the cop and abduct Nina instead. Or, the killer arrived with the intention of pulling Nina out. In which case either Reidel's presence was unexpected – and he got killed just because he was there – or the killer went in already expecting one fatality, one kidnapping. Either way, he succeeded in doing what he wanted.

So: assume Nina was the target. What did that mean? And who did it point towards?

Everybody's assumption had been that it was the killer at large in Thornton. From some hidden vantage he had observed Nina on the investigation, decided she was a danger to his safety or that he'd like to work on her next. I didn't like this last idea at all, but thankfully there was a problem with it – a complete switch of MO and victim profile: from the stealth killing of two middle-aged men to forcibly abducting an armed and female federal agent.

So: consider instead the idea it was somebody else.

Monroe's suggestion that it might be Paul had shaken me but it didn't stand up. It was true that my brother was capable of the attack on every physical and moral level. I just didn't make him for it. Partly because I believed he would have been there waiting when I returned to the hotel room. Also I didn't want to believe it because I knew if it was Paul then I would never see Nina again, no matter what I did next.

So who else? Other agents of the Straw Men? They'd doubtless have other people who would kill police officers without qualm: I had seen one of them empty his gun into Charles Monroe in a public place six months ago, and I had been to a location where the dead bodies of their victims had been buried in the gardens of high-value real estate. These were not people who understood boundaries on behaviour.

Then something clicked in my head.

*　　*　　*

I had no problem getting out of Thornton: I don't know which three exits were supposed to have been covered, but I evidently found some other way without any trouble. I put my boot down and got to Owensville fast. I dropped speed once I got to the main drag because there were more cop cars around here – Monroe's alert had evidently had an effect. I found the Days Inn and forced myself to enter the building slowly enough to look casual.

Three o'clock in the morning and the Inn still had someone behind reception. He looked dozy, to be sure, but he was there. Maybe if the place in Thornton had the same policy Nina would still be in her room, and I'd be there with her.

'I'm in 211,' I said, coming on tired and a little drunk. 'I lost my key someplace. Can you run me off another?'

'I'm sorry sir, I didn't see you check in. I'd need to see ID.'

I kept moving, pretended to fumble in my pocket. 'Oh – that's okay, I found it.'

'Goodnight, sir.'

I hurried up the stairs and down a corridor until I found room 211. I knocked on the door and put my hand in my jacket.

No response. I knocked again, harder. Put my head up close. No sound from the interior. I suddenly started feeling cold inside.

'Carl? It's Ward.'

Nothing. I stood back and gave the door a solid kick. The door barely registered it. I gave it another kick with no more effect. I don't know how to hack that kind of lock and wasn't fool enough to try shooting it out.

I ran back down to reception. 'Some problem with the key,' I said. 'It's not working. I need another one.'

'Then I'd still need to see ID.'

I pulled out the gun. 'Will this do?'

I saw him reaching to his left.

'Don't touch the phone. I'm investigating a homicide in Thornton.'

'You're a cop?'

'No. FBI.'

'You should have said.' With visions of making local news as Owensville's most helpful citizen, he was a different proposition. His fingers rattled over the keyboard in front of him. '211?'

'Yes. Carl Unger.'

He frowned. 'Um, no.'

'I really have to get inside that room.'

He grabbed a card blank from the pile and swiped it but didn't hand it to me. Instead he came out from behind the desk. Evidently he was coming too. I had neither the time nor the inclination for punching him out, so I followed. He was quick up the stairs and went straight to the door. He swiped the card through the lock and opened it.

I walked in. The room was empty. The bed untouched. The bathroom was spotless and the toilet still sanitized for someone's comfort and convenience.

I swore and rounded on the desk jockey. 'Tell me,' I said.

'Mr Unger made a reservation by phone late this afternoon. He called a little before ten o'clock this evening and cancelled it. It was too late and he had to pay but basically he checked out without ever entering the hotel.'

I sat bonelessly down on the end of the bed. I felt too angry and foolish to speak. Unger had separated the two of us effortlessly. He booked a room in the hotel so it looked like he was *in situ*, and to give him a place to draw me and Nina to the following morning if tonight's business hadn't gone as planned.

But it had. And so now he was gone. And Nina was gone.

Leaving just me.

When I got back to Thornton the parking lot of the Holiday Inn was jammed with police vehicles and two television trucks. A ring of pre-dawn rubberneckers stood on the pavement outside. I drove straight past. There was nothing for me there.

I drove to a place I'd already visited once that evening. The lot above Raynor's Wood. I sat in the car with the windows down, listening to the sounds of the forest. Nina's name kept swimming into my mind and my heart clenched tighter and tighter with panic.

'What do I do, Bobby? How do I find her?'

I asked before I'd realized I was going to, and silence was all that came back. Asking was foolish, but I knew that now was not the time to suddenly comprehend that people dear to me could become actually and permanently dead.

On impulse I got out my phone and hit the speed dial number for Nina's phone. It went straight to voicemail. I knew it would: Monroe had already tried to locate the phone via beacon signals and got nothing. The phone was switched off. There are conspiracy nuts who think you can trace them anyway. Sadly they are wrong.

So then I did the only thing left, and tried another number. I tried it again, and again, at five-minute intervals until finally at 7:03 it was picked up and I heard a voice for the first time in five months.

'What the hell do you want, Ward? I got your SMS and I don't know the guy's name.'

'John, I've got to talk to you.'

'We have nothing to say to each other.'

'They got Nina.'

There was a long pause. 'Who did?'

'I don't know. But they got her.'

'Where are you?'

'Thornton, Virginia. John, get here fast.'

Chapter 20

'It's business as usual. We just do what we do.'

'Man, you're dreaming. Nobody has called me in the last twenty-four. Two parties I know of have been cancelled just this week. People's parents are freaked, big time, and with the cops hassling people left and right . . . It's just not a party atmosphere, Lee. People are staying home and watching TV.'

It was twenty before nine in the morning and they were sitting in Lee's car outside the Starbucks from the night Pete died, working their way through vanilla lattes again. This morning they seemed sickly and over-sweet. Being there at all was Lee's idea. He had some theory that they should go places that connected with that night, to overlay any memories people might have from then: so the last impression the staff or any patrons might have – assuming they noticed or gave a shit – was of two guys being casual, at one with their world, not two whacked-out people who'd just buried their best friend. Brad didn't know whether this made sense or not. He thought trying to second-guess the cops was a game for people with a lot more experience. Lee's confidence was beginning to worry him a little. Since his one-to-one with this Paul guy, he seemed to be disconnecting from reality just a bit.

'Didn't they realize it was going to be tough?'

'Of course,' Lee said. 'But it's about turnover. Money in, money out. They got a shitload of pills and they don't last forever.'

This sounded like bullshit to Brad. 'I guess I could go check Stacy and Josh,' he said, without any enthusiasm. 'They didn't know Pete so well. They could still be partying.'

Hudek shook his head. 'Not the Reynoldses, no.'

'How come?'

'Just no.'

'Well, Lee, you got me. Take the drugs back to your friends and explain that what with some upstate shithead having blown Sleepy's *head* off, the market isn't so fucking buoyant right now.'

Lee turned to look at him. 'You okay, bro?'

'No I'm not okay, Lee. And I miss Pete. I really fucking miss him.'

'I know. Me too.'

Brad wasn't sure he believed this. It seemed to him that in Lee's universe Pete had become merely a problem to which a solution was being bought. 'His mom was on the phone to mine yesterday evening, asking if she knew anything.'

'She's calling everyone.'

'I don't care about the general fucking situation, Lee, okay? Right now I don't care about you or Steve or about the man on the street in Baghdad. I'm talking about *me*. Last night it was *my* mom she called. And so then Mom comes and sits in my room and – shit, man: you know the score. This is bad.'

'It's going to be fine.'

'No, Lee. I'm really not sure it will.' He hesitated. 'I had Karen on the phone last night too.'

'You guys are fucking. Talking comes with the territory. Deal with it, dude.'

'That's not what I mean.'

'I guessed that. It was a joke.'

'You think this is funny?'

'What are you actually talking about, Brad? I'm smart but I'm not a fucking mind-reader.'

'She keeps asking me things.'

'What kind of things?'

'After they found Pete's body she called me and we were talking, this and that, about how fucked-up it all was, and suddenly she asks me if I know anything about what happened to him.'

'What did you say?'

'I said no, of course. But . . . she heard something, Lee. I was out the front waiting for you that night, and she was there, remember? When you walked up you said "He'll be here soon", or "in a minute", or something like that. I don't specifically remember it but she sure as hell does. She knows we were waiting for someone and she thinks it was Pete.'

'Christ. So why didn't you say it was Jed or Matt or Greg?'

'Because I didn't think fast enough, okay? I just said that we went for burgers alone. Which is the way anybody watching would have seen it when we got back, right? So why bring any of those guys into it, especially if they're just going to say no, we didn't go?'

'Yeah, okay. So what was she saying last night?'

'Nothing else. Except . . . she said she hoped if anybody did know anything about it, they'd go to the cops. She said the cops seemed serious and it would probably be better for that person in the long run if they just told what they knew, even if it looked kind of bad.'

'You think she was talking about you?'

'I guess so. But I agreed with her and we left it. It just makes me nervous, man. And it makes me feel . . . guilty.'

'You're not, I'm not. She's just doing what she thinks is right. Our friends are going to make this go away and Karen will see we didn't know anything, and everything will be cool again.'

'They'll do that even if we tell them we can't sell their drugs?'

'This isn't about the drugs. They've got something else in mind. I don't know the details right now. But something's coming up. These guys are connected. They're like the Mafia, or something, but not Italian or Columbian or any of that shit. White guys. They got some big thing up ahead and we're going to help. None of this will matter.'

'Pete will still matter, Lee. Sleepy Pete will *always* matter.'

'Yeah, of course,' Hudek said, and Brad realized he barely remembered who Pete was.

Hudek's pager went off and he glanced down and read the message. He kicked the engine up.

'That's them,' he said. 'Time to go.'

There was something surreal about walking into the Belle Isle food court. It was a place Brad knew well. Limitless taquitas and egg rolls had been ingested there in the last five years, innumerable sodas and berry smoothies sucked up during slow trawls with the gang or with Pete or lately just him and Karen. Look back far enough and he'd come here with his mom and dad and sister too, withstanding their boring shopping imperatives by asking if he could go to the court and get a chocolate shake and wait, which had generally been allowed.

At this early time of day the food concessions were still being fired up and the seating area was largely empty, just a few housewife kaffeeklatches in progress and a seat-busting monster already hunched over the detritus of enough burgers to feed a small family, fries hanging out of his mouth like the remaining legs of insectile snacks.

And there was a guy.

He was sitting in splendid isolation at a table right in the middle of the floor. This surprised Brad until he happened to look around again. Widely spread around the seating area were three other individuals who didn't look like they were there to hunt for bargain animal calendars in Waldenbooks. None had anything to eat or drink. All were looking his and Lee's way. Casually. Kind of. They ranged from forties down to very early twenties. This youngest was eyeballing them the hardest. There was something about him Brad really didn't like.

Lee had the drug bag with him. Brad didn't like that either – but that was what the pager message had specified. When he got to the main man's table Lee went as if to hand the bag over straightaway. The man shook his head, one single movement.

'In a moment,' he said. 'Take a seat.'

Lee and Brad sat opposite. Funny: the way Lee had described him, Brad had been expecting someone who looked like a famous actor or something, a person you'd notice across a crowded room. Brad thought this guy could fade into background anywhere.

'Brad, right?'

'Yeah.'

'Good to meet you, Brad. I'm Paul.'

'Okay,' Brad said. Thinking: *There is something not right about you.*

The man turned his attention to Hudek. 'So you're not having much luck with sales.'

'We've done our best, but – with Pete dead it's just not the time.'

'Surely you didn't used to sell only to close friends.'

'No, of course not. But we sold i̅ a controlled area. And to a certain class. Look, we'll keep trying if you want.'

'Don't worry. The Valley's loss is West Hollywood's gain. We'll move them over there instead.'

Hudek felt pained. This didn't feel like it contributed to the upward progression he'd begun to enjoy. 'I'm sorry,' he said. 'Things are just screwed up at the moment.'

'It's not a big issue,' the man said. 'And it won't affect the Plan, don't worry.' He turned to Brad. 'Do me a favour, would you, Brad? Go get me an espresso?'

Brad's first inclination was to say hell no, he didn't run people's errands. But he got the sense that with this guy, you sort of did.

Also, as he opened his mouth, he got derailed by a cramp in his stomach, and winced.

The man watched him closely. 'Not feeling so good?'

'Had this gut ache a few days,' Brad said, feeling abruptly nauseous. 'Just can't seem to shift it.'

'You're under considerable stress.'

'You could say that.'

'What are you taking for it?'

'Oh, you know.' Brad's mom had dosed him with the greatest hits of her medicine chest, as usual leaping at the chance. The man's interest made him feel awkward. 'Pharmaceuticals in depth.'

'You should try something herbal. Scutellaria, maybe.'

Brad nodded, his irritation subsided, and he realized he was going for coffee after all and somehow didn't mind. This was what the guy had. It wasn't looks. He had the quality Lee aspired to and sort of possessed, but multiplied by a factor of a zillion. He was the alpha males' alpha male. You just did what he said.

Brad headed to the nearest concession which had no one in line. As the woman got the machine whirring he looked back over to Lee. He and the man were deep in conversation. Presumably about this 'Plan' thing, whatever the hell it amounted to – Spring Break? What the fuck? Brad didn't care right now. He wanted to get this meeting over with and maybe head to Karen's and hang out. Things seemed more tethered when he was with her. He noticed that two of the men he'd seen earlier seemed to have disappeared. Only the youngest remained. He looked full of himself and as if he could leap at the chance to do people harm. Brad wondered what on earth he and Lee could help these people with, and couldn't come up with anything that sounded credible: which made him wonder whether it was not help they needed, but cannon fodder. People they could send out on deals that might go bad, like the other night. Drugs were exactly like the film business, for which Brad's father had been careful to inculcate in his son a healthy scepticism. As a battle-weary entertainment lawyer, he had reason to. People seemed to assume their stardom slot was ready and waiting for them, and all they had to do was seize the day and use a little get-up-and-go and all that talk show crapola. Actually both industries were the same as large predators everywhere: you were snackfood to them, naive morsels seasoned with hope and greed. He hoped sooner or later Lee would get this. Brad could suggest it to him ahead of time, but his friend had a way of not really hearing any sentence that hadn't started inside his own head.

He trooped back over to the table, carefully carrying the little cup of coffee. When he got back there, Lee was nodding.

'Whatever way you want it,' he said to Paul.

'You know the big sports store, level two, by the escalator? I forget what it's called.'

Lee knew it. The crew had bought a lot of gear from there over the years. 'Serious,' he said. 'Of course.'

Paul took the coffee from Brad. 'That's the one. There's a rack of bags on the side wall. Hang it there. Near the back, where it won't be noticed. One of our people will swing by for it in a short while.'

Brad frowned. 'Isn't that risky?'

'Not on a morning like this, and not with last season's bag. None of you Valley princes would be seen dead with it, right?'

The man winked and put the cup of coffee to his lips. He drank the contents in one smooth movement. Brad tried not to gape. He'd seen the stuff come steaming out of the machine and had been surprised the cup hadn't melted.

Then the man stopped suddenly, cup still at his mouth. He was staring at something. Lee and Brad turned to look.

Outside Branigan's Irish Bar a large flat-screen television was slung from the wall. Though the bar wouldn't be open for hours, the television was on to make sure no one missed a chance to be advertised at. The sound was muted, and it was set to CNN. The picture showed a bunch of cops standing somewhere in what looked like a hotel parking lot. Yes – there was the Holiday Inn sign. Some on-the-spot news monkey was talking sombrely into a microphone.

Looked like somebody got killed. Brad found this concept wasn't as empty as it had once been.

Lee turned back from the screen to look at Paul. 'We'll talk later, right?'

The man nodded, still staring unblinkingly at the screen. They were dismissed. Lee seemed like he really wanted to shake hands with the guy, make some concrete gesture of comradeship, but the man's attention had left them, apparently for good.

'Later,' Lee said. There was no reply.

Brad followed Lee across the court and up the escalator. On the second level they went into Serious About Sport. Brad walked over to the desk and busked a long and complex enquiry about snowboard arcana, a matter upon which the clerks were more than happy to lavish the gravity of their slacker intellect.

They were showing him a third board when Lee wandered over, without the bag.

'Got to go,' he said.

Brad shrugged at the sales dudes, and they left.

'Kind of cloak and dagger, isn't it?' Brad said. 'How come we couldn't just hand the bag back over in the court?'

'Guy had his reasons,' Lee said.

Which he probably didn't even have to tell you, Brad thought, as he pushed the door and walked out into the warm lot. *Because you are now all about doing whatever he says. I wonder what you think that's going to buy you. I wonder if I'm set to get a cut. And if so, how small it will be.*

'So now what?' he said.

'We chill,' Lee said. 'The cops are going to get a tip-off this afternoon. They're going to hear how there was a deal with Pete Voss and a couple of kids from upstate he met at a party on Friday, the night before Karen's. A thousand-dollar deal they killed him for on Saturday night. The kids are set up and ready.'

'And why are the cops going to believe that?'

'Because it's slightly true and also the tip will hand them the position of Hernandez's body, who was Pete's accomplice, killed as part of the same deal. It's a package.'

That didn't seem too great to Brad. 'So Pete's mom is told her son got wasted while taking part in a drug deal.'

'Yeah, well, he did. Remember?'

'Can't it just be an accident or something?'

'No. It's too late. And if it was then no one but his friends would have buried him.'

'Not true, Lee. It's . . .'

'Brad, this is your get-out-of-jail card. You can't dictate what design it has on the back.'

'And what's it going to cost us?'

'Nothing.'

Brad shook his head.

He got dropped at home and got in his own car. Pulled the roof back and set off into the morning.

Karen's car wasn't in the drive when he got to the Luchs house. He'd tried calling on the way but got busy signals and/or voicemail redirect. He considered reversing right back out again but it would look rude and anyway the car could be in the shop.

When he rang the doorbell Mrs Luchs opened it. She seemed a little subdued. 'Hello Bradley,' she said.

'Hey, Mrs L. Is she here?'

'She went to the pharmacy. She left a note for you.'

He thanked her and took the note back to the car to read. It was a folded piece of white paper, inside a sealed envelope.

It said:

> B—
>
> *Mom probably told you I went to the store but that's not true. I told her that because I wanted to get out. I've been doing a lot of thinking and we need to talk. I know what you said but I know what I heard. Mrs Voss is on the phone*

the whole time to Mom about how it was our party that Pete was last seen at, like it's Mom's fault or something, and it's getting to her, plus if someone knows something it's just not right that the police don't know too. I think you and Lee know where Pete went that night. Pete deserves his killers to be found. I've looked into my heart and I think I really have to tell the police something. Let's talk before.

I'm going to go somewhere quiet to think. Please come find me.

Love you – K x

Brad stared at the paper for a full ten seconds after he finished reading, the message whiting out in front of his eyes. In a semi-trance he reached for his cell phone and speed-dialled her number again. It rang, not busy, but then flipped to voicemail.

He threw it on the seat and reversed out of the drive at fifty miles an hour. He went looking. And looking. His knuckles growing white. Praying to gods he hadn't known he believed in.

Trying not to cry.

After an hour and a half he had entered some kind of weird mental zone that felt like a blurry purgatory. His head ached with sunshine and reflections. He had looked everywhere he could think of. *Everywhere.* He had been to every mall except the Belle Isle because he knew she wasn't there. He had been over the hill to Santa Monica because there were places there he knew Karen liked to hang with friends, and he'd looked up and down the 3rd Street Promenade and even run down the pier because they'd spent a date there once. He had called his own home to check she wasn't there or sitting outside. He had called all of her friends he had a number for, and as he supplied drugs to most of them that was a lot of numbers. None of them knew where she was. A couple actually asked if he had any pills but it was too fucking late now.

And Karen still wasn't picking up her phone.

He didn't know what the hell to do. He was finally heading back towards the valley through Universal City because he couldn't think of any other direction to try. If he put his mind to it, if he *really* tried, he could believe that maybe his and her paths had crossed earlier, and that she'd been pulling into the parking lot of the Belle Isle just as they were leaving and that she might still be sitting there waiting. They'd been there a lot together, after all. Maybe she thought it was their place. Maybe it was. Brad wasn't sure. That kind of decision is always made by girls.

The traffic was slow but he was going to stick with it. If she wasn't there . . . he didn't know.

Had either of them ever written the L-word before? Committed to it on paper? He didn't think so. He had been back and forth over the contents of her note in his head and he believed she really did want to talk to him before she went to the cops. He knew her, and he trusted her. He realized now that it didn't matter whether she'd been with Lee. It had never *really* mattered to him, in fact, except that no guy likes knowing someone else has been where he is. The important thing was he loved her. She loved him, too. They'd talk this through and he'd get her to see there was no big deal, and then by the end of the day the cops would have a story and everything would go back to the way it had been. Brad was well beyond caring that Pete would come out of the story badly. Pete *had* been out on a drug deal. He'd already paid the price, and it was too high for sure but there was no point spreading the cost around those still living. Brad would come out of it older and sadder and wiser but he could deal with that, and this was fate telling him it really was time to find a job that didn't involve selling illegal substances. Karen would help him, he knew. It was all fine. It was all containable.

So long as he got to her before she went to the cops.

The traffic started to dawdle to a standstill. To save himself from going insane with the delay he tried to think himself around everything else, for something like the thirty-fifth time. Karen evidently hadn't said anything to her mom, or his conversation at the Luchses' would have been very different. She had a lot of friends, but he really believed she'd have kept quiet about something like this: after all, weren't *they* each other's best friend now? The fact Karen's phone had been off for so long maybe suggested she'd gone somewhere to think and had turned it off. Well, it kind of did. Actually that made no sense – and it hadn't the last three times the thought had occurred to him. If she wanted to talk to him, she'd have kept it on. Battery dead? Not very likely.

Maybe she was somewhere out of signal.

Shit, he hadn't thought of that before. She could have gone to the Santa Monica Mountains, maybe, be taking a drive through the Malibu or Topanga state parks. She liked it there. Always had. What did it say in the note?

Somewhere quiet . . .

Christ. And now he was headed in the wrong direction entirely.

Brad stood up in the car and saw that the traffic was starting to ease a little up ahead. He was split evenly between carrying on over to the Valley in the direction of the mall – the notion had reached a talismanic status in his head, not least because he could go check the bag had been picked up from Serious About Sport, he didn't like the idea of it just hanging there even though he'd never touched it and it could never be traced back to him – and the new idea.

There was nowhere to turn for a long block anyway. He'd make the decision then.

Gradually the traffic started to bear a little left, and he realized the right lane had been closed off ahead. Cool. Once he was the other side of this, he'd be able to pick up some speed again.

Mountains? Mall? Mountains? Mall? Maybe the mall still made more sense: he could always come back around this way if it was a bust.

He could see the lazy flick of lights now. Cop car. His heart had become so used to the heavy double-thud the sight now produced that it took him a moment to realize there were actually two cars, stationary on the right side of the road. And an ambulance.

Then suddenly Brad's car was level with the obstruction, as he drove slowly past it. Drove past it in a glittering daze.

A car lay smashed up against a post on the side of the road. It had a big, sharp dent in the other side. The front end was mangled to hell, windscreen long gone, fragments splattered red-brown.

The car was a nice new BMW. It was electric blue.

The cars behind him blared, but his foot had slipped off the accelerator. Brad wasn't going anywhere.

Not after he realized it was Karen's car.

Chapter 21

She is in a room and the air is dark and soft. The room is at the top of a wooden house, a place where dust motes hang and spin. The door is open, revealing an upstairs hall. Hazy light comes from here, seeping through a window which is dirty and also obscured by a pull-down blind. A narrow plank of wood is propped up beside it, one end splintered as if by great force.

The door to the room is painted white, as are the walls. Over time, and in this uncertain light, the walls have come to resemble the bruised grey of a heavy storm coming in off the sea: still distant, but unavoidable. Despite its size, the room has little sense of being an area in its own right. It feels as though it and the floors and even the house's exterior walls are arbitrary divisions in a wider space; one which perhaps even extends a little beyond the boundaries of the dwelling, though not as far as the trees which she believes surround it. Occasional noises come from out there, hoots or growls or swishing sounds: but so quiet and distant and muffled that they do not seem in the least real, or any argument for the existence of an outside world.

The floor of the room is covered by old, dusty carpet, which in turn supports a patchy collage of other materials. Pieces of glass, small fragments of fallen plaster, half a broken mirror, and some leaves. It's not clear how the latter got here, as the two big windows at the front end are firmly shut, and evidently not broken. On the other hand they allow no view of the outside world either, so they may not be trustworthy. A lampshade lies on the floor near the inner wall. Its garish 1970s purples, now faded a great deal, were once intended to complement the narrow stripes of the carpet, a pattern now similarly subdued.

On its own stands a wooden chair. It is facing away from the door and tilted at an angle. It is a dark green chipped by many years of casual use and would be unexceptional were it not for its status as the only complete object in the room, apart from the single bed frame pushed tight into the corner. The chair is not quite in the centre, but seems to have been placed to leave a larger area in front than behind, as if in anticipation of something. Did someone sit there and watch something, or were they made to watch?

Then she realizes someone *is* sitting in the chair.

It is a woman. Her face is turned away. She is twisted in a position that looks uncomfortable: back quite straight, knees bent. Nina walks quietly and carefully around to the front, to find out who the woman is.

She is only slightly surprised to see it is herself.

She sees she is a little slimmer than she realized and also that she looks very tired and pale. Her eyes are open and she is staring fixedly at the floor near the corner of the room. After a while her right eye seems to twitch. The movement gradually gains in strength and determination until it is something like a wink.

Yes. She is trying to wink, trying to say hi, I know you're there and that's okay. Nina knows that this does not mean she is all right, however.

223

And then she is in herself, in her body on the chair.

The air in the room seems to get darker and more dense. She cannot move and her feet are cold. She feels unbearably heavy and cramped. She is not looking at the floor in the corner after all, but at the wall just above it. She can see something fluttering there. She thinks perhaps it might be a bird but then she realizes it is a hand. It is flapping slowly, its fingers straightening and curling, as if trying to reach for something – or as if it was trying to understand its location in space, attached to the wall, about nine inches up from the floor. It opens, closes, silent and pale.

Then the hand is still.

It turns a little, as if listening.

Nina heard the noise too. It was a door opening and closing. The door sounded heavy. It was the door to the outside.

But it is not someone leaving. No, it is someone coming in.

The footsteps are heavy. They reverberate loudly and this sound too has a strange quality. With each step she seems to become more awake, and with that, loses her vision – the previous images, the room itself, merely phantoms seen on a confused inner eye. She sees a last movement of the hand at the wall; then she can see nothing at all.

As Nina struggles to separate what makes sense from what doesn't, she manages to establish only the following:

What she has been looking at is only a memory, a snapshot of somewhere she does not remember being. Either she has lost most of her sight, or she has been blindfolded. She has been tied to something. Her feet are bare.

And she feels very sick.

She tries to breathe normally. He is already very close. This tells her the room is smaller than she thought, or that she is now in a different place altogether. Perhaps she passed out again.

He is quiet. He does not want to speak to her. She knows this may be because some find talking to their victims confers a reality they do not wish to confront.

'I'm awake,' she says. Or tries to. It comes out as a mush of sylla-bles. She tries a couple more times until it becomes intelligible.

He does not reply.

She is assuming it is a 'he'. Men and women smell different, whether they are kempt or not, but there is too much of a pervading odour of dust and oil for her to make that call with complete confi-dence. She feels his/her/its hands on and around her, but soon real-izes they are merely checking she remains firmly secured. As he tightens the knot behind her head, she is glad to have it confirmed that something has been tied around her eyes. Blindfolded isn't good, but blinded is worse. Her vision of the world beyond the cloth is not quite nil, but is no better than shadows at midnight, the darkest soot falling across jet black. The only place he seems to linger is at the inside of her left elbow. He holds her tightly there for a moment, between what must be his thumb and forefinger. The strength of this pressure is enormous. This suggests he is a big man, and strong. She has no recollection of what he looks like. He arrived in the hotel room like a tidal wave hitting a beach house. She had barely a glimpse of a moving presence before her world went black. She has no idea what happened after that but she's wise enough to understand that her being in this place means it's unlikely it was anything good. Her being alive still, at this moment, is the only thing she can count on.

Everything else has to build from there.

'My name is Nina Baynam,' she says.

He seems to move away a little. She can sense him standing looking down at her. Her position is awkward. She is on her back, but her hands have been secured slightly behind her head. Her thighs seem to slope downwards, and then bend at the knee.

'My feet are cold.'

No response, and she decides not to speak again for the moment. Her consciousness does not feel stabilized. Presumably she received a blow to the head, and then was drugged. She has never experi-enced Rohypnol and is unfamiliar with its effects, but thinks this must have been something far stronger. Bubbles of strangeness are still surfacing. She cannot yet quite clear her mind of the impression that she is in the upstairs room with the chair, though this seems very unlikely now. Maybe that was earlier. Maybe she was never there.

She is getting no response when she speaks and so for the time being it's better to be quiet, so as not to encourage him to drug her again.

The man seems to move a little distance from her, to sit – she hears something settle under him. It is quiet for a spell, though she can hear things from the outside. These are the sounds she could not interpret when she first started to come back to herself, sounds that she thought came from a forest. They don't. She's still not sure exactly what they are, and tries not to reach for them yet. She needs to get things right. She needs to not make false assumptions and build illusory structures on them. She is not in a position in which she can afford to make mistakes.

There is another noise suddenly, shockingly loud.

It is the ringtone of a cell phone, surreally prosaic. She recognizes the melody, one of the standard factory presets that have become part of the background hum and clatter of modern life.

It rings and rings, and then it stops.

Soon afterwards she hears the seat relax as the man stands up again. Her body tenses. She wonders whether to say something else after all, to reason with him. Not to plead, not yet.

He comes closer. She can hear him breathing.

'Open your mouth.'

His voice is quiet and calm. Quite deep. Impossible to age. But it is a man, for sure.

She has no desire whatsoever to open her mouth. She purses her lips. She knows this is partly the urge of the powerless to exert power. She doesn't care. This is all she's got.

'Open it.'

The fear of what he might be about to do is powerful: far worse is the fear of what will happen if she continues to refuse. If he wants her mouth open, it will be opened. A common hammer will achieve that, quickly.

She opens her mouth.

Something is introduced into it. It has a dry, water-leaching quality. As it is pulled around behind her head and tied, she realizes it is a gag. She swallows with a click and understands her position is going to be a great deal more uncomfortable now.

Ten minutes later he is gone. She hears him open a door and close it. Again, there is a strange quality to the sound.

She is less angry with herself. Maybe she could have pretended to have still been knocked out, but chances were he would have taken the precaution regardless. It's perhaps odd he hadn't before. It suggests either that he wasn't expecting the drug to wear off so soon – which might be good news – or that he'd done this before, and knew the drugged will sometimes choke themselves if there is something in their mouths. Which would be bad news.

Either way, the gag may not be her fault. Excellent. Point for her. What else does she know?

She knows Reidel is likely to be injured, possibly dead. This is bad. She knows her abductor was able to come into the hotel and take her back out again without being stopped. This is bad too.

She considers a speculative timeline. Assume a couple of hours' unconsciousness, though it felt longer. The further she comes back into herself, the more she experiences faint recollections of time away. Of things that were not dreams but chopped-up memories: including experiencing once again the time, a year before, when a man had come for her in the dark at the development up in the Montana mountains, and nearly killed her. She shoves that recollection away but knows she has been here at least a few hours. No one has come to rescue her. This is bad. It is doubly bad because it gives her assailant time to have moved some distance from where she was abducted.

227

There are probably more bad things. But that's enough. It's bad all around. Except . . .

Ward had not been there. He had not been in the hotel room with her, and so presumably was okay. That was good.

Unless . . .

Nina felt a sudden, sick swirling in her stomach. If Ward's meeting had been fake, to separate them, then the pile of bad could swell to fill the sky. If this was not Thornton's killer, as she had been assuming, then it might be the Straw Men.

In which case Ward could be . . .

Dead in a room, sprawled wetly across a bed. Dead in a backstreet, partly hidden with trash. Lolling dead in a car, brains blown mottled over the side window, his face waxy and pale.

No.

No. She suddenly tensed every muscle in her body, made an all-directions spasm of movement with every ounce of strength. Her bonds didn't even stretch, but she triggered enough jags of pain around her body to haul her mind out of the mine shaft it had threatened to plummet down.

She resolved to lie quietly for now, to empty her head. Bad never gets better through thinking about it. Bad never gets better through trying *not* to think about it either.

You just have to think about something else.

She spaces out as best she can, but soon realizes something. There is a presence in her head. Some thing has come to make a home in her, an emotion she has vigorously defended herself from for most of her life. As yet it is a sly newcomer, and it knows it has work to do, deeper inroads to forge. But it's there.

She tries to breathe deeply and evenly. It helps, but not much. She has to accept this thing as a fact.

She is scared.

She is very badly scared.

Chapter 22

I sat in the car in the Mayflower's parking lot smoking cigarette after cigarette. I'd driven past the Holiday Inn on my way back into town and it was already heaving with busy-looking men and women in windcheaters with FBI printed on the back. There were cop cars in strength too, and there would soon be enough media people to cover the Olympics. The situation had been handed up to a world I didn't understand or trust. I couldn't have got close to Monroe even if I wanted to. Need arose, I had his phone number. For the time being it was just me, hunched in a car in the lot of a stupid bar.

I'd tried to snatch some sleep in the car in the small hours. It felt like betrayal but I had no useful way to deploy awareness and my mind was beginning to judder like a plane running out of gas. It didn't feel better for the forty minutes or so I'd managed. It ran the same old tracks, as if there was comfort to be had from repetition. There wasn't, not when the questions were 'Had I helped by getting

Unger to meet me somewhere other than Thornton, where I could have been closer to Nina?' and 'What kind of guy did you send to do what had happened in that hotel room, and what manner of thing might he do next?' Worse was the knowledge that I should have gone back to Nina: that after our heated words outside the police station I should have walked back and kissed her, said goodbye properly. It would have been a ten-yard walk then. Now it was not.

And yes of course I'd tried calling Unger's phone. Soon as I got a chance I would email the fucker too. Apart from the small thrill of threatening him from a distance, I might as well bark at the sky.

'Jesus – are you okay?'

I nearly wrenched my neck, turning to see where the voice had come from. Someone was standing by the car. The window was clouded up and I didn't see who it was until I opened the door.

Hazel was standing there. She eyed me warily.

'Not really,' I said.

'Is it something to do with what happened at the Inn?'

I didn't have to answer. She could see it was from my face. 'I got the keys this morning,' she said. 'Come inside.'

I pulled myself out of the car and followed her.

As I entered I caught sight of myself in the mirror along the wall. I saw Hazel's point. I did not look good. I went straight into the restroom and washed my face and hands, keeping the water cold to stoke my head. There wasn't anything I could do about the residual blood on my clothes. I kept my eyes away from the mirror for fear I might not recognize the creature reflected there.

When I got back out a coffee was waiting for me.

'I put a heap a sugar in it,' she said. 'I advise you drink it whether you like it that way or not.'

I did. Taste and warmth seemed to flood from my mouth down as far as my chest. For a moment I felt better.

'Was she your girlfriend?'

'Is,' I said. 'She still is.'

She looked dubious. 'They got any idea where she's at?'

'No.'

'This the guy who killed the two guys here?'

'I don't think so.'

She appraised me for a moment. 'You're not a cop, are you. Nor with the FBI neither.'

'No.'

She nodded, then frowned, seeming to look at something over my shoulder. 'Lloyd's not due till lunch,' she said. 'Plus, that's not his truck.'

I turned. A black car had turned into the lot. It pulled slowly around in an arc and drew to a halt on the opposite side, close to my own vehicle.

I got my gun out. Checked it.

'Stay here,' I said. 'And keep away from the windows.'

I walked out into the lot with my right hand held down by my side and somewhat towards the back. I made a slight curve as I went, moving towards the rear of the vehicle. If someone inside had in mind to shoot me, I hoped this would make their angle a little more difficult.

I stopped about five yards away from the car.

The engine died. The driver's side door opened and a man got out. He walked around the front. His hair was short and his face was lean and his eyes were sharp.

He was John Zandt.

'Hello, Ward,' he said. 'You look like shit.'

'I feel it.' I took a couple of steps closer, held out my hand. He'd take it, or he wouldn't. 'Good to see you, John.'

He nodded slowly, and shook.

'Never thought I'd say it, but it's good to see you too.'

We took a booth near the back of the bar. Hazel fixed more coffee and offered to make food, or find us some, but we both said no. I found it hard to imagine eating ever again.

'Tell me,' he said.

231

I told him everything I could think of, from Monroe coming to fetch Nina from Sheffer to what I'd observed and heard her tell of the investigation since. I told him of Unger's apparent attempts to contact Bobby and myself, and of what we'd spoken of in the bar in Owensville. I told him of the look I'd caught on Julia Gulicks' face through the cell window in the small hours, I told him about the condition Reidel's body had been left in, I told him about the two bodies found in the woods around Thornton.

He listened, eyes down, hands clasped on the table. When I finished he said nothing for a moment, then looked up at me. 'Have you considered the idea that Unger might not be a part of what's happened?'

'Not yet. But I will if you make me.'

'I'm just not sure why he'd have this conversation with you if he was a point guy for the Straw Men.'

'To sound convincing.'

'Why give you information you don't already have? The spam technique sounds feasible. I suspect also it's used as a fishing net, on the theory if someone is stupid enough to respond then there's a chance – on the promise of some great deal or other – they'll be stupid enough to come meet a guy down a dark alley someplace and not tell anyone where they've gone. Either way it sounds more like Unger was feeding you stuff to open you up. If he wanted to take you out he would have done it right there in the bar and hang the consequences. And you got no bad feeling off him, right?'

'He seemed like a regular guy. Convincingly gung-ho for the Company, too, though that could just have been him running interference. Judging character is an inexact science.'

'When was the last time you got it wrong?'

I thought about it. 'I can't remember.'

'Right. From what I've seen, you tend to make decent guesses.'

'Maybe. The jury's still out on you, though. What's your point?'

'The only thing implicating Unger is that Nina got taken. But that's not proof: could be the abductor was watching the pair of you closely and picked his moment when you were out of the way. Could even just be a coincidence. Judging by how he conducted himself when the time came, it could be he wouldn't have cared much if you were there. This is someone competent and insane. He might have enjoyed fucking you up too.'

'Which brings me to the thing I haven't yet mentioned,' I said. 'Paul's escaped.'

I don't know what I expected from this revelation. Fury, incomprehension, John storming straight back out into the lot. In fact he just nodded.

'I expected that to make you as unhappy as it did me,' I said. 'But I guess you figure this gives you another chance of killing him, correct?'

'Underneath it all, you're really quite smart.'

'Doesn't it worry you they can break someone like Paul out and leave the Feds just scratching their heads?'

'Doesn't surprise me in the least. I've spent the last year researching these people. I know things about them you wouldn't believe.'

'John, spare me the weird shit, okay? I'm not in the fucking mood. If you now think the Straw Men are space aliens from beyond Orion's Belt, keep it to yourself. These people scare me enough without giving them tentacles.'

'They're human, Ward. That's the worst thing. Have you tried calling Unger since last night?'

'Yes of course I have.'

'Dead?'

'Voicemail redirect.'

'You emailed him?'

I shook my head.

'I think it would be a good idea.'

'Why?'

'Nothing to lose if he's one of them. Plenty to gain if he isn't.'

'He didn't seem to know a great deal, John.'

'He knows their name. Right now that puts him about fourth most knowledgeable in our circle and maybe the whole US. That makes him useful – especially if Monroe isn't prepared to go to bat against them. Unger's already on the case, and probably knows more than he let on. He has government backup. And if he *is* a bad guy then our going to him for help makes us look more stupid than we are.'

'Okay. We'll go to a Starbucks and wi-fi from there.'

'There's a Starbucks in this place?'

'There's one everyplace, John. Where the hell have you been? They're building new towns just so they can put coffee houses in them. Come on, I want to get moving.'

I went out back quickly and thanked Hazel. I tried to pay her, too, but she wouldn't have it. She wished me luck and said she'd pray for my friend to be okay, and I thought that if her boss Lloyd had any brains at all, it would be Hazel he was chasing.

We took Zandt's car, after I'd called Monroe from the lot and established that absolutely no progress had been made in any direction. The agent sounded harried and angry and exhausted and it wasn't hard to tell he was doing the best he could.

I directed John to the historical district and we parked directly outside the coffee house. It was full of people who looked like they were from the media. A big old guy with grey hair was sitting in the window staring out with tired eyes. Luckily the signal was strong enough that we could piggyback internet access from the car. I sent an email to Unger, telling him what had happened and asking him to get the hell in touch. I still hadn't dropped him as a factor in Nina's abduction, but as John said – there was nothing to lose. When I was done I looked up to see Zandt was frowning at his own screen.

'You got a problem?'

'I don't know,' he said. 'Can you check something for me?'

He read me out a web address and I typed it in. The browser went to a badly-laid-out page with type in a numbing variety of sizes and colours. It was supposed to have a lot of pictures on it too, but each space came up blank. 'Doesn't look good,' I said. 'What is this anyway? Who's Oz Turner?'

'The lack of pictures – that because the signal's weak out here?'

I tried a few things and shook my head. 'No. There's placeholders for them in the page's HTML, but the pictures look like they're missing from the server.'

John closed his machine and took out his phone. He got hold of someone and asked to talk to Oz Turner. Evidently got the response that the guy hadn't got in to work yet. Left a 'deliver this or else' message, telling Turner to call him immediately he showed up. Closed his phone looking sombre.

'What's that all about?' I asked.

'Hopefully nothing,' he said. 'We should get moving.'

'Moving where? I've looked. Believe me, this guy's not just sitting on a street corner having brunch.'

'I know that,' he said. 'We can't go looking for her. We don't know where he's got her, assuming it is just a "he" and not a team. We don't even know where to start. I want to go look at something else.'

I waited for him to tell me where, but he said nothing more. I turned to see he was looking through the windshield. Fifty yards up the street, kids from Thornton's high school were milling around the spacious grassy area inside the gates, filling time between classes, making hours fly as the young do.

'John?'

He didn't seem to hear, and I realized he was looking for Karen, the daughter abducted by the Upright Man on 15th May 2000 and never seen again in one piece. She would have been about nineteen by now, had she not been murdered. The oldest kids we could see were maybe sixteen, seventeen, and so Karen would have been too old to be emerging with them this morning: unless perhaps she had simply been held up inside for a long, long time, getting some piece of classwork just right, talking to a teacher about costumes for the school play, taking a couple of years out to help a fellow pupil who wasn't quite as smart as she was. Being in all things and all ways the perfect person she was free to be, since she was not alive any more.

'You okay?'

'Fine,' he said, and looked away as he drove past the school.

John told me where he wanted to go and I directed us as far as I could remember. Then Zandt got on the phone, called the Thornton sheriff's office and impersonated an FBI agent. He had been in law enforcement before, a homicide detective in Los Angeles, and he knew the language and protocols far better than I did: but I was still intrigued by the ease with which he assumed the role.

'Been doing that kind of thing often, have you?'

He didn't answer. He kept driving north-west. Eventually we hit the long straight road out into the wet woods, and I started recognizing things.

'What are we doing here?'

'Something you said when you told me about the second victim,' he said. 'What were the forensics on the body?'

'I don't know any more than what I saw on the night,' I said. 'I was only there on sufferance. Nina didn't have a chance to update me the next day because the Gulicks thing went wide. Forensics may not even be back yet. They probably switched to examining what was left of Reidel.'

I saw a stretch of gravel by the side of the road that looked sort of familiar, and I told Zandt we were getting close. A hundred yards later I told him to stop.

I got out the car and looked out into the damp forest. 'This is it,' I said. 'It's in there.'

He got out and went around the back of the car. He opened the trunk and reached for something inside.

I looked back along the way we'd come. 'Anything strike you about the drive we just made?'

'Not really,' he said. 'Other than I felt no real pang in leaving that town behind.'

'We didn't get stopped.'

I called Monroe again. He had neither the time nor the inclination to talk but I wouldn't go away until he'd got the message. If the town was supposed to have been secured, it wasn't working. He put the phone down in the end.

Zandt shut the trunk. A long canvas bag was slung over his shoulder.

'What's in there?'

'Tools,' he said. 'Which way now?'

I set off into the woods. The going got boggy real soon, the previous night's rain having turned the ground even more mushy. I wasn't too sure of where I was going but just when I was beginning to doubt myself I caught sight of incident tape in the distance. I walked us to the point where the boards had been laid to create a bridge onto the little island. One of them was now broken. We got ourselves across without incident.

John stood a moment, looking around.

'Shirt was over there,' I said, pointing. I led him to where it had been, and turned him round to see what I'd shown the others the night before last. 'It's hard to get the picture now, but it seemed pretty clear at the time.'

'I believe you,' he said. 'It was hung out over these branches?'

'Yeah. Facing back that way.'

John looked out over the rear end of the semi-island. All you could see was more trees marching up a hill, though in the distance they seemed to thin.

'What's that way?'

'Some small town, I think someone said.'

'The cops went through all possible exits from this position?'

'I assume. But as I said – I heard nothing on this yesterday. And if they didn't get it done then or that first night, it's not going to happen. All available manpower is otherwise engaged. Seriously, why are we here, John? I don't care how the dead guy got on this island. I care about where Nina is and I feel like I have spiders under my skin.'

'I know you do. But you were right. Putting that shirt there was not an accident. The killer was making a point about something. Why here?'

He walked back to where the defleshed body had been found. The area had been largely cleared of undergrowth, and the ground was uneven where shallow soil samples had been taken in a vain attempt to establish where the body had been kept previously.

I watched as he unslung the bag from his shoulder and pulled the long zip which ran along its side.

'So what's your theory?'

He put his hand in the bag and pulled out a shovel.

'John, if we screw up this crime scene they'll throw us in jail.'

He started digging.

The ground was very soft and within fifteen minutes he'd made a complete mess.

'Cool,' I said. 'So, underneath the mud you've found a bunch more mud. I'm out of here. This is a waste of time and . . .'

'And Nina's out there somewhere.' He kept digging, like a machine. 'I really do get it, okay? I came a long way this morning and not because of you.'

'If this is such a good idea, why didn't the cops do it?'

'Because they had no reason to.'

'So why do we? If the ground looked like it had been disturbed recently, they would have dug it up. They didn't, so it can't have looked that way.'

He straightened, and perhaps saw that I was a beat from walking away from him. He spoke patiently.

'This is how investigations work. You do what you can and hope that eventually it takes you where you want to be. If you're going to go, just go. Otherwise you can either stand there going insane over a problem you *cannot solve right now* or you can grab another shovel and help.'

This derailed me. 'You've got another shovel in there?'

He started digging again. 'Of course.'

'Why would you have two shovels?'

'I've got two of everything, Ward. I've got two shovels and two cameras and two of most types of gun. I've got two maps and two laptops and a lot more than two sets of ID.'

'I asked why, not for a stock list.'

'Because if you're out by yourself the one thing you *cannot* afford is not having the thing you need. You have two of everything to make up for there only being one of you.'

The set of his shoulders spoke of too much time spent in an empty car, of evenings in chairs outside silent rooms in cheap motels, of dark hours lost in contemplation. I didn't know him well but it was obvious he had changed: as if he had been through his soul and thrown out everything that didn't help lead him where he needed to go. He looked like a one-man patrol unit, the lone mercenary of his own lost cause.

'You didn't have to be out there on your own.'

'How have you spent the last six months?'

'Hiding. In a borrowed cabin up near where we saw you last.'

'I guessed it would be something like that. Did you need me as a neighbour, someone guilty of three homicides?'

'I thought it was two.'

'You remember Dravecky, the real estate developer?'

'The one you sold out to, for information on where Paul might be?'

'I didn't sell out. I made him think I had. I went back for him later.'

'And killed him.'

'He was a very bad man.'

'I wonder whether you're in a position to make that kind of call any more.'

'I believe I am.' He stopped, looked up at me. 'Three is a lie too. There have been another four since.'

'Jesus, John. Why don't you just apply to *join* the Straw Men? You must about qualify by now, right? Seven murders? These are decent numbers.'

'These people *were* Straw Men. When I took out Dravecky I left with a stack of his computer records. Each of those four guys was in the organization, and also someone very evil. And yes, I do mean "evil" – murderous and deranged but too rich or powerful for the law to ever touch. So I did it. I'll likely do it some more.'

'They probably want to kill you pretty bad by now.'

'My point exactly. You didn't need me around.'

'We tried to call you, regardless.'

'Yeah. The woman I used to live with called me. The man who didn't kill my daughter's murderer called me. Some days you're just not in the mood to take those kind of calls.'

He turned away and kept on digging. I took some deep, even breaths, then went and got the second shovel.

Another twenty minutes turned the scene into even more of a mess without revealing anything useful. The mud was wet and sticky and heavy and shovelling it got increasingly hard.

I looked up from my section of the landscaping carnage to see John had stopped digging. 'There's nothing here,' he said.

I was reminded of the time the two of us had walked out onto a high, desolate plain south of Yakima and found a cabin which had been used as a storehouse for the dead, and used that way for many years. It was John who'd taken us out there looking, on a tip I wouldn't even have listened to. But it was me who'd kept us going. I have a certain lazy doggedness: sticking to the task in hand saves you the work of deciding what else to do instead. Right now I was warm despite the cold, and the rhythmic movements of the shovel had helped blank my mind of other things.

I moved six feet away and started digging a new hole.

After a moment, he went back to work.

'Ward,' he said, suddenly. 'Come here.'

We were fifteen feet apart by then, and had been digging for over an hour. I walked over to where he was standing.

He was maybe nine feet from the point at which he'd started. At his feet was a hole about two feet deep. The bottom had an inch of water in it already. But you could see there was something in there.

I bent over and looked more closely. Looked up at him. 'What the hell is that?'

We both started digging, much more quickly. Water seeped in through the sides of the hole almost as fast as you could slush it out, but after only a few more minutes it was obvious we'd found something sizable. John went to his bag and got out a pair of trowels and we both went down on our knees and spent another ten minutes clearing material away. The nature of our discovery became hard to deny. We stopped and stared down at it.

'Is that what I think it is?'

'Yes,' he said. 'That would be a ribcage.'

'Christ. Human?'

'Looks like.'

I oriented myself in relation to the body by the direction of curve in the revealed sections of seven ribs. I started digging with the trowel again, moving to an area two feet to the left.

'What are you doing?'

I didn't answer but kept going until I found the upper arm. I moved further left and found the bones of the lower arm. These ended in a pair of jagged lines.

Then nothing.

'Okay,' I said. 'No hand.'

He got the connection. We stood up.

'Christ, John – what's going on here?'

'I don't know,' he said. 'But check this – there's no smell. At all. And you see the colour of the bones, their texture?'

'Stained brown. Porous-looking. Which means this has been here a while, right?'

'At least ten or twelve years, maybe a few more. How old is this suspect they got for the other two bodies? The red-haired woman?'

'Twenty-five.'

We both stood there quietly, and did the math.

241

Chapter 23

Lee was sitting in his kitchen. It was as clean as it was going to get. The reason his house always looked spruce – and he knew that this mildly freaked Brad out – was simple. He spent a lot of time cleaning it. First week he moved into his own house, Lee realized it was going to have to be that way. All his life there had been a maid or two around: he had never seen his mother do anything more strenuous than rinse out a martini glass, and that had been desultory and *in extremis*. But he didn't want a maid. He was twenty years old. It would be ridiculous – not to mention there were sometimes things in his house you wouldn't want a nosy Mexican to lay her hands on, maybe start thinking she could parley the information into a favour with the immigration services.

So he cleaned it himself. He soon found he was good at it. Liked it, even. Kind of a gay thing to get into, maybe, but if you did it yourself, you knew it was done. Nowadays, whenever he needed to think properly about something, he cleaned. It was his guilty secret. He guessed everybody had one.

The house was absolutely quiet. He liked it that way too. A lot of his friends – their parents too, and younger sisters especially – seemed incapable of spending time without aural wallpaper. Had to have the TV on, or the radio. Failing all that, conversation. Something. Anything. Lee was not that way, just as he was not someone who had to take drugs to go out and party. He took a line of coke every now and then, to show willing. Otherwise, he stayed away and stayed clean. You needed to be sharp in this life. You needed to be together. You needed to have your ducks in a row.

Boy, but he was going to be happier when he heard the Pete thing was dusted away. Then everything would be in profit, that stupid evening nothing more than an event which had brought him a lot closer to the guys that mattered, and which had – by happy accident – also got rid of Hernandez. This evening should be a time for celebration. He wondered what he'd do. Maybe give Brad a call, though the guy had been unusually flaky that morning. Problem with getting close to people, chicks in particular, is it gave them the power to rock your boat. First your boat, then your world.

Lee thought maybe he'd get a piece of paper and make notes about stuff to talk to Paul about next time. Get the Plan moving into higher gear, now things were getting back to normal. He stood up to go fetch some from the right side of the second drawer under the silverware – everything had a place – and realized a car was driving *fast* along the road towards the house.

He recognized the car.

It skidded to a ragged halt. The door opened and Brad climbed out. He was all over the place. He looked like he couldn't even walk properly. He was shouting something. And he was headed straight for the front door.

Hudek walked quickly out into the hall and had the door open before Brad had a chance to bang on it. Brad's face was red and wet and his hair was sticking out all over the place.

'You fucking,' he shouted. 'You fucking . . .'

Then he burst into the house and was on top of him. He just went postal. It was like being attacked by a tiger on meth. You didn't always remember it but Brad was two inches taller than Lee and had maybe an extra five to ten per cent of strength at his disposal. He was screaming, his voice rasping out so much it was impossible to hear what he was saying.

Lee tumbled backward into the hallway and was battered quickly down onto his back. However out of control Brad was, it wasn't stopping him piling blows into Lee's face and neck and chest. He punched back as best he could, all the while trying to push out with his knees and roll out from under the bigger boy, trying to get out so he could restart this whole thing at less of a disadvantage: and also before Brad grabbed his head and smashed it on the floor, which he showed every sign of being willing to do.

He managed to gasp out a single sentence, panted out word by word: 'Brad – *what the fuck is your problem?*'

Brad wasn't saying. Brad was all about causing damage right now.

Finally Lee managed to connect a fist hard enough to get him to rear back, just for a second, and Lee shoved him hard to the side and kicked him again and then struck out hard with his arm. Brad's head connected with the wall and that was enough for Lee to pull himself out and up onto his feet.

He'd hoped maybe that would be enough to earn a time-out, but Brad just lunged straight after him.

Whatever this was it was *serious.* Lee turned and ran back through the house. He made it into the living room and saw he'd left the doors to the yard open. He'd never tried climbing the fence down the end and it would freak the hell out of neighbours he'd trained to think of him as a very nice young man, but it could be they were just going to have to deal with it . . .

Then from nowhere Brad tackled hard from the side and brought him down in the middle of the living room. Started whaling into him again, punches less and less accurate but still very, very hard.

Lee managed to roll him off again and reconsidered – on a straight run Brad could always catch him.

He turned and ran back towards the kitchen, still shouting at Brad and trying to get him to tell him what the hell was going on in his head.

And that was when he got a glimpse of Brad's eyes again and heard the growling sound coming out of his throat, and knew this was non-negotiable. He wasn't screwing around: Brad really was trying to fuck him up, and trying to fuck him up for good.

He turned around the corner and headed down the corridor. Yanked open the door at the end and stepped quickly into the double garage. He could hear Brad coming on fast behind him but knew if he just kept his head and got to the storage unit . . .

He got there. Grabbed the drawer open and pulled out the gun.

Turned around and pointed it straight at Brad's head.

Brad hesitated. For just a moment it looked like he was going to come on anyway, as if he was just going to run straight at the gun.

Lee was now panting heavily. 'Brad, what the fuck?'

Brad was a mess. He was crying and snot was running out of his nose down over his mouth. He didn't seem to realize or care.

'You killed her,' he said. His voice was a croak.

'What are you *talking* about?'

'Don't fucking lie to me. You killed her. You got her killed.'

Lee kept the gun trained firmly on Brad's face. There was only about six feet between them. If Brad lunged, he was going to have to shoot very fast. 'Brad, I have no idea what you are talking about. Got *who* killed? Who's dead?'

'You know who. Kar . . .'

Brad's face crumpled and his speech was lost to comprehension for a moment, stretching into a long, moaning sound that finally resolved into a recognizable name.

Lee stared at him. 'Karen? Karen's dead?'

Brad screamed at him. 'Of course she's dead, you prick! You think

245

she was going to survive that? Or didn't they tell you how they were going to do it?'

'Brad, you have to calm down and tell me what you're saying because right now I have no fucking clue what this is about.'

Brad pulled his hand viciously across his eyes, sniffed hard. Blood had started to run out of one nostril.

'You told them.'

'Told them what?'

'You told them Karen was asking questions. That she thought we knew something about what happened to Pete.'

Hudek opened his mouth, shut it again. Guilty as charged.

Brad nodded tightly. 'I knew it,' he said. 'You turned her in. You thought she was going to blow it for us, and you turned her in.'

Lee licked his lips, spoke carefully. 'I'll be honest with you, man. Yes, I mentioned it to Paul. I did mention the situation. While you were getting his coffee. I thought he should know, that's all. I told him it wasn't a problem, that she wouldn't do anything to hurt you, and he said it was fine, everything would be cool by the end of the day anyway and nothing would matter.'

'But that's bullshit,' Brad said. 'It didn't matter if the cops had been spun some other story. If Karen told them we'd lied to them, they'd have come for us anyway. They'd have come for us and the other story would have fallen apart in seconds. You knew that, and he knew that, and so you got her killed to stop her talking.'

'Brad – I didn't.'

'You know how they did it? Right in public. Right in the fucking street. Some guy in a Humvee just rams her car in broad daylight and then drives off. Her face got squashed flat. Her fucking arm came off, Lee. Her fucking *arm*.'

'Look, Brad, for Christ's sake, I'm nothing to do with this. I told the guy but it was just information. You don't know it's them anyway. It could just be an accident. Did you even think of that?'

'Yeah, right. Don't treat me like an asshole, Lee.'

'I didn't mean for them to do anything to her.'

'I don't believe you,' Brad said. 'And it doesn't matter anyway. You told him. You got her killed. You killed her whether you meant to or not.'

'It's not my *fault*.'

'Nothing ever is, right? What's the fucking problem, Lee? You couldn't stand the fact she was with me instead of you, or what?'

Lee laughed. 'What? Man, I didn't care.'

'Yeah you did. Yeah you *fucking* did. Ever since I've been seeing her you've been an asshole about it. Telling me you screwed her. Dropping hints all over the place. Yeah, you thought she might talk and you wanted her gone because of that but it was personal too, wasn't it? Just fucking admit it.'

Lee went light-headed. 'You were *welcome* to her, you asshole. Fucking ice queen. She couldn't blow for shit anyway.'

Suddenly Brad went quiet.

Ominously quiet. He was no longer crying either.

'You're dead,' he said, matter of fact.

Hudek could see Brad's body gathering to explode. The tendons in his neck stood out like wire. He knew if Brad came at him now, he really was going to die.

'Brad, don't make me do this,' he said, keeping the gun steady. He wished he could remember how many shots he'd fired that night in the parking lot. 'Don't you fucking make me do this.'

'I loved her,' Brad said, with eerie calm. 'That's something you're never going to understand because you're screwed up in the head. I loved Karen. And you got her killed.'

'Brad, we have to . . .'

And then Brad hurled himself at him.

Lee pulled the trigger like they did on television. Two quick pulls, bang bang.

The reports were deafening in the confined space and the gun was pointed direct at Brad's face and not wavering more than a degree.

Brad smacked into him like a train and threw him into the back

247

wall. Both heads hit it hard and then fell to the ground and Lee started to struggle immediately, feeling nightmarish with the other man's body on top of him.

Then he realized there wasn't any blood.

And that Brad was still moving, not twitching but shoving just as hard as he was.

They pushed each other away, wound up sitting a couple of yards from each other on the concrete floor.

They looked at each other. There was a spray of something that looked like soot across one side of Brad's face. Lee's eyes were open wide and he still had the gun in his hand.

Then Brad started to laugh.

It was a quiet, horrible sound, the noise a mind might make if it came unhinged and started flapping in the wind.

'Blanks,' he said. 'They were fucking blanks.'

Lee just stared down at the gun.

Chapter 24

'We don't know who the second victim is yet,' Monroe said. 'Nobody's missing that we're aware of. A picture has been shown around with no hits. There was no ID in his pockets, no tattoos or distinguishing marks left and his prints go nowhere either. His clothes are no help and the lab got nothing off them to help us with where he was kept after death. He's either a transient or a citizen from some other town or he dropped straight out of the sky and landed there on that island.'

'The picture was shown around the Mayflower?'

'Yesterday afternoon. But people aren't good at recognizing dead faces. He certainly never made an impression like Widmar did.'

Monroe and I were sitting in the lobby of the Holiday Inn. The crowds of the morning had dissipated. Scene-of-crime teams had gone, local cops moved out, and though there were still a couple of reporters in the parking lot most had determined this was old news now and gone to find somewhere nicer to park their bags and flirt with each other while they waited for fresh and juicy developments. There were Feds present but they had retreated to the temporary HQ in the hotel's business centre. The only people around in bulk were staff, and their voices were especially perky this late afternoon, as if loud greetings and broad smiles might somehow undo what had happened in one of their suites: but it still seemed like most of the guests had checked out.

Monroe had agreed to give me ten minutes. He looked more tired than I felt. He had not changed clothes since that morning, when I'd got the receptionist to roust him out of bed. It felt like about a hundred years ago to me, and I hadn't had to deal with the stuff he had. He had a pot of coffee on the table and was drinking it steadily, crisply – only the slightly robotic timbre of the motion giving away the fact he wasn't tasting it any more.

'We're going to find her, Ward,' he said. 'We really are.'

'You don't even know who's got her.'

Monroe's coffee cup went back up, and back down again.

'Do you even have a clue?'

'We've started doing a house-to-house, Ward. If Nina's in town or nearby, she's got to be in a building, a dwelling. We'll find her. Her abductor has to keep her somewhere.'

'Who isn't Julia Gulicks, that's for sure.'

'You shouldn't have gone to see her last night.'

'I had to check she was there. And I saw something.'

'What?'

'She must have known what had happened. The cops in there were so freaked out she'd have been able to sense it through the walls. And she looked up through the window in the door to her cell and she gave me a look that I can't explain.'

'She's guilty of two murders and has spent the last two weeks chopping bits off people. Who knows what's going on in her head.'

'Did the search of her apartment turn up anything?'

'It's ongoing.'

'Which means no. No basement for her to keep a body in. No hunks of discarded flesh. No cleaver embedded in the stairs.'

'She evidently did it someplace else.'

'There been another case of a woman doing that kind of thing? Ever?'

'I know what Nina thought about this. You don't have to do her job for her.'

'Why'd you bring her here?'

Monroe hesitated, for just a fraction of a second.

I leaned forward. 'I just don't get it, Charles. She explained it to me and I *still* didn't understand. Maybe you can do a better job. You know about the woman in Janesville when Nina was a kid, and so you realize she's conflicted over the subject. So how come it's this case you choose to use to drag her back into the world?'

Monroe started trying to speak, but I suddenly found I was too angry to let him. 'A world where three days later she's abducted from a hotel room by someone who slaughtered a city cop with a gun? Explain that, please, and make it simple and make it good.'

Monroe shook his head, and for a passing second I felt sorry for him. He didn't have any way of undoing what had happened. All he could do was wait while houses were searched.

He looked out the big window into the parking lot, where the light was beginning to die. It had started to rain again too. I hoped Nina could hear it, wherever she was – and that the sound would reassure her that time still passed, and that if enough did, I might get to her.

'She's the best investigator I've ever known,' he said. 'She carried me. I handled the system and local protocols, she solved the actual crimes. You know how messy it got with Aileen Wuornos in the end, petitions and documentaries and the whole nine yards. I just wanted to make sure we were watertight here if it came to a media clusterfuck. Nina was going to kick against the idea of it being a woman from the get-go, which meant we had to prove the case rock hard.'

'And now Reidel's dead, and Nina's gone, and the case makes no sense.'

'It still makes . . .'

I shook my head. 'There's stuff going on here that none of us understands. I don't know whether it relates to Nina, but at the moment it's all I have to think about.'

I reached to the bag I'd set down next to my chair when I arrived, and pulled out a series of colour prints I'd had done from stills taken with a digital camera early that afternoon.

I laid the first one down in front of him. 'Recognize this?'

He frowned. 'It looks like the second scene.'

'That's right.' I put down a second print. 'And this is looking back across the island, from where the shirt was hung.'

'I don't see anything here that . . .'

Third print. 'This is what it looks like now.'

He stared at the picture. 'What the hell happened?'

'Took a shovel to it.'

His eyes were wide. 'You're joking. This is somewhere else. You didn't really do that to it.'

'I surely did. And actually, it's worse than it looks.'

'I don't believe you've done this. I just don't believe it.'

'Someone had to. The shirt had to mean something. But you just looked at the surface and determined that's all she wrote.' I put another picture down. 'What do you see here?'

'Just mud, Ward.' His voice sounded hollow, aghast. 'And a hopelessly compromised crime scene.'

'Look again.'

Despite himself, he leaned over and looked at the picture more carefully. 'There's something in that hole.'

I put the next four down together.

He looked along the row, blinked, looked back the other way. 'Oh Christ.' He looked along again, then back again. 'No hand.'

He stood, looking like he was about to start moving in three directions at once. 'You should have told . . . we should have had a proper team on this. You've completely screwed this up.'

'If this is to do with where Nina is then I don't have time to wait for it to be done properly. I've got something else to show you too. It's outside.'

'I have to . . .'

'You are now officially playing catch-up, Monroe. Follow me right now or I will go into town and find the stupidest reporter I can and start telling them everything I know.'

I headed off towards the main doors. He was level with me by the time I stepped out into the lot. I walked quickly over to the side where my car was parked.

'Get in,' I said.

When we were both inside with the doors shut I started the engine.

'What are you doing?'

Then he heard the sound of the rear door opening, and someone getting in. Monroe wrenched himself around in his seat and stared at Zandt as if he was the devil himself, bearing hotdogs.

'Hey, Charles,' John said. 'Been a while.'

I flipped central locking on, drove over a flowerbed and straight out of the lot.

It was raining harder now and there was some unattractive skidding as I joined the main road. Luckily this distracted Monroe for a moment as he held onto the dash with both hands. Zandt reached over from the back seat, dipped his hand into the agent's jacket pocket and came back out with his gun and cellular phone.

Monroe grabbed his seatbelt and put it on. 'I don't know what you think you're doing,' he said. 'But it's a bad idea.'

'No,' I said. 'You're not going to like it, but that's your problem and you've got a ten-minute drive to come to terms with what's going to happen.'

'Give me my gun back.'

'No,' John said. 'Hold this instead.' He tossed something over to land in Monroe's lap.

'What the hell is that?'

'You tell me.'

Monroe gingerly picked the thing off his trousers. It looked like a short, curved stick, but you didn't have to be a forensics staffer to tell that it was not.

'I went to Richmond this afternoon,' Zandt said. 'Pulled in a couple of prehistoric favours. Had someone look at this and a couple other of the bones we found.'

'Where's it from?'

'Didn't Ward show you the pictures yet?'

'Christ,' Monroe said. 'So you've not just screwed the scene, you've defiled the body too. Or are you so far in the outfield now that you don't understand that kind of thing any more?'

Zandt ignored him. 'The sciatic notch from the pelvis says the body was female. Dating this kind of thing is inexact. My friend said he needed to have seen it *in situ* and we were dumb to remove it, so you and he would agree there. But in his opinion it would have been hard for that bone to have reached this condition in fewer than fifteen years, plus or minus a couple.'

'Say that again?'

'You heard me. This bone came out of the ground near a spot indicated by material left at the site of a murder you're attributing to the suspect in Thornton jail. But this body was put in the ground at a time when your only suspect was between eight and twelve years old.'

Monroe looked at the object in his hand. 'Assuming I take your word for all of this.'

'Why would we lie?' I said, taking the bend which led over the hill past the school towards the centre of what passed for this town. 'I don't give a damn about your killer except in how it relates to Nina. She nailed this from the start. She said a woman didn't kill those two men. This says maybe she was right.'

Monroe rubbed his forehead with both hands. 'And so why am I in this car with you now? Why couldn't we have had this conversation in the hotel?'

'This is the part you're going to have to get your head around,' I said. 'We're about to do something untoward, and you're going to help. John wants to talk to Julia Gulicks.'

'No way,' Monroe said. 'Absolutely no way.'

I'd been expecting him to say no, of course – but I was still surprised by his vehemence. I'd hoped the bone would just push him to the next step, that he'd see it was the obvious way to go.

'We're three minutes from the sheriff's office,' I said. 'You're going to have to change your mind fast if we're not going to waste time. My understanding is that even you would admit that John was a good homicide detective. The way I hear it, he nailed at least one case for you back in the day. So what's your problem?'

'Forget it,' Monroe said. 'He's not a policeman any more. He has outstanding murder warrants, he's actively dangerous, and over my dead body am I letting him *anywhere* near . . .'

'Look,' I started, but then realized I could hear an odd, melodic noise. I didn't work out what it was immediately, as it wasn't one I was used to hearing.

Then I swerved straight over to the kerb, nearly skidding the car. I reached in my jacket and yanked out my phone. Read the number off the display.

But it wasn't Nina.

'It's Unger,' I said, feeling like I was about to walk out over a long drop.

'Take it outside,' John said.

I opened my door and stepped out into the rain. I flipped open the phone.

'Ward,' he said immediately. 'It's Carl.'

I was silent for a second. What did I do here?

'Ward? Are you there?'

'I'm here.'

'Your friend Agent Baynam. Is there any news?'

'How did you know she was the person I'd told you about?'

'Because the second I left the bar I started calling around.'

I wished he was in front of me. 'You put her in danger. You may have killed her.'

'It's a risk I had to take. I'm not screwing around with this. Your privacy means dick right now. You held back on me last night. So I did what I had to do.'

'What did it get you?'

'Nothing. I still have no idea what is going on. I'm in Langley. Why don't I come back to you? I could be there in two hours tops. We need to talk. I may be able to help.'

I closed the phone on him.

When I got back in the car I expected to enter a full-blown shouting match. Instead it was eerily quiet. Monroe was putting his gun and his phone back in his jacket pocket.

'And?' John said to me.

'Unger was bandying our names around last night but that was after the fact. Reidel's blood was drying by the time I got back to the hotel. It depends whether Unger's lying and I can't make that judgement over the phone. He wants to come to talk.'

'So?'

'He'll come or he won't.' I smacked the steering wheel viciously with both hands. Part of my head was still spinning from the stupid hope it might have been Nina calling me. '*Shit*. I don't know where to go with this. I don't know who's doing what.'

'Drive to the station,' Zandt said.

I looked at Monroe. 'You going to let him talk to her?'

The agent didn't say anything. Just sat there looking out at the night, face sallow-lit by a streetlight. I kicked the car up and drove the last half mile.

The cop behind the desk in the station was the one I'd pushed past the night before. He half-stood as he saw me coming in, but then clocked Monroe was with me this time.

'Sir,' he said, 'this is the guy who . . .'

'I know,' Monroe said. 'Is anyone using the interview room?'

'Not right now.'

'Get Gulicks in there.'

John and I followed him through the access door and into the corridor.

'You want to be in there when she arrives?' Monroe asked. Say what you liked about him, if circumstances changed, he went with it.

'No,' John said. 'I want to see her first.'

Monroe led us into the observation room. We waited ten minutes while John scanned through the transcripts of the previous day's interviews. Then I heard the sound of the door into the suite being opened. Two cops led Julia Gulicks into the interview room, sat her down. One left. The other stationed himself in front of the closed door.

Julia sat in the middle of the long side of the table, as she had the afternoon before. Her face looked almost pure white. Her hands seemed to tremble a little as she placed one on top of the other in front of her. Then they were still. She looked up, straight at the one-way mirror. Cocked her head a little on one side.

I watched John as he watched her. He stood with one elbow supported in the other hand, a finger up straight against his nose. I don't know how long I watched, but he didn't blink.

'Still no lawyer?'

'No,' Monroe said. 'She asked for and was appointed one. But now she won't talk to him.'

'No family visit? No friends?'

'No one. We had the semi-boyfriend in for questioning late yesterday. He declined the opportunity to speak to her. He said she never talked about family. Don't screw this up, John.'

John left the room. A minute or so later the cop in the room turned and opened the door. John walked in and told the cop to stand outside. He waited until it was just him and Gulicks in the room and then sat on the chair at the end of the table.

After a few moments she turned her head to look at him.

'You're a good-looking guy.'

'Thank you,' John said. 'While since I was paid a compliment.'

'Poor you.'

'I survive. What about you?'

'What about me . . . what?'

'You going to be okay? You don't have any family or anything, someone who can come by and see how you are?'

'No,' she said. 'Never had any siblings. My parents are dead.'

'Sad story.'

'Depends how it's told.'

'You grew up in Boulder, that's correct?'

'On the money.'

'And you moved to Thornton six years ago?'

'Beautiful place, don't you think?'

'Haven't had time to get to know it, but it doesn't strike me that way.'

'Oh – but all the trees! The pretty little houses?'

'I've never believed picturesque is the same as good.'

She smiled. 'Then maybe cute doesn't equal stupid. This place is all wrong.'

'You understand how much trouble you're in, right? You're not trying for some kind of insanity plea?'

'Wouldn't be half-assed, believe me.'

'See, that kind of thing is probably supposed to help your cause. But it just makes me think you're jerking me around.'

'I'll try to do better.'

'Want to show you something.' John reached into his pocket, took something out, and placed it in the middle of the table.

Standing next to Monroe, I heard his intake of breath. 'Christ,' he said. 'I don't believe this guy.'

Personally I thought John was approaching things right. Gulicks looked and sounded very different to the way she had when I'd first observed her through this glass. There were dark shadows under her eyes, as if she had not slept at all. Shadows in them, too.

She looked down at the object John had put in front of her. 'I already ate,' she said.

'You know what that is?'

'It's a bone.'

'It's a rib. A woman's rib. Where do you think I got it from?'

'Your collection?'

'It came from out in the woods north-west of town. A body was discovered there a couple nights ago. There are people here who want to put that murder on you, along with that of Lawrence Widmar. I see from the notes that Detective Reidel already talked briefly to you about this.'

Gulicks didn't say anything. She was still looking at the bone.

'But this bone isn't from that victim,' John said. 'Because he was male. And the female was buried two feet below the ground.'

'So where did it come from? Please elucidate.'

'You recall Agent Baynam?'

'I do. Nice lady.'

'She is.'

'Have you fucked her?'

I don't know what it felt like being in that room, but where Monroe and I were standing, it felt cold. Not because of him. Because of her.

She smiled brightly. 'I bet you have, right? She looked like hard work, I must say, but maybe that's your type.'

'No, Julia,' John said. 'You're more my style. Nothing I like better than a woman who white-knuckles it through every day and spends the evening sitting in the dark. Who's in front of me now with her hands clasped to stop it from being obvious how much she needs a drink. That kind of thing – you have no idea. Every guy's dream.'

Gulicks' face went blank. Not angry, not distressed. Just blank.

'Quitting is for quitters,' she said, suddenly dropping her voice a quarter octave. 'Everyone knows that.'

'Reason why I brought Agent Baynam up,' John continued, his voice at the same conversational pitch, 'is she's been called away on other business. This is not good news for you. Agent Baynam was convinced that you were innocent. Others around here are not. Detective Reidel for one.'

'He's dead,' she said. 'So who cares what he thinks?'

'How do you know that?'

'Talk of the town. I have nothing to do in here except listen. I have always observed. You want to know which deputy is being unfaithful? Who takes cash to forget speeding tickets? You want to know what they think of my tits? Because they *do* think about them. They think about the breasts of a murderer who hasn't had a shower in forty-eight hours. But still . . . the tits, right? What are the *tits* like? The TITS. Men really are something else, aren't they? Not big enough, by the way, is the general consensus.'

'Women are capable of bad things too.'

'No,' she said, and for the first time looked heated, dislocated. 'Retaliation is a ricochet. Doesn't count.'

'So who are you getting back at?'

'I was talking on a larger scale. Nothing personal.'

'Really? It sounded that way.'

She was calm again. 'Nothing's personal with me, handsome. I have no personal skills. Ask my boss. Comes up time and again in appraisals. Good little worker but you wouldn't want to have to sit next to her at a dinner party. Yada yada yada.'

'Mark Kroeger evidently did. He dated you, right? A few times?'

'He did, yes.'

'He walked down to the woods with you. At your suggestion, but he went.'

'That's correct.'

'Julia, are you protecting somebody?'

'Why would you think that?'

'Because I'm not sure you killed these people. I think maybe somebody else did, and it's something to do with this third body. I wonder whether for reasons of your own you're covering up for him.'

'Well you're wrong.'

'Wrong about what?'

'Everything.'

'Really? I hate that.' Even over the intercom John sounded genuinely irritated. 'I don't mind being a little dumb. But wrong about everything? That can't be good.'

'I know something about you,' she said, smiling down at the table. 'You should be able to look at me and tell the same thing.'

'And what's that?'

She said nothing for a moment, and then turned her head to look John directly in the eyes. 'You've watched.'

'Excuse me?'

'They seep, and then they stop. Only when it dries do you know they've gone.'

'What are you talking about?'

She slowly raised one hand and pointed at him. 'Killer,' she said. 'You're a killing man.'

Monroe and I looked at each other.

Back in the room, John seemed unperturbed. 'What makes you think I've killed people?'

'Are you denying it?'

'I'm asking you a question.'

'It's obvious. It never washes off.'

John leaned his elbows on the table, friendly and open. 'You're obviously trying to tell me something, Julia. I want to know what. But I have to get it right. I don't want to misunderstand you, and so you're going to have to make it a little easier for me. Will you do that?'

'Okay,' she said, and then spoke very clearly. 'I killed them.'

John blinked. 'Say again?'

'I killed Larry in the wood. Took him for a walk and got my tiny tits out for long enough for him to think he'd got it made. He wasn't thinking straight because I dosed him with a potion I got from an online pharmacy. Not Viagra, I should add.'

261

'If you killed him in Raynor's Wood, how come the body was clean of blood?'

'I killed him at the stream. He fell straight down into it. I thought he would look better washed off. Don't you think?'

'Why did you take his clothes?'

'To embarrass him. He was a prick. I saw him drop some other woman to come over and hit on me. I have no idea who the other guy was, sorry. I picked him up from the bus station in Owensville two weeks ago. He was a practice run and just too . . . fucking . . . *heavy*, in retrospect. Larry was a little more manageable.'

John was trying not to look as surprised as Monroe and I felt, and largely succeeding. 'Something about the other victim has not been released to the media,' he said. 'Perhaps you'd like to tell me what that is?'

'Hard for me to be sure because it's been a while since I saw a newspaper, but would it be to do with him missing large parts of his body? Really horrible job, but I couldn't have got him out there otherwise. I'm sure there must be a more efficient method, but I couldn't find a single tip on the subject in *Real Simple*.'

'You realize there are witnesses to this conversation?'

'I assumed so.' She looked up at the glass and waved. 'Hi, guys.'

'You're confessing to the murders of these two men?'

'I'd prefer "telling". I have nothing to feel bad about. Apart from the fact I just wasn't very good at it. Two is a crappy score. Especially when you consider all the dead ladies everywhere, at all times, all around us. That pisses me off.'

'So why are you telling me all this?'

'Because you're so damned cute. Plus you really got to me with that whole good cop/bad cop all rolled into one.'

'Really?'

'Oh yeah. And you smell just like me.'

'Julia, it would help me a lot if you'd just stick to simple, declarative sentences.'

'No,' she said. 'No, no, no.'

'You *want* to talk about it. I think talking about it is all you want to do right now. At least explain the deal with the hands.'

'Fuck you.' She sounded hurt, angry. 'I don't know. You tell me. You work out why.'

John looked levelly at her. 'What if I don't care?'

She leapt at him.

She had about twenty seconds before the two cops from the corridor burst into the room and restrained her, and she made the most of it. Considered, focused, silent. Fists, elbows, nails.

John just sat there under the onslaught, not even raising his hands. He knew no mark could be left on her – not in here, not by him: accidentally or otherwise, even in self-defence.

When the deputies got hold of her she finally seemed to lose it. She started making a sound I would find difficult to describe, something between a shriek and howling laughter, and three big men found it hard to get her out of the room.

Monroe stayed in the station, setting in motion the next three days of incarceration for Julia Gulicks, now officially charged with double homicide. John and I walked outside and stood on the pavement. I gave him a cigarette. We lit them and smoked in silence for a while.

'So where the hell does this leave us?' I asked, in the end.

John rubbed his forehead, accidentally smudging the blood still seeping from a long gouge there. He pulled his hand away and looked at it.

'I have no idea,' he said.

Chapter 25

Lee drove. Brad's head ached too much to consider it, and now the moment had passed, it was always Lee who led and it was always Lee who drove. The streets seemed oddly empty, as if they had been cleared to take them where they had to go. Both boys had shiny welts on their faces where the other's fists had connected. Hudek was trying to conceal it but he thought Brad had cracked at least a couple of his ribs, and he wasn't hearing too great out of one ear either. Brad had washed the gunpower residue off his face and the blood from under his nose. He still looked like he had been through a threshing machine.

They didn't talk. Nothing had been said since Lee made the call to set up where they were going. There was little that could be discussed. Hudek had told Brad in every way he knew that it had not been his intention that these people would harm Karen. He had apologized for his other comments. Brad had offered nothing in return. Brad's head was like a wide open space. His phone started to ring after a while but caller ID said it was his parents and he turned it off. He would have to deal with them eventually, as he had already dealt with the Luchses: would have to find it within himself to keep faith with the pretence that Karen's death had been a random piece of hit-and-run hell, fate tragically cutting short a blah blah blah. Could he do that? Could he speak false to her memory, turn his back on her and walk further away with every lie? He didn't know. Time would tell.

Right now, there were other things to attend to.

There were people who had to learn that these two Valley boys did not take shit lying down. They had to learn that wealthy and privileged did not mean stupid or weak, and that young did not mean without power or will. They were going to learn that the strength of purpose which had made the class of 2003 frankly unbeatable in any sport could be translated out of school and into the real world: transmuted into a sharp tool for use in adult situations, and brought to bear with decisive force.

Lee and Brad were going to teach them these things. They were going to a meeting and they had the gun, and this time the bullets inside it were real. Brad had loaded them himself.

They pulled straight around into the lot behind the building at the junction of Roscoe and Sennoa. Parked close to where the tarp had been lying the last time, the one under which Pete and Steve had been stashed, tied and gagged.

'Should have known it then,' Brad muttered, speaking around the end of another cigarette. 'What kind of people would do that?' They got out of the car. 'I still don't like meeting him here.'

'It's the only place he would see us.' Lee breathed out heavily. 'Are we really going to do this?'

For a second the world shivered, as Brad remembered asking something similar the first time they came here, an evening that didn't seem that long ago. He thought about a little K swinging round someone's neck, about the fact he would probably have to withstand being given that necklace back, at some point.

'Yeah. We are.'

'But if there's a bunch of them we play it cool and bide our time and act like we know shit. Tell me you're going to stick to that.'

'Lee, let's just get in there. I don't want to die any more than you do. I just want to hear what this asshole has to say.'

They walked across to the door on the side of the building. Lee grabbed the handle and pulled. It was unlocked.

Brad followed him into the building. Walked quietly through a big room and down a corridor and then into a space that was larger yet.

Unlike the last time Lee had been there, this room was well-lit by a set of strip lights. Now you could see the space properly, it looked less like an abandoned storeroom and more like a high-tech office. There was a line of desks along one wall with a rack of computers and flat-screen monitors, something that looked like it might be an internet web server, a couple televisions, a suspicious number of cell phones. All the TVs and computers were turned off, and cables were trailing all over the place.

Somebody was moving out.

Standing in front of one of the desks was the man they had come to see. He didn't look up at first, but continued with what he was doing, which was putting data CDs into a bulky shoulder bag.

Lee and Brad walked as far as they had to, and then stopped.

Paul looked up. 'Hey, boys,' he said. 'What's the problem?'

Brad had thought maybe when he saw him he would just go at him, the way he had with Lee. He knew straight away this was not the way it was going to be. There was something about this person's presence which made the idea of attack seem invalid.

'You here alone?' Lee asked.

'Just me,' the man said. 'There's work to do. So I'm going to have to ask you to get right to bottom line.'

Brad wasn't going to wait any longer. 'Why did you do it?'

'Do what, Brad?'

'Kill her.'

266

'Kill who? You're going to have to narrow it down for me.'

'Don't fuck with us, man,' Lee said, and went into what they'd agreed. 'Look, we want things to be cool here. We understand you got some plan going on. She's no big deal. Just tell us what's going on. We just need to understand.'

The man finished up putting things in the bag, zipped it, and set it on the floor. He folded his arms and looked at them.

'Tell me what's on your mind, Lee.'

'I told you this morning that Brad's girlfriend had been saying some stuff, could make things difficult for us. You said it wasn't a problem. Then a couple hours later, when she's on the way to talk to the cops, she gets slam-sided in broad daylight and killed.'

'I'm sorry to hear that,' Paul said, looking at Brad. 'You must be bereft.'

'Fuck you,' Brad said. He started to tremble, and thought he might just go ahead and go at him after all. 'Fuck . . .'

'Hang on,' Lee said, grabbing his friend's shoulder. He turned back to Paul. 'And so Brad and I get in a big fight because he thinks I turned her in deliberately, which I did not. It gets out of hand and . . .'

He put his hand in his jacket and pulled out the gun. He held it so Paul could see it. 'Recognize this?'

The man shrugged. 'I see so many, you know?'

'This is the gun Hernandez gave me the night Pete got killed. When I got back home that night I hid it away. I fired it this afternoon, I fired it twice, and guess what happens?'

'I'm agog, Lee.'

'The gun is full of blanks.'

'How strange. I wonder why Hernandez would do that.'

'Bull*shit*. I don't believe he ever did anything you didn't tell him to do.'

'So what's your theory? I want you to put it together yourself, Lee. I think you already have.'

'This was a set-up from the minute Pete died,' Brad said, flatly.

'You sent us on a whacked-out deal but didn't trust us enough to give us a gun that worked. Pete got killed and then Hernandez took advantage of the situation and deliberately put us in a position where we were guilty for hiding his body. After that, we're your bitches.'

Paul just nodded. 'Very good.'

Hudek was staring at the man with an odd expression on his face, and Brad realized – with something approaching joy – that for once in his life, Lee was furious.

'Is that true?'

Paul smiled vaguely. 'Yes,' he said. 'It is.'

There was a long pause.

'You are so history,' Lee said. He held the gun up slowly, pointing it directly at the man's head. 'You . . . are . . . gone.'

'You're going to shoot me?'

'That's exactly what I'm going to do.'

'Despite the fact there are people who know who you are and where you live and who will have no compunction about killing everyone you've ever even spoken to?'

'I don't care. You fucked with us, man. Pete died because of you and you got Karen killed. You're screwing with our heads and you've been doing it from minute one. So I'm going to kill you.'

'Excellent,' Paul said. 'I knew you could do it.'

Lee's face was flushed. 'Don't fucking patronize me, you fuck.'

'I'm really not, Lee. I'm genuinely delighted.'

Lee glanced at Brad and Brad saw in his eyes that Paul had finally managed to pry a trapdoor in Lee's mind, opening a gate that maybe might otherwise have forever remained closed. Lee's eyes were glittering and dark, and Brad knew him well enough to be convinced that Paul's last seconds of life would be all about discovering that when Lee said he was going to do something, it was going to get done.

Lee brought his left hand up to cup the right from underneath, steadying the gun. 'Goodbye, asshole.'

Brad braced himself for the sight. But then someone spoke.

'No, honey, you're not going to do that.'

It was a new voice, and it was female.

Lee turned so slowly it looked like he was having to push against a strong wind, as if knew that by seeing what he was about to see, nothing would be the same again.

His mother was standing at the back of the room, a few yards from the door. His father was by her side.

Mrs Hudek looked composed, upbeat – her husband's face was a little harder to read.

'Mom?' Lee's voice was quiet, and sounded very young. 'Dad – what are you doing here?'

'Lower the gun, son. You're not going to need it right now.'

The suggestion didn't appear to connect with anything in Lee's head. His hands stayed where they were.

Brad meanwhile remained motionless. He knew he wasn't dreaming. But still – it was hard to be sure. Mr and Mrs Hudek had appeared. Maybe Karen was still alive, after all. Maybe he had a cool job in television and was married to her and hadn't seen Lee in years and at some point he would wake up with a mild hangover and go jog it off before starting a bright new day.

Slowly Lee began to lower his arms. 'What's going on?'

Lisa Hudek walked forward until she was close to him. 'We knew you were going to be confused, so we wanted to make sure you didn't do anything silly.'

'You . . . you know these guys got Karen killed?'

'Yes, we're aware of that.'

'But . . . so why are you here? How do you know . . . *why are you here?*'

She gently took the gun, and handed it to Paul. Then she spoke directly to her son. 'We're here to say goodbye,' she said. 'You're going on a journey now, and we wanted to wish you good luck.'

'I am?'

'That's right,' Ryan Hudek said. There was something like resignation in his voice. 'Been a long time coming.'

Brad found he suddenly had to speak. 'I don't know what you people are on,' he said, and pointed at Paul. 'But this guy's not walking out of here.'

Lisa looked at him as if he was a pool cleaner who'd become a fixture in her domestic life, and semi-impossible to fire, but who habitually did a very poor job. 'Bradley, could you stay out of this?'

'No, I can't, Mrs Hudek,' he said. 'Not really. Whatever "this" is.'

'I don't have much time,' Paul said. 'And you people need to be back home soon, ready. Showtime is about to start.'

'Ready for what?' Lee said.

Paul shook his head. 'Not you. Your folks. They're returning home from a spree over on Rodeo. Got hung up in traffic.' He winked at Brad. 'You know how that can be.'

'Why have they been shopping? Why traffic?'

'Because that's how they won't have seen the news or know the slightest thing about it until they get to their street and see the cop cars waiting outside.'

'Know about what?'

Paul leaned over to the desk and turned one of the televisions on. Flicked through channels until he got the 24/7 news.

Lee and Brad watched the screen. It showed the exterior of a building they knew so well it took an oddly long time to recognize it – though they'd been there only that very morning. It was a large commercial structure, designed for viewing from the inside.

'Is that Belle Isle?' Lee said. 'It kind of looks like . . .'

The channel had put together a rotating segment which they could cut in and out of as fresh information arose. The story it presented was compact. An hour and a half previously a small bomb had gone off on the second floor of the Belle Isle mall. Firefighters had got the blaze under control easily. The destruction had been limited to the Serious About Sport store and those either side of it, with collateral injury to a few people walking past, who had been caught in the shower of shattered glass. There were no fatalities – the sales clerks and three customers were being treated for minor blast injuries and the effects of inhaled smoke.

The news anchor cut in to detail how scene investigators were beginning to understand what had happened. They believed the incendiary device had been planted in the store that morning, hidden in a canvas shoulder bag. Footage from security cameras in the store had provided them with a suspect. They were double-checking identity before releasing a name to the public.

A still picture came up on screen. Grey, blurry, shot from above and to the front. A young man covertly hanging a bag up on a rack, taking care to make sure it was well hidden – not realizing his position put him in clear view of two cameras.

It was Lee John Hudek. And just like that, he was different. He wasn't just Lee any more. He'd become something bigger.

'But the bag was full of drugs,' Lee said.

Paul turned the television off. 'Of course. The one behind it wasn't. The one we put there, rather more carefully, the night before. They're going to be at your house soon, Lee, if they aren't already. They'll find Brad's car outside and start to think he was in on it too. Sooner rather than later they will get around to searching the Metzger house, which means they'll find Pete Voss's cell phone thrown in bushes down the end of the yard.'

'But, the cops have been told . . .'

'Actually, we didn't get around to that.'

Brad stared at him. Every cell in his body felt cold. 'What are you doing? Why . . . I don't understand.'

'This is kind of hard on you, Bradley,' Ryan Hudek said, quietly. 'We know that. But sacrifices have to be made.'

'But . . . you're his *family*. You let this happen? You're always going to be the parents of the guy who did that.'

Mrs Hudek smiled. 'Oh, I think you'll find society's to blame. And videogames, and carbohydrates and the Bush family and Bin

271

Laden and doubtless poor old Charlton Heston too. Not us. Never us. Only those who know will give us our due.'

'Who do you mean, "us"?' Brad asked, but nobody answered.

'You know what?' Lee said. He hadn't spoken in quite a while. 'Brad is not the only person who has *no clue* what is going on.'

'All that matters is this,' Paul said. 'Your old life is over. It's no loss. You were going nowhere. Your Spring Break "plan" was the most naïve piece of nonsense I have ever heard. We can take you somewhere useful instead.'

Lee looked at the floor. 'We did meet before, didn't we? When? When was it?'

'Long time ago. But you had to see there's nowhere else to go. In the process you've demonstrated you're our kind of man.'

'For what?'

'You and I are going on a trip. I'll explain on the way.'

'Excuse me,' Brad said. 'Where do I fit into all this?'

Paul looked at him. 'You don't.'

He raised the gun smoothly and shot Brad in the centre of the forehead.

Brad stumbled backward and slowly slewed to the ground. For a moment he almost looked like he was trying to stand back up, but then he slumped on his side. His legs bucked, slowly, pulling him around in a lazy circle, leaving a trail of bubbled red.

His mind was a burst of colours and lights and memory, place and time crashing together and compacting eternity to a rotating point. He felt lucid and warm and as if everything was going to be okay, perhaps even better than that. He was very close to understanding it had all been some unwelcome fantasy. He heard a voice, echoing. It was familiar. He tried to open his mouth to say something, probably her name, or just, 'Hey'.

Paul shot him again, and the body was still.

There was quiet for a moment, as the echo died too.

'Wow,' Lee said, quietly.

Neither of his parents seemed phased by this, though both had made Kool-Aid for Brad since before he was old enough to hold his own glass. Lee looked down at his friend's remains. He supposed he was maybe in shock or something, but he was surprised by how little he felt. Brad always had been kind of weak. Mentally weak. At school he had been physically stronger and probably a little smarter too, had he but realized it. Certainly better looking. And yet Brad just coasted. He'd had no idea there were places to go, big things to do. Would he have had the strength of purpose to grab a gun when attacked? Lee didn't think so. Though actually, he had tried to kill Lee that afternoon. So, like, fuck him.

'It's better this way,' Paul said. 'His life was going to hell soon anyhow.'

Lee nodded. 'Whatever,' he said.

He pushed his hands back through his hair. He actually felt okay. The last few days had been murky, confused by all the difficulties and the strain of trying to glimpse a clear road ahead. Everything seemed simpler now. There was only one door.

'So what happens now?' he said.

'We've waited a long time for this,' his mom said. 'The Day of Angels. And you're going to be a part of it.'

She reached out, as she had after the policemen had left their house, and touched his face. Her eyes were clear.

'You're going to make us so proud.'

Part 3: The One

The commonest and gravest error of modernity
lies in believing that antiquity is dead.
Clarke Ashton Smith
The Black Book of
Clarke Ashton Smith

Chapter 26

Finally Jim tried to eat. He parked outside the Renee's again. He checked the alleyway around the back. There was no sign of the child, of course. She had not been there in the first place. He ordered a Hearty-Ho breakfast and sat at the table nearest the window and stared at his food when it arrived. It looked too much like the picture on the menu, and it smelled foul. He got about five, six mouthfuls of it down and then had to stand up hurriedly, walk stiffly out into the john, and throw up.

Wiping his mouth on his sleeve, he went back into the restaurant and sat down. He didn't consider trying to eat any more. Just the smell was enough to make him have to turn his head away. Nobody else seemed to have a problem. A couple of truckers and local early birds were slinging it down like there was no tomorrow. Jim was so hungry it was making it hard for him to think straight. It was partly this and partly the fact that James had never been that good at joined-up thinking. That was what Jim was for. James was mainly still seventeen and did what he wanted too much of the time. Whenever Jim looked at something now he found it hard to remember whether it qualified as food or not. He couldn't eat this crap, for sure. He needed something, but it wasn't this.

Jim knew what James was thinking of. He'd been thinking of it for two days. It wouldn't have to be much. Just enough to settle his stomach. And if you've slipped this far then why not . . .

No. Absolutely not.

He drank his coffee and paid and left.

The vehicle was in motion again.

Nina was ready for it this time. The first time the vehicle had moved she had been lying in her twisted position, half-asleep. Perhaps sleep was not the correct word: it was more like a condition of standby, a dulling twilight fear that was better than being fully awake. She'd dimly heard a door opening, noted again the sound's metallic timbre, and heard an engine being turned over. Before she'd had time to process this the vehicle was suddenly moving. She'd been thrown onto the floor into a cramped space, banging her head on the way down. She'd cried out because one of her legs was twisted so that it felt like the knee might pop, but she was still gagged and almost none of the sound made it out of her head. All she had been able to do was wait it out, trying to push away the pain, while she gradually managed to shift her weight so it didn't hurt so astonishingly any more. When he eventually stopped driving he must have noticed what had happened. He came in the back and shoved her onto the bed, table, whatever it was. He was not gentle. It was as if she was a thing. Her knee continued to ache for some time. Worse was a semi-permanent feeling of nausea, caused by unexpected movement while she couldn't see: either that or the vehicle was leaking a lot of gasoline fumes. She thought she might vomit, but she did not. She just lay there. She lay and lay and lay. She felt too sick to play her game, which was remembering all the things Ward had put in the stupid salad that time back in Sheffer, imagining eating more of it this time, eating it all right up, making him happy. So instead she imagined sitting and talking with him at the lake outside the cabin that had been theirs, until she realized it would never happen again and that made her too sad to play any more.

This time she had readied herself when she heard him get back in the van. It *was* a van, she now believed, the sound of its engine very much like an old VW camper. She let the forward motion of the vehicle slide her backward, and then braced for the gentle slide back. She got it right. Always been a quick study.

The van was in motion for some time. Maybe twenty minutes. Then it stopped. The engine was turned off. The front door opened, and then shut. Was he going off somewhere again?

No. There came the metallic sliding sound of the side door opening. She caught a quick breath of air that smelled very fresh, and heard the sound of birds. He had driven to somewhere out of town. Why? Was it going to happen now?

Was this it?

Then the van shifted as he climbed inside, and shut the sliding door again.

He was close to her. She felt her whole body tense. What would he do first? Where would he do it?

'Don't be scared.'

Okay, Nina thought. I'll not be scared. Funny how that sentence works about the same as saying 'I'm not drunk'.

She made what sounds she could with her mouth, hoping her meaning would be clear.

'No, I'm not going to let you see or talk,' he said. 'Sooner or later you'll say the wrong thing. I've made mistakes already. The hotel did not go right and I know Forward-Thinking Boy's going to make me pay. But . . . look, just lay there. Be quiet. It's all going to be okay.'

Nina doubted that. She doubted it very seriously. He was not talking to her. He was talking to himself. The thing about reassuring yourself about your own intentions is that you're very forgiving when it all turns out to have been a lie.

But she kept quiet, and she listened when, after a while, he began to talk. He started slowly, as someone who'd had no audience in a long, long time: no audience except himself.

He had a teacher in high school who said something that evidently stuck. This guy was trying to make a point this one time (later James could never remember what it had been, only that it was a warm afternoon and no one was listening very hard), and he got off on a tangent and said something about how the same difference could represent different types of difference. Though this didn't sound promising – or even intelligible – the words meandered into James's consciousness, and he wound up hearing what the guy asked next.

'Example. What's the difference between two and three?'

There was silence for a while, the fug broken only by the noise of a blowsy fly at the window which ran the side of the classroom.

Someone, a girl, probably, eventually offered the answer 'one'.

'Correct,' the teacher said, nodding briskly. 'Their values differ by one unit, and that's about all there is to say about the matter. But now tell me: what's the difference between one and two?'

And someone, likely the same girl and after a similar interval, said the difference was 'one', again. The teacher nodded once more, but with that jaunty half-smile which said he had something up his sleeve he believed was going to make you think he was cool as all hell, your very own Mr Chips, whereas in fact it just increased your vague desire that he have a coronary, right here, right now.

'Also true,' he said. 'But let's think about that. The difference between two and three just says you've got more of something. Three dollars in your pocket, better than two. Three assignments overdue instead of two – that's worse.' Nobody laughed. One of the girls maybe smiled. Girls are kind. They pretend to be, anyhow. 'It's a unitary difference, and it's a little better, or slightly worse, depending what you're counting. No biggie. Right?'

There was no response. The teacher glanced wearily out the window for a moment, as if counting the years to his retirement and finding them too many. But he ploughed on.

'The step between one and two is bigger news. It's the difference between one and many, between unique and commonplace. If someone says there's two gods, and another guy – or girl, of course – argues that there's three, or five, everyone will remain calm. Polytheists are basically on the same side. But a *mono*theist runs into a polytheist, it's time to take cover. One true god versus a handful of weird-ass heathen idols? These people have a funda-mental disagreement. Fur is going to fly. You're sleeping with one guy, or you're sleeping with two. These differences *matter*, okay? You see what I'm saying?'

Nobody did, at least not sufficiently to vocalize. The fly was still buzzing. It stopped for a while, then started again, in that way they do.

'But then we come to something way more crucial,' the teacher said. 'The difference between zero and one. And again – don't worry, Karla, I'll do the math this time, it's why I get paid the big bucks – superficially we're looking at a difference of one. You've got zero, you add a single unit, so then you've got one. Right?'

James was looking at him now. What the guy was saying was beginning to creep into his head, almost as if James was actually listening. This was a novel experience. It felt compellingly odd.

'But actually,' the teacher said, holding a finger up, '*it isn't one at all*. We say it is, for mathematical convenience, but it really isn't, and that's because we're out of the world of sums now and into what the philosophers call "ontology". You're not talking about numbers any longer, about quantity: you're talking about *quality* – you are saying something about the nature of the world.'

'What?' someone said. 'Saying what?'

'Could be lots of things. Example. The difference between having one kid or twins is not such a big deal . . .'

'You think?' said one of the girls, indignantly.

'Not in the way I mean,' the teacher said, hurriedly. 'One or two is a matter of degree, and of course it makes a huge difference with costs, and practical considerations, strollers, and stuff . . . but: pregnant versus not-pregnant, *that's* the real life-changer. It's the difference between being a woman and being a mother. When zero changes to one, that's where the universe flips and life changes. See?'

'Okay,' the girl mumbled, either mollified or falling back asleep.

He pressed the point. 'You get what we're at here, people? The bottom line. There is *a* god, there is *no* god. Existence versus nonexistence. Life or death.'

'True or false,' some guy said, quietly.

'*Right*, James,' the teacher crowed, delighted, and only then did James realize the speaker had been himself. '*Thank* you – and here was me thinking you were in a coma. Zero, one. On, off. True, false. Something's never happened, then the world is one way; but if it *has* happened, it's another. The step between none and one takes creation and changes it forever.'

James stared back at him, understanding.

And then the bell for end of class went, and everybody split.

The man was silent for a little while then, as if considering the memory. Something about the way he had spoken made Nina think he had not revisited it in quite some time.

'Everyone remembers their first,' he said, eventually. 'Which was Karla. Don't get the idea that I don't like women. I do. Just not very many of them. I get on fine with the ones I like. I had a wife, I had a . . . I had a wife. It's just it's only once in a great while that a woman does something for me. She has to be very special. It used to bother me that other guys would be looking at a waitress or something and saying how hot she was and I could see her face was okay and she had good tits or ass or whatever they thought was so great about her, but that would be it. It would be like someone offering you a sandwich and you think 'Yes, that bread's nice and fresh, little crusty at the edges, and the fillings look good and are piled high and there's a grind of pepper just to round it off. That's a fine sandwich you've got there. But . . . I don't want one. It's not that I don't like sandwiches. I do. I just . . . don't want it.' It's like that. And then you see one you really do want. That you have to have. One with wings. And it always ends up going wrong.'

He breathed out heavily. 'I'm hungry,' he said. 'I'm trying very, very hard. It wouldn't even hurt you, but it would be bad for me to start.'

Nina had no idea what he was talking about. She was badly dehydrated, and concentrating was hard. It was especially hard if you were constantly vigilant for the possibility that he might underline some point by slipping a knife into your skin, or under a fingernail, or into one of your eyes. She had no intention of engaging with his world. She had spent many hours talking to the psychopathic, and if you had a thick wire screen between you it could be fascinating – though most of them wound up heading inexorably down similar tracks, damaged rolling stock shunted towards the same dark and bloody station. Stuck in childhood, believing theirs so much more meaningful than everybody else's. The mechanical tic of recalled injury and slight. Whirling round some momentous event like a rabid dog chained to a post, unable to understand that outside their own heads it was just a past moment of unremarkable time. Inside, the event beats like a psychic heart.

He was quiet for a while longer and then she caught a scent of dry tobacco.

'This is bad enough,' he said, but his voice said he was a man losing a battle. She heard the sound of a match being struck, and then the smell of a cigarette smoked. She didn't mind him doing that. It reminded her of Ward.

Then he was a little closer, and she tensed. He seemed to hesitate, and then his hands were around the back of her head. A quick movement, and the blindfold was off.

It took long seconds for her eyes to adjust, even though the light in the van was very muted. Out front she could see trees. Between them and her, a man. Not young. Big. Sad eyes. But his compassion was for himself, not her.

She blinked and looked around the interior of the van. Sparse, no windows along the sides. A few thin rusty scratches across the inside of the door, short parallel lines. As if someone had once scraped it with their fingernails, while trying desperately to escape.

Maybe even more than once.

Slowly he started talking again, and though he had taken the blindfold off, he never looked anywhere near her eyes.

You remembered the last, he said – and faltered a little, as he said it – but most of all you remembered your first. When zero became one. It's like your first beer, or lying beside a girl having done it for the first time – confused, excited, slightly let down: her seeming a little more grown up now, you feeling even younger and smaller than when the evening started. All those nights were anticipated, key battles in the campaign into the foreign hills of maturity. You're not sure where you're going, or why. You just are. Everybody else is too. Alcohol comes first. You come to realize adults drink stuff that you're not supposed to – and the occasional sip you score at home reveals it tastes strange. But that's sort of the point, you gather, and there's something grown-up and delicious about this: you drink this gloop even though it's not too nice? How sophisticated and unchildlike is that! Then suddenly someone at school will make the phylogenetic leap, acing you out by months. There will be quiet, jealous tales told about some party at the weekend, an older boy passing a six-pack around, a boy in your class drinking half of it, not puking, and then kissing a girl . . .

The kissing part will not be true. Small boys always go one lie too far; big boys too, of course. But the rest of it will be, and the identity of the kid in question will not in the least surprise you.

It will be the Forward-Thinking Boy.

Every class has one. The one who always gets there first, who will forever have left his trash on your mountain top; the one on some fast-track to adulthood, his voice trailing in his wake.

After he's broken the ice it suddenly seems conceivable for the rest of you, and comes the night when you and your buddies are outside a bar and one of them gets away without being carded and you're all suddenly holding these big cold glasses and it's completely different to being allowed a try at a warm bottle out in the garden last summer: and you take a mouthful and it's metallic and foamy and tastes like it might have leaked out of a machine but it's *beer* and you know – as you biliously work your way through a glass that will, in only a few years, disappear in a couple of unthinking swallows – that a box has been ticked.

You have the first of your magic cards. You know the beer spell now.

Overnight you become one of the guys who's had a beer, who chugs it like a fish all the time – Jeez: sometimes you worry you might be turning into a fuckin' juicer, you're drinking so much – though it still tastes soapy and sour, if you're honest, which you're not, because nobody else says anything and you don't want to sound like a pussy, especially now you've proved that you're not.

By now the Forward-Thinking Boy you all want to be acknowledged by (and also slightly fear, and kind of hate) will have leapt whistling over further horizons. He'll regularly smell of cigarettes, or will have weaselled his hand up some pretty girl's shirt – and then, finally, he'll have done *the thing*. The Big One, the World Series of adolescence, the event that carves men from boys, takes the doers and takers and puts them in the VIP enclosure of adolescence: fenced off by experience, lustrous with action, immediately taller and cooler in a way you will never, ever feel, regardless of what you do in the rest of your life.

But you do not understand that, not yet, and this is a time of credits which have to be earned. So you will try cigarettes one afternoon, and hate them, or not, little realizing this small difference will cost you tens of thousands of dollars, countless coffee breaks standing in the cold and rain with your fellow pariahs, and finally your life. And eventually, under one circumstance or another, your hand will cup the surprising warmth and softness of a breast, disbe-lievingly, as if you have been allowed against all odds to pet some small, bald, mythical creature, in its nest. You're not sure what to do next – there doesn't seem to be a self-evidently logical next step – but it's done. And finally you will screw, and it will be embar-rassing, but it will be over quickly and you will be ejected out the other side into a land where there is little left to do, all but two of life's major boxes already ticked.

Sooner or later you will start drawing new boxes for yourself, as a way to fill the time: and they may be sketchy and on show to all – big car, big house, big job – or small and intimately detailed and kept largely out of sight. The hand that draws those boxes will look like it's yours, but it will be much younger. It will be the hand that held the first cigarette, the hand placed on that first breast by a girl who was growing cold and bored and would have preferred you to be someone else. It is the hand that pulls the sheets up to your chin when you go to bed in your parents' house at the end of the night when you have first had sex; lying in bed as the planet turns, knowing the world is different now and wondering why it feels so much the same, whether you perhaps did something wrong, or *not quite right* – wondering why the idea of it felt so much more momentous than the actuality turned out to be.

The hand is the key. When you look at someone's hand, look carefully and long, you see everything they are and have been and done. Hands are action. Hands are doing. When you take someone's hand you own them entire.

Just as holding that first cigarette can be a life sentence, so can the other thing. You liked it well enough that first time, but felt you didn't really get to the bottom of it. That there must be *more* to be had, something that will bring the reality in line with the idea; that will align the world outside your head with the way it is inside.

Most men will find ways of engaging on this quest which they can share, and their lives will follow their timeless course, still and forever in the wake of the Forward-Thinking Boy. For he will be

286

the first to tick the penultimate box, too, that of getting a girl pregnant – thereafter putting aside forward-thinking things in return for the adult glees of earning a wage and putting up shelving and sitting alone on the back porch some evenings and drinking beer that now tastes much like water, as he stares out into the yard as if wondering what on earth the next day could be *for*.

He'll often be first to return to the home plate, too, to leap over that final horizon unto death, but they never tell you that at school. Back then, first was always better: it's only later in life you realize the value of idling further down the pack. And in some senses that boy never dies, even when he winds up drunk-tangled in the metal of his car down some country lane. He is immortal, the dark seed embedded deep inside: your endless opinion of yourself. He was the person who made you understand you were not exceptional and that you would never be first in any race that other people could know about. He is gone, but you will meet him again. He will be older then, and gaunt, but some day you will realize that many of the actions you believed had been yours had actually been his. He will always be that one step ahead, knowing you better than you know yourself. Pulling strings, guiding you down dark alleys, his hand drawing new and strange and awful boxes for you to tick.

And when you have done his work and stand panting in the night, staring in a mirror that reflects a world from which you can never now escape, it will be his face you see looking back.

His phone rang suddenly, stopping him in mid-sentence.

He let it ring. He had done this once before, earlier in the day, or perhaps it had been the night – Nina hadn't been able to tell the difference between the two. Both were murky. The ringing had reminded her that her own phone might be somewhere in the van. Also that it was turned off, and she was tied up. Her phone was a dead end, but she had not forgotten about it.

There was quiet for a few minutes.

Then the phone rang again, and this time he answered. He listened for some time, and in the end said only 'Okay.'

That was the end of the conversation.

He lit another cigarette. Nina could tell immediately that there was a marked change in the ether.

'Well, he's coming,' he said. He sounded different, hard once again. 'Talk of the devil. Forward-Thinking Boy himself is on his way. And so . . . I'm going to do this after all.'

Nina tried to say something. Anything. Only gurgles made it past the gag. He quickly tied the blindfold back around her eyes, and everything was inky charcoal again.

The van swayed as he got up and moved past her. She heard what sounded like a drawer being opened above her head. Other, quiet noises for a while, and then he moved back in front of her. There was a dry, rasping sound.

It sounded like a Polaroid photo being taken.

A clunk as something was put down. Then he was very close to her. He took her right arm in his hands and she could hear that he was breathing quickly and this did not make her feel very safe.

Something was tied around her upper arm, tightly. She tried to kick, to jerk her body away. Then something shockingly sharp slid into the inside of her elbow. She went rigid, terrified.

Still his breathing, shallow and fast.

The sharp thing stayed in her for some time, several minutes, five, perhaps ten. Then it was pulled out again.

He stayed motionless for a few moments, standing over her, as if this was his last chance to not do something. Then he moved away.

Now what? What was he going to do now?

She heard the sound of some pieces of equipment being taken from a cupboard. She could not tell if they were knives. A clank, a screwing sound, a brief wisp of something that smelled like gas. Then the sound of a match being struck, though this time it was not followed by the smell of a cigarette.

She tried very hard to make her mind go away someplace else. To go back to the lake. To see its shiny black surface under a cloudy sky, to believe that if she could just wake up and turn her head, she would see Ward sitting next to her, a half-smile on his face, amused at the way she had cried out while she was dreaming.

She couldn't get there. It was too far away.

She had to remain here, to stay in the van with this man. She could not fail to understand what he was doing. She didn't even particularly mind the sound of her blood draining into a metallic-sounding receptacle, though the realization of how much he'd taken made her stomach turn. That was bearable.

Far worse was the smell as it cooked.

Chapter 27

I had slept very badly. I tried hard to get some rest, because I didn't know any faster way of making it day again. Getting a room in the Holiday Inn was not difficult and I lay on a wide, flat bed and stared at the ceiling and willed it to shade away and let me float up into some place where my head did not ache with absence. It did not want to do so, and perhaps I didn't really want it to either. A period of unconsciousness could only make Nina seem further from me, time fading reality's colours like a wind blowing autumn leaves away. Some time after 2 a.m. I got up, took my phone out of my jacket, and tried her number again. There was still no answer, just the redirect to voicemail.

In the small hours I must have stumbled into something close to sleep, because I spent time in places that were not Thornton. I stood for a while on the precarious balcony of Nina's house in Malibu, waiting for her to join me. She did not, and when I went inside I discovered the outside was connected instead to the interior of the house I grew up in as a child, hundreds of miles north of Los Angeles in Hunter's Rock. The house was cold and empty and damp patches of neglect had settled into the corners of the ceilings and some of the walls. One room had a bed in it, and a telephone on the bedside table, but the phone steadfastly remained silent. I waited there for a while, thinking that if nothing else my mother might call. Then for a time I walked through trees, not like the scrubby local woods but the deep endlessness of the forests around Sheffer. It had snowed recently and there were fleet shadows behind some of the tall and silent trunks, and these shadows had minds and knew my name: but it appeared none wanted to talk. They just watched, not unkindly, as I struggled deeper and deeper.

Finally I was on the couch of an apartment I had lived in for a while in Seattle ten years before. Five storeys up, with a view over Elliot Bay, it was one of the most pleasant places I have lived. I spent my time there with a woman, the longest relationship I have ever managed. Most of the time this woman was businesslike, can-do, a scourge to the indolent and pessimistic. I had a nick-name for her: Hope. Partly because she looked like the actress who played a character of that name in *thirtysomething*, but also because that's what she had. A hope, or confidence, that the world was a good and sensible place: that it was organized for the benefit of the right-minded and fair, and would always see them okay in the end.

But every now and then something would crash a little inside. I would see her staring into space in a bar, or down at her hands, or not looking properly at the television. Her movements would become tighter and defensive, her eyes wide. I would ask her, when I noticed, if something was on her mind. She'd say there wasn't, and I'd go back to drinking beer or chuckling at Chandler or eating potato chips – the important stuff.

But then a little later and apropos of nothing, she would ask: 'Will it be okay?'

'Will what be okay?'

'Everything,' she'd say, quietly, and I'm sure each time she was unaware we'd had this exchange before. 'Will everything be okay?'

And I'd say that it would be, and hold her a while, and steer us back to the mundane – and usually in the morning I'd wake to hear her singing in the shower. She sang like a frog, but I was glad to hear it.

We made it to ten months, then slowly spiralled apart. In the end things were not okay. Not for us, not in general.

In this world, everything is never okay. But I'm glad I didn't know that then, and I'm glad I never told her.

I woke at five thinking I heard someone in the bathroom of the suite. I half-fell off the bed, dragging myself towards the sound. But there was no one in there. Any singing I thought I'd heard must have come from some other room, or another time. I knew there was no point going back to bed so I stood under the shower for a while. The exchange of information in hotels is very efficient, and when I turned up at the hotel café well before opening time the people setting up there rapidly provided me with coffee. I probably did not thank them well enough. I was not yet ready to accept the solicitousness offered to the bereaved, and became monosyllabic in the face of kindness. I took my cup of coffee through the lobby doors and stood outside.

The parking lot was largely empty and looked like a winter sea, cold and grey and flat. As I stared across it, willing Nina to somehow appear, I knew that if I didn't find her then nothing would ever be okay again.

And I knew also that time was running out.

'You got her to talk once,' I said. 'Maybe you can do it again.'

John shook his head. 'I don't think so.'

I was still in the parking lot, where John had found me ten minutes before. I had drunk a good deal of coffee and smoked some cigarettes and felt a little more alive, though not necessarily in a good way. The morning was very crisp and cold and the temperature had fallen ten degrees overnight. If we'd chosen today to go digging in the woods we'd have needed pickaxes to break ground.

'I don't see how it would help us,' he added. 'That woman didn't abduct Nina.'

'Some guy told me once that investigations proceed by pushing in any direction you can, in the hope it will take you where you need to go. Oh, wait – that was *you*, right? Yesterday?'

'Do you have any idea how annoying you are?'

'People regularly try to kill me, so I guess that's a clue. John . . .'

'Monroe's not going to let me interview her again.'

'Why not? You got a confession out of her. Which is more than he or Reidel ever did. Or Nina, come to that.'

'I didn't get anything out of her. She elected to tell me what may or may not be the truth, for bizarre reasons of her own. And then she stopped talking. You saw what happened next. I could spend another week with her and get nothing.'

I turned away, frustrated. 'But what else do we do?'

'Nina's probably not even in Thornton any more. Why would an abductor keep her in town?'

'Because this is where he lives.'

'Assuming it's a local crazy person, yes – but there's already someone in custody who's confessed to those killings, Ward. If this is related to the Straw Men instead then Nina's most likely miles away by now. You understand that, don't you?' He looked at me seriously, and visibly made the decision to broach a subject. 'You also need to prepare yourself for the idea that she could be . . .'

'Don't you *fucking* say it.' Suddenly I couldn't hold anger back. 'I know damn well what she could be. Every time I shut my eyes I believe she's dead. But until I feel it and know it, she isn't.'

'Ward, I'm just trying to . . .'

'You're not the only guy who's lost people, you know. Come down off the fucking mountain.'

'What do you mean by that?'

'The way you look down on me and the rest of the world from

the moral high ground of having lost your daughter. I get that's a bad thing, John, I really do, and I'm sorry my brother did it. But the Straw Men killed my parents, too, remember? They cut my life off at the knees and I'm not letting anyone else go. Nina is alive until I have no choice but to accept otherwise. You can gently kill her off in *your* head if that suits you, but it's not fucking happening in mine.'

John pursed his lips and looked away. Then he walked quickly back into the hotel. I'd just had time to smoke another cigarette, and calm down, when he reappeared.

'It's confused in there,' he said. He was holding a slip of paper. 'They're split three ways on a serial killer, a cop-killing and an abduction, and have no clue about any of them. Plus someone left a kiddie bomb in a mall in LA yesterday so they're twittering all over that.'

'A bomb?'

'Nothing serious, apparently, just some random kid playing with a pipe bomb instead of a gun. Anyway. Charles Monroe left the hotel very early this morning, it turns out. They wouldn't tell me where he went.'

'So I'll call his cell phone,' I said. 'I could have done that without you bothering the Feds.'

'Didn't go in there for him. I've got another idea.'

'Yeah?' I said, dubiously. 'And what's that?'

The building was a few blocks the other side of the historic district, an easy walk from the Starbucks and yet just a little down at heel. Whatever regeneration programme had converted it out of old business premises had not outlasted the early nineties. We got there just after eight and waited for ten minutes. Didn't see any cops around.

'Shouldn't they have someone posted outside?'

'I guess they're busy,' he said.

As we got out of the car John's phone rang. He answered it and listened for a while.

'No,' he said, quietly. 'It wasn't me.' He listened some more. 'The further the better. Don't tell the local cops anything. Don't even call them. And don't go home or to the office without checking with me first.'

He ended the call and stared out of the window a moment, biting his lip.

'Who was that?'

'That site with the missing pictures? Oz Turner runs it. The pictures aren't there because his server has been wiped. Yesterday some suspicious-looking Hispanic guy turned up at his office looking for him. Luckily Oz was feeling paranoid and hadn't gone to work. Last night he stayed with a friend. This morning he goes back home and finds his back door is missing, along with all of his files and his computer.'

'So who is this guy? What's the big deal with the pictures?'

'It's a Straw Men thing. Background.'

'How deep background?'

'The kind of thing you dismiss as weird shit.'

'Okay. In that case I don't want to hear about it.'

The entrance to Julia Gulicks' apartment was up a separate staircase around the side of the building. The door had been sealed with police tape and plastered all over with DO NOT ENTER signs.

'Monroe said they've tossed this already,' I said.

'The local cops went through after she was arrested, yes – but it was only a search for primary evidence. Since yesterday morning priorities have changed.'

I watched the street as Zandt ran a blade down through the tape, then pulled out a ring of slender metal implements. Within a couple of minutes the door was unlocked. We slipped inside and closed the door behind us.

It was not a big apartment. The exterior door gave directly into the largest space, a sitting room with a kitchen area at the far end. Bookcases lined one wall and a large wooden table evidently served for both eating and working. Two doors at the other end led to a bathroom and a bedroom. The last was extremely small, with space only for a narrow walkway around a queen-sized bed. You could barely open the doors of the closets to their full extent. Each room showed signs of organized search.

John and I had taken a first look around the entire place and were back in the sitting room in less than a minute.

'Thoughts?'

'Only that we're not going to learn anything here,' I said. 'The cops have been thorough. Plus according to the coroner the nameless victim lay somewhere for a while before she cut his flesh off. And where are you going to put a body in here?'

'The sitting room floor. Across the dining table or on her bed, with her lying right beside. You can't guess the circumstances under which lunatics lead their lives.'

'Assuming she really did it. Nina didn't think so.'

'Nina was wrong.'

'I'll look forward to seeing you explain that to her.' I walked over to the wall holding the bookcase and rapped it with my knuckle. It made a flat, hollow sound. 'Cheap partitions,' I said. 'I wouldn't want to kill someone in here with sound-proofing that basic. Not that I'm an expert.'

'She drugged Widmar. Probably the other guy too.'

'But she didn't kill Widmar here, did she? Which maybe makes my point. And unless someone's actually out cold there's no telling they won't suddenly cry out – and then you've got neighbours calling the cops and all hell breaking loose. So – assuming she did whack these guys – there's some other location we need to be more concerned with.'

'You know where that is?'

'No.'

'Right. So let's search this place.'

Zandt went into the bedroom. I worked quickly around the kitchen and sitting room. I looked in the drawers and in the cupboards and saw small quantities of decent-quality silverware and canned goods, all within use-by date. I looked on top of and underneath things and found dust and three elastic bands. I moved the furniture and felt inside and discovered nothing of note. I went through the bookcase, opening and shaking every book and upturning every small vase and decorative gewgaw. Four paperclips, seven magazine subscription cards used as bookmarks, the back of a broken brooch. The books were generic: paperback novels, unread success-in-business-and/or-dieting-and/or-life-in-general grimoires with near-identical balding shysters on the front, an idiot's guide to Windows and two expert books on a commercial accounting package. In a lower drawer I found a small wooden box stuffed full of photographs, showing people who looked just like everyone else, with or without Julia amongst them. I took this over to the couch and waited for Zandt to finish in the bathroom.

He came out empty-handed. 'Nothing obvious,' he admitted.

'Of course, we have no idea what the cops have already taken.'

'I haven't seen anything like an address book or journal.'

I shook my head. 'Nearest is this.'

We flicked through the pictures for a couple of minutes. The clearest proof you can get of the fact you are not somebody else is by looking at the images they value. They seemed generic to the point of fake. Red-eyed women with curly hair, shiny-faced guys holding up a beer, random old people looking unsure: everyone offering pro forma grins as if bracing themselves for injury. I lost interest quickly, caught in a bad reverie, wondering if there existed a single photograph of Nina and me together, if we had somehow failed to make even so small a mark in time.

'Look at this.'

I glanced at the picture John was holding. Unusually, there was no one in it. It showed a patch of woods, taken on an overcast day. 'And?'

'Doesn't that look like where the second body was found?'

'In that it's a wood, yeah, kind of. I don't think it's the same place, though. The trees look different.'

'But look at the tones. Either that picture was in sunlight for a long while, or it's older than most of the others in that box.'

He was right. I looked more closely, turned the photo over. 'Can we get a year off these numbers on the paper?'

'It's worth a try.' He stood up. 'We're done here. I'll make some calls on the way.'

'Where are we going?'

'To talk to her again.'

'I thought you said there was no point?'

'Maybe there is now. If this is a photograph of the crime scene it might demonstrate prior motive. If attacking me and her overall weirdness is the groundwork for an insanity defence, then this is going to hurt. It may be enough to rattle her.'

'I don't see this being our magic bullet,' I said. 'I'm still not convinced it's the same place.'

'Doesn't matter. It just has to be possible.' He turned, framed in the open doorway. 'You shoot accurately enough, you can use bullets made of air.'

'She's not here right now,' the cop behind the desk said. He was one of the policemen who'd helped pull Gulicks off Zandt. He looked very defensive.

'Where is she?'

'In the hospital.'

I stared at him. 'Why?'

'Look, guys, I really shouldn't be . . .'

John interrupted. 'Is this your fault?' He sounded for all the world like he had his own locker in the station and ran the morning roll call.

'Shit, no, sir,' the guy said, hurriedly, and was suddenly all about telling us everything he knew. 'Christ, I told . . . I did the rota. I checked on her at four and she was sleeping. She was fine.'

'So then what happened?'

The cop breathed out in a rush. 'Sometime after that, she tried to kill herself.'

'How?'

'Stood on her bed,' he said. 'Put her hands behind her back and let herself fall forward. Onto her head. They think she did it three times. Didn't make a sound at any point.'

'Great. Chalk one up for the insanity plea,' Zandt said. He sounded pissed.

'No way,' the cop said, firmly. 'You think you could do something like that? Twice? Three fucking times? I couldn't. She tried to die, man. She tried *hard*. That woman just doesn't want to be here any more.'

'What's her condition?'

'Same as yours or mine would be. Not fucking good.'

He turned to deal with a ringing phone and John and I walked away from the desk. I rubbed my face with my hands as if trying to keep my head on.

'So much for the new plan. *Now* what?'

For once Zandt looked at a loss. 'The hospital, I guess, though I'm now assuming that's where Monroe rushed off to first thing this morning. Which probably means they don't think she's going to be around for long. She may not even be able to talk.'

'She's got to. If she doesn't . . .' I took a deep breath, started again. 'We're losing this, John. This whole thing is out of control.'

My phone rang. I checked the screen hoping it might be Monroe, but it wasn't.

'It's Unger,' I told John, and answered it. 'What do you want, Carl?'

'Where are you?'

'In Thornton.'

'I'm near town. I'd like to talk to you.'

I was long past the point of wondering if Unger was some kind of Straw Man. If he was, so be it. Either John and I would take him, or he'd take us.

'Fine,' I said. 'I've got to go somewhere first. I'll be back in an hour. Meet me at a bar called the Mayflower. It's on the Owensville road.'

'You got it.'

'One thing,' I said. 'You had better be on the level, Carl, or we're going to kill you there and then. Count on it.'

I closed the phone to see both John and the desk cop staring at me.

I shrugged. 'Just want to make sure everyone knows where they stand.'

Chapter 28

They had landed in Huntsville, Alabama, very early in the morning. Walked out of the airport and straight to the parking lot, where three cars were waiting with engines running. The rear door to the first of these opened as they approached, and a guy got out. Early twenties, confident-looking. Lee recognised him from somewhere. Either the first time he'd met Paul, or maybe he'd been one of the guys spread around the food court the previous morning. Lee wasn't sure.

Paul took a seat in the back and Lee sat next to him. The young guy sat opposite, next to another man, older and sleek with sharp blue eyes. This guy nodded at Paul.

'Hey, Lee,' he said. 'Glad you're on board.'

They pulled out of the lot like a motorcade and headed across country in a loose convoy. Not right after one another, of course. Three big cars driving fast and steady in a line could not have helped but attract attention. The drivers made sure there were generally a few cars in between each of them. Lee realised these people didn't seem overly cautious, however: if it had been him, he might have arranged to have different models or colours or something, or headed to wherever they were going from different directions. He got the sense these men basically just didn't give a shit.

They took 231 north into Tennessee and then cut east into craggy hills. Lee looked out of the window. He was tired from the multi-hop journey from LA, not to mention that all the stuff that had happened yesterday seemed to have left him kind of wiped out. Brad was dead, and Lee was sitting next to the guy who had killed him. And Karen, by extension or command. That was a little weird.

The two other guys in their car spent the initial part of the journey having short conversations on mobile phones. These seemed to be conducted in a kind of code. Paul made a single call in which he told someone simply that he was coming. Lee couldn't have worked out what any of them were talking about even if he wanted to, which he didn't, particularly. He was going where they were going. He was doing what they were doing.

It would all become clear, he assumed.

After two hours they took a turn off the highway and headed along a succession of smaller roads. These eventually led to a ramshackle house in the backwoods, the dirt yard in front of it dotted with long grasses and surrounded by rusted-up vehicles from decades past. The cars pulled to a halt side by side. Everybody got out.

There were five people in each of the two other cars. All were dressed in dark suits and coats but moved like soldiers. They, Paul, and the two other guys headed straight into the house – which looked as if someone enterprising but strictly loopy had lashed it together out of stuff they'd found in dumpsters. Lee wandered off into the bushes to take a leak, then walked back and leaned against the car and waited.

Fifteen minutes later everyone came out carrying stuff. Some had wooden boxes, which they carried like short stretchers. Others had heavy-looking shoulder bags. Nothing was labelled and nothing looked like it had arrived in this place by a regular channel. It was loaded into the trunks of the cars, and then everyone got back inside and three engines started at once.

The cars retraced the route back to the main road and were soon spread out over half a mile with cars in between, as before. They kept east for a while and then took a little jag north, into Kentucky. Not far over the state line a similar thing happened, the lead car turning off the main road again, with the vehicles following it into the countryside. This time the house was a lot fancier looking, a colonial pile with two-storey pillars and a quaint little pond in front, secure in the middle of manicured grounds. The cars pulled up and again everybody got out. Lee waited twenty-five minutes this time, watching a pair of young teenage girls on horses as they cantered around the meadow. Long ponytails bobbed up and down in the morning sun. The girls didn't look his way, not once. It was as if the cars weren't even there.

Everybody came out again, carrying bags. Not so many this time, but they were carried carefully. There was one further stop, which involved briefly halting in front of an abandoned gas station. Somebody had left two small, angular bags hidden in back. The difference after this stop was that the two guys from their car got into one of the others instead, leaving Lee and Paul alone in the back. The sun was in the middle of the sky by now.

Not long after that, they entered Virginia.

Paul stared into space like he was meditating or something. He hadn't moved in a half hour, not a muscle, and it was getting freaky. Lee had been well trained in the art of keeping quiet unless spoken to – the Hudeks entertained old-fashioned values – and didn't want to piss the guy off. Plus he remembered a party at the Metzger house one time where he'd met some screenwriter client of Brad's father. The guy was called Nic Golson – he kept dropping his own name, bizarrely, as if he thought that would help you remember it, which evidently it did, now Lee came to think of it. He'd told Lee his theory that when you took the Big Meetings, instead of running your mouth straight away, trying to impress people as friendly and accommodating, you came across better if you kept your mouth shut and sat there looking moody. Anybody can be friendly and accommodating. This way forced people to come to you, pushed you up the pecking order, made you someone to be reckoned with. Or so the guy claimed, though Lee noticed his pockets were stuffed full of food when he left.

Lee had tried this over the last six months and found it worked. You could get many people to do what you wanted just by not making it easier for them to do something else. After another hour of driving and not a word being said, however, it was Lee who finally cracked.

'So, are the cops looking for me, back in LA?'

Paul's head turned slowly towards him. 'I imagine so.'

'You know, you could have just asked if I'd go with you guys. Help you with this deal.'

'This deal?'

'Yeah. Or whatever. You didn't have to do all that shit. Fuck me up back at home.'

'What if you'd refused?'

'You know my folks, obviously. And how is that, by the way? How do you know them?'

'Old friends.'

'So they could have talked me into it, right? Did they *know* you were going to do all that crap to me?'

Paul didn't answer the direct question. 'Men of your age are notoriously hard to influence. They need a *force majeure*.'

'You evidently got drugs in depth. I've never seen so many bags and boxes, and these are some serious-looking dudes you got carrying them.' Lee noticed that the man was smiling faintly at him. 'My point is what fucking difference do I make?'

'You're going to be key, don't worry.'

'Maybe you could tell me what's going on?'

'Well, what do you think?'

'You've got some major deal going down. Some big festival or something. You're gathering up a whole bunch of gear . . .'

'Lee, these are not drugs. Try to think in the longer term.'

'I thought you guys were all about drugs.'

'They've been useful over the last few decades, that's all. They generate money and they're a lot less effort than mining.'

'Mining?' Lee tried to rethink. 'So this isn't about drugs?'

'It's about old times and a new start. A more personal form of breakage. Bringing the fight close to home.'

'See, you're just, fucking . . . *saying* things again. And I have no idea what you mean.'

'Oh, well. I'm sure we'll survive.'

Lee thought a moment, and then reached over and grabbed the door handle. He opened the door and pushed it wide.

He had no intention of jumping out – the car was going over seventy miles an hour – but it had the desired effect. The car wavered for just a moment as the driver struggled to cope with the sudden change in aerodynamics.

Paul reached out calmly and shut the door again. 'Don't do that,' he said.

'So don't treat me like a kid.'

'Actually, you would do well to think of me as a father figure, Lee – though one who will burn your soul to ashes if you fuck him around.' He smiled brightly. 'Are we clear?'

Though Paul's voice was still level and pleasant, it made the hairs on the back of Lee's neck rise.

'I get it. But I already got a dad, thanks.'

Paul nodded, and – just like that – it was okay being in the back of a car with him again. 'True,' he said. 'Well, Lee, I'll tell you something, part of why we're going to this place right now. When I was very young I lived in Northern California. My father was an important man. Not rich, like your father, but important. And one night some men and a woman came to the woods where he was living, and they murdered him. They stole me and kept me for a little while, but then they got to thinking they didn't like me so much any more, so they left me on a city street corner.'

'Shit, man, that sucks.'

Paul nodded. 'Thank you, Lee. Yes, it does. Luckily I survived, and in part because I got to know a group of people. We had similar interests, but it became a lot more than that. I was able to contribute some notions. They're like a family. Your mom and dad are part of it. You are too. We really have met before, Lee, though you don't recall it. We met not long after you were born, and again when you were three.'

He reached into his jacket pocket and pulled something out. Lee got the impression it had been there waiting for this moment, and wondered how it had come here so smoothly. It was a photograph showing much younger versions of his father and mother standing in a garden with another man. This man was Paul, though he looked barely into his twenties. A toddler stood unsteadily on the ground, holding Paul's hand.

'Is that me?'

'Already part of the team.'

'What team?'

'We look out for one another. Sometimes you quarrel, like any family, but when it comes down to it you're on the same side. We're strong right now, but there are always enemies. One man in particular isn't good for us. He's killed a few important members of our family.'

'Well, we should fuck him up.'

Paul smiled. 'We might just do that. You're a good kid, Lee. You've been raised well. You get on with your old man?'

'Yeah. He's pretty cool. He's got a good sense of humour.'

Lee was surprised to see Paul laugh, apparently despite himself. He grinned, glad things seemed to be getting a little more relaxed.

'You got that right,' the man said, after a moment. 'You never think about your name at all?'

'Hudek? What about it?'

'I meant the rest of it.'

Hudek looked at him. 'No. What's the big deal?'

'Say it.'

'Lee John.'

'Right. So tell me what your name is.'

'My name is Lee John.'

Paul just stared at him, waiting, then finally shook his head. His voice was cold again.

'Jesus. You kids. You really do know less than *shit*.'

And finally the cars slowed.

They had been driving for a half hour along a featureless road that cut through mile after mile of scrubby-looking forest. A call came in to Paul's cell phone, seemed like it was from someone in the leading car. He agreed to whatever was being said, and soon afterwards the three vehicles pulled over, just ahead of a side turning. Paul opened his door and got out. Lee followed.

In the road all of the cars' doors were opened. Lee was reconciling himself to another inexplicable period of waiting when he realized something.

The people in the cars had changed.

He stared, open-mouthed. They were different. Dressed differently, different-looking . . . None of them was the same. There were two *women*, for a start. These were simply not the same people who had been in the cars all along.

Except . . .

Suddenly he recognized the young guy who'd opened the door for them, when they hit the lot at Huntsville airport. He was now wearing a hooded sweater, unlaced sneakers and baggy-ass jeans, with a little red backpack. He walked past Lee to go get stuff out the back of their car and he looked just like any teen you'd see outside a strip mall anywhere in the continental USA, complete with a skateboard and the I'm-too-cool-to-walk-upright shoulder roll.

Lee looked back at all the other people and slowly began to half-recognize other faces. The sleek guy – the one who'd been in their car at the beginning – was now dressed as a cop, so convincingly that Lee's heart missed a beat when he spotted him. Two other men were in cheap business suits, another in grimy mechanic's overalls. This last opened the hood of the second car and smeared oil over his hands. The first woman Lee saw was dressed in head-to-toe Banana Republic with a big, soft sweater. Her hair had previously been tied back in a style so severe he hadn't even noticed she was a chick. She pulled off a hair-tie as he watched and shook it out. By the time she was finished she looked like she should be pushing an up-market stroller along a nice village street, on her way to sip a skinny latte with others of her breed, maybe go hog wild and have a lo-fat muffin to spend the day feeling guilty about. She smiled briefly at no one in particular, as if practising. Then her face went blank again. The other woman was wearing a kind of pale green coat, looked like she worked in a grocery store.

Everyone was carrying something. A briefcase. A big handbag. A tool box. A long oblong carton with the UPS logo on it. A mail bag.

After a couple of minutes all the car doors and trunks were shut. Two of the cars reversed slowly up the road and performed graceful turns. They drove quickly back the way they had come, leaving the people standing in the road, looking even more odd without the vehicles to give them context and remind you how they'd got there. It was like aliens had decided to return a random selection of the population they'd abducted over the last few years, and zapped them down on the side of this nowhere road.

Lee watched as Paul walked amongst them. He spoke to each in turn. There was some nodding, a few handshakes. The homemaker smiled when he spoke to her, and this time it looked a little more convincing.

Then, without anything in particular seeming to trigger it, they all set off into the forest. At first they walked largely together as a group, but soon they split off in twos and threes, heading somewhere – Lee had no clue where – as if to arrive eventually from different angles, at different times.

Paul walked back over and motioned Lee to get into the car.

Twenty minutes later they arrived at a town. It wasn't big. Just one of those places you find everywhere, the kind you gas up in and grab a coffee from and then leave, thanking your lucky stars you live in an environment where the Halloween parade isn't the year's biggest deal. The car wound its way in through streets of wooden houses and then entered what appeared to be the centre. Old-looking buildings. A police station. A kindergarten. A Starbucks. This and that.

Lee watched as they passed through. This didn't look like a place where much interesting would happen. Not according to his value system, anyhow. 'Jesus,' he said. 'What a shithole.'

'That's harsh, Lee.'

'You must see something different to me.'

'I see the homes of hard-working, television-watching, product-buying souls. Commerce and service industries ticking over nicely. And many years of history, with a few dark corners. This place is more interesting than it looks. Older, too.'

'Whatever. It's still a dump.'

'It's where people live, Lee. Real people. True blue folks. Real *Americans*, or so they think. Small towns are the backbone of this country.'

'Maybe a hundred years ago. Urban is where it's at now, dude.'

'That's what a lot of people seem to think.'

Eventually the car passed a Holiday Inn, and Paul got the driver to go a little more slowly. This perked Lee's interest. He thought he recognized the hotel from the television – from when Paul had stared at CNN in the Belle Isle mall. There were a couple of cop cars parked near the entrance, plus a few anonymous-looking sedans. Then he saw a guy in a blue windcheater with the letters FBI on the back.

'Uh,' he said, nervously, 'do we really want to be here?'

'Maybe later,' Paul said, and the car picked up speed once more.

It hung a left and left town again. After a time it took a side road which took them in a long sweep out around some woods. Eventually this led into a tiny town called Dryford. A vague collection of houses, decently sized, but still the place looked like its glory days were fifty years past.

Another turn-off led them down a couple of hundred yards of road that ended abruptly at a gate. Just before the end was another gate. The driver got out and went to open it. Lee could see a deep yard on the other side, hugely overgrown. Way back in amongst all the grass and a bunch of trees that had been allowed to do whatever they liked, stood a house. A little bigger than the ones in 'town', and somewhat falling down. The driver got back in and drove them onto the property. It quickly became evident that this house had not been inhabited for quite a few years. Boards were slipping on the front. Shingles were missing from the roof and the glass in the windows, though unbroken, made it look as though old mist was trapped inside. A white VW camper van was parked out front, also looking like it could have been here a while, though presumably not.

'Behold a pale horse,' Paul said.

They got out of the car. As they approached the van its side door opened. It was dark inside. A man got out, slid the door back most of the way shut. The man was tall and looked old, kind of, because he had grey hair and was a little rounded over the shoulders. He was big, though: big and strong-looking. Kind of like that guy in *The Hitcher*, plus twenty years.

'Hello, James,' Paul said. His voice was flat. 'I trusted you.'

'It was an accident,' the man said. 'It's been a long time and I'm out of practice. It got out of hand.'

'Maybe you're too old for this.'

'Maybe I am. Should have had one of your baby zombies do the job instead.' The man turned his gaze on Lee, and Lee was surprised to feel a strong tickle of fear. When he looked at you, the guy didn't look so old. At all. 'This isn't the same one, is it?'

'No,' Paul said. 'This is our new special friend.' He raised his head, sniffed. 'Been cooking in there?'

'I would have been okay, if it wasn't for you.'

'No, James, you wouldn't. Remember the talk we had, the night I saved you? You are what you are. You know that. And you know that one never changes back to none.'

The older man looked at Paul for a while, as if enduring advice from someone he'd known all his life.

'No,' he said, in the end. 'I guess it does not.'

Paul walked over to the van and slid the door open. Curious, Lee followed. The old guy didn't seem to like them doing this, but evidently didn't feel there was anything he could do to stop it. Closer to the van Lee could smell something too. Kind of earthy, but a little sweet. He wasn't sure what the old guy had been cooking in there, but even though he was hungry he thought that if offered a mouthful, he'd probably decline.

Then he realized someone was in the van.

Right at the back, tied in an awkward position, lay a tall, skinny woman. She was blindfolded and gagged.

Lee felt uncomfortable. This looked wrong. The kind of thing you saw re-created in documentaries on cable, viewer discretion advised.

Paul stepped up into the van and squatted down in front of the woman. He reached up and undid the blindfold. Lee was close enough to see the woman's eyes widen when she saw who it was.

'Hey, Nina,' Paul said. 'Remember me?'

Chapter 29

The hospital looked as though it had been opened with great fanfare ten years before and then promptly forgotten. It had been designed by an architect with an eye to posterity and a good straight ruler, who must have kicked himself when he realized he'd forgotten about windows and the fact that people might have to spend time inside. The lobby smelled of chemicals and sounded like rubber heels squeaking on linoleum, and the walls held lots of small posters about things that were either tedious or dire. I don't like hospitals. In my life nothing good has come out of them. It's where you go to be sick, or be told you're about to be.

And of course it's where you go to die.

The first glimpse I had of Julia Gulicks said this last was the job she was here to do. We walked up a long, grey corridor on a high floor to a private room near the end. A policeman was sitting outside but through the small, square window in the door above his head you could see a body lying on a bed, immobile as a model of a mountain range made out of sections of wood and a sheet. Most of the face was wrapped in bandages. The only confirmation it was her was the red hair straggling over the pillow, but even that was thin and muted now, as if her vitality was leaking elsewhere.

Before the cop had the chance to start telling us to get the hell away, we heard footsteps heading towards us up the corridor. 'What are you doing here?'

The voice was Monroe's. He was carrying a foam cup of coffee. I remembered Nina telling me once what a bear he was for the stuff. The memory didn't help much.

John held up the photograph. 'This.'

'What is it?'

'We think it's a picture of the woods where you found the second body.'

'Where'd you get this?'

'Her apartment. On the way here I got someone to look up the product code on the paper. The photograph was printed five years ago. It's premeditation, Monroe. It slam dunks your case.'

Monroe shook his head. 'It's landscape photography, that's all.'

'I want to . . .'

'She can't see it, Zandt. Have you *looked* in there? Her eyes are wrapped in gauze and even if they weren't it would make no difference. She's got a grossly fractured skull and massive lesions on both frontal lobes. They drained her and kept her alive but that's all medical science has on offer right now.'

'She doesn't have to be able to see,' John said. 'Just hear. I only want to talk to her.'

'She isn't listening. Next big thing she's going to do is die.'

Nonetheless he thought for a moment, and stepped aside. 'If there was one person here to speak for her,' he said, 'I wouldn't let you do this.'

'I think she wants to,' John said.

* * *

313

Monroe stopped at the end of the bed. I stood well back, near the wall. Gulicks was hooked up to a bank of machines. Probably their purpose was reassurance, but if you ask me they don't work. Being connected to a machine is never a sign things are going well. Even the comatose know that. John perched on the side of the bed.

Gulicks seemed to register a shift in the mattress. Her head moved to the side a little. Her mouth opened with a quiet pop as gummy lips separated.

'Julia?'

She closed her mouth again, and moved her head back the other way.

'I'm the person you talked to last night. In the police station. Do you recognize my voice?'

Nothing.

'Julia – why did you do this to yourself?'

It wasn't the question I was expecting him to ask. Monroe either, judging from his face. You made assumptions. She'd done it because she was nuts. Or because she was guilty and didn't want to stand trial. But maybe not.

She turned her head back towards him. Suddenly her tongue rolled quickly around her mouth, a little too fast. John reached to the bedside table and got a glass of water. He let a few drops into her mouth. Her tongue kept moving for a while, then slowly stopped.

'Rowboat,' she said, clearly. 'Penguin in the bank hall. It's a shitty mix, you need more butter.'

I looked at my feet. It wasn't the words so much as the way her tongue moved. It was too autonomous. It looked like a rat trying to desert a sinking ship.

He asked her other things. He asked her if she remembered the pictures she kept in the box in her apartment. He asked if she remembered taking a photograph of the woods near Thornton, and if so, when that might have been. He asked if she'd kept that picture pinned up on her wall, and why.

She said nothing in reply. There was little evidence that she hadn't

314

gone back to sleep or, if she was awake, that her mind hadn't wandered somewhere else and gotten lost in a basement corridor. I didn't know what effect brain injuries had, and I didn't know whether they were always permanent, but something told me Julia was gone and wasn't coming back. I guess if I was Lawrence Widmar's wife then this might have made me angry: you want someone to blame, to rail at. Gulicks was beyond good and evil now.

'Here's here,' she said, suddenly.

I looked up. Though it didn't make any sense, it was the first thing she had said in over ten minutes.

'What's that?' John said. He leaned towards her.

The second time she was easier to understand. 'He's here. Isn't he?'

Monroe spoke. 'Who's here?'

'Where am I?'

John held a hand up to stop Monroe confusing her. 'You're in the hospital, Julia.'

'Am I being born?'

'No.'

'Did you say something about a photograph?'

'We found a picture which shows some woods. Do you remember taking it?'

'There's lots of woods. Always have been. Ever since I was a little, little girl.'

'Why did you take the picture, Julia?'

'What picture?'

'The picture of the woods.'

'Make memories. Right? Right? Right? Wonderful.'

'I don't understand what you're saying.'

'Did you ever go to Disneyworld?'

'Yes,' John said. 'Long time ago.'

'Nobody would take me when I was young. I took myself when I grew up. It's not the same.'

'No.'

'Nobody should have to take themselves to Disneyworld.'

'Julia . . .'

'Did you shit on me? Everything smells wrong.' Her tongue started to loll again. Her chin trembled. 'Oh, it's bad.'

'Julia – why? Why did you kill them?'

'I got it wrong, okay? None of it helps. It's a fucking, fucking disease.' Then suddenly her voice changed, dropping almost an octave. 'Twelve step me to hell, you nigger.'

She laughed uproariously, arching her back. Then it became a cough, and suddenly she was being sick.

Monroe slapped the attention button and John quickly rolled her onto her side. Very soon afterwards the room was full of medics and we were shoved out into the corridor.

We waited in silence while the people inside did their thing. After a half hour they started to leave, although a nurse was left by her bed. The last person in a white coat was a woman who glared at us as she shut the door firmly behind her.

'I told you she couldn't be talked to right now.'

'She's a suspect in two murders,' Monroe said.

'Your problem,' the doctor snapped. 'She's dying. The damage to her brain is compromising her autonomic nervous system. That's the part that controls the things we don't normally have to do deliberately, like *breathe*. I don't care what she may or may not have done, you don't have the right to hasten her death. Disturb her again and I'll call the police.'

'Ma'am,' said the uniform still sitting in a chair to one side of the door, 'um, I am the police.'

'More senior police, then,' the doctor said, and strode off down the corridor.

After she'd gone Monroe turned to Zandt. 'So. Was it worth it?'

'She took the picture. She killed those men because of something that took place a long time ago. Something that made her want to record a particular part of the woods for later reference. She saw something happen there.'

316

'She saw whoever killed the victim we found,' I said. 'And she's the only person who might be able to tell us who that was.'

'The body was definitely a woman,' Monroe said. 'Mid-forties. They lifted the rest of the skeleton last night. And the signs are you were right about when it happened. So who is she? Who killed her?'

'I don't know,' I said. 'But I believe there's a fifty-fifty chance he's the person who took Nina.'

'If not him, then who?'

'Ghosts,' I said, bitterly. 'People you don't believe in and nobody can ever catch.'

We left the hospital. Monroe evidently felt it wasn't worth waiting there any longer, and I believed he was right. Julia didn't strike me as someone who was going to say anything useful again.

John walked straight over to my car. I hung back, wanting a last word with Charles. I was surprised at how he looked. Tired I'd seen before, but now he looked defeated.

'You've got to find something, Charles,' I said.

'I'm doing everything I can.'

'I hope so. We're running out of time. And if I don't find Nina, your life is not going to be worth living.'

I left him standing there and walked over to the car. Before I climbed in I pressed the speed dial for Nina's number one more time.

Still nothing. And wherever her phone was, whether it was switched on or off, sooner or later the battery was going to trickle out.

Chapter 30

The cellar was worse than the van. Nina knew life had come to a sorry pass if she looked on the VW as the glory days, but there had been movement, at least. There was the possibility she might be taken somewhere and released: pushed out into the wilderness, or rolled out onto the road at speed. Neither were great options, but they were doors to other realities – if you were strong, and if you were lucky. Perhaps a line-caught fish felt the same, right up until it was knocked on the back of the head. When you are lying on the floor of a cellar, it does not feel as if strength and luck are nearby. Instead there is damp, there is coldness, and there is the unforgiving sense of being underground.

Being under the ground is not good. Under the ground is where you go to be dead.

She knew she was lying in a space about thirty feet square. She'd gotten a glimpse of it when she was brought down the wooden staircase, and tried to look around before the door was shut again, returning the cellar to darkness. Immediately she closed her eyes, so as not to be misled by shadows. She felt the space around her, pictured where the supports were, thought about how you might try to get to the staircase: assuming you weren't lying flat on your back with your wrists and ankles tied. She tried to lock these ideas in her mind, but it had been a long time since she'd slept and there was a ringing in her ears. She felt physically wretched. Being short a pint or two of blood didn't help, but that shouldn't make you vomit, which had happened five minutes previously. She didn't know what damage petrol fumes could do, but whatever it was, they had evidently done it.

She had to remain alert. The guy who'd taken her had failed in some way. She had heard Paul called him 'James'. He was supposed to have done something else, either instead of, or as well as, abducting her. What? Not killing her, it seemed, otherwise Paul would have done that right away. He wasn't someone who kept people alive for the fun of it. Quite the opposite.

It was not a good question to have to ask yourself, but why was she not supposed to be dead? And what could she do to try to stay . . .

Then she remembered something else. She recalled that in the van she'd realized that she probably still had her cell phone. She knew she'd turned it off prior to the meeting with Reidel, so it should still have charge. Hopefully. In the van she'd been too constrained and sedated to dream of actually finding the phone.

Here it might be different. If she moved fast. She didn't even have to get a call out. If they had a beacon trace on it, or if Ward had been trying to call her and suddenly got through at last . . .

Nina craned her neck, turned her head on the dusty, splintered floor. When she'd been brought down into the cellar a bulky bag of her abductor's stuff had come too, everything out of the VW. It was lying against the wall, she thought. She'd been wearing her coat when he came to her hotel room. The phone would have been deep in the inside pocket. It must now be in his bag.

After being able to do nothing except withstand discomfort, she had a job now, a proper one.

Get hold of the phone. And not die, of course.

*   *   *

The best way would be getting herself to a sitting position. That way she could shuffle across the floor in the direction of the bag. Wouldn't be the fastest method, but it gave her a little control.

It took five minutes to wrench and turn herself upright from where she'd been left. Then she oriented her feet in the right direction, and wriggled her ass.

It worked, kind of. It was slow. The floor was uneven. There were things lying on it. Neither became obvious until she ran into an obstruction, and then she had to work her way around.

But slowly she kept moving, until her feet met the wall. Swivelled right a little, reaching out. A rustling sound.

The bag.

Now what? Couldn't use her hands and feet. Coat might be buried deep in there. It was thick, too – Ward had bought it for her against the coming cold of a Pacific Northwest winter. There was going to be no way she could actually get the phone out. But maybe if she put pressure on the bag . . .

Then she heard the sound of footsteps approaching up above.

She fell back onto her side immediately, straightened her body out, and rolled. She rolled fast. It didn't matter what she hit on the way, she had to get back to where she'd been. They couldn't suspect there was any reason for her to want to get over to the bag.

She made it, via thudding and scraping collisions with every single unseen obstruction. Something caught at her wrist and she had to yank it hard to keep going. She was in pain, and breathless. But she got back to where she'd started. Made sure she was lying flat. Forced her chest not to heave up and down.

She heard the sound of the cellar door being opened. She raised her head, still trying not to pant. She could see two men standing at the top of the stairs. The Upright Man and the older one. She got a glimpse of the younger kid standing well back.

Could he be a help to her? There had been something in the kid's face which said this was outside the world he understood. Could she try to tap some kind of older sister vein in him? Yeah, dream

320

on, Nina. But how old would his mother be? Could she be his defenceless mom instead, some pie-wielding sweetie? Would it help?

But when the two older men started down the stairs, the boy remained behind, and after a moment disappeared from view into some other part of the house.

Paul didn't come over to her when he reached the basement, but walked off to one side. He squatted down and seemed to inspect a portion of the ground for a while, reaching out and pulling his finger through the dirt.

'Don't think our wannabe is going to be a problem any more,' he said to the older man. 'Again, no thanks to you.' He stood up again and looked down at Nina. 'We might as well keep our agent for the time being. There will come a time when that's no longer the case. I will call you then, and if I tell you to kill her you'll do it immediately. No playing. Understood?'

The man nodded.

'He was supposed to kill us both,' Nina said, quietly. 'Is that it? He mistook Reidel for Ward, and killed him, but then decided he wanted me for himself.'

Paul came so he was standing directly over Nina. 'You're sharp, Agent Baynam. Sharp and super-smart. But wrong. James was supposed to kill you. But Ward wasn't his other target.'

'Who was?'

'I'll leave that as an exercise for the student.'

'You're a lunatic.'

'No. And I'm not the one tied up in a basement and stinking of stale sweat and fear, so right now nine out of ten cat-owners would prefer my reality to yours.'

The men left soon afterwards, and she heard the door to the house being slammed and the sound of a car driving away. Nina made herself wait before she tried for the phone again, to make sure they'd all gone. In the meantime she tried to think calmly, see if there was anything to learn from what Paul had said. A classic 1930s text she'd read once described a psychopath as a 'reflex machine', which could mimic the human personality so effectively that it was impossible to say what about them is not real. You saw something of this in the eyes of the men who end up in fights in bars. If you passed by early in the evening – assuming you were incautious enough to look their way, which is a bad, bad idea – you could see a restlessness in their faces, a blankness washed with slippery good cheer. The silent are usually misanthropes or depressed or serious drinkers getting on with business. There is a cold and hectic charm about the dangerous ones, like the blurred numbers on a computer read-out: forever spinning to the conclusion of some complex calculation, but never settling on a result. A result would be a fixed personality, something you could reason with. There is no such thing inside such men. They are pockets of violence waiting for an excuse, demonic whirlwinds in human wrappers.

The truly mad are something else again. With them, there *is* something inside – it's just not clear what it is. Dr Cleckley's 'reflex machine' model begged a question: what was it that was doing the impersonating? What was this 'machine', and what was it doing when it wasn't impersonating humankind? What were its normal responses? Where did it come from? *What did it want?*

Was it actually something different in each of them, or was it possible that it was the same thing, the same demonic substance or insane spirit, staring out of all of their eyes? Everything in Nina's training and belief system said otherwise, that these were damaged humans, manifesting individual psychoses and pathologies.

But when someone like Paul looked down at you . . . sometimes you had to wonder.

She had just decided she couldn't wait any longer when she heard the sound of the cellar door opening again, and light leaked down. Her heart sank. They hadn't all gone after all.

Heavy footsteps descended. It could only be James, the one who'd taken her blood. He stopped at the bottom of the stairs, where he sat in silence for some time, smoking.

'What happens now, James?' she asked, dully. 'We wait until your leader says you can kill me?'

'He's not my leader. And I'm not James.'

'That's what he called you.'

'I'm Jim Westlake. I take photographs.'

'My father was a photographer.' This was not true, of course. 'What kind of pictures?'

The man hesitated, then got up and went over to his bag. He took Nina's jacket out and laid it on the ground, and Nina's heart caught in her throat.

So it was here. That was great news. But lying on the floor, it could be knocked. The phone could fall out and be discovered. But if she could get to it . . . or have it brought to her . . .

'I'm cold,' she said. 'This floor is so cold.'

He didn't seem to hear. When he straightened he was holding a small box, something that looked as though it once held a pair of children's shoes. He sat back on the bottom stair and opened it. He looked through the contents for a while, as if he'd forgotten she was there. Then, without even looking at her, he held up a few Polaroid photographs so she could see.

Nina couldn't tell much except they were of women or girls, of various ages, taken somewhere that looked sunny.

'I didn't do anything,' he said. 'None of them. For years. I even lived next to . . . Look.'

He flipped quickly through the pictures for a moment, then yanked a single one out. 'Look.'

He held a picture so close to her face she could barely focus to make out what it showed. The picture was of two little girls, maybe four, five years old. Smiling.

'Cute.'

'My neighbours.'

'Really? Next door to here?'

'No. I haven't lived here for a long time.'

'So how come you can just walk in?'

'I still own it but . . . I lived here with my wife.'

'You're married?'

'Not any more.'

Nina opened her mouth to ask another question, but closed it again slowly. She was not in charge here. This was not an interview with a man awaiting trial. She let silence settle.

Eventually he spoke.

'We met when I got out of the army. We moved around for a few years, all over the place. Then we found this area and it felt right. I got myself a teaching certificate. I'd always been good at numbers. I taught math at the school. But . . .'

He left a long pause before he continued.

'I'd been okay all that time, overseas. In the army I could have . . . but I didn't. But something . . . after I'd been here a while I just wasn't right any more. Couldn't get my head to add things up properly. The sums started going wrong again.'

Nina couldn't help herself. 'What? You're saying it's Thornton's fault? The town made you do it? Take my advice, that defence just won't play.'

'I don't care. For a long time I was like everybody else. I knew I could be wrong if I let myself. But I didn't want to have to do it. I . . . I did my best. But then.' He put his head in his hands. 'A student. At the school. She reminded me of Karla. That's all it took. She looked like Karla. That was all. Bang. Just like that.'

'Who's Karla? Your wife?'

'My wife was Laurie. Aren't you listening?'

'I'm sorry. So who was Karla?'

'A girl I knew a long time ago. At school. She was my first.'

'The first girl you had sex with.'

'Yes.'

'But that's not what you meant.'

'No.'

'You killed her.'

'Yes.'

He told Nina about the girl, this Karla. He could remember her face in bitter detail. He could remember the way she walked. He could recall preparations, too, undertaken under erasure in his head while apparently doing and thinking something else entirely, something normal. He remembered, too, sitting on the edge of the river afterwards, a waterside where he had played as a kid. It was dark and cold that night and spitting with rain. He sat on the hard, pocked mud, her severed hand beside him, and there was no light anywhere apart from a few distant twinkles in the windows of houses right up along the opposite edge of the water. If you turned away from those and looked out and listened to the wind you could believe that the whole world had disappeared, that you had gone back in time to a place when the things you now held dear had yet to be brought into being, when men and boys were free to be themselves. The specifics of what he had done were already fading around the edges, and he was oddly unconcerned with the notion of capture (that too would return, and in spades). For the moment he felt he was sitting to one side of creation, and it was hard to understand how it could impinge upon him any more. When he turned and looked once more at the house lights he knew they could not see him, just as he knew that if he knocked on their doors the inhabitants would neither hear nor see him. Their life was closed to him now. There was nowhere else to go. He just sat there in the rain and listened to the sounds of wild nature until he was too cold and walked the long mile back home, where he ate a piece of cold chicken and then went to bed.

Nothing like it happened again for a very long time. It could possibly have ended there, stayed at one, remained true but unique. It didn't. Karla was his first. She was a long way from being the last.

He tried. He went in the army. He travelled the country when he got out and eventually settled down into a job in a nice town with a wife and a kid.

It was too late. It had always been too late.

'She was a stupid girl anyway. The one who looked like Karla. Really, really dumb. People were happy to believe she'd run off somewhere, gone to California like all the other lazy whores.'

'How long ago was this?'

'Fifteen years,' he said. 'It didn't happen often. I didn't let it. Never women from Thornton or Dryford, either. A waitress from Owensville, once. They're in the woods now. No one's ever going to find them. But once I'd started . . . I thought I was handling it. Of course it wasn't good, but it was under control.'

'Your wife didn't know? Didn't guess?'

He was quiet for a moment. 'She left.'

'Did she?'

He looked away. 'No,' he said.

Then suddenly he frowned, turned his head upwards. 'Did you hear that?'

'I didn't hear anything,' Nina said. 'What did you think you heard?'

He shook his head. 'Sometimes when there was a storm in the night she would get so upset.'

'Your wife?'

'She would hear the thunder and think it was the sky shouting. She thought the night was angry, and looking for someone to hurt. I said it wasn't that, it was just a sound like children make when they play. I said thunder was just the sound of the sky playing, far away.'

He was quiet for a while, and Nina realized he was crying.

'Jim,' she said, gently. 'I'm really cold. I don't feel well. You couldn't . . . would it be possible for me to have my coat? You could just lie it over me. Keep me warm. I'm sure he wouldn't mind.'

But he still didn't hear her, and Nina had a sudden vision of her smashing a metal bar over his head. None of them ever heard anything above the jabbering inside their own minds. They talked and talked, but no words ever made it in the other direction. Nothing ever went inside.

'I lost . . . It all just got to a point,' he said, his voice thick. 'You understand, don't you?'

'No,' she said, coldly. 'And I never will.'

*   *   *

A while later Paul returned. Nina heard a car door slam outside and two sets of footsteps enter the house. She heard someone walk over to the door and open it. She thought that now maybe time had run out.

But when he got down to the cellar Paul bent down and helped her to her knees, and then her feet.

'What now?' she said, hating the confidence in his gentleness.

'Going to bring you along.' He tied the gag around her mouth again. 'I don't have time to savour any of your deep thoughts. Sorry if that's disempowering in any way.'

'She's cold,' Jim/James said, suddenly.

He was not looking at either of them, or at anything that Nina could see. He had another cigarette in his mouth and seemed focused on that. She wasn't even sure he was talking to Paul, or about her.

Nonetheless Paul reached down and picked up her coat, the coat Ward had given her a lifetime ago. He hung it over her shoulders. 'Better?'

Nina nodded quickly, warmly, gratefully, the most well-behaved she had ever been in her life.

When the coat was on, she could actually feel the slight heaviness on the left side. Her phone was only inches away. All she had to do was find a way of pressing the ON switch through the fabric, and then a speed dial button. It wouldn't be easy but it wasn't impossible. Ward wouldn't even need to hear her voice. He'd know from the number that flashed up on his phone . . .

'Oh,' Paul murmured. 'Mustn't forget this.'

He reached into the pocket of her coat and pulled out her phone. He watched her face as he did so, and though she tried, she could not hide the crushing disappointment.

'Give me some credit, Nina.'

As he carried her up the stairs, towards an uncertain light, Nina dismally accepted that he had always been a step ahead of her, of all of them.

Maybe always would be.

Chapter 31

When John and I pulled into the Mayflower parking lot Unger was already waiting right in the middle. He was dressed more smartly than when I'd seen him last, an expensive-looking charcoal suit and a sober dark tie. He looked different. I led John over.

'Good timing,' Unger said. Even his voice sounded more clipped.

'How did you get here?'

'Cab. I don't like to drive.'

'Really?'

'It's dangerous.'

'Worse than flying?'

'Pilots are trained. I'm not.' He turned to John. 'I'm Carl Unger.'

'John Zandt.'

'I know who you are.'

John frowned. 'What do you mean by that?'

'Several things.' Unger looked at the Mayflower. 'We going to take this inside? It's cold as hell out here.'

The Mayflower was barely open and Hazel hadn't arrived for work. Instead there was a girl with platinum blonde hair, a tattoo and a tongue piercing. And attitude. In depth. I assumed this was the Gretchen who was currently withstanding some of Lloyd's good loving. He was welcome to her. Even getting her to pour coffee was uphill work.

We settled into a booth in back. Unger put his hands on the table in front of him. 'No sign of your friend?'

'No,' I said.

'I'm very sorry to hear that. But to be honest I'm here to talk about other things.'

He pushed a piece of paper across the table towards us. John and I read it:

> It is our day. We are in America, but we are not
> Americans. We are in Europe. We are not European.
> We are not Asian, Arab, African: we are not Christian,
> Moslem or Jew. We are the real humans. It is time to
> teach the way.

'Another coded spam mail?'

'Sent out at six a.m. this morning. Book-coded out of the Koran, no less.'

'Messianic, but so what? Carl, I'll be honest right back at you: Nina is my priority.'

'Yesterday afternoon a bomb went off in a sports store in a mall in California.'

'We heard. What about it?'

'They have a suspect on video but he's disappeared. A rich kid from the Valley. His name is Lee John Hudek.'

John stared at him. 'Hudek?'

'I take it the name means something to you?'

'Ryan, not Lee John. Ryan Hudek is mentioned in files I got from the house of a real estate developer called Dravecky.'

'Whom you killed.'

It was odd seeing Zandt caught off guard. 'How do you know that?'

'I didn't for sure. Just an educated guess. A few other people have died this year in suspicious circumstances, men whose names I knew from unusual contexts. I had a theory someone was going around whacking people they believed to be senior Straw Men. True?'

John didn't say anything.

It was my turn to stare suspiciously at Unger. 'Seems to me you know a hell of a lot more than you were letting on when we last met.'

'My job is to get information, not give it out. Only thirteen people in the world know the full story on this right now. We're not trustful of others. Me especially. My father and grandfather were killed over it.'

'Who's "we"? If the CIA know . . .'

'It's not the Company,' he said. 'Like the FBI, they're too heavily compromised to involve.'

'Okay, so who *is* "we" then?' I said, irritably. 'Carl, this is going to go a lot faster if you stop only responding to direct questions.'

'I'll get to that,' he said. He looked at Zandt. 'I've been trying to talk to you for a while. You're hard to track down.'

'Tell me about it,' I muttered.

John did not exude openness. 'Why do you want to talk to me?'

'First help me trust you,' Unger said. 'All I know is you're a friend of Ward's, you used to be a good homicide detective and now you're a dangerous man to get the wrong side of. I've seen the autopsy report on Dravecky.'

John considered, then reached in his pocket and pulled out two plastic bags. They looked like the things scene-of-crime people used to collect evidence in. Both contained small and undistinguished-looking objects. I picked one up. Could just be a lump of earth, though it had a few threads of strong colour in it. Blue, green.

'There are stone structures in New England,' John said. 'Usually

330

described as root cellars. The contents of those bags came out of one in Massachusetts.'

'Is this to do with this Oz Turner guy?' I asked.

John nodded. 'I got him to take me to the first one ever found, up in Webster County. It was lost for a very long time, almost immediately after it was rediscovered, and is far less tainted than the others. Some of the photographs that disappeared from his website were pictures I took that day. When I went to see my contact in Richmond about the bone we found out in the woods here, I also got him to tell me what he could about the contents of these bags.'

I picked up the second one. 'This looks like a scrap of bone too.'

'It is. From a skull.' John looked at Unger. 'Can you tell me what's in the other one?'

'It's a small lump of copper,' Unger said. 'Mined out of the Great Lakes region, a couple thousand years before the birth of Christ.'

'Oh for God's sake,' I said. 'Not you too.'

'Yes,' John said, ignoring me. 'The bone's also very, very old. And human. I didn't have time for radiocarbon dating.'

I was beginning to feel like the dumb kid in the class, which I don't enjoy. 'And so why are these things in a root cellar?'

'Because it was never a root cellar,' Unger said. 'None of them were. They're ancient burial chambers.'

'By "ancient", you mean what?'

'Some are only five, six centuries old. Others go back a few thousand years or more. They're where key leaders of the Straw Men have been laid to rest.'

'*What?*'

'I don't think it's that simple,' Zandt said. 'I believe they also interred their victims in them. A collection, an exhibit. A work of art. Then finally the murderer would be laid to rest with the remains of a lifetime of kills.' He looked at me. 'You remember that place we found south of Yakima? That was similar. And I found a reference in a journal to an archaeological site in Germany: a collection of bodies buried about ten thousand years ago, arranged in an

331

orderly pattern. It's possible that even some of the more innocuous-looking ancient burials may be the same: instead of chieftains being buried with servants so they can have staff in the afterlife, like everyone thinks, it's serial murderers and their victims.'

'Why?' I asked. 'Staking ownership to the area? We bury our dead here, so it's ours?'

'Probably, but not just that,' Unger said. 'If you plot the distribution of the chambers in New England it looks like they were placed to circumscribe certain areas.'

'They thought they were creating some kind of force-field around their strongholds? A wall of blood?'

'Something like that.'

'Are you kidding me?'

'Serial killers have similar rituals today, from what I gather. This is just the idea raised to a way of life.'

'Now make me trust you,' John told Unger. 'I thought I was the only person who knew this kind of thing about the Straw Men. If I'm wrong, tell me what you think you know.'

'Okay,' Unger said. 'But you're just going to go with it because I don't have time to give you chapter and verse, or dull stuff like proof. You've just got to believe what I'm telling you.'

I put my head in my hands, and just let the man talk.

'Fast version,' Unger said, taking and lighting one of my cigarettes. 'As you doubtless know, the last ice age ended a bit before 11,000 BC. End of the big freeze – the planet is finally a comfortable place to live again, and the human race can afford the luxury of culture. Over the next five thousand years we started knocking the world into shape. We got the farming thing going. There was trade, communication, we pulled ahead of the Neanderthals for good. That's why you find bits of ancient cultures in unexpected locations all over the Earth: they're not anomalies, that's *the way it was*, a pan-global civilization. Every culture in the world has a legend of this halcyon period: the Garden of Eden, the Dilmun, the Airyana Vaejo, the Dreamtime. But there have always been men and woman who were different, and they coalesced into a power that was the precursor of the Straw Men. Around 6,000 BC they decided to attack the key global centres of culture. Their ambition was astounding. They said: "We hate this new world order, and we're going to fuck it up." It took them five hundred years and happened over the entire planet, taking one land mass after another, like killer ants.'

'They took over the *whole world*?'

'No. They didn't invade. They didn't want dominion: they wanted everyone else dead. They just destroyed and moved on. The thing about the Straw Men is that they will never, ever stop – and bear in mind these are people who *individually* can be sick beyond belief. You want to know what the last battle with the Straw Men was like? Think Hieronymus Bosch and multiply it by the Holocaust. They torched our cities and lands with such efficient *horror* that this era gave rise to every culture's myths of hell. This reversal of millennia of civilization was so traumatic that its memory eventually got tangled up with other epoch-ending events – like the flooding at the end of the last Ice Age, the previous worst thing in human history. That's why the Atlantis legend ends in deluge, for example – and note Noah's Ark here too – and also why the Atlantis story got mistakenly placed back in time to around 11,600 BC, when sea levels rose catastrophically all over the world. You take this and add memories of volcanic and asteroid conflagrations over the millennia (hello, Sodom and Gomorrah) and it all gets spun into an era-spanning disaster myth. The defeats the Straw Men inflicted on the rest of the world were so appalling and conclusive that they came to be seen retrospectively as the work of the gods – a punishment for not living right. The world has spent the last *eight millennia* coming back from that apocalypse. By three, four thousand years ago we'd got them on the back foot again, and they retreated into the shadows. In *Timaeus* – the first recorded version of the Atlantis "old ones" myth – Plato talks about "mountain copper". He says it coated the walls of the city, made up the pillars on which their rules were inscribed. Almost like it's a defining characteristic. And why?'

'The prehistoric Great Lakes copper mines,' John said.

'Exactly. It's a confused reference to the fact the Straw Men had gone on to establish their mines in the US, the place they claimed for their own. Right fact, wrong era – because remember Plato was writing around 400 BC, a couple thousand years after the mining had started here, and a whole five thousand after the war. The two were already getting muddled. Come on, Ward – this stuff is there in plain view. What's the name given to the body of water that kept a safe distance between Europe and the Straw Men's lair? The *Atlantic*.'

'That's a coincidence. Or a . . .'

'There are no coincidences. Most of the world's myths, right down to vampires and werewolves and demons, are attempts to comprehend this endless fight – to remind us there are people who move against us in the night, who stalk us with deadly intent. Christ didn't literally cast out demons. That's merely code inserted into the Bible logging the fact that the Church was formed to help keep the Straw Men at bay: to form a wall against the *real* demons, the people who are all mankind's enemy.'

There was a pause while I attempted to absorb all this. 'So I'm guessing you don't actually work for the CIA after all.'

'No, I do. It's as good a way as any of plugging into the global underworld. But it's a cover, yes. I work for the Masons. I unofficially liaise with the Bohemian Grove Organization and try to keep the peace with the Jesuits from time to time. The point of *all* these people, even the Bilderberg Group – though they are indeed globalist scum these days, and are sort of running the world behind everybody's backs – is stability. And the most important thing is they don't even understand that's what they're for. Each one of them *thinks* they're just in it for the money and the power – but the combined effect, and the original point of the whole structure, is to form a barrier against the Straw Men.'

'So even the guys in the conspiracy don't know what the conspiracy is really about?' I shook my head. 'Fabulous.'

'They don't *have* to know. It just has to *work*. You can't under-mine something you don't know is going on. Like Heraclitus said – yes, he was one of us – a hidden connection is always stronger than an obvious one.'

I looked at Zandt. 'The great thing about Carl is he makes you sound positively level-headed.'

Zandt sat staring at the table, looking like someone who was finally being vindicated, albeit to an extent he hadn't anticipated. 'I don't hear anything I can't believe.'

'John, you'll believe anything.'

Unger gripped my shoulder. 'Ward – do you think it's a coinci-dence that the Roman Empire officially adopted Christianity just as it was losing its grip? Of course not. It was a deliberate handover, negotiated by the Emperor Constantine and his mother. The Roman Catholic Church was created to carry forward the structural legacy of the Roman Empire, just as they'd taken over from the Greeks and the Egyptians before them. It was organized by the dominants of its time, as the European Union was created by the hidden rulers of ours. Like all human institutions the Church curdled and went bad eventually, but in the beginning Paul – the biblical Paul, of course, not your brother – saw the potential of a Jewish rebel's teaching as a tool for international organization: and he got it *right*. Centralized power, extending out through smaller and smaller units that put a priest in every town, reporting back to mission control. The Catholic Church shaped Europe for the next fifteen hundred years, kept it vigilant for signs of the Straw Men. The Masons grew out of the Knights Templar, one of the enclaves who stepped into the breach when the Church started to fade in the back straight. The Church was still powerful enough to fuck up the Templars, using the pretext of the Cathar Heresy, so they covertly reconfigured into the Masons – and are still in business eight hundred years later. Almost no Masons today know the organization is more than a back-scratching club: only three members of the 33rd Degree understand its original purpose. The on-going pissing match between the Masons and the

Church is because both were set up – in different times and by very different people – to combat the same menace. The Church had a nice long ride and got fat on the proceeds: it doesn't want to yield the reins to anyone, which is how come the West has had five hundred years of internecine crap between the two. The world only has room for so many hidden elites, when they're competing for the same hearts and minds and money – and especially when they've *forgotten why they exist in the first place*. Yes, the Masons are part of it and Bilderberg too, along with the Trilateral Commission and the Bank for International Settlements and La Défense and el-Rashjid and Yom Pek and others which hopefully you haven't even *heard* of. One person from each of these knows the truth, along with three Masons. We are what stands between this world and the Straw Men.'

He suddenly looked very tired. 'And the thing is they're so much *better* at it than us, because sooner or later we all get greedy and forget what we're about. Time clouds everything. Yes of course Christ studied in China and yes, he escaped to France after the crucifixion, and yes he wound up in Kashmir, where he died. Who fucking cares? It's not the point. He was just one good guy, like Mohammed and Buddha and Jimmy Stewart. This is about the many. We have to hold the Straw Men back. Nothing else matters. This is the meaning of life. We've muddled on for a long time but now technology has finally done for us. With the internet we can't stop the Straw Men gathering. They care more. They hate harder. That's just the way it is.'

He sat back in his chair. There was silence for a moment.

'So tell me,' I said. 'How do UFOs fit into all this?'

'They don't exist, Ward. Don't be a prick.'

Never let it be said I'm not open to new ideas. I spent five minutes trying to work with what Carl had said, mainly to see if it made any difference to the task of locating Nina. It didn't, and I decided it was of no real interest to me. When I tuned back in, John and Unger were still deep in conversation.

'What was actually in the files?'

'Contracts, for the most part,' John said. 'Ryan Hudek didn't seem like a big deal. If anything it looked as though Dravecky was actively putting business his way. Like a favour.'

'Or a payment,' Unger said. 'I think yesterday's bomb in LA was a warm-up.'

'To what?'

'I don't know, but . . .'

Suddenly a bulb went on in my head. I looked up. 'This is why they broke Paul out.'

Both turned to look up at me.

'Think about it,' I said. 'Six months ago Paul had gone feral and become a problem to the Straw Men. Dravecky sent guys up into the forest to kill him, remember? And now they go to all the trouble to take out an armoured transport, just to get him back? Why would they do that?'

'He knows everything about them,' John said. 'They wanted him wiped from the board in case he tried to plea-bargain on the Jones and Wallace murders. He could have blown the Straw Men wide. So they got rid of him.'

'He wouldn't have betrayed them and they knew it. So do you. You don't think he's dead or you wouldn't be hanging here with me. If they wanted him killed they could've had him whacked in Pelican Bay with a phone call. They need him. It's the only thing that makes sense.'

John was silent for a moment, and then it looked as though someone hit him on the back of the head.

'What?' Unger said.

'How did you not guess this already? This "Day of Angels" – it's Los Angeles. The day of angels, in the city of angels.'

Unger was staring at him. 'They're going to attack LA?'

'Paul knows the city,' I said. 'It may be where he first started killing. He certainly gathered victims for the Straw Men there. He murdered Jessica Jones there too.'

'Dravecky, Hudek and at least four others are or were based in the city,' John said. 'They have sufficient influence on the FBI there to get Nina suspended earlier this year.'

I stood looking out onto the parking lot. My stomach felt cold with panic. 'And four days ago Nina, I and the one FBI agent we've tried to tell about this stuff – Charles Monroe, also based in LA – get hauled to the other side of the country to investigate a murder that looks like it might be a serial killer. Two days later Nina disappears. I call John, and so he's here too. All of us together, and all of us in the wrong place.'

John and Carl were already standing.

'There's time,' Carl said. 'I'll find a local airfield and have a plane for us in an hour. John – do you have an address for Ryan Hudek?'

'Yes. But LAPD will be there already.'

'Guys . . .' I said.

'Of course,' Unger said, to John. 'But they'll have quizzed the parents for the whereabouts of their son, and then dropped them. Who's going to suspect they're in on what the kid did?'

'Can you get them secured in their house?'

'I can try.'

'I'm not going to LA,' I said.

Zandt turned impatiently to me. 'Ward, you just said . . .'

'I know what I said.'

Carl had his phone to his ear and was looking at me with the flat, steady gaze of the zealot. He and John had already gone through a door in their heads. 'Ward, this is not a hard decision. It's the one or the many.'

'I choose the one. I always will. The many are just going to have to look after themselves.'

John looked at me and shook his head.

I walked straight past him and past booths which had begun to fill with people come to hide their first drink of the day with a sandwich. I was walking fast and angrily. On the way out of the door I nearly knocked over some guy in a fifty-dollar suit. He didn't even look me in the eye.

As I went across the lot to the car I heard someone call my name. I glanced round to see Hazel getting out of a car on the other side. With so little idea where I was going, any hesitation could stop me for ever. I waved instead. She waved back. Then I got in the car and drove straight out onto the road.

Half a mile away my cell phone rang. I got it out expecting John or Carl: vainly hoping they might have decided to leave LA's problems to LA. Instead it was Monroe.

'Where are you?' he said. He sounded very focused.

'Driving into Thornton. What's up?'

'Pick me up at the station. I think we've got something.'

Chapter 32

I left the car outside the sheriff's department and ran inside. Monroe was in back talking to some cop I'd never seen before. The agent saw me and broke off the conversation immediately to head straight over. The policeman gave me a stare laced with cop superiority. I didn't like the look of him even from ten yards away.

Monroe took me by the arm and led me back out onto the street. 'Is that your car?'

'Yes. Who was that guy you were talking to?'

'Sheriff from some town the other side of Owensville.'

'What's he doing here?'

'To be honest, I don't know. But he seems a lot more clued up than the locals.'

'Which wouldn't be hard.'

'Right. Except finally someone's been doing some good work. In the statement Julia Gulicks gave to Reidel she said she came to live in Thornton six years ago. Which checked out with when she took the lease on the apartment here and joined the company in Owensville. But she also told us she grew up in Boulder.'

'And?'

'She lied. We've been looking for the last day and a half and there's no sign of her there. Birth, college, jobs, nothing. Then a half hour ago the one cop in Thornton still working the case finally came across a record of a girl called Jane Gillan, who was born and went to school in Dryford.'

This was evidently a big deal for Monroe. It didn't trigger anything in me. 'Dryford. You got me. Is that in Colorado too?'

'No. It's a little over six miles away, just the other side of the woods where the second and third bodies were found.'

I opened my mouth, shut it again with a click.

'Right,' Monroe said. 'That's what I thought. So let's get moving.'

I waited until we were on our way before I asked: 'What do you have on this Gillan person?'

'Not much, but it works. Last we know is from when she was twelve. Jane Gillan's father died in 1992 in mildly suspicious circumstances, which is how the cop here flashed on the connection. Dad fell downstairs drunk one afternoon. Broke his neck. His young daughter was the only other person in the house at the time. Allegedly when Mom got home she found a dead heap in the hallway and Jane in the kitchen doing homework. Walter Gillan was a violent alcoholic and a racist pain in the ass and he was known to regularly beat his wife, so basically nobody pushed too hard on solving what might not be a crime. The wife and child moved out of Dryford immediately afterwards, never heard from again. But in 1998, a woman called Julia Gulicks moves into Thornton.'

'She's really not very good at this, is she?'

'What do you mean?'

'The world's reddest hair and she doesn't think to disguise it when she meets her second victim in the Mayflower. She believes it's smart to be the person who discovers Widmar's body, whereas it just puts her on your radar. She chooses a new name with the same initials as her real one, for God's sake.'

'Happens all the time with fugitives, or normal people trying to start again. Makes it easier to sign cheques and recognize the new name when you first start hearing it.'

'I think I'd take the risk and go a little more left field.'

'Not all murderers are professionals, and very few are even at all smart. They don't always think ahead.'

'Makes you wonder how many serial killers get caught first time, then, before they've had a chance to get into their stride.'

'That's not something I want to think about. And I don't want to die before we get there, either, so please will you *slow down*.'

I did, but only to get us across the big junction opposite the Renee's. As soon as I was heading through the woods for Dryford I dropped my foot again and ignored Monroe's increasingly white knuckles.

'I have the address where Gillan lived as a child,' he said, not watching the trees as they whipped past. 'It still doesn't help us explain what happened after we'd already got Gulicks in custody.'

'There's always been someone in the background,' I said. 'Remember when John asked her about the hands? "At least tell us about the hands," he said. That's when she started to lose it.'

Monroe shook his head, not getting where I was going.

'She doesn't know,' I said. 'She doesn't *know* what the deal with the hands is. She saw something bad a long time ago. Maybe she tried to tell someone about it, and got hit or screamed at and so it got sealed in her head as something she couldn't forget. Now she's acting out someone else's psychosis and is flailing and lost because she doesn't really have one of her own.'

'She still killed two people.'

'Really? Like the woman Nina knew in Janesville, the one who killed men who abused her? Is killing always the worst thing you can do? Regardless of what's come before?'

342

'Neither Widmar nor the John Doe did Gulicks any harm so far as we know.'

'No. But someone sure as hell did.'

Dryford was a small and desiccated town that looked baffled to still exist. The road out of the woods hit Main at a right angle. Two turns brought us onto Jefferson Avenue, a long narrow road sparsely dotted with small houses on either side. About a hundred yards before it ran out, Monroe got me to pull over outside number twenty-three.

We looked out the window at a yellow-painted wooden house. It was not big, but it looked well cared for.

'What exactly are we hoping to find?'

'Anything, Ward. Just anything we can.'

We walked up the path together and Monroe rang the bell. The door was opened by a middle-aged woman who looked like she baked a mean brownie. Monroe asked her how long she'd lived in the house and was told it had been eight years. He discovered neither she nor her husband were relations of the Gillans, nor had they heard of them. Luckily he had the subtlety not to mention that someone of that name had died falling down the staircase we could see over the woman's shoulder. Nobody unusual had come visiting recently – apart from us, of course – and the owner hadn't noticed anything odd in the neighbourhood. She plainly had no idea what we were talking about. In the face of this there wasn't any justification for asking to look around the house and yard. What could we hope to find?

We thanked the woman and walked back to the car. I stopped at the end of the path and looked back up the road the way we'd come. Thought for a minute.

'I wonder how long it would take to walk to the forest from here,' I said. 'If you were a little girl who was allowed to wander.'

'Not long,' Monroe admitted. 'But going back that way is going to take you east.'

343

'You could double back,' I said. 'But yes, that's true.' I turned and looked up the remaining length of road in the other direction. 'Let's take a look the other way instead.'

We walked to the end of the road. On the other side of a wide gate a large patch of open ground sloped down towards the woods. A rough path headed across it.

'That'd get you there,' I said.

'Not a short walk.'

'I suspect you'd be amazed how far a kid will go when they don't feel safe at home. And that if you followed that track you'd find yourself pretty close to the place the body and the shirt were found.'

'So maybe we know more about Gulicks than we did.' Monroe rubbed his face with his hands. 'But now what?'

'Now nothing,' I said. 'Brick wall. Again.'

I turned away and started walking back towards the car. After ten yards I stopped. Looked at the house right at the very end of the road.

Monroe stopped a few yards up the street, turned to see what was holding me up. 'What's on your mind?'

Like a lot of roads in towns like this, the further the houses were from the centre, the less well-kept they were. Dryford was barely a town, and the effect was accelerated. Number twenty-three was two minutes' walk up the road, and was spick and span. The house at the very end of the street didn't look that way at all. It was behind a gate of its own, a little bigger than the rest but very unloved. Trees pressed up against the side. The front yard was deep, a good hundred and fifty feet, completely overgrown with long grasses and bush. It didn't look like anyone had lived there for some time.

But there was a white van parked right in front of the house. A white camper van with no windows in the sides.

'I've seen a van like that before,' I said.

'You see them everywhere,' Monroe said, unimpressed. 'My brother-in-law has one. Calls it a Combie. He's Australian.'

I shook my head. 'I've seen that particular one. Somewhere specific. A couple of nights ago, I'm sure.'

Monroe got that I was serious. He came back the couple of paces to stand next to me. 'Can you remember where?'

'In Thornton. Somewhere . . . Yes. It was up the road from the police station the night Nina disappeared. I assumed it was the first reporters hitting town on the Gulicks arrest.'

'You're sure this was the same van?'

'Pretty sure.'

'Still could just be a local. I can run the plates.'

'Whatever,' I said, walking towards the gate. 'I'm going to take a look at that house.'

I opened the gate, watching the house for signs of reaction to our entry. The house looked dead, the windows on the upper floor a dark and opaque grey. The grass the other side of the gate had been flattened in an obvious track. We walked across the yard, swish, swish through the long stalks. Stopped after over half the distance, and looked around. Back up near the road some bird made a random twittering sound in one of the trees.

'The van has been out more than once in the last few days.'

'But if it lives here,' I said, 'and comes in and out every day, how come the grass it's knocked over is so high?'

Monroe considered, and reached in his jacket. He pulled out his gun, checked it. I did the same.

'Let's do this carefully,' he said.

'You don't want backup?'

'On the strength of bent grass?'

He smiled, and I realized that he did want to call in but knew it would look twitchy. That he had to prove to himself he was still whole after being shot earlier in the year. And that Nina meant a lot to him, too.

'Lead the way, chief,' I said. 'I learned this stuff watching TV.'

He headed straight for the front door. I approached in a wider arc that took me far enough to the side that I could check along it. Nothing to see except more slipping boards and overgrown bushes. Either the owner was very down on yard work or he/she had returned recently after a considerable absence.

I followed Monroe up onto the porch. The windows to the right of the door were dusty and cobwebbed inside. I stood up against the wall, ready to move fast if need be. Monroe reached out and knocked.

There was no response. He knocked again. Nothing.

He gently took the door handle in his hand. Gave it a turn. The door clicked open. He steadied it with his fingers so it wouldn't swing too far.

He looked at me. I knew what he meant. Either someone was inside and not responding to summons, or the house was empty.

I gestured with my head. *We're going inside.*

He knew that anyway.

I stepped away from the wall while he opened the door. Nothing untoward came of this, so I followed him as he stepped carefully inside. I took the door from him and pushed it quietly shut after us.

Listened to the dust.

Ahead was a dark hallway. Open doors either side, leading to living areas. Monroe nodded to me to take one. He stepped sideways into the other, gun held out and down. I don't know what he saw, but the room I looked in had more dust, very thick, and yet with furniture and pictures in place. Books still in a case along the back wall. Old novels and mathematics texts.

We re-entered the hallway and walked down it, trying not to set off the floorboards. A couple more rooms – dining, small study – both much the same. A large kitchen in the centre back. This too looked like it had been tidied long ago, but as if someone had forgotten to take their stuff with them when they left. No signs of vandalism. Either the local kids were remarkably well behaved, or it was a place they didn't like.

Monroe and I looked at each other, then went around the corner to the bottom of the stairs to the upper floor. I waited at the bottom while he moved carefully up them, keeping his back close to the wall and his head and gun facing upwards. When he held the top, I followed.

There were three bedrooms. We split up to look them over. All had beds still in place. One of the beds had been stripped long ago, and lacked its mattress. A wooden chair stood near the middle of this room, and a lampshade lay on the floor. There were some leaves and bits of glass lying around.

When I came back out into the upper hallway Monroe was still in one of the other rooms. I checked the bathroom, which was as quiet and faded as everywhere else. I stepped back out and was just beginning to relax a little when I thought I heard something.

It was coming from one of the rooms I'd already been in. The one with the chair.

A sniff, or soft ripping sound?

I straightened my arms, bringing the gun up a little higher. Walked very quietly back to the bedroom at front right. Stood outside the door a moment.

And saw a small shadow slide across the wall inside.

Monroe came out of the main bedroom. I quickly held up a hand, first finger straight. He stopped in his tracks. I indicated the room. He gave a single upwards nod of his head.

I took a step in, gun pointed down the far end. Turned quickly back to sweep across the long wall. Went back. Took another step. Dropped to one knee to stare uncertainly under the bed, the one which had been left without a mattress. There was nobody in the room.

I turned to see Monroe standing at the door. 'Did you hear anything?'

'Nothing,' he said. 'What was it?'

I shook my head. 'Nothing, I guess. Never mind.'

I let out a long overdue breath. The whole house seemed to exhale around me.

We walked back down the stairs. Took another look around the rooms there and wound up back in the kitchen.

'I think we've drawn a blank, Ward.'

347

'It's still the van I saw,' I said. 'The fact nobody's home doesn't change that.'

'It doesn't make it into anything we can use, either. We . . .'

He stopped talking, looking over my shoulder. I turned to see an unobtrusive door set into the back wall.

'Cupboard?'

'Don't think so,' he said, his voice low again. 'It's under the central stairwell.'

I reached out and pulled the door. It opened onto blackness. Cool air floated up towards us. I put my hand through the opening and felt around for a light switch. Found one. Flipped it.

Wooden stairs led to a cellar.

We walked down. The basement was a large, rectangular space and it was empty. I was about to turn straight around and head back up, but Monroe stopped me.

'Wait,' he said. 'Look at the floor.'

The harsh light from the single hanging bulb made it obvious to anyone who knew what to look for. The dirt and dust on the floor was not evenly distributed, but scuffed up in a series of large and irregular swirls. Kind of like what might happen if someone had recently moved around over it, someone whose movements were constricted. Something made me drop to one knee and put my hand gently in amongst it. Stare down at it, and listen.

Monroe had moved to a further portion of the floor and was doing something similar.

'Okay,' he said, his voice tight. 'I think we might have found something here.'

I looked up reluctantly. 'What?'

'Blood smear, faint. Someone did a decent job of trying to clear it up. But there's staining evidence of volatile fatty acids too. As if a body lay here for a while.'

'Alive or dead?'

'Immediately after death,' he said. 'Okay. We might have found where Gulicks stored her first victim before she took off the flesh.'

'You think this disturbed dirt came from him?'

I didn't want him to say yes, and he knew it.

'I don't know, Ward. But it probably is. This place is maybe to do with Gulicks. There's nothing concrete to put Nina here.'

'But the van moved here after she was in custody.'

He thought. 'True. Let's go take a look at it.'

He trotted up the stairs. I waited a moment and looked down once again on the swirls in the dust. Had Nina made them? Shouldn't you be able to feel the presence of someone you loved, even if they weren't there any longer? Shouldn't that be what your senses were for? I tried, but I couldn't tell. I could feel something in this house, but I couldn't tell if it was an echo of her.

I started towards the stairs but on impulse reached up and knocked the dangling bulb with my hand, just to provoke a change in the light. The bulb swung irregularly back and forth, throwing its glare into different corners. It made the staining Monroe had noticed a little more obvious – and forced me to wonder if it had been a man's body after all, or more recent, and a woman's.

And something glinted up close to the far wall.

I stepped quickly over to it, through thick and dodging shadows. I squatted down and felt around with my hands. My fingers brushed over something sharp. I grabbed it.

It was a bracelet. Cheap, plated silver ringlets, mottled pieces of indifferent turquoise. The chain was broken, as if it had caught against something and snapped.

But it was not tarnished, which said it had not lain here for years. And it looked a lot like something I remembered Nina picking up for six dollars in a small town we passed through when we took one of our vague road trips east from Sheffer.

I wasn't sure. Nowhere near. But suddenly the shapes in the dust looked like somebody I recognized.

I ran up the stairs. I knew this probably wasn't going to be enough for Monroe. But for the first time in two days, I felt I'd been close to her.

I made it out onto the porch and then stopped in my tracks. There was something in the yard. Something large, lying half-hidden in the long grass.

My gun was back in my hand. I moved sideways along the porch, trying to get a better angle to see what the thing was. Glanced across at the van. Called out softly:

'Charles? Where are you?'

Nothing but the wind moving the leaves at the very tops of the trees. I quickly swung from far left to far right. Nothing to see there either.

I stepped carefully down off the porch and walked towards the shape lying on the ground. I kept my gun on it until I recognized the colour of the suit.

Monroe was lying face down. He was not moving. The grass around him was flecked red, as if with tiny wild flowers.

I pulled him quickly over onto his back. There was blood everywhere. There were deep, straight channels hacked into his forehead and face and neck, revealing meat and chipped bone. A tooth glinted through a hole in his cheek, clean, polished.

His jaw sagged slowly to the side, releasing a dark clot of something from inside, and his last breath shaped a word.

Sorry.

I said his name but his eyes were already flat, and not even looking in the same directions.

I knelt, staring down at him, not knowing what to do or who had done this. I reached for the pulse in his neck but it was beating in some other place now. He had gone. The person called Charles Monroe wasn't there any more, just a thing that looked very like him, a dead thing adrift and a thousand miles from home.

I heard the swishing of long grass. Loud.

I looked up –

A man was running at me from the left side of the house. A big man, with a huge knife in his hand.

I swivelled my arms up and right and fired before I really took in what was coming at me.

The bullet hit him in the shoulder. I shoved myself backward, barely making it up to my feet.

The man tried to keep coming, and almost had the momentum to make it far enough to strike. I kept backing up and shot him in the thigh, and he swivelled and fell and slid.

I didn't give him a chance to get up but ran over and stomped on his hand until it no longer held the knife. Picked it up and threw it as far as I could into the long grass.

I stood back out of arm's length and pointed the gun at the man's face. His hair was grey. His hands and face were spattered with Monroe's blood and his own.

'Tell me who you are,' I said. 'And tell me where she is.'

He stared up at me, as if confounded. 'It's you,' he said. 'It's always you.'

'You don't know me.'

'It was always you.'

'I don't know what you're talking about, and I'm not . . .'

'Just get it over with. Please, please get it done.'

'Oh, I'll kill you. Count on that.'

I stepped onto his chest and pressed the gun against his forehead with all of my weight. 'But you have tell me first.'

He was a man called Jim Westlake. He was a man called James Kyle. He/they had lived here and he/they had killed eighteen women over twenty years, ending with his wife, who had lain in the woods fifteen minutes' walk from here, until John and I found her. Things had come to a point. Did I understand? Things had just come to a point. He had not realized back then that people had known about him for a long time, people who were not the police but who understood why women in Owensville and Rackham and further afield occasionally disappeared. They even knew where he had buried them, and they approved. Someone he called the Forward-Thinking

351

Boy had come on the worst night, the last of that old life, the night when he was alone in his house with no wife any more and a child who ran to hide from him because she had realized he was all wrong, who ran up to her bedroom and crawled underneath her own bed as if he was a storm come to get her. He had buried his wife only two nights before and he knew he was lost and everything had unravelled and come to a point: as he placed Laurie in the ground he had looked up and in the moonlight he thought he saw a pool of dark blood hovering four feet in the air on the other side of the island. Blood, like the blood he had taken from them all, the blood of his angel women, the blood he had taken inside himself. You can't eat a hand, it's too bony, but you can eat blood and find it good. He chased the apparition but it was gone, running away through the woods. So he finished his business, but what do you do then? It is inexorable. One leads to two and finally to many. Maybe if it had not been for this town he would have been okay, and Karla would have been the one, long-ago Karla, back when everything happened for the first time. But if the land wants you to renew its power you have no option but to comply, and when your beloved discovers your secret one night there can only be one conclusion to the situation, and then you are trapped in the burning shell of a life with your own little girl terrified of you . . .

'I don't understand,' he said, racked with shivers as shock began to set in. His face was pale, slicked with cold sweat, contorted with whatever it was he could not comprehend. 'I told her about the storms. I made her feel better. I loved her. But I still did what I did. I just don't understand.'

'What happened then?'

'When?'

'After you'd killed whoever it is you're talking about.'

'You came along.'

'I'm not . . . okay. What did I do?'

'We buried her close and you helped me clean everything up and move and you used contacts to make it all fade away. You made me kill people for you and then you stopped asking and I heard nothing for years and years. I didn't kill. I took pictures. I was like everyone else. I thought you had gone for ever. For every year that passed I tried to imagine one angel subtracted away. I thought maybe I could get back to none. But you never go. You're always there. You're always fucking here.'

'It's not me. It's someone else.'

'It's you. You look different, but it's you. It's always you.'

'Why did you come back here?'

'You made me come. I was supposed to deal with the girl who saw me back then, who had started killing in my way. But she had already been arrested. And . . . you wanted me to do other things for you.'

'You killed the cop at the Holiday Inn.'

'Yes.'

'You abducted Nina, the FBI agent. Brought her here.'

'For a few hours, but then we drove. We could have driven for ever. No one would ever have found us. I wasn't going to . . . Then you came, and I had to come back here to my house. You made me.'

'Who?'

'You.'

'It's *not me*.' I stared at him. 'Wait – came *here*? To Dryford? When?'

'This morning.'

'Paul came *here* this morning? By himself?'

The man stared at me, and finally seemed to get I was not the person he'd been talking about. 'In a car with some kid,' he said. 'They don't know what he's really like. They don't understand he's not even real.'

'Where is he now?'

'I don't know. He went.'

'When?'

'Two hours ago.'

353

'Does he have Nina with him?'

Jim/James suddenly tried to pull himself upright, catching me off guard. I kicked him back down again.

'Tell me or I swear to God . . .'

'He's got her.'

'She's alive?'

'She was when they left.'

I pressed the gun harder into the head of someone not much younger than my father had been when he died. 'Where are they? Where did they go?'

'I don't know.'

'What kind of car?'

'Big. Black.'

I tightened my finger on the trigger but I looked in his eyes and saw there was nothing in there worth killing.

Instead I left him crawling into the long grass and went quickly back to Monroe. I was going to close his eyes but then realized there are worse things to look at forever than branches waving gently across a cold blue sky.

Then I turned and ran back to the car.

Chapter 33

Lee was getting pissed off. Lee was getting confused. Lee was beginning to feel that none of this was making much sense.

They'd put the woman in the back of the car and Paul had got in with her. The windows were tinted. Nobody could see who was in there. Paul told Lee to sit up front with the driver. This guy was short and had heavy brows and a hook nose and was basically the kind of person Hudek usually went to some trouble to avoid. The flat smile he gave Lee when he got in the car said he felt much the same way about him.

They drove back through the woods to the bigger town and cruised around. Occasionally Paul's phone would beep: he looked at the screen but didn't answer. Once in a while Paul would ask for something. The car would stop, and Lee would go get it. The driver came with him and stood just outside the door each time. Presumably this was in case Lee decided to run off, and the precaution made him mad. He wasn't going anywhere. He just wanted to be told what was under way, and what this job he was supposed to do was. They went to the Starbucks and Lee withstood the usual wait to bring back coffees. They went to the grocery market and Lee was sent in for cigarettes. Lee was told to go take a digital photograph of the inside of the church, and the outside of the police station, both of which he did. He went and bought batteries from the Radio Shack in the strip mall on the edge of town, and onion rings for the driver from the Renee's up the road. At each of these places the people were friendly to him. They smiled and nodded and wished him good day like they were in some advert for small-town living. None of this dissuaded Lee one iota from his view that the place was utterly lame.

Finally they headed back into the centre and the car pulled up outside a long run of iron railings with an ornate gate in the middle. On the other side was an open patch of tended grass leading up to the school. Kids of various ages were milling around in front of it, stretching a few extra minutes of freedom out of lunch break. On the opposite side of the road was a smaller building in the same style. A super-friendly sign said this was a kindergarten.

Paul told Lee to come have a seat in the back. Lee got out, came around, climbed in. The woman was sitting where she'd been put, tied hand and foot. Lee looked her in the eyes for a moment and thought that for someone in her position, she seemed remarkably unafraid.

'You going to make me kill her?'

Paul look at him, eyebrows raised. 'Why would you think that?'

'Like a blooding thing, or something.'

'That's not what I had in mind. Hand to hand I'd bet evens, anyway. At best.'

'So – what?'

Paul reached beneath the seat and pulled out a small black bag. Looked like the kind of thing you might tote an iPod around in, or a CD player. He handed it to Lee. Inside were four small jars of pills.

'What's this?' Lee said. He looked out the window at the school. 'You want me to go sell drugs?'

'No. I want you to give them away.'

Lee was about to tell the guy he didn't have to be sarcastic but then realized he wasn't joking. 'Why?'

'Priming the pump.'

'*That's* the big job you've got lined up for me?'

'Just a warm-up, Lee. I'll be back in an hour, and then we'll get to the main lesson for today.'

Lee got out and watched as the car drove away.

He knew he would do what he'd been asked – told – to do, but the situation was really beginning to try his patience. This didn't seem like enough for someone who'd been through what he had, who'd had his life cut out from under him. He was a guy who wanted to make his mark. Up until a week ago he'd been going in the right direction, heading along a good, straight track of his own devising. He had a crew. He had friends. He had a life. He had a plan.

He was the one who drove.

For a moment he hesitated right there on the sidewalk, and realized how much he missed Brad. Sleepy Pete, too, a couple others, but mainly Brad – even though his ribs still ached from their fight. They had been friends a long time, and Lee never had too many friends. Brad had a way of saying things, subtly and offhand, that Lee had eventually taken on board. He had sort of understood that this process took place, but never as acutely as he did now. He wished Brad was here to say 'Shit on this, man, it sucks,' or 'Okay, it's weird but let's get busy.' Or that he could hear Pete droning on about the hidden rooms in some game or other, or even see Karen passing by on the other side of the street. He wished he'd made more of an effort after that one time they slept together. He had felt awkward afterwards, emotionally exposed in a way he was unaccustomed to. Natural response – don't call. He hadn't even realized he'd like to see her again until it was too late and she'd moved on to Brad, and Lee's dad had always been one for saying you can't go home again.

For one bizarre moment Lee even thought about calling his old home, talking to his parents. Saying: *I don't understand what's going on. What am I supposed to do?*

But something told him they'd just gently put the phone down. He wasn't their kid any more. He was Paul's. He belonged to this bigger family now and maybe always had. He should really ask: *What was the conversation you were having in the photograph I saw this morning? What was going on? What deal was being made? What did you get?*

What was I ever to you?

It wouldn't be any use. Did anyone ever really get what went on in their parents' HBO lives? Did they understand your MTV main event? Or were you always walking tracks parallel in direction but separated by time, once in a while waving across a distance about the length of a misty football field?

Whatever, he supposed. In the end, you walk alone.

He unzipped the bag and got out one of the little jars. Loosened the lid for easy access, and slipped it into his pocket. He walked up to the gate and ran an eye over the few kids he saw dawdling inside. They dressed the same as kids everywhere. He wouldn't stand out, as Paul had evidently known. Worst case and some teacher called him on what he was doing there, he'd be someone's older brother with a message from home. He'd done this before, in the old days, back when he was eighteen and just starting out. Maybe Paul knew that. Maybe Paul knew everything.

Lee turned at the familiar rocky sound of hard little wheels, and saw a kid clacking down the road towards him on a skateboard. He was about to give the guy a wave and get straight to business with him, when he realized the boarder was a little older than he looked, and his red backpack looked familiar. The guy winked as he passed and went sailing down the hill, just part of the scenery.

So Lee turned back and walked in through the gates.

*   *   *

Paul took her gag off soon afterwards.

'Going to ask you to do something for me,' he said. 'You're not going to want to, which I can respect, but if you don't do it I will kill you immediately. No second chance.'

Now Lee was out of the car, Paul's manner had changed abruptly. Nina realized he put on an act for the young man, that he put on a different act for everybody. He was probably doing one for her now, without even realizing. The machine, doing its job, impersonating.

'What are you doing here?' she asked. 'A town full of innocent people. What's here for you?'

'Getting it back,' he said. 'Don't you *feel* it? Can't you tell?'

'No,' she said. 'Just feels like a regular town to me. Guess you must be imagining it. Probably a side-effect of being insane.'

He smiled coldly. 'You feel it well enough. There's other places like it. Areas we lived two thousand years ago or more. Then we moved on. We like to roam. Sometimes we come back, but we always move on. There was plenty of room before everyone else arrived. But in they flooded, and they found useful piles of stone, and tracks, and they said how *convenient* for the Indians to have left these lying around for us to build our little farms out of, our stupid little towns. Not realizing they're picking through things that *belong to somebody else*. That *we* put it here for a reason. That it was all *ours*.'

'You should really sit and have a proper talk with John Zandt. He has some pretty whacked-out theories about you guys too. Of course, he would probably want to kill you first.'

'Oh, I'm looking forward to meeting him again. I've gone to some trouble to engineer it. It's going to be a brief conversation, though.'

His phone beeped and he paused for a second to examine a message on the screen. 'Not long,' he said. He got a gun out of his jacket pocket, efficiently loaded it and flicked the safety off. Kept it in his hand.

'Whatever it is you have in mind,' Nina said, 'I'm not going to do it.'

'Yes, you will,' he said, calmly. 'Or I'll find a way of getting your heart to Ward, with a note saying you didn't care enough about him to stay alive. That it meant more to you to play the heroine. That you only ever slept with him to get closer to me. And that you did it on a suggestion from Charles Monroe.'

Nina looked quickly out of the window, trying to focus on the town as it passed gently by.

'That's not true.'

'Maybe. But he'll never know.'

Chapter 34

They didn't believe me at first. Unger was a man with thousand-year timelines in his head, and flat-out said he thought I was trying to stall them in town when they had far more important business elsewhere. I had to shout down the phone to get them to stay around long enough to talk to them. They agreed to wait only twenty minutes. I drove to Thornton as fast as I could.

When I got to the coffee house they were sitting tensely inside, bulky and incongruous on a burgundy sofa by the window, surrounded by normal people. Unger was talking urgently on the phone. He was turned to the window in an attempt to be discreet, but vigorous hand movements were involved and he was red in the face. He looked like a man who was experiencing difficulty in getting people to take him seriously. I wasn't surprised.

'What?' John said. 'What the hell happened?'

I sat close and spoke fast. 'We found where Julia Gulicks grew up. And we found the house of a guy I suspect she saw kill his own wife when she was eleven years old. We went in the house and found a basement, and that's where Nina was this morning. She was in a van the rest of the time. The FBI were never going to find her in a house-to-house search: the abductor had her on the move.'

'Hang on.' John held up a hand, trying to slow me down.

I took a deep breath, knowing I had to sell him on the idea of staying here. 'I shot the guy who took Nina,' I said. 'And he says Paul is *here*. Here in Thornton. Right now. He has a kid with him and he also has Nina. And two hours ago she was alive.'

'Why would you believe this guy?'

'Because he wanted me to kill him and I said I would if he told me the truth.'

'Did you?'

'No. Fuck him.'

Unger ended his call. 'Ramona didn't show up for work today,' he said. 'The woman I worked on the email stuff with? She's not answering at home either. Everybody I want to talk to at Langley seems to be elsewhere. The line went dead twice.'

'What about LA?' John asked. 'Are they going to move into position for us there?'

'We're going to have to go there and work it in place. There's too much obtuseness going on over the phone.'

'That means "No",' I said. 'They don't believe you and they're right. Nothing is going to happen in LA. We've got to . . .'

'Forget it, Ward,' Carl said. 'We've been through this. I have orders from elsewhere. I'm going to the restroom and then I'm out of here.'

He got up and walked quickly out to the back.

I turned to John. 'For Christ's sake . . .'

'I'm sorry, Ward, I just don't buy that Paul is here.'

'I've just *spoken* to a man who . . .'

'. . . is a murderous lunatic. Their grip on reality sucks. Also, they lie. Meanwhile I got another call from Oz Turner. He checked his server again and suddenly it's full of hardcore child pornography. He wiped it and pulled the plug and has now got the hell out of the state. These guys are on the move, Ward. They're locking down for something big. I just do not see why Paul would be in this town today.'

'Because *we* are,' I said, angrily. 'He wasn't getting us out of the way: he was gathering us in one place. You know what the last thing Monroe said was?'

'Whoa,' John said. 'Last thing?'

'Yes – the killer killed him,' I said, light-headed. 'He took most of his face off with a great big fucking knife. I thought that would be obvious from the fact Monroe isn't here with me right now. Do try to keep up, John. Charles Monroe is *dead*.'

'Christ. Look, slow down, Ward. You've got to . . .'

'We don't have *time*.' Around us I was aware of people going up for refills, switching to the sports section, living explicable lives. 'The last thing Monroe said was "Sorry". Got any idea why that is?'

'Because . . .'

I threw up my hands. 'You know. Of *course* you do, but you didn't think to tell me. When you wanted to talk to Gulicks that night and I got the call from Carl, you got me to take it outside. Because you suspected Monroe had gotten a push from somewhere, that he was told to get Nina to come with him out here.'

'Yes.'

'And you confronted him and he didn't actually admit it, but it suddenly became okay for you to talk to a murder suspect.'

'I just suggested to Monroe that if you got to thinking he'd brought Nina there under anything like an order or suggestion then you would probably kill him right there and then. But I didn't know for sure. It was just a guess. I didn't tell you because . . .'

'. . . you don't trust anyone and think I'm kind of slow and maybe you're right. But *I'm* right about this. And what the hell is taking Carl so long? We need to get out and start looking.'

'For what? Even if this is all true, how are we suddenly going to find them?'

'A big, black car. In a town full of pickups and compacts, it

363

can't be impossible to find. It's worth a *try*. We've got to do something.'

Zandt frowned. 'Carl's been a while, you're right.'

We waited another thirty seconds then got up and walked through to the back, where a twenty-foot corridor led down to the restrooms. We went through into the gents. Three sinks, three urinals, three stalls. No sign of Carl.

'Strange,' John said.

'He split on us,' I said. 'He knew you'd waver if I told you Paul might be in town, and so he's taken off for LA without us.'

'No. That guy needs us. We believe him.'

'No, *you* do. And anyway – isn't every hidden elite in the world backing Carl? From the Masons to the charter members of the G8 summit? Can't he just call 1-800-GOOD-GUYS?'

'No, Ward. They have no idea what's going . . . Weren't you listening to a single word he said?'

He pushed the door of the first stall. It was unlocked and empty. 'He needs us,' he said. The second stall was empty too. 'We've dealt with these people face to face. For everyone else they're a myth. Plus, there's no way out of here. Carl would have had to come back out past where we were sitting.'

He pushed open the door to the third stall. Carl Unger was sitting inside.

His legs were outstretched, arms hanging straight down. He was leaning back against the cistern, head thrown back. There was a neat hole in the middle of his forehead. It had been made by a bullet from a small-calibre weapon, enough to ruin the contents of a skull without blowing a messy hole out the back.

We both stepped unconsciously back, stopped, went forward again. The guy was dead without a doubt.

'How?' I said, feeling very scared. Death knew exactly where I was today. 'How . . . how did this happen?'

We hurriedly pulled the stall door shut and stepped warily back out into the hall. John pushed open the door to the female restrooms, went inside. I held the corridor while he checked. There was nobody in there.

We confirmed there was no exit out back. The corridor dead-ended in a solid wall. The only other access was through the front door.

We turned and looked over the seating area.

A couple of grey-haired guys were jawing at each other. Young mothers sat chatting in threes and twos, admiring each other's Baby Gap spending sprees; a sprinkling of homemakers were out by themselves, reading magazines and nibbling at cranberry scones as they watched this hour of the day drift by in cocooned ease. There was a middle-aged guy with a notepad. Two tourists peering at a big map and worrying about making time. An old woman serenely reading the local paper. Nobody looking at us. Like they were all happily in someone else's dream.

'We're getting out of here,' I said, quietly.

'Yes we are.'

We walked out the middle of the coffee shop, straight through the warm, cosy centre. We stayed close together, fast, stiff-legged. A young woman in a fluffy sweater laughed suddenly, and I twitched in her direction and came this close to yanking my gun out, but she was just charming some other woman's kid. In the background the coffee machine hissed and spluttered and baristas shouted about extra shots and soya milk, and ethically sourced coffee remained available.

We got out onto the sidewalk and turned to look for any sign of someone looking out at us, watching, following.

There was no one even glancing our way. It was as if we hadn't left, or hadn't been there in the first place. We walked up the hill, fast. Both of us had our hands inside our jackets, guns in our hands.

John couldn't restrain himself from glancing back. 'What *happened* in there?'

'Did you see anyone acting weird?'

'No – but I wasn't looking for weird. It's a fucking Starbucks.'

'It has to be Paul.'

'What – did he come right by us, dragging Nina by the hair? No. *That* I'm pretty sure I would have noticed.'

'There's a younger guy here with him too.'

'That must be Hudek. I guess it . . .'

'But no one came in or out, John. I was facing the door. I would have seen.'

We got to the car and I unlocked John's door and ran around to jump in the other side. We sat stunned for a moment.

'Unger's dead.'

'So much for the fucking cavalry.'

'We're going to want to put some serious distance between us and here,' I said, turning the ignition. 'Before long someone's going to go in the restroom and find a dead man that you've been sitting next to for the last half hour. We should tell the Feds.'

'Forget it. Monroe's dead, and he's the only reason we ever got through the door.'

'True. And I don't see the cops being much help, either. When I was there to pick him up this morning, there was a new guy in there, some cop from out of town. He didn't seem to like the look of me.'

'Right, but you're certifiably paranoid.'

I turned to stare at him.

We did a rapid U-turn and drove back past the Starbucks, slowing a little while we were level. It looked like a happy fishbowl. Nothing had happened for the people in there. They were inside the post-card, looking out.

Zandt had recovered fast and had his gun out in his lap. He looked like he wanted to use it.

'We should go back.'

'And do *what*? I said. 'Whoever killed Carl will cut us down before we have any clue who they are. Half the other people in there will get taken down in crossfire, and it won't get us any closer to Nina.'

'So what, then?'

'We keep moving.' I picked up speed and followed the road down the hill. People walked up and down on either side. Trees shook autumnal leaves in a light breeze. A UPS van made a delivery, a guy in brown carrying a long flat box into the Christmas store. The whole town was like a moving billboard, an image you couldn't get past, somewhere we didn't belong.

'Ward, where are you going?'

'I don't know. We have to find where Paul's taken her. In the meantime we need somewhere where we won't get shot. We're running out of good guys fast.'

'Is that what we are now? The good guys?'

'Close as we're going to find.'

Ten minutes took us to the edge of town and I drove up a hill to a turning that led down a single-track road. At the end was the vague parking lot that looked down over Raynor's Wood. It was empty, which I liked.

I parked at the far end. Got out of the car and walked in tight circles for a while. I saw I still had some of Monroe's blood on my fingers. Tried to rub it off.

John got out after a couple of minutes.

'We should really call the cops anyway,' I said. 'Tell them there's a body. And also about Monroe. Alert them to what's happening here.'

'In the last week this town has had a cop killed and an FBI agent abducted, plus two dead guys found in various woods. If they're not alert already it's just not going to fucking happen.' John looked down over the forest, shook his head. 'There's something wrong with this place. It's . . .'

He walked a few yards down the slope, peering down into the forest below.

'What are you looking at?'

'There's a little hillock down there,' he said. 'Just in the trees.'

'It's where Lawrence Widmar's body was found. Somewhere down there, anyway. What about it?'

'It looks like the things I've been all over New England searching for.'

'John, this is not the time for . . .'

He put his hand up, listened. 'What's that sound?'

I put my hand in my pocket. Pulled out my phone.

The screen said NINA.

My fingers had turned to rubber and it took three tries to press the right button. I put the phone to my ear slowly. My head was ringing as blood rushed around it, not yet knowing where to go.

'Nina?' I said quietly. 'Is that you?'

'Hello, Ward.' It was a man's voice.

'Who is this?'

'Who do you think?'

It could only be him. 'Paul.'

John looked up quickly. I held up a hand to keep him quiet.

'You got it,' the voice said. 'Thought I'd see how you are. You never write, you never call . . .'

'Where's Nina? Where are you?'

'Where do you think I am?'

'There's a theory something major is about to go down in LA.'

'Wow – you guys are good.'

'It's not my theory. I think you're a lot closer than that.'

'Then you're even better than I thought. Got someone who wants to say hi.'

I gripped the phone tightly.

'Hey honey,' she said.

'Hey,' I said. My throat felt like it was clutched in someone's fist. 'Are you okay?'

'I'm fine.' Her voice sounded weak.

'Where are you?'

'He's holding a gun at my head, Ward.'

'Don't tell me then. What does he want? What do I have to do?'

'He wants John.'

'Stay alive,' I said. 'Stay alive for me.'

'I'll do my best. I really will. You live and learn,' she said. 'You live and learn. I love . . .'

Then she was gone.

'So there's your motivation,' Paul said, back on the line. 'Is former-detective Zandt with you right now?'

'No,' I said. 'He went to LA.'

'*Really*. That's such a shame. He's gone in completely the wrong direction. He's going to feel such a fool. And I did so want to talk to him.'

'That's the risk you take playing stupid games. What would have happened if you hadn't got hold of Nina's phone? How would you have contacted me?'

'I had your number already, Ward. And listen.'

There was a two second pause, and then I heard an unfamiliar ringing sound from close by.

John got his phone out. It was ringing. He looked at me.

Paul laughed down the line. 'Hey, what do you know? I just heard someone else's ringer down the line – which I guess proves the two of you *are* still here together. Of course I have his number too, Ward. You really don't seem to have a clue what you're dealing with.'

'Nobody does. Not even the Masons, from what I gather.'

'Ah, Mr Unger. Strange, deluded guy. Still, he's dead now, so, whatever. Didn't you see me? I'm always there somewhere, in the background. Always will be. We are legion, brother. Put John on the line.'

I held the phone out and John took it. He listened for a minute, and at that moment I admired him like never before. He listened to the voice of the man who had killed his daughter and he did not interrupt or shout or threaten. He knew the man had Nina, and so he listened.

Then he handed the phone back to me.

'Call the cops,' warned Paul, 'and I'll know. Fuck me around and I'll kill Nina and not even quickly. You know that's true.'

'I believe you. But you should know something too,' I said. 'I shot your psycho pal an hour ago.'

'Meaning?' His voice sounded very slightly hesitant, just for a moment.

'Over in Dryford. Jim, James, whatever. The guy was spilling blood all over his yard when I left. And talking. It's possible that even around here he may attract some attention before long.'

'It won't even make page seven,' he said, and then the line went dead.

John lit a cigarette, stared out over the forest. His face looked tight, composed, as if he'd made a decision. My head was shining white from having spoken to Nina. I knew that would fade fast. But at least she was still alive. For now.

'What did he say to you?'

Zandt didn't turn. 'That if I came to him he'd call the other thing off. He said he'd let Nina go. He wants you alive anyway.'

'What's "the other thing"?'

'That's all he said. Maybe nothing.'

'No. This isn't about you. You're not enough for all this.'

'He wants me to go to the Holiday Inn. He'll come and collect.'

'And you're thinking of going, right?'

'What else are we going to do?'

'It's not that. You think that you'll be able to take him down.'

'The hotel is still half-full of Feds. When am I ever going to have a better chance?'

'And you think he doesn't know that?'

'If we get over there now we can tell them what happened to Charles. Get them ready.'

'They won't believe us. They'll probably arrest you. They'll . . .'

I stopped talking, tried to leave room for a thought to make it through from the back of my head. 'That's what he wants,' I said. 'He wants you there, and he knows I'll go with you as backup. That means he will be somewhere else. He wants us, yes, but that's not

370

why he's really here.' I put my head in my hands. 'Nina said some-thing.'

'What do you mean?'

'She said . . . she said something weird. Right at the end. She said "You live and learn". She said it twice.'

'So?'

'Does that sound like Nina to you? Does she normally talk like a fortune cookie?'

'No,' he admitted. 'But . . .'

'And it was out of context. Living and learning has nothing to do with staying alive. Why would she . . .'

'She didn't say anything else?'

I ran back our too-brief conversation in my head. Claimed she was fine. Gun to her head. Staying alive. 'Nothing like that. She got about thirty, forty words. And she spent eight of them on that.'

Zandt stood there, waiting. Finally it came through.

'The message Carl told us about this morning,' I said. 'What do you remember about it?'

'Something to do with them not being American. Or European, or anything in particular. Plus there was a part about . . .'

'It's time to teach people, or teach the way.'

'They've got a young guy with them. Someone who could pass as young enough to get inside somewhere and plant a bomb, like he did in LA yesterday. Not a small one this time. Something that's really going to make a sound. That's why Paul wants us on the other side of town.'

I started to run back to the car.

'They're going to do something to the school.'

Chapter 35

I parked fifty yards up from the school, in front of the big church. We got out and stood buffeted by a cold wind which came up the hill. From this position you had a vantage over half the town. I couldn't see anyone. Not just anyone suspicious-looking, but anyone at all. It was as if everyone happened to be around the corner or indoors or down the street, out of sight. I checked my watch: quarter of three, the business-as-usual hour, that time in the afternoon when things either happened earlier or will happen later. In the meantime everyone works, or shops, or studies, and waits for time to pass. If you were landing in a space ship, three o'clock sharp would be a good time to invade Planet Earth.

We checked our guns. In the previous fifteen minutes I'd driven John up to the Holiday Inn. We'd moved his vehicle so it could be seen parked there from the main road – in case Paul had someone looking out. Then we covertly transferred back to my car, bringing John's ammunition and small arms in a black bag. Probably the car being there would make no difference, but the idea seemed good at the time.

I ejected the partly spent clip from my weapon and refilled it. We loaded our pockets, black coats weighed down with things from which no good can come.

John looked at me. 'Ready?'

I nodded. 'But if I get the faintest *hint* that Nina is somewhere else, I'm out of here.'

We took a right down the side of the church. This led via an alley to the road which ran parallel to the main drag. We walked along this until we were fifty yards from the back of the school, then stopped. Still nothing happening and nobody to see.

We crossed to the other side of the street and walked along it looking across at the rear of the school, a block-wide collection of buildings dominated by the main structure, with a big rectangle of asphalt between it and the road. Unlike the lawns around the front it did not look as if it was used for playing or hanging out. Railings ran along the street, with two wide gates at either end allowing access to delivery trucks. One of these was in position now but the goods being ferried in by a man in overalls looked real enough. Frozen pizzas, pulled on a trolley down a slope into an underground loading bay. He re-emerged and embarked on a cheerful exchange with the guy who'd accepted delivery as they leaned against the wall with a cigarette apiece. They evidently knew each other of old.

We walked quickly up to the far end of the block, turned left and up the side street until we hit the main drag again. Looked up the hill. Saw the bulk of the old buildings, safe behind their stretch of leaf-strewn lawn.

Saw also a guy standing just outside the school gates. A young guy, who hadn't been there before. He had a skateboard under his arm and could have been anywhere from seventeen to twenty, maybe even a little older. Neither John nor I had seen an image of Lee John Hudek to compare him with.

'What do we think?' I said, quietly.

'School day isn't over yet. Why's he standing there?'

'Going to the dentist. Waiting for a ride. Bad-mouthed a teacher and been told to stand there for an hour.'

'Kind of tan, don't you think?'

'You're right,' I said. 'Let's get him face down on the sidewalk. Sorry, son, you're insufficiently wan. Going to have to shoot you.'

Nonetheless I walked up the hill until I was a couple of yards from the kid. I took my time. He made a big deal of not looking up as I approached, but anyone his age would have done the same.

'Got a light?'

'Smoking kills,' he said.

'Need a ride someplace?'

He looked up. His skin was without blemish and his eyes were blue and cool. He looked at my face curiously. 'Man, you've got to be kidding me.'

'School's not out yet.'

'What the fuck is it to you?'

'What the fuck it is to us,' John said, having appeared at my shoulder, 'is we wondered why you're standing out here.'

'So are you like the sidewalk police, or what?'

'Yes,' I said. 'That's what we're like.'

The kid just shook his head. 'Jerk-offs.'

Then he caught the way John was looking at him. He turned on his heel in his own good time and walked back through the safety of the school gate.

John and I watched. 'That went well,' I said.

He didn't respond. Just stood there, watching the kid as he strolled across the lawn. The boy didn't turn around at any point, to eyefuck us or flip the bird. I was trying to work out whether this was surprising or not when he did something noticeable.

All the way across the grass he'd been heading for a structure to the right of the main school building. But when a couple of school kids appeared out of a doorway there, he made a diversion in his course so as not to come into contact with them.

John looked at me. 'Yeah,' I said. 'I saw it.'

We walked in through the gate. Our guy was moving more quickly now, heading for an archway which led into a courtyard within the main school building.

'Hey!' John shouted. 'Lee!'

The kid didn't turn. But one of the others did.

One of the two standing over on the far right glanced up imme-diately. Stopped what he was doing with the other kid, and looked straight at us. My heart sank.

'John,' I said.

'I saw.' He started heading quickly in the new kid's direction. The boy slipped something back into his jacket and turned to head quickly into the building. He did this with a grace and confidence that suggested he knew his business. He wasn't a school kid. Recently, maybe, but not any more. Add his response to the name, and it had to be Lee Hudek.

John went straight into the building after him. I saw the third kid wandering off to the side with signposted nonchalance and hurried over to intercept him.

'That kid you were just talking to. You know him?'

The boy shook his head. He evidently harboured delusions of cool but was no more than fourteen and looked very nervous. 'Not really.'

'So what were you discussing?'

'Nothing.'

'Bullshit. I saw him put something in his pocket. What was it?'

'Don't know what you're talking about.'

'Fine,' I said. 'So it definitely wasn't drugs.'

The guy's face said all I needed to know. 'Whatever it was, don't take it,' I said, and ran inside the building.

The entrance gave into a wide and gloomy lobby which split two ways into a corridor, with a stone staircase at the back down which grey light filtered. Entering was a step back in time. Doesn't matter what you build a school of, it still smells of school. You don't notice it when you're there but if you go back as an adult it's like the place is a stable for unwashed aliens. There were classrooms either side with frosted glass panels in the doors, a bank of battered lockers down the end, the muffled and measured background cadence of speech designed to be heard rather than interacted with.

I paused a second and listened. Heard footsteps above. I ran up the stairs to the next level and found the same layout there. John was down the far end of the corridor next to a bank of windows.

'Where'd he go?'

'I don't know,' John said, heading back my way. 'I thought he came up here.'

'He didn't have a bag,' I said. 'So either we got it wrong and he's just some twitchy kid dealing weed or he's already planted whatever device he came here with. This is dumb, John. It's time to warn someone on site and then get the hell out and look for Nina.'

'Okay,' he agreed. 'Let's find the principal's . . .'

He stopped talking.

I looked out the window and saw a police car was parked in the street directly outside the school. A big policeman was walking quickly across the lawns below.

'This we don't need,' I muttered. I headed back down the stairs, John close behind. We walked quickly back out of the building. The cop saw us emerge and diverted to head straight towards us.

'Interesting,' I said. We kept walking towards the policeman. 'I'm pretty sure that's the guy Monroe was talking to this morning.'

'He looks like a regular cop to me.'

'Put me in a uniform and I would too.'

'Kind of. The sort Internal Affairs takes an interest in.'

The policeman stopped a few yards short of us. He was definitely the one I'd seen earlier. Sleek, big-chested, flat-eyed.

'Who are you and what are you doing here?' he asked.

'What's it to you?' John asked, sounding more like the skateboard kid than he probably realized.

'You get that I'm a policeman, right?'

'What's the problem, officer?' I asked.

'I just got a call from a teacher. One of his kids told him that two strange-acting guys had accosted him outside the gates. I'm thinking that would be you.'

'We believe there's a potential danger to this school.'

The policeman grunted. 'There is. It's *you*. I'm not asking here, I'm telling you. We're leaving right now.'

Neither of us moved.

'Now, gentlemen.'

'Where were you when you got the call?' John asked, casually. 'Back at the station?'

The cop just looked at him.

'You must have moved fast,' I agreed. 'We spoke to that kid what, five, six minutes ago? He had to get indoors, talk to a teacher, convince him it was worth bothering the cops about. Teacher called the station, call got relayed, and you arrive.'

'That's some fast service,' John said.

'Or maybe the kid didn't report anything after all,' I said. 'Maybe someone's been watching us. In which case why would he lie about getting a summons?'

'You going to call for backup?' John asked. 'That's what I'd be doing. Two strange guys with a warning? I'd want other officers here with me right away. Assuming I was here for the right reasons.'

The policeman's eyes grew colder.

'Does the name "Paul" mean anything to you?' I said. 'We heard someone of that name was hanging around. A very dangerous man. Maybe it's Paul you're really looking for.'

'Never heard of him,' the cop said, and his hand was around the top of the gun in his belt holster. 'And I'm done listening to you.'

'You're right,' I said, and held up my hands. There wasn't any other way of handling this and we were wasting time that Nina didn't have. 'We don't want to get off on the wrong foot here. This is an important matter. We should go to the station. Talk it through properly.'

'Let's do that.'

We followed him back across the lawn and through the gates and back onto the street to his car. He started opening the back door of his cruiser.

John signalled me with his hand, blind-sided from the cop. I glanced up and down the road. The time was now.

I grabbed the door and swung it hard, crunching it into the cop's stomach. He saw it coming and nearly got out of the way, but side-stepped straight into a smack in the head from John. His eyes started to roll but he locked back in again just in time for me to punch him in the face. John shoved him into the rear of the car.

I opened the driver's door and climbed in. 'No keys,' I said.

I watched out the windows to the sound of muffled grunts and a short series of blows. Then the grunts stopped.

'Catch.' John tossed the keys over from the back.

I drove sedately up the road as far as the corner of the school grounds, then hung a left to go down the side.

'His ID looks good,' John said. 'If it's a fake, it's very well done.'

'He was an asshole either way.'

I stopped the car halfway down the street, got out and helped John pull the unconscious man out of the car. I opened the trunk and we lifted him in. He was a big guy. It was a tight fit. 'You want to gag him?'

John shook his head. 'Just in case he's not.'

We shut the trunk. 'He's bad,' I said. 'You know he is.'

'Which means something really is about to happen here.'

I knew he was right, and that meant Paul wouldn't be too far away.

'So let's go get that school shut down.'

Chapter 36

We ignored the building we'd already entered and went through the arch to the other entrance. A staircase on the right of the courtyard here took us into more promising territory. This was the school's biggest and oldest building and it made sense the ranking staff would have their lairs here. The ground floor held classrooms arranged on long corridors at right angles. They were deserted. In my recollection someone was always wandering the halls at school, skipping this class, faking that injury, goofing off pure and simple: Thornton High evidently ran a tighter ship. I finally saw a kid in the distance, walking across the far end of one of the corridors, but he didn't respond to a shout and was gone before we got there. The layout on the floor above was the same, with the addition of a big empty room that looked like a science lab. At the top of the building we found offices with panelling on the outside, and down the end a door of a size that could only mean one thing. It was slightly ajar. The sign said A L SINGER, PRINCIPAL.

We entered an anteroom in which a matronly woman sat behind an ancient word processor. She looked at us disapprovingly and I felt about twelve years old.

'Who are you?'

'We have to talk to the principal,' I said. 'Now.'

'She's on the telephone.'

I followed John over to the second door, which was shut. He opened it to reveal a bigger space with a lavish desk in the middle. Behind it sat another woman, who was of course not on the phone. The walls held ranks of serious books and black-and-white photos of worthy predecessors and people formally shaking hands. A window beyond her gave a view out onto the front lawns.

'You have to evacuate the school,' John said.

The woman stared at us. She was tall with bouffant hair and would have looked equally at home kicking butt in the boardroom of a Fortune 500 company.

'What are you talking about? Who are you?'

'Someone's about to launch an attack on this school.'

The woman stood slowly. 'Someone . . . how? What on earth makes you think that?'

'We don't have time to go into it,' I said. 'Please just take our word it's a very strong possibility.'

The woman reached for the phone on the corner of her desk. John got there first and put his hand on it. The principal pursed her lips and spoke to someone over my shoulder.

'Jane, call the police, would you, and then get Ben up here right away. Tell him we have intruders.'

I turned to see the woman from the outer office was standing in the dooway. 'Please don't do that,' I said.

Something distracted the woman and she ducked out of sight. I turned back to the principal.

'Ms Singer,' I said. 'I know this is weird. But you have to believe what we're telling you.'

'Of course I don't. If there's a threat to this school the police would have contacted me.'

'We just discussed the situation with one of them,' I said. 'It's not certain they can be trusted.'

'Can't be . . . good grief. Jane, get Ben up here. Right now.'

There was no response from the outer office, but then we heard the older woman's voice querulously upbraiding someone. The door was abruptly pulled wide.

A kid walked in. It was the kid with the skateboard we'd encountered outside the gate – except by now it was clear to me he was not a kid and he did not attend this school or any other. He started talking straight away, injured and self-righteous.

'Ma'am, I was standing outside the gate and two guys came and hassled me. These two guys right here.'

The woman stared at him. I sensed her days didn't usually go like this. 'Who are you? I don't remember you.'

'Jason Scott, ma'am. These men tried to get me to go with them in their car.'

The woman swept her gaze back to John. 'Give me back my phone. The police can deal with this.'

John kept his hand on the handset. The woman opened a drawer in her desk and pulled out a cell phone instead.

'Okay, fuck it,' I said, angrily. 'Call the cops, Ms Singer. Whatever. But in the meantime please get everyone the hell out of this building. What's *wrong* with you? We're telling you the school is in danger. Are you hearing that? Do you want to take the risk?'

'I wouldn't listen to them, ma'am,' said the kid. He giggled suddenly. 'One of them showed me his dick.'

I tried to get through to her. 'You've never seen this kid before. Come on, think – have you? He doesn't go to school here. Do you recognize him at all?'

'I can't remember every . . .'

'Look his name up. See if there's a Jason Scott on the school roll. But do it fast.'

She turned towards the computer sitting on the end of her desk, but without any real sense of purpose. I used all my reserves of patience not to leap at her.

'Ma'am, either evacuate this place or we'll do it for you.'

A voice called: 'Principal?'

It was the woman in the outer office. 'There's something wrong with the phones,' she said. You could hear her tapping her handset impatiently. 'I can't get an outside line.'

The principal looked at me. Suddenly I wasn't the strangest thing in her life.

'Really,' I said, holding her eyes. 'Do it, and do it now.'

'All right, Jane,' she said. 'Sound the fire alarm. Right away.'

The young man with the skateboard smiled thinly. 'Jeez, but you guys are a pain in the ass.'

He dropped his skateboard and pulled a gun with a snub silencer out of the front pocket of his sweater. He shot the principal in the head, turned and ran straight out the door.

By the time John and I had our guns out I'd heard the soft clap of another muffled gunshot. I ran out into the other office to see the older woman lying sprawled against the wall, legs still moving but her face pressed down into the carpet. The back of her head wasn't there.

'Find the alarm,' John said, and went running out past me.

I searched all around the office but couldn't find any way of setting the alarm off. Then I realized there must be triggers out in the hallways. I hurried out and down the corridor, banging a fist on every door as I passed. By the time I got to the stairs there were puzzled heads sticking out of most of the rooms.

'There's a fire,' I said, as calmly and convincingly as I could. 'Get everybody out.'

'Where?' someone asked. 'What fire?'

I abandoned calm and pointed a gun at him. 'Just fucking do it.'

I ran down to the floor below and saw John tearing across the next intersection. I headed after him and soon passed an alarm box.

I smashed the glass with my elbow and jabbed hard at the big red button.

Nothing happened.

I hit it again, this time with the palm of my hand. Then pushed it more gently, but still driving it in as far as it would go.

'Oh Christ,' I said, and went running up to the next intersection. I found another alarm point and broke the glass with my fist. Palm-hit the button again and again.

Nothing. I turned and saw John heading towards me, gun out.

'They've disabled the alarm system,' I said. 'Forget that other guy. We're going to have to alert people ourselves.'

He went running off down the corridor and yanked open the first door he came to. I heard him shouting at the people inside. I went the other way and did the same. I opened the door on a roomful of people sitting staring at the front as if hypnotized.

'Evacuation,' I said, back to calm and convincing. 'We believe there's a fire. Get out of the building now.'

The school's fire drills must have been good. Everyone got up quickly but in an orderly fashion. 'Tell anybody else you see,' I added, as an afterthought. 'Nobody run. Just get out of here and be careful.'

This is going to be okay I thought, as they filed quickly past. Ten minutes, and this place will be clear and I can get on with what matters.

Out in the corridor I confirmed other classrooms were emptying. Then out through a window I saw John had left the building and was walking purposefully across the lawns below, heading back to the first building. Maybe he was just on the way to clear that one out too, but he had a look in his eye and I decided I'd better be with him.

I pushed my way through a loud buzz of kids and got down the stairs as quickly as I could. The lower hall was full of milling bodies and their movement was far quicker down here: quicker, and a little out of control.

I heard shouting and realized somebody had found out what had happened to the principal and her assistant. A middle-aged man in a tweed jacket was stumbling down the stairs, blustering to another teacher, far too loud. He looked like just the kind of guy who'd have to check with the principal before following a simple instruction to get the hell out of a building that might be on fire.

I shoved my way back to him, grabbed his lapels and got my face up close.

'Shut it,' I said, quietly. 'Stop talking now.'

He stared at me. 'What? What happened to . . .'

I spoke low and fast. 'Ms Singer is dead. But these people do not need to know that right now. Don't cause a panic. Just help them leave the building as quickly as possible.'

The man stared at me. 'You don't work here. Who are you?'

'Just some guy,' I said, pushing him on his way. 'Now *move*.'

Chapter 37

Lee wasn't sure what to do now. He'd done his job, talked to a few people, come across like a friendly person and passed out party favours for them to try. He still didn't understand how this was worth doing when it didn't seem even slightly likely they'd be here to sell the next batch, but he'd done what he was told – as a prelude to not doing it next time. He'd been on his way out, ready to latch up with Paul outside the gates and demand to be put on something more worthwhile, when he heard somebody call his name. He looked up to see two extremely suspicious-looking dudes in black heading quickly through the school gates and across the lawns.

They were after some other kid at first – too far away to see if it was one of the ones he'd passed drugs to – and Lee could have kicked himself for looking up the way he did. It was amateur. Even Sleepy Pete would have had the presence of mind not to do something like that. But once it was done, you had to make the best of it. Lee ducked back into the school building as smoothly as possible, and made himself scarce in the maze of corridors. He heard one of the guys running into the building after him, but the familiarity of the layout made it easy for him to keep some distance ahead.

He'd been crouched down the end of the lower corridor, waiting to see what direction he should head in next, when he saw something that spun him out. It looked a hell of a lot like Paul, running into the building. Lee blinked, and it still looked like Paul, even though he was dressed differently and he was sure it was one of the guys in black from outside. The guy stood absolutely still for a moment, like a listening animal, and then sprinted up the stairs to where the other guy had gone.

Lee waited until he heard them come back down again and leave the building in a hurry. Then he slipped back upstairs. He decided he wasn't going anywhere until these two new guys were good and gone. Neither came across like a person it would be advisable to meet.

He'd just decided he'd waited long enough when he noticed there'd been a change in the sound of the world. Previously it had been real quiet – hell of a lot quieter than his school had ever been, that's for sure. Now he could hear people talking. At some distance. Outside?

He went to one of the windows in the side of the corridor, and looked down to see a bunch of kids were beginning to come out of the back of the next building, to stand together in the big area at the back. He looked at his watch and saw it could hardly be the end of the school day. Plus, why would they all be leaving via the back? It looked like a drill or something, though he hadn't heard any alarm go off.

Whatever. Things were getting weird. It was time to be somewhere else.

He was approaching the top of the stairs when he realized someone was coming up them. He was too far committed to make it back to his hiding place. He reminded himself that the two men couldn't have got that good a look at him. He'd been in the bathroom, that's all, seen the drill assembling outside. He was leaving the building, like you were supposed to.

He started walking again and nearly ran slap into the person coming up. It was the young guy with the skateboard, except he didn't have it with him any more. He looked pretty hyped.

'What's going on?' Lee asked.

'We've got a problem,' the guy said. He was trying to keep his cool but riding close to the edge. 'The plan's hitting some turbulence. I've got to check in with Paul.'

He pulled a tiny radio out of his pocket and stabbed at a button. Turned away from Lee and started talking fast in a low tone. He walked away down the corridor, listening, and then glanced up at Lee.

And that's when Lee saw it.

That's when he realized why the guy's face had looked familiar. Yes, he'd been one of the guys in the Belle Isle court, and yes he had probably also been one of the guys who'd stepped out of the shadows the very first time Lee had met Paul. But he'd seen his face in between those times too.

Seen it down the end of an isolated parking lot at night, lit by a car headlamps. He was one of the three guys who hadn't come forward the way they were supposed to, but who hung back and then suddenly went ape.

Lee stood staring at him. Tried to see the guy's face some other way. He couldn't. The picture had locked.

The man pocketed the radio, grinned. He was way into character as a skate slacker, bobbing from foot to foot.

'Apparently this *is* the plan,' he said. 'So, like, upwards and onwards.'

Lee nodded. 'And when exactly did the plan start?'

'What do you mean, bro?'

'I mean, I *thought* it began after a friend of mine got killed and we did the wrong thing and hid his body because we were told to. Hernandez gave us a bad steer on purpose, and I thought things started after that.'

'Right, yeah. Look, we don't have time for . . .'

Lee started walking towards him. 'But it started a lot earlier, right?

Sure, my parents have something to do with it. I got that part. I don't really understand it, but I got it. But now I'm talking about the night where me and some friends went to a parking lot up in Santa Ynez and someone I've known since I was a kid got his fucking head blown off. That wasn't some random crew of gangbangers from upstate. That was you.'

The other guy was standing still now, his back straight. He didn't look like a kid any more.

'What's your point?'

'My *point* is that you or one of those other guys killed my friend.'

'Great work, smart-boy. Yeah. It was me. It was my shot.'

'And so right from that night you people have been screwing me around. Pushing me in this direction and that. Fucking up my entire life.'

'You never *had* a life,' the guy said, and Lee realized this person had never had anything but contempt for him. 'You've been bought and paid for since day one. Since the day you were . . .'

Lee threw himself at him.

Lee Hudek was good at fighting. Lee had what it took. He was strong and he had confidence and he was willing to hurt people. But this other guy had far more than that. He actively enjoyed it. He came back at Lee like a switch being thrown.

Both were silent, intent, making little more than grunts. Lee's first couple of blows landed in the ballpark but after that the other man slipped into movements that only long and dedicated practice can make second nature. Lee knew enough not to try to land Hollywood-style punches. Fighting isn't about looking cool. Fighting is about fucking somebody up. Lee knew you grabbed at hair and clothes and eye sockets and tried to bring someone down to the ground as fast as possible and then got dirty with kicks and fists and any sharp objects you had to hand. But he just couldn't seem to get a hold on this guy. Wherever he went for, he just wasn't there – and in the meantime the guy was getting closer to pulling Lee down, and kept cracking Lee's face and stomach with his fists and elbows and the sides of his hands.

Finally one of these caught Lee square in the throat and he couldn't breathe. He slipped down to one knee and had barely time to yank in one long rasping breath before a foot scythed up and caught him full across the face.

He fell over onto his back, head spinning. He saw the other guy standing above him, a gun in his hand.

'I'm not supposed to shoot you,' he said. He was barely out of breath. 'But I might anyway. I can always dig the bullet out.'

'Fuck you.'

'Yeah, right,' the guy said, and stamped on his head. And then did it again a couple more times.

When Lee was unconscious the guy put his gun back in the pouch in his sweater, leaned down and got his hands under Hudek's armpits. He pulled him quickly up the corridor to the far end. He knew the layout of the school intimately, having studied its plans for many hours in the previous weeks. He knew exactly where he needed to go. A storage cupboard just around the corner. Wasn't supposed to happen quite like this, but he'd had no choice. It would do. It was within tolerance.

He opened the door to the cupboard and pushed Hudek's body in. Closed the door on him, and locked it with the external bolt. Nobody would be trying to get in from the outside.

He finished just in time, about ten seconds before he heard one of the troublesome guys from the principal's office come running in the building, shouting about fire. This was not good. The Upright Man hadn't mentioned this kind of trouble once the gig actually started, and these two guys were just not going away. These looked like they were in it for the full mile, especially the one who looked like Paul, and who he was theoretically not supposed to shoot.

He got himself in position and reloaded his gun. Instructions were always open to interpretation. Whatever happened next, he had no intention of dying cheaply.

That was not what people like him did.

389

Chapter 38

I was only a few yards behind John as he ran back into the first building. He split right and I went left, opening doors and telling people to get out. Everybody kept doing what they were told. It was great. John did his half very fast, and I still wondered whether he'd seen someone and was in here partly to give chase. I left the last classroom on my corridor unopened and just banged on the door. They'd get the message – the noise of departing kids was getting loud. I pushed my way through the emerging crowds and ran up the stairs after Zandt. A whole crowd of children started rushing down as I was turning the corner, and I had to put my head down and shove up against the tide as fast as I could.

'John?'

'He's up here,' he shouted, heading fast down the upper corridor. I assumed he must mean the person we'd encountered in the principal's office. I pushed my way after him. Finally got to the end of the corridor and confronted a heavy door I hadn't noticed the first time.

On the other side I found myself in another section of the building, at a right angle to the first. There was a set of three long, frosted glass windows on both sides of the corridor. More science labs.

John was flat up against the wall, gun held against his chest. He flapped at me with his other hand, keeping it low. I got the message and moved quickly up against the wall on the other side of the corridor.

'He's in the one on the left,' he said, quietly.

'So leave him there.'

John looked blankly at me.

'I don't care about this guy,' I said. 'We just need the school cleared and locked down. The police or FBI can deal with it. I'm done here. I'm going . . .'

'You've got nowhere else *to* go, Ward, and this guy could lead us to Paul.'

I hesitated, and heard a clanking from within the lab. We held our breath together, guns trained on the door down the far end. The I realized it would make sense to pick different targets and swept mine across to aim at the middle of the three opaque glass panels on that side.

'Okay. Let's get him. But be careful.'

Zandt almost smiled. 'I've always valued your advice.'

'You know what? Scrub that. Be as rash as you like.'

Shooting out the frosted windows would either reveal the guy's position or make it harder for him to hide. It would also make it easier for him to fire accurately at us. The alternative was going low up the corridor, keeping under the level of the glass, getting to the door to the lab and just taking it from there.

We did both. John went down low and scooted up the corridor. Meanwhile I fired at each of the three windows in turn, starting with the furthest in the hope this would drive him back towards me, deeper into the room away from the door. As the second window collapsed into shards I caught a glimpse of him heading exactly that way. As soon as I'd shot out the third window I headed after John.

By the time I was halfway there John was standing in the doorway and he and the guy were shooting at each other. I saw John knocked back against the wall, and I turned and emptied my gun into the room. The first couple of shots were random but then I saw the guy trying to get behind one of the long benches and I held still and tight and kept pulling the trigger.

When I stopped firing he wasn't firing back.

John held his arm up and I saw he'd just been grazed across the wrist. I reloaded and then the two of us moved carefully into the lab.

We walked slowly down opposite sides, towards the back, and rounded the last bench at about the same time. At the corner I found a handgun with a snub silencer lying on the floor, and kicked it out of harm's way.

The skateboard guy was sitting wedged up against the back wall, arms straight down by his side. There was a lot of blood on the floor. More was joining it.

'Where is he?' I asked him.

The guy shook his head, businesslike. 'You're too late,' he said, thickly. 'It's started. The Day of Angels.'

'Not for you,' John told him. 'Your days are coming to an end. You're going to tell us where Paul is. I don't give a damn how badly we have to behave to get this information. You're going to tell us if I have to start shooting your limbs off one by one.'

Another shake of the head. John moved his arms so his gun was pointing at the man's leg.

'I'm not kidding,' he said. He wasn't.

The guy closed his eyes for a moment, as if summoning strength. I raised my gun to keep him pinned.

Slowly the man lifted his arm.

'Don't do that,' I said. 'Keep your hands where they are.'

But then suddenly he moved much more quickly, slipping his

right hand into the pouch in the front of his sweater. It was out again in an instant, holding a knife.

'You're not getting anywhere with that,' John said.

The man took a deep breath. 'Enjoy your world while you can,' he said, and then plunged the knife into the left side of his neck.

John lunged forward and tried to pull it back out, but the man had committed his last bit of strength. Once the knife had gone in as far as it could, he yanked it back out from left to right.

The mess was bad, and he was dead very quickly.

John searched the body. He found a wallet with a little money but no ID. He found a half pack of cigarettes, one of which I took and lit. He found something that was evidently a compact radio, but one of my shots seemed to have hit it square on and it was misshapen and bent and I couldn't get it to make any noise. Presumably he'd used this to contact the fake cop outside, the one now in the trunk of his own car.

There was nothing to lead us to Nina.

I turned angrily away from the mess to the window along the other side of the room. This gave a view down on the open space to the rear of the school, and I was relieved to see the near end was full of milling kids. More were joining them from various buildings.

The children were being organized into neat ranks within a marked-out area in the shadow of the school underneath my window. A few hundred of them, maybe. The top end of the open space was clear.

And a car had just driven in the gate.

At first I thought, thank Christ – the cops have finally arrived and we can get out of here, but it was a dumb thought that only lasted a nanosecond. The local cops wouldn't drive around in a large black car with windows tinted black.

'John,' I said. 'Come look at this. Quickly.'

The car drove across the open space at a measured pace. Nobody was watching it. Everyone was too busy marshalling each other into orderly rows, enjoying the lark that fire drills always seem to be.

'Oh Christ,' John said. The car cruised over to the back of the school and entered the sloping runway we'd seen the pizzas taken down. Within seconds it had disappeared from view as if it had never been.

'Basement,' I said. 'Or loading area. Why is he bringing her . . .'

'The bomb hasn't been planted yet,' John said, dismally. 'We just saw it arrive.'

A car full of explosives is a very big bang. Best case it would take the school down to shower in burning chunks over the kids in the open space. Worst, depending on the layout and extent of the basement area, it could detonate right underneath them.

We hadn't achieved anything at all. Paul was still at least one step ahead.

I grabbed the handle on the window but it had been painted shut many years before. I banged on the window with both fists but no one was paying any attention.

'Leave it,' John said. 'We know where we've got to go.'

We ran out into the corridor and back into the other arm of the building. I thought I heard someone shouting somewhere as we sped through but I couldn't work out where from and didn't have time to worry about it.

We raced down the steps to the ground floor and searched for access to a lower level. There wasn't any. We ran out onto the lawn and around into the main structure, turned left into a corridor that went past a big open space that seemed to be the cafeteria.

Which meant kitchens. We dodged in and across it to where the food was dispensed from. Behind this was the food preparation area, battered stoves, big refrigerators. And way in back, a door to a stairway. We got out our guns, and went down into the basement.

394

Chapter 39

When Paul directed the driver to drive into the back of the school, Nina realized that anything she said would be a waste of time. Pulling the car down into this subterranean space could mean only one thing. She knew there was no appeal to reason she could make, and that this was not because Paul was too insane to follow an argument. He'd comprehend perfectly, but disagree. Like Wittgenstein said, if the lion could talk, we would not understand him. Paul had reached this place through his own rationality, simple and logical steps in a mind that was simply wired differently and organized around other values. This thing was going to happen. There was an almost sexual charge about his conviction now, and Nina realized she was probably entering the last few minutes of her life. Good to have spoken to Ward, then, however briefly. Shame he had not picked up on her reference to the school, but it had been a subtle hint. There really had been a gun at her head.

There wasn't a great deal she could do about it now either way.

Not much she could do about anything. She had to just be, for whatever time she had left.

Sometimes the decision not to pursue hopeless action is the bravest act of all.

The car was driven down into a space beneath the building, four cars wide and lined either side with access stairways and a series of bays twenty feet deep. Parts of the walls were lined with old, shiny tile. The lighting was gloomy and intermittent. The driver pulled the car into a bay at the end, next to a wall with an archway leading to a further section of the basement. The engine was turned off.

Paul turned to Nina.

'Upside is that it's going to be very fast,' he said. 'Pow. Vaporized. Downside is you're going to have to wait for it. I could just kill you, of course. Partly I'm just not inclined to make things easier for you, but on the other hand I suspect you'd like to keep those moments, however imperfect they may be. Correct?'

Nina looked steadily back at him. 'Thank you, Paul. Yes, I would.'

'Done deal. I can't give you an actual timing, because I'll be triggering it myself. Still, that should keep you on your toes. Make each thought a happy one because, you know, it could be the last.'

The driver got out. There was a finality about the sound of his door closing. Things were starting to happen for the last time.

Nina kept her eyes on Paul. 'You realize that how ever much you pretend otherwise, your leaving me alive is basically a deed of compassion?'

'And?'

'So you can do it. You can empathize. Do it more often than not and you could become a real boy. Just like Pinocchio.'

'I'm more real than you'll ever understand.'

'No, you're not. You're the same as me or anyone else. There's no genetic difference between you and Ward. You do not behave the way you do because you're part of a master race. It's just because of what has happened to you in life. You could be like everyone else.'

'Right,' he said, curiously. 'And who would these normal people be? You should have spent more time watching the news and less time hunting down people like me. Your species has been stealing and killing since it walked on two legs. It has been lying since it could talk. We're not the only ones who war and rape and murder. Only difference is you pretend it's a bad thing.'

'Paul – you really *aren't* a different species to us. You know that, don't you? Somewhere inside your head you must understand that you're human too.'

'No,' he said. 'We are the song of God. We've been tied to you for far too long and now we're cutting the cord. You're not going to be around to see it, but trust me – it's going to be wild.'

He opened the door and got out. He exchanged a few words with the driver and then went around the back of the car. He did something inside the trunk and Nina heard a beep she could only assume was the sound of a device being armed. The driver walked quickly away.

Paul came back to the door and leaned down to look in at her.

'You may think that you might be able to get one of these doors open,' he said. 'Even though you're tied up and they'll all be locked. Seems like a long shot to me, but maybe you'll hope it isn't. So I should explain that each door is wired to the bag of tricks in the trunk. Open one, and it all goes off. Do me a favour? Give me time to get out of the building before you try.'

Nina looked back at him and tried to work out, finally, what it was that looked out of his eyes.

'Paul,' she said. 'Do you even remember who you are?'

He shut the door. There was the sound of central locking being engaged.

And then his footsteps, going away.

Chapter 40

The basement was a warren of storage designed for a time when you couldn't get goods delivered seven days a week. The stairwell from the kitchen led down into a space filled with metal racks. There was a pile of packing materials from frozen pizzas: also a small room entirely filled with old wooden chairs. No school employees to be seen.

John and I ran through this section trying to get through to the loading area at the back. Finally we found a corridor which was brighter at the far end. We hurried along it until we were a couple of yards from an open door. John motioned with his head and I took the side.

He stepped through, looping around to the right. When there was no sound of shooting, I followed through.

We found ourselves in a long, open space that seemed to stretch the width of the school. This was intermittently lit by strip lights on the low ceiling: tiles and mildewed stretches gave the whole area a greenish cast. Over to the left it became lighter where the sloping access road entered from the rear of the school. You could hear the distant sound of a couple of hundred kids filtering down from above. Still no sirens. Where in Christ were these people?

'You should go warn them,' Zandt said.

'I will when we've found Nina,' I said. 'Or you could do it right now.'

'If Paul's here, the bomb isn't going to go off yet.'

'You don't know what he's prepared to risk or do. And if he's not here it could go off any second and you're not going to find that out until too late.'

He just shrugged and ran off to the right. I realized I wasn't sure what John was prepared to risk either. I wished Bobby had been here with me instead. He had been a better man than John and a nicer one than me. He could be trusted to do the right thing, he had always put others before himself without considering the cost, and he had a level of expertise in violent situations that had been frankly disconcerting. I was an amateur and I knew now was not the time to make a single mistake.

People had to be warned.

It was going to have to be me who did it.

I swore and started running towards the slope. I was only a quarter of the way there when I realized a shortish figure was standing in the shadows by the wall down at the far end.

He shot at me. Three measured clicks from a silenced handgun.

I was moving fast so I just threw myself headlong across the remainder of the central space into the opposite bay. I hit the side wall hard and crash-slid down onto the floor. I tried to roll out of this and get in a position where I could fire back at the shooter, but he just kept up a steady rate of bullets past the end of the bay.

'Ward?'

John's shout rebounded so much off hard, echoing walls that I couldn't tell how far away he was calling from.

'I'm okay,' I yelled back. 'Can you get him?'

The answer was a volley of gunfire that went on for ten seconds. Loud claps from John's weapon interspersed with soft clicks from the other guy, the exchange laced with the flick and whine of ricochets.

Immediately after the last of John's shots rang out, I heard him shout 'Now, Ward!'

Before I could think about it I ran out of the bay and banked left, holding my gun out to the right and firing again and again. John was providing covering fire. Halfway across the central space I made him out, hunkered down at the entrance to a bay about thirty yards up on the opposite side. The last few feet were accompanied by the sound of the shooter firing at me again.

Then I was in the bay, bewildered to still be alive. I was surrounded by old desks. My ears were ringing. 'Jesus.'

'Who the hell is this guy?' John said.

'No idea,' I panted. 'But we're not getting anywhere near that exit until he's dead.'

'That's not going to be easy,' John said. 'He knows what he's doing. He very nearly nailed you.'

'Thanks for the information.'

'He missed. It's a happy story.' He stuck his gun out of the end of the bay and fired again. The return shot came a second later.

At the back of our bay was a door. I went over, yanked it wide. Beyond lay a passageway heading left.

'It's not going to get us closer to him,' I said. 'But it might get us in the other direction. Which frankly suits me fine.'

I went through first. John followed, backing away from the mouth of the bay, gun held out in front in case the guy decided to run into the bay after us.

When we were both through I shut the door. We hurried along the narrow passageway, reloading feverishly. About every ten yards there were further doors on the left side: the ones that opened gave onto bays just like the one we'd come from, stacked half full of stuff the school didn't need right now. I opened each in turn but couldn't see any value in going through any of them. Then the corridor ended abruptly in a flat wall.

'Shit,' John said.

'I guess we're going out one of those doors after all.'

'We at least need to know where that guy is now. We're trapped. If he comes across to that first bay and into this corridor then we're fish in a barrel.'

I opened the final door. It opened onto another bay. When I stepped out into it I saw there was another exactly opposite, and that it did not hold boxes or chairs like the others, and yet was not empty.

It held a big black car.

'We've found it,' I said.

None of the car's lights were on. From our position the tinting of the glass and the low light made it impossible to see what or who, if anything or anyone, was inside.

I stuck a foot out of the bay and jumped back just ahead of a bullet which came immediately down the central aisle. The guy with the gun was holding his position up at the top. Presumably his job was partly to stop us getting to the car, which was why he'd passed up the chance to run down into the passageway and take us out in there. He could see us the moment we tried to break for the other bay. He was some distance away now, however, and if we ran fast enough and asked for luck, we could still make it across. Probably.

John was already tensed, ready to make the run.

But I suddenly realized it wasn't that simple. To the right of the bay in the end wall was an arched doorway. This gave access into another section of the basement, under the next part of the building. It was very dark through there and we couldn't see if . . .

'Wait a second,' I said. 'Paul *must* be down here too.'

'How do you know?'

'If he got out of the building then this other guy would have left too. So assuming Paul was in that car when it came down here, either he's in it still or he's somewhere down there on the right.'

John got what I was saying. If Paul was still down here then the car could be checkmated in their lines of fire. Either the guy down the end shot us as we were running across to it, or we ran straight into a trap which Paul had in his sights from a location just the other side of the arch into the next section.

John nodded wearily. 'We only get one try at this.'

I didn't know what to do. We were twenty feet from a bomb that might have Nina strapped to it, and we couldn't get out of the building to warn anyone outside. There was no way back or sideways. We were going forward from here. The only question was which direction we took those steps in, and how many we had left. I sent up a thought, a question, hoping someone with more guile than me might see a way ahead.

Now would be good, Bobby. Now would be really good.

The seconds ticked by. John took a step forward. Another bullet whined past the end of the bay.

'We're just going to have to take the risk, Ward . . .'

And finally my old friend answered.

'His phone,' I said, slowly. 'Paul called your phone. His number will be stored. You can call him back.'

'He'll have the ringer off.'

'Maybe, maybe not.'

'Getting a signal down here . . .'

'John – it's all we have.'

He got his phone out and hit the button which showed previous incoming calls. The number listed last had come at around the right time and had no entry in his phone book.

'Got it,' he said.

'Wait.' I took a deep breath, tightened my grip on my gun. 'This is bang and go. You dial. If it rings and we hear it and the sound suggests he's not right there waiting to mow us down, we go that instant. I'll run across to the car. You go through there and find Paul.'

He thought about it, knew this was it. 'Okay.'

'Stay alive,' I said.

He looked at me with eyes full of the reflections of people long gone. His smile was sad but real. 'This isn't living.'

'It's better than nothing.'

'Get Nina out of here, if you can. Don't you dare come after me.'

'I know that's what you want.'

He breathed out heavily. 'You call it.'

I waited a beat, and then said: 'Now.'

John pressed the button on his phone. There was a series of quiet tones as it dialled the last incoming number. Two, three seconds of silence.

Then we heard a phone ring. It was in the area on the right, way back in there. Twenty, thirty yards or more.

'Go,' I said.

I ran straight across the aisle. John went just as fast but angled right to take him through the arch into the other section. Three, four shots fizzed through the air between us. None ended in a dry slap.

I made it into the bay and skidded to a halt near the back of the car, spun round immediately to be ready in case the guy down the end had orders to come running down here and duke it out.

'John?' I called, but he was gone.

Gone into the other section, gone away down the road he had always meant to follow to its end.

I gave it thirty seconds and then risked turning away from the aisle to the car. I went quickly to the back door on the right and reached for the handle.

My hand was actually on it when I heard a soft thud.

I started back, not knowing what I was hearing. Then it came again, and I realized something was impacting on the window from the other side.

I pulled my hand back from the door, squatted down and got my face as close as I could. Used my hands to shield out the light.

Saw Nina's face inside.

I couldn't see her hands and she looked awkwardly out of position, as if stretching against something. She'd banged her head against the window to alert me.

She pushed her face up as close as she could and mouthed something urgently. It took three tries, but I got it.

She was telling me the doors were wired.

Chapter 41

Dust, first, and then the smell of something damp. Darkness and a heavy and dismal ache across his head.

Lee sat upright, slowly and painfully. He had no idea where he was. He tried to stand but the space was confined and his legs were unsteady. He crashed back again, bringing down a pile of something noisy off the hard wooden shelves behind.

He tried again, using his hands to help himself up. Got to a standing position, head spinning. White lights in front of his eyes. Felt strange and claustrophobic. Felt like he was somewhere small.

He put his hands out to the right. Shambled carefully in that direction for a couple of steps, before hitting another wall of shelves. Some of the things on there felt soft, like cloths or towels. His foot hit something with a clang. There was another thing that had to be a mop.

He was in a cupboard.

He tried to go the other way and half-fell against a door. He had a vague feeling that he might even have done this before, that he might have woken up a little earlier and shouted a while, before checking out again. His head felt like it could wobble out on him at any moment. His head hurt really fucking badly.

He felt . . . not good at all.

He fumbled around the door with both hands, trying to find some way of opening it. Found a handle and turned it, but it didn't seem to do anything. It must have been locked on the other side.

He banged against it with his fists for a while but the impacts seemed to reverberate up through his arms and into his head, turning it into a dark sea of crashing waves that made no sound.

There was no response from outside.

He reeled back from the door, intending to stand still for a moment, to stand and breathe deeply and let his head get back together. Instead he found himself slumping down to land heavily on the floor, mainly on his ass, partly on his side.

It was better down there, if the truth be told. He wasn't going to be getting out until someone came to fetch him. So he might as well sit. They would come, sooner or later. Paul would turn up. He'd notice Lee wasn't outside the school and he'd come see what the problem was. Or Lee's dad might, maybe. Not his mother. That didn't seem likely. She had always been slightly out of reach: had always, now he considered it, seemed to be thinking about something else. But maybe his dad would. His dad had liked him. Or Brad, maybe. Yeah, Brad. He was solid. He was Lee's friend, always had been. If everything else failed, Lee knew Brad would make it here sooner or later, unlock the door, come find him and take him somewhere else. Go and get a burger. Go and watch the sea.

Until that happened he'd just sit here and wait. It was warm. It was a small room, and held you close.

There were worse places to be.

I stood back from the car door. I'd made Nina mouth it one more time to be sure. Paul had wired the car so any attempt to open the doors would detonate the bomb.

But Nina was inside.

I put my hand up against the window. She did not put hers there to meet it, which confirmed she must be tied. But she did rest her head against it, getting as close as she could to where my fingers were splayed. Were it not for the glass, I would have been able to touch her hair.

I knew nothing about bombs. Nothing about how you wired anything or defused anything. Any of the children in the playground above would have been in as strong a position as me to disarm the car. If they'd listened in physics class, probably stronger. An explosion could be due to go off within seconds. In the very next second. In each new second that was born, the world could go white.

But Nina was inside the car.

The only way I could open the trunk would be by shooting out the lock. I'd have to stand far enough away not to take a ricochet, which would put me directly in the line of fire of the guy down the end. Putting a bullet into a trunk full of explosives was also a very high-risk strategy.

I stood as far back from the side as I could, looked at the car, willing it to tell me something I could believe in, and tell me fast.

There were four doors I had been warned not to trust. There was a trunk I couldn't access, containing devices I did not know how to disable. There was unlikely to be much time. If Paul had left the vehicle, it meant it was armed and ready to go.

I realized it came down to this:

Did the door triggers work on electrical contact or motion detection? Did a connection have to be broken, or were they also geared to detect sudden physical jolts to the vehicle as a whole?

There was no way to find out. True, the impact of Nina's head against the window had not triggered anything. But she'd done it as softly as she could. What I had to do would not be gentle.

I just had to hope it was electrical. The idea was true or false.

407

Our future was long or infinitesimally short. I had no option but to put it in someone else's hands.

I went back to the window. Put my face up against it again, found Nina's eyes in the murk inside. Told her that I loved her, and then gestured with my hands to get as far back in the seat as she could, away from the windshield, and as far down, while staying as close as possible to this door. She didn't question me. Just held my eyes, then disappeared into tinted gloom.

I stood back. Swallowed. Walked up to the front of the car. Held my gun in both hands and aimed it at the middle of the other side of the windshield.

Fired.

John Zandt carefully traced his way into the darkness, through a basement that felt like everywhere he had been in the last three years. There were bays in this section too but they were smaller and full of the lost and forgotten and not-needed-anymore. It was quiet and damp and cold and neglected and felt more like a forest than anything man had made.

He stopped in the centre of the aisle. Forty yards away he could see a dim, milky light, filtering down from some dirty glass pane. Presumably there was a way out there, an emergency-access stairway to the outside world. If so, it was possible Paul had already made his way up it. But John did not think so. He could feel him nearby. He had always known it would come to this, known since the day the Upright Man had taken his daughter from him and destroyed everything he had considered to be his life. He had known that, unless someone took him down first, it would end this way. That the two of them would meet, and leave only one. Or maybe none.

And so he did not feel afraid, or unhappy, or as if anything worthwhile was about to end. Sometimes a death is the only viable answer to a question you never actually heard. You just have to hope it is the death of someone else, and not your own.

It was going to have to be trial and error, and the time was now.

He heard Ward shooting in the other section and the sound of a strange impact. Time was getting on.

So he walked up to the first bay and fired into it.

The windshield took a lot of punishment. It took several shots to get beyond its first bulletproof shatter and make a hole.

But the bomb did not go off.

I heard the sound of shooting from down in the darkness. John sounded like he was methodically making some kind of progress deeper into the basement.

And so I climbed up onto the hood and pulled off my coat and started shoving at the glass with my hands, using the fabric to protect me. I pulled until there was a big enough hole to lower myself through and I went straight in, slashing myself on every side rather than take the risk of landing with an impact. But Nina was there, in the back, and I got through to her and kissed her once, hard, in case that was all we had – and then I untied her hands and feet and started pulling her out back the way I had come. She was vague and very pale and moving awkwardly from being in twisted positions for too long, and every moment was backlit with the knowledge that it could be the one that the question of how the locks were wired became irrelevant as someone, somewhere, pressed a button. It didn't matter. I hauled Nina through the windshield and out over the hood and cut myself all over again. I tried to keep her from the sharp edges but the shards got her too. We slid together off the car and fell onto the ground and still the car didn't go off.

I got to my feet and pulled her up with me.

'John?'

'I don't know,' I said. 'Is the bomb on a timer?'

'Paul's got the trigger.'

'Then Nina, we've got to go.'

'Okay,' she said.

I reached in the pockets of the remains of my coat and found another gun. Loaded it. Gave it to her.

'Can you run?'

'I can try.'

'Then let's move.'

I wrapped my arm around her back so I would be between her and the gunman and then pulled us into a run straight across the central aisle. The guy down the end fired at us but I fired back and then we were in the opposite bay.

I helped Nina to the back of it and opened the door and ran straight into the passageway and right down to the end – as quickly as I could, in the hope we'd get there before the shooter decided to run across and be in the bay when we arrived. I kicked open the door Zandt and I had come through and into that first bay. I made sure we were flush against the left wall, cutting out his angle. Waited a second for Nina to get back her breath.

'Okay,' I said. 'This is where we just have to do it.'

She smiled. 'Always is.'

And we ran out shooting.

When he was well over halfway down, John heard a sound from the last bay on the left. Something like a desk or chair, scraping along a concrete floor, accidentally bumped by someone refining his position in the dark. Paul knew what John was doing. He knew he was on the way, working through the bays one by one, emptying half a clip into each. He knew that John would not be turning back. Paul was getting ready for him.

John wondered whether the man felt any fear at all, and suspected probably not. If he did, he might make a break for that ladder, might try to get out of this place and back into the air. In that case, John would nail him. If Paul was without fear, and waiting until the very end, then it was in the hands of whatever negligent spirits nodded and dozed at the tiller of this world. Spirits that had let Karen die but which had also let John find the Upright Man again. Spirits who either didn't care, or were obsessive about never playing favourites.

John reloaded once more. He closed his eyes for a second, and thought of certain people and places and times. In the background he heard the sound of Ward firing his own weapon, a long and sustained burst of shots which sounded further away than before, and he hoped that this would turn out to be a good thing.

Then he walked on to the last bay.

'Hey, John,' said a voice in the darkness. 'Got your daughter in here with me.'

And after that it was just guns talking.

Nina got the shooter, I think. One of us did, anyhow. I saw him spin and fall before I realized there was nothing flying past us any more.

Nina stumbled and nearly fell and I got a better hold on her and dragged her faster towards the sloping access ramp. Though it was uphill the light seemed to pull us, as if we were falling up a waterfall.

When we came into the open air and the area behind the school I started shouting and waving my free arm. It took a moment before anyone understood what I was trying to say – but then it passed through them quickly and everyone broke out of their fire-drill formation and went running out the gates at either side. It was like watching a wall of glass shatter sideways. Slow, and then very, very fast.

As soon as I knew they were going, all of them, and quickly, I concentrated on getting Nina out the nearest gate. She was moving better already and I saw her glance across at all the other people and wonder if she shouldn't be doing something, as if this was her responsibility, and so I put my hand in the small of her back and shoved her. We ran out through the gate and into the street, across it and into a road on the other side.

We turned then and looked back at the school. Kids and teachers were still streaming across the road but there was no one left in the area on the other side of the fence. The buildings looked to me like balloons, expanded to the limits of their endurance.

'We don't know,' Nina said. 'John could have . . .'

Then it went off.

It was as if the whole world shook, like someone kicked the planet against a wall.

There seemed to be two explosions, one a fraction of a second after the other. The area at the back of the school erupted straight up into the air, at the same time as every window in the school was blown out. The glass had just started to fly when the roof and upper floors collapsed and blew out at the same time, destruction in all directions at once.

People who had still been running in the street behind us turned to stare and then started to back up again, and turn and run, as brick and wood and glass and earth and fire began to rain down. I pushed myself up against the wall of a building with Nina, trying to get shelter, and realized she was shouting something at me.

'Phone,' she was saying. 'Give me your phone.'

I handed it to her as the earth seemed to shake again. The school's tower dropped like a slow and irrevocable hammer, adding to a huge plume of smoke that had started to rise into the sky over the shrouded and collapsing remains of the school buildings, coalescing as if with dark intent, as if it was forming into a face. People were still running past us in the street, white-faced except where the blood of fresh injuries had started to run. The world sounded like thunder laced with screams.

'I can't get anything,' Nina said. She jabbed at a series of buttons, tried again.

'Who are you calling?'

She just grabbed my arm and pulled me back up the street towards the school. I ran with her against the flow of crying children. Fires had burst into twenty-foot waves across the whole school, new ones following them into life effortlessly, leaping out from nothing as if touched into being by somebody's hand. It was scorching from a hundred feet away.

'Where's your car?'

I pointed left and we ran along the back of the school, dodging piles of burning debris. Dust and hot ash had started to snow down. We made it to the end of the block and ran up the street past the side of the school. The trees that surrounded it were all on fire. There was a long, squealing groan as some other part of the building collapsed. I couldn't understand why the earth still seemed to shudder unless the movement was in my own head.

We ran past the big old church to the top of the street, to the road that ran over the hill and past the front of the school down into Thornton, and we stopped. Our steps faltered, and finally we were still.

We turned around, slowly, looking down over the town, and I understood why it felt as if the explosion was still going on. It was.

The whole town was on fire.

Columns of smoke rose on all sides and in every direction. I ran down the street until I could see past the curve. The police station was gone. The historic district was in flames. When I turned in the other direction I saw a huge spilling thundercloud pouring up from the direction of the Holiday Inn.

I saw Nina still trying to get a call through to someone, somewhere, trying to talk to authorities who were no longer there to talk to. I kept turning, not knowing when to stop, and saw a huge field of fire joining the sky from the direction of Raynor's Wood.

Two seconds later we were blown halfway across the road when the church exploded into a blizzard of joyous stone.

Sheffer

It is cold now. We are back in Patrice's spare cabin, hidden in the forest. We have been here nearly three weeks. In that time winter has come down out of the mountains, creeping closer every night as we sleep. The time for eating on the porch is long gone, but we still spend some evenings down by the lake. We sit and look out over the icy water, watching dark clouds reflected from above. We sit close together, but we don't usually talk very much.

Nina is out there right now, waiting. I am standing at the window watching her. I am not making dinner.

We're going to eat out.

I follow news coverage of the aftermath of events in Thornton very closely. It is impossible to miss. Many days there is no other news. Estimates of the number of dead still vary so widely as to be meaningless. It is certainly well over a thousand, and it seems inconceivable it will not end up far higher than that. Individual explosive devices are now known to have been left in the police station, the church, the school, the Starbucks, the Holiday Inn, the Renee's, the kindergarten, the fire station, two restaurants in the historic district, the main grocery market, the Radio Shack of the strip mall on the road to Owensville, the public library and the Masonic hall. Amongst others. One was also left in the Mayflower bar: Hazel, Lloyd and Gretchen died, along with everyone else inside. Diane Lawton died with them, having stopped by for a coffee after work to prove to herself she could do this without it turning into a full evening drink. Maybe she could have. Maybe not. The receptionist I scared at the Holiday Inn died, along with the seven FBI agents using the hotel as a base, and a young guy I briefly met when he came to check the minibar in Nina's room the second day I was there. He was hopeless at what seemed like a very simple task, but he was personable and had a nice manner. Both qualities are gone now, persisting only in my memory. The number and nature of the other dead defies comprehension. I suspect that Thornton is a place not unused to such things, and something Nina told me, a thing Paul said to her, seems to suggest I might be right. It may have started there long ago. It may always have been a place where people died.

We did what we could, that afternoon and night. We ran down into town and tried to help people out of buildings, to pull them out of the way of the fires which had started to burn everywhere. Everything broke down. Every system, every valued way of being. It was an endless hell. The town dissolved into a fragmented mass of burned and bleeding individuals trying to escape in every direction at once. Even those who wanted to be heroes discovered their nerve deserting them, found themselves dropping people they'd started to help and running away instead. There were no policemen left. There was no fire service. Fires spread quickly, with no one to put them out. Soon it was impossible to tell where they had even started, where the initial explosions had been. It all just went up together.

The best I can do is tell myself that we got everyone out of the school. There were a score of injuries from falling debris, and a heart attack, but it would otherwise have been far, far worse. Hundreds worse. Some days that helps. We went back twice more and tried to find John. We did not find him. You simply couldn't get close enough.

There was no organized assistance until people started making it to Thornton from neighbouring towns, and the eventual arrival of the army. They came in droves, and they came with guns. No one was sure who to trust or who the enemy was. For a time it seemed like everyone might be. In the meantime we helped try to get people to safety. Some of them were saved. Many were not.

We did what we could until we were falling down with exhaustion and the relief had finally arrived. Then we found my car and drove. We drove all the way back up here, over several days, through a country in which many roads were blocked and all air travel was grounded, where every television screen showed one picture, where everybody in every town was wondering if they were next.

So far, nobody else has been. But how long will that last? Nobody knows.

No one has any idea how a terrorist group managed to infiltrate a town and plant so many bombs without anyone being aware of what was going on. Conspiracy theories abound. I see occasional reports of two men, or sometimes one man and a woman, allegedly seen on school grounds immediately prior to and after the explosion there. Some say they issued a warning, but more often it is claimed that they were carrying guns and shouting slogans common to Islamic extremism. The remains of an unknown man were found in the trunk of the remains of a cruiser parked right next to the church, burned out as the fire from there spread. It's believed on the basis of his uniform that he had been a policeman, though due to the confusion and the high number of fatalities amongst members of local law enforcement, this has not yet been confirmed. There are many, many bodies. It is going to take a long time to work out who every one is, or was.

But one has been identified already, of course.

In the debris of a cupboard on the second floor of one of the

416

school buildings, firemen came across the scant remains of a young man. Dental records have confirmed this to be the person responsible for what is now regarded as a diversionary attack on a mall in Los Angeles, on the previous morning.

His name was Lee John Hudek.

It is now a name which no one will ever forget. Even if his remains had not been discovered, his face was already familiar, one which local survivors report seeing around town on the day of the attack. Positive IDs from a score of reliable witnesses put him in the grocery market and strip mall, the Starbucks, near the church, and at a number of other locations which were later destroyed in the initial explosions – apparently accompanied at these places by a short, Arabic-looking man. He was also seen by a number of pupils at the school, to some of whom he gave drugs. It has become obvious to everyone that this behaviour was a cover for planting the devices which he and his associates deployed. Hudek is also believed to be responsible for the murder of a former friend, one Bradley Metzger, whose body was found in a warehouse in the Valley. The deaths of another young man from their circle, and a young woman, are considered to be connected, though no one seems certain how. Testimony concerning an overheard conversation, submitted by local businessman Emilio Hernandez, has led to the working assumption that they were co-conspirators disposed of by Hudek before the final attack.

One thing is for sure. There is now a public face for what happened at Thornton. No one will ever be able to see behind it, to wonder quite how this thing came to be. There may be something else going on. There probably always is.

Ryan and Lisa Hudek have appeared on television on a number of occasions, carefully shielded by lawyers at press conferences. There is a degree of hatred towards them, but many Americans seem to feel they are victims too, loyal citizens who lost their only child to a foreign darkness none of us can understand. Neither Hudek has any idea why their son might have become involved in a terrorist organization. His mother has tearfully confessed that Lee John had been behaving oddly over recent months, and recently admitted that on one occasion she heard him become heated in a discussion of certain episodes of recent US foreign policy, characterizing them as 'acts of war'.

But they have no explanations. Ryan Hudek in particular appears numb.

Julia Gulicks is still alive, barely. She's never going to wake up, but as she confessed to two murders they'll keep her going as long as they can. They need someone or something to stand trial eventually. I wonder if sometimes across her cloudy sleep comes the memory of an afternoon when her father shambled drunkenly to the top of the stairs of her old home in Dryford: and I wonder if in her endless dreams another little girl comes to visit, one who would have been a few years younger than her back then, but who evidently never left their street.

Because a man called James Kyle was apprehended, in the back yard of a house he had occupied before abruptly leaving Dryford twelve years before. It was believed at that time he had left town with his wife and young daughter, though this has now been thrown into serious doubt. On the afternoon of the attack on Thornton, a neighbour reported a man behaving strangely in the garden of the old Kyle house. He made this observation from the road and did not get close enough to detect the presence of a dead FBI agent in the long grass. If he had, and reported it, it's possible that police would have made it to the scene more quickly: though more likely not, as when they finally arrived in the area there was far more pressing business elsewhere. On that particular afternoon dead law enforcement officials were commonplace. When someone eventually responded they found a badly wounded man in his sixties sitting by a shallow hole he had dug with his hands in the corner of the property. He was extremely distressed, and holding the bones of what appeared to be an eight-year-old child.

Matters in the Gulicks case have been somewhat complicated by the fact Kyle is now claiming responsibility for the two dead men discovered around Thornton over the previous week. While he is unable to provide any corroborating evidence for this, he firmly maintains they are his fault. He also claims there are other bodies to be found in the local area. Very many bodies.

Nobody is deeply interested in that side of things just at the moment. Thornton has become enough of a town of the dead without going back a decade to find more. So for the time being Julia lies in the hospital, marking time, neither guilty nor innocent, neither dead nor alive. I am careful not to mention her name to Nina.

Charles Monroe has been buried, one of many. We sent flowers.

I have no idea if Paul is still alive. I know that when Nina and I left the basement of Thornton school I could still hear the sound of John hunting for him. It's very hard to imagine how Paul could have escaped in time to avoid the detonation he triggered, sending a signal not just to the explosives in the back of the black car in the basement, but also all the other devices planted around the town.

If he died, I'm sure he died happy. The Straw Men got their day, spilled the blood of many angels. Nobody is talking about anything apart from what happened in Thornton. Somehow the fact that the attack was explicitly designed to destroy a small town, that it was directed at where normal people live, seems to make it much harder for everyone to take. This was not an attack against a symbol, or some place you only see on the television. This darkness came and found people where they lived. The fact the terrorists destroyed a place which had a significant FBI presence at the time just means the public at large is even less convinced of the government's ability to protect them, regardless of increasingly strident daily statements on the subject. Maybe that was intentional too, along with having members of the media already in place so they could show the horror right from the beginning so no one could possibly be mistaken as to how it had been. Was this good fortune, or were these parts of a big puzzle put meticulously in place? With Paul, you just don't know. As James Kyle told Nina, he was a forward-thinking boy.

I have tried calling John's phone. Every day, and I know Nina has too. All we get is a dead tone. He was never good at returning calls, but at least you could leave a message.

Probably in time we will stop trying. You have to stop, in the end.

Agent Nina Baynam is provisionally listed as a fatality in Thornton, given that she had already been missing for several days when the attack took place. She has not yet decided whether to contradict that assumption.

In the meantime we help Patrice and other neighbours with manual work. I don't let Nina do heavy lifting. Unless she insists. We have quiet dinners down in Sheffer, and sometimes get a little drunk over the pool table in Bill's bar. We sit close on the bench out by the lake, or in the chairs inside our cabin.

And we spend time with each other.

In not a single report have I seen a reference to a dead CIA agent found in a coffee house restroom. The Starbucks was burned to the ground. In photos you can't even tell where it was. Carl Unger's remains are likely mixed with those of the others who died there, returned to dust in the hidden undertow of history.

I have spent a lot of time thinking about the story he told us, trying to conceive of it as a possible truth. The problem is that I don't believe in Edens. I don't believe in hells either. They're both attempts to explain who we are, and who we are is not a question: it is a fact. The dark kernel at our centre is a death dream, and individual killers are merely its isolated priests. Every now and then some lunatic will attempt genocide on our behalf and the world will quiver for fifty years in his wake; in the meantime the lone gunmen are quietly getting the job done. Once in a while we catch one, and kill or incarcerate him or her or them; there will always be others. There will always be death because it is in our hearts. We do not fight wars and kill our neighbours and destroy other species because we are stupid or short-sighted, or at least not only because of that. We were the first animal to comprehend death, and we feel a need to demonstrate we are not powerless in its face. Maybe our thirty-thousand-year murder spree is an act of defiance, an attempt to own our nemesis: we know death is coming for us and so sometimes we take the fight to it. Or perhaps Paul and his kind are right, and there is nothing wrong with it. Maybe killing is what we do.

But that is not all we are; and death is never simple. What would I have done if I had been given a straight choice between Nina and the school?

Don't ask me that.

Right now, I do not know what to think. But I don't believe, as Carl seemed to, that history repeats itself. There is no cycle. History is permanently doing the same thing. Sometimes we don't notice what's going on, that's all – and sometimes we have no choice but to see. Every attack kills the innocent. Every counterattack does the same. We cower in the centre of a circle of spite, not knowing which way to turn. Killers of all denominations and faiths and eras stand around the edges of our world, firing inwards. They see only the people on the opposite side of the circle, their chosen foes, the demonized others. The rest of us are invisible to them.

How unreal we must seem, we normal folk, how lacking of their bright cleansing fire. How unheroic we are, in our small-minded wish to be allowed to get on with the short lives our various gods have allotted us; in our simple desire to last our span without being shot or starved or blown to pieces over vested interests or ideals about which we neither know nor care.

Yet still they kill us. It's how they live, and it's what they do. We must resist them, always and forever. We must find a louder way of saying no.

Three days ago, one question at least was answered. For two weeks after we got back up here, Nina suffered intermittent periods of nausea. She remained quite weak and found herself prone to

421

headaches. We hoped these were merely a temporary result of her incarceration in an old vehicle leaking fumes, but when they failed to fade, I eventually persuaded her to go see a doctor.

And we found out she is pregnant.

So I'm going to go outside now, collect Nina, and take her for something to eat. Not a salad. Something substantial and nourishing. She can be picky but I can be relentless. I'm hard to resist. Maybe we'll talk a little about what's going to happen, about the future we're going to have to find.

We're getting there slowly. I have no idea whether I'm ready to be a father. I suppose I'll find out. It's going to be a strange world to bring a child up in.

But then, I guess it always was.